# BECKY

Sarah May's previous novels include *The Nudist Colony* (short-listed for the *Guardian* First Book Award and winner of the Amazon Bursary), *Spanish City* (shortlisted for the RSL Encore Award), *The Internationals* (longlisted for the Women's Prize) and bestselling *The Rise and Fall of the Queen of Suburbia*. She teaches creative writing at Faber Academy and has launched many brilliant new voices in fiction. Sarah also runs a young people's theatre cooperative, Play On Productions, with her partner.

# BECKY

## Sarah May

PICADOR

First published 2023 by Picador

This edition first published 2024 by Picador
an imprint of Pan Macmillan
The Smithson, 6 Briset Street, London EC1M 5NR
*EU representative:* Macmillan Publishers Ireland Ltd, 1st Floor,
The Liffey Trust Centre, 117–126 Sheriff Street Upper,
Dublin 1, D01 YC43
Associated companies throughout the world
www.panmacmillan.com

ISBN 978-1-5290-6693-7

Pan Macmillan does not have any control over, or any responsibility for,
any author or third-party websites referred to in or on this book.

1 3 5 7 9 8 6 4 2

A CIP catalogue record for this book is available from the British Library.

Typeset in Celeste by Jouve (UK), Milton Keynes
Printed and bound by CPI Group (UK) Ltd, Croydon, CR0 4YY

Visit **www.picador.com** to read more about all our books
and to buy them. You will also find features, author interviews and
news of any author events, and you can sign up for e-newsletters
so that you're always first to hear about our new releases.

*For you, the reader*

# ORPHAN
# 1989

# English Rose Nanny Agency

Here I am. All eighteen years of me so far on a single piece of paper:

---

## CURRICULUM VITAE

---

| | |
|---|---|
| Name | REBECCA SHARP |
| Date of Birth | 18/07/1970 |
| Address | 7 Shelley Court, Haversham, West Sussex, RH12 7FL |
| Telephone | 0403 53486 |

---

| | |
|---|---|
| EDUCATION | Chilston House School for Girls (1981–8) |
| | A Levels: French A / Music B |
| | GCSEs: English C / Maths C / French A / History C / Music A / Biology C / Chemistry C |
| WORK EXPERIENCE | 1988–9: Part-time nanny to the Crisp family where I was responsible for three children aged 1, 3 and 5 |
| | 1987–9: Office Assistant at the *County Times* and solely responsible for compiling the weekend TV Guide |
| OTHER ACHIEVEMENTS | I have passed my Grade 8 piano exam with Distinction |
| | Fluent French |
| REFERENCES | ON REQUEST |

---

This CV was produced on my Olympia SF portable typewriter and posted, a fortnight ago, to the English Rose Nanny Agency at their Knightsbridge offices. The agency was recommended to me by one of my referees, Mr Crisp, for complicated reasons that have nothing to do with his three children. Childcare isn't what brought us together.

And only some of the information on my CV – currently in the hands of Jemima Pinkerton, the woman interviewing me – is true.

Jemima has a cold that she's combatting with heavy make-up and the tissues stored in the cuff of her cardigan. A matching navy Alice band keeps the mane of greying chestnut hair in place. There are no rings on her fingers. I notice this because my mother was a bare-fingered woman as well. Something that caused us no end of trouble. Not that Jemima looks like a troublemaker. Far from it.

I scan the desk separating us – a mug rimmed with coral lipstick prints, full ashtray, and a desk calendar stuck on January's picture of a foal in a snowbound field. It looks unsteady on its feet, like an orphan with rickets.

'Chilston House School,' she sniffs. 'Not Feathers, but still good.'

'House' is pronounced 'hearse'. Something I've been practising. 'Feathers' is pronounced 'futhers', and is short for Featherstone Hall. These things have been carefully researched because, although I'm familiar with Chilston House, I never went to school there. It's where my mother worked as a cleaner.

When it comes to my past, I enjoy being flexible with the truth. Most people call this lying, but I view it as an exploration of possibilities that circumstance has robbed me of – a creative redress to the accident of birth. For my mother, living truthfully was a major preoccupation. She built an entire moral code around it. But since her unexpected death just over a year ago, I've been freed from all that.

Now, facing Jemima Pinkerton, I give an apologetic shrug. Credentials, I've discovered (even fake ones), are to be shrugged at. Compliments require a wince. What I'm really trying to affect here is a sort of dead-eyed insouciance. Anything to stifle the stench of need coming off me, because if there's one thing I've learned in life, it's this: need is off-putting. It makes people feel responsible for you in ways they do not want to be made to feel. Especially when there are no obvious gains. Which is why it's essential that Jemima doesn't for a moment suspect just how badly I need this job.

'You'll know that my sister, Barbara Pinkerton, is headmistress at Chilston,' Jemima says, giving in to a yawn.

I do know this – Mr Crisp mentioned the connection.

'What did you think of it? School, I mean?'

The question catches me out. I'm not used to being asked my opinion.

'I survived.'

Jemima smiles. Quick. Complicit. She leans forward on her elbows and whispers, 'Barbara can be hell.'

She pushes a pack of Marlboros across the desk between us and soon we're straining together over a lighter advertising a nearby auction house, Jemima giving in to a hacking cough as she exhales.

Smoke hangs in the small, carpeted office like fog.

She returns to my CV, trailing ash across it. 'Fluent French?'

'Proficient' would be more accurate, but like the rest of my academic achievements, I've risked overplaying it.

'My father was French – and a pianist,' I say, stubbing out the cigarette in the now overflowing ashtray. 'He died when I was a child.'

'Oh, I'm sorry.'

I bat at the smoke between us, dismissive.

And my father might have been French; he might have been a pianist as well, for all I know. I never met him. Sometimes, I have him dying in a car accident, conjuring up images of an Aston Martin flying off a hairpin Alpine bend. Other times, he has a terminal disease. My mother, I recast as a Russian ballerina who defected from the Bolshoi only to have him die in her arms. It depends on who I'm speaking to, but with two parents gone, the possibilities are limitless.

'Hence the piano.' Jemima nods, glad to have my musical and linguistic abilities accounted for. 'Could you give lessons?'

'Of course!'

I really do play the piano – used to be rather good at it, actually – and my eagerness is hard to conceal. My posture is all wrong, suddenly. Too alert.

Jemima, thumbing the small photograph I was asked to send with my application, hesitates. But then her attention returns to my CV. 'No NNEB qualification?'

'No, but I've had extensive experience with young children,' I say, trying to keep my voice level, briefly terrified that I'm about to be summarily dismissed and sent back to the small town I left earlier this morning. 'The family I worked for has three under-fives.'

Her face is unreadable despite the earlier flash of intimacy and the shared Marlboros. She looks at me for what feels like a long time until finally, moving now with a new and unexpected sense of purpose, she opens the desk drawer.

Still holding my breath, I watch as she runs her fingers over the row of hanging files inside, before selecting a buff folder with CLEVELAND scrawled in caps across the top right corner. The Clevelands are a banker's family living in Sunbury-on-Thames. Jemima lists their credentials, trying to sound disinterested but unable to prevent awe from slipping in: a riverside estate located on the private island of Wheatleys Eyot; access to five acres of idyllic grounds including tennis courts and a heated swimming pool; accommodation in a separate guest annexe with en-suite and a self-contained kitchen; my own VW Golf and no responsibility for the Clevelands' dogs – they have their own nanny.

Despite all this, I hear myself say, 'I was kind of hoping for London.'

It sounds like an apology.

Jemima blinks, as if surprised to find herself in the Knightsbridge office when only seconds before she was stalking the sun-ridden lawns of the Clevelands' riverside mansion. A place where all of life's missed opportunities were gathered. Clearly.

'London,' she repeats. Her face tightens, the mouth puckering. 'Well.' With an aggressive thrust, the Clevelands are refiled before I can change my mind. 'There *is* a family.' She rifles, distracted, among the graffitied folders in the drawer once more. 'Although, I should tell you—'

Finding what she's looking for, she stops abruptly. Her fingers tap on the buff folder. 'They've had three girls previously. None has lasted longer than a couple of months.'

The way she says it – *girls* – makes them sound somehow culpable.

'The first two had nothing to do with us.' She screws up her nose. 'But I'm sorry to say that the last one was an English Rose – with a vivid imagination. If we move forward with this, you'll be living with the family as an employee. That is something you need to be clear about. It will help you to establish and maintain boundaries, which are of course essential to the smooth running of any household.'

She relinquishes her grip on the buff folder. It lies on the desk between us as she grabs at the box of cigarettes again, draws out the last one and lights it, eyes thin with relief.

'It helps in case things get fuzzy.' She turns away, blowing smoke sideways out of her mouth. 'And of course, if things *do* get fuzzy, there's no need to become hysterical. Hysteria,' she persists, sounding suddenly irritable, 'especially the girlish sort, is so disruptive to the general order of things. Not at all what's expected of an English Rose nanny.'

She pauses in her cautionary tale, giving me time to agree with her.

'Of course.'

Our eyes finally meet. Her mouth twitches. Almost a smile.

'Most of these husbands aren't predators. They are simply opportunists. A cheerful refusal will suffice.'

Her eyes seek out the buff folder again.

Tipping my head to one side, I read the name CRAWLEY. '*The* Crawleys? The newspaper people?'

My voice rises. Far too excited. The Crawleys own the country's biggest-selling tabloid, the *Mercury*. I first heard of them one hot afternoon in the offices at the *County Times* when it was announced that our little local paper was being gobbled up by the Crawley Corporation. The announcement was made by a pale but impassioned Mr Saunders, the newspaper's editor. 'Gobbled' was his word. He likened it to an act of cannibalism.

Hauling a tissue covered in lipstick smears from the sleeve of her cardigan, Jemima gives her nose a fretful dust and says, 'I think you'll be the perfect fit, Rebecca.'

# Haversham

The school I went to had a flat roof and a broken boiler. It boasted a pigeon infestation and asbestos in the classrooms, over half of which housed cookers, sewing machines and ironing boards. This was a girls' comprehensive in the eighties and domestic science was a big part of our curriculum. We were taught how to darn socks, sew our own clothes, iron shirts (men's shirts) and prepare family meals that were nutritious as well as economical, by two women who had not only failed to recover from post-war rationing as children but who had likewise failed to have families of their own. We also learned shorthand and touch-typing in case domestic bliss evaded us and we needed to fend for ourselves. Most girls left at sixteen to work in the local supermarket or in one of the factories on the town's industrial estate. Some left pregnant. Those who remained, and very few did, took A Levels with a view to being recruited by Sun Alliance, an insurance company with headquarters in the town.

As far as I could tell, each of these avenues was, in its own way, a life sentence rather than a life.

Chilston House School for Girls was about five miles out of town. A Palladian villa set beside a lake in rolling Sussex Weald, this was a sequestered world surrounded by high walls and fences, boundaries that enclosed endless courts, pitches and tracks, long lawns splashed with cedar, rhododendron and magnolia.

The girls themselves were like distant figures from books

and films to me. I saw them sometimes, in town. Their distinctive uniform – the navy skirts and red blazers – set them apart. Of course, there were other things beyond the uniform that also set them apart. Things I sensed but didn't fully come to understand until later.

They were fortunate.

An accidental achievement so much more alluring than anything hard-won or striven for. I would follow them into shops where smiling assistants jostled to attend to them. Nobody told them not to touch things or tailed them between aisles to stop them from shoplifting.

They had other places to go and were only passing through our small town.

Although I didn't realize it at the time, the school's ambitions for its pupils weren't too dissimilar from those of my own school. The well-carpeted seclusion of Chilston House was billed in the 1989 *Good Schools Guide* as 'a haven for daughters of well-born, conventional parents for whom the social result is more important than the academic'.

Six days a week, it was a haven my mother cleaned, wearing regulation blue overalls embroidered with the Chilston House emblem – a swan – the two pouch-like pockets packed with Golden Virginia tobacco and Rizla papers. She subsisted almost entirely on a diet of roll-ups, black tea and slim shakes. Never that interested in food, she ignored all my attempts to feed her solids – toast and beans, mostly, along with the occasional can of ravioli.

'Have to look after my figure, Becky,' she would say. 'It's all I've got.'

Every Saturday up until I turned thirteen, she would take me to Chilston House with her. Sometimes we gave a lift to Caroline, one of the other cleaners. Caroline used to bring a white poodle to work with her. He sat on her lap and looked out of the window during the car journey, panting with excitement by the time we turned through the school gates and into the avenue of horse chestnuts – the girls, who were only allowed to keep small pets, made such a fuss of him.

Caroline had a husband, Joe, who liked to tie her up when they were having sex. My mother and Caroline loved to talk about Joe. They would light their cigarettes in unison, wind down the windows and drop their voices to a whisper. I was told to listen to my music, my mother checking in the rear-view mirror to make sure my headphones were covering my ears. But while staring out of the window, affecting disinterest, I would turn down the volume.

Caroline liked to show my mother the rope burns on her wrists and ankles, the bite marks on her neck and, once, hitching up her cleaning overalls, her thigh. Caroline pretended to be upset, and my mother pretended to be sympathetic. But she forgot to match her face to her voice. It wasn't sympathy she felt as she took her eyes off the road to peer at the legacy of Joe's passion on Caroline's body. It wasn't envy either. Although this is what Caroline – preening herself in the passenger seat – mistook my mother's curiosity for.

It was pity.

She would seek out my eyes in the rear-view mirror, knowing I was listening in to every word, and shoot me a quickfire smile. Too fast for Caroline – lost in her Joe-ish fug – to notice.

My mother had boyfriends. I never met these men and none of them lasted. But for months at a stretch, she would go out on Saturday night dates. The flat would smell of bubble bath, blow-dried hair, perfume and lipstick. Her excitement at going out. There would be music playing on the stereo – Bruce Springsteen, usually – that she sang along to as she moved between bathroom and bedroom with me traipsing after her, made increasingly anxious by her imminent departure.

'Becky, I really need this,' she would pout, running her hand down the side of my face, before flying downstairs in a clatter as soon as Angelina, our neighbour, arrived to babysit.

Which is why I guess she never said anything to Caroline and why Caroline, in turn, pitied my mother. For her silence, for me – the kid she had to cart around everywhere with her – and because Caroline's life was in better shape than my mother's. This was the unspoken rule of their friendship. Caroline lived in a house she owned, not a council flat, and she was married. She had an upstairs and downstairs, a poodle, and a husband who was into S&M. So, Caroline got to do the talking and my mother got to do the listening. This was how things worked.

They were popular with the older girls, who were no doubt treated to the same tales of Joe and his predilections. But it wasn't Joe who made them popular. Alongside cleaning, Caroline ran a lucrative business selling contraband vodka and cigarettes to the sixth-formers at vastly marked-up prices.

I never knew whether my mother was involved in the racketeering because after getting out of the car, we parted ways.

She would pull me to her and kiss the crown of my head before pushing me away with an embarrassed smile: 'Now piss off and stay out of trouble.' This was for Caroline's benefit. Caroline, who would stand beside the car clutching her white poodle, impatient at this show of maternal affection. But I knew that when my mother said, 'Piss off' in that rough way of hers, what she really meant was, 'I love you.'

Every Saturday was the same. After my mother and Caroline cut me loose, I would go straight to the music block where I spent the rest of the morning practising piano. The music block was a new building, shaped like an octagon and never warm. In the winter months, I had a small electric fan heater that I would take with me, the hot air burning my ankles and heating little else.

Being able to practise on one of the school's well-tuned uprights was a privilege my mother had secured for me by accident one bright frosty morning when she was hurrying past the music block, cigarette in hand.

As she passed, someone called out asking for a light. She stopped in her tracks. There was a man leaning from a practice room window.

'I don't know what got into me, but there I was telling him all about you, Becky,' my unusually excited mother said later, blushing, her hands stuffed into the pockets of her cleaning overalls. She was pleased with herself and her bravery, breathless with it still. 'About your piano playing and stuff. I told him that we didn't have a piano at home and asked if you could use one of the practice rooms at the weekend.' She paused here for dramatic effect, licking at a frond of tobacco stuck to her lip. 'He said yes. He said yes, it would be OK.'

I met this teacher – the smoker – shortly afterwards, half-way through Debussy's 'Clair de Lune'. One morning, the door to the practice room opened and a man appeared briefly, a cigarette clamped between thin lips. Despite my mother's constant warning that I was to remain invisible – something that made me increasingly anxious about contact with others – I didn't really register him. He felt distant as things often did when I played. The door shut again, the man vanished, and I forgot all about him. When I finished, I unplugged the heater and checked to make sure I'd left no other traces of my presence in the room. My mother was very particular about this. 'We don't want to get into trouble,' she would say. Trouble being something she was prone to.

As I turned out the light, plunging the room into February gloom, the door opened once more. It was the man from earlier. He apologized for disturbing me (the first apology I had ever received from an adult). He had been listening from the corridor outside and felt compelled – he used that word, 'compelled' – to find out who was playing.

His eyes shone. 'It's Rebecca, right?'

I nodded, embarrassed. I was at an age when it was always embarrassing to hear my name spoken.

He didn't introduce himself but this, I realized, must be the music teacher my mother had spoken to.

He stepped into the small practice room, the door shutting behind him with a tidy click. Patting the piano stool as he passed it, he sat down in a plastic chair pushed against the wall and crossed his legs. There was something almost feminine about his posture and I couldn't decide whether I found this reassuring or unnerving. Either way, I understood how hard it must have been for my mother to speak to him. He wasn't anything like the men I overheard her discussing with Angelina when she came home late on a Saturday night; men who seemed to take up too much space in her life, making it feel messy. I couldn't imagine this man taking up so much as a centimetre more than he needed. Even his silhouette felt tidy.

I hesitated, unsure whether I'd read the gesture right.

'Go on,' he urged. I was hovering with the heater in my arms still, and then he flashed me a smile. Expectant.

I put the heater back on the floor and sat down, becoming uncomfortably aware of my shoes suddenly. They were the ones I wore to school and the only pair I owned. Black. Scuffed. I tucked them under the piano stool.

Neither of us thought to switch on the light. Perhaps it was because of this – the lack of light creating a false sort of night – that I chose to play a Chopin nocturne.

Afterwards, he said, 'Has your mother heard you?' He

sounded distracted, almost as if he wasn't talking to me at all. 'You're really very good.'

I didn't know what to say. I never knew what to say when I was paid a compliment.

'I'm Mr Crisp,' he continued into the silence that followed. Then he asked who taught me.

In later years, I would tell people that my father was a pianist with the London Symphony Orchestra and that it was him who first taught me piano. But Mr Crisp knew – because my mother had told him – that we didn't have a piano at home, he knew that my mother was a cleaner, and he knew that made it unlikely that she had ever been married to a successful professional pianist. I knew enough about the world at eleven to know this. So, mumbling and ashamed, I told Mr Crisp the truth.

My mother used to clean for an elderly neighbour and ex-piano teacher called Cyril Byrd. While she cleaned his cramped, book-bound flat, he let me play on his piano. It was out of tune and had a buzzing middle C, but I didn't care. Everything about the instrument excited me. I couldn't explain why, I just felt drawn to it. My mother watched this newfound obsession unfold at a preoccupied distance, unsure whether to encourage it.

After a while, Cyril offered to formalize the arrangement by giving me two lessons a week after school. Payment in kind, he suggested, for the cleaning and – increasingly – shopping my mother now did for him as he became less and less mobile, something she refused to accept any money for. Not even when he grabbed at her hand and forced the notes into her palm – she would slip them under the dish in the hallway as we left.

Although his eyes barely moved as I spoke, I felt somehow processed by Mr Crisp.

At first, he said nothing. Then, lighting another cigarette, he began to speak about the music he liked, encouraging me to do the same. We talked about Chopin, Bach, Beethoven and Brahms, who – I confided to Mr Crisp – I didn't understand. There were specific recordings he recommended I listen to, cassettes he said he would lend me. We spoke in a way I'd never spoken to anybody before. Not even Cyril Byrd.

Usually, adult attention was something I curled up under. But this – this was different. I could feel myself quite literally unfurling in the face of his enthusiasm. Blossoming, unseasonably, on the spot. My stomach so tight with excitement it was starting to hurt. Eleven pent-up years of solitude breaking all over the floor of that tiny practice room.

Then he started to explain about the music scholarships available at the school.

And although I didn't understand everything he said to me that morning, I understood this: the fifty-two white and thirty-six black piano keys were my way out. And in. A bridge linking our damp, disorderly flat to the magic kingdom that was Chilston House School.

# Leaving

Stranded between the flat's lounge and hallway, I watch as Paul hauls the first of my two towering suitcases, packed with everything I own in the world – including the Olympia SF portable typewriter, a last Christmas present from my mother – out of the front door.

'Jesus, Becky, what's in here?' he pants, shouldering the weight of it before disappearing step by step down the block's main stairwell.

Outside, it's barely morning yet and freezing cold.

'Will someone please shut the fucking door!' Angelina calls from the armchair in the lounge.

She's sitting in fluffy pink slippers watching a breakfast show, whose hosts smile, fixedly, at the camera. She stares back at them, motionless apart from her right hand, which holds a cigarette and moves between her mouth and the ashtray balanced on the arm of the chair. The ashtray is painted with a black Scottie dog and was a honeymoon gift from Bute.

Unlike my mother, Angelina was once married. There are photographs on the sideboard of her husband in uniform – he fought and died in the Falklands. Formal wedding photos, silver-framed, and smaller informal ones of them on holiday together. Angelina before she was sad; before she became frayed around the edges. Her thin, tanned arms slung around a handsome man who looks a lot like Paul. Sparkling in a way I find hard to believe possible, despite the photographic evidence.

My mother used to say that the reason Angelina's flat was so meticulous was because of her time as a military wife. Perhaps. Or perhaps it was just in her nature. Either way, life in these well-maintained rooms has always felt ordered to me. Time is demarcated; objects have a home, and furniture a fixed purpose.

There is no clutter.

There are no teetering piles.

The carpet is not obscured by heaps of discarded clothes, kicked-off shoes and wet bath towels.

Unlike next door, on the other side of the wall where, up until my mother's death thirteen months ago, chaos reigned. Inside our flat, the shabby rooms and even shabbier furniture littering them had long since lost any sense of their original purpose. Every now and then – usually in preparation for a visit from Mark – my mother would make an effort and rush around trying to tidy the place. But she never achieved anything close to the order of Angelina's flat. Not even temporarily. How could she when she was at her happiest leaving a perpetual trail of debris in her wake? An empress in a council flat.

The disorder in which we lived used to make me anxious, but since my mother's death, I've not only missed it, I've come to understand that it marked her ongoing attempt to live a life less ordinary, something I fought as a child when ordinary was all I wanted. Now, living with Angelina, I'm beginning to see that ordinary has its limitations.

Paul reappears, humming to himself. He's gone through his Robert Smith phase – messy make-up; hair like plumage – and come out the other side. Now he looks like the sort of young man who upends social order in a Forster novel. George's influence. Today, however, his slight form is made bulky by the anorak he's wearing over his work uniform: dark trousers, short-sleeve white shirt, red tie and name badge.

'You off?' Angelina says, standing with an effort and shuffling towards me in her slippers. The shuffling is new. Something I've been too preoccupied to notice until now.

She wraps me in a hard embrace. Shutting my eyes, I push myself into her woolly shoulder. I remember how she would make popcorn when she used to babysit me. The bowl between us on the bed, and Angelina asking me the sort of questions my mother never asked about school. Peering around the room at the certificates Blu-tacked to the walls. She was openly impressed. Admiring even, in a way my mother wasn't, which is why I started saving up my achievements for Angelina instead. I loved the bright, eager look on her face when I gave her my most recent test results. The wide-eyed pleasure she took in me. More than that, the possibility she saw in me.

Whenever I hurt myself, it was Angelina I took my cuts and bruises to. They only irritated my mother, who didn't have the energy for anyone else's pain. More importantly, she didn't have the treasure trove of a first aid kit that Angelina kept in a cupboard beneath the kitchen sink. When I ran to her, sobbing with shock, a knee or elbow bleeding, she would bundle me into her lap at the table and we would rifle through the contents of the tin together, deciding on the best course of action for whatever wounds I bore. There was an eight-month gap between my mother's death and my eighteenth birthday. During these eight months, Angelina made arrangements to formally foster me.

The truth is, I have debts I can't possibly hope to repay, and the realization of this now only makes me push my face harder into Angelina's jumper. She smells of the best parts of my childhood. If I was able to, I would bottle that scent and take it with me.

'Come on,' she mumbles into my hair. Even though she's the one doing all the crying.

Finally, she pushes me away with a series of untidy sniffs, holding me at arm's length. Her voice is suddenly urgent, taking on the edge it does when she's being affectionate. The same voice she once used – head hanging, intent, over a fresh wound on my leg – to tell me that she'd always wanted a daughter of her own. Words that made me feel coveted. A rarity. 'You'll be all right, Becky, you hear me? You'll be all right.'

'I'll phone.'

'No,' she almost shouts. 'You won't phone. And you won't write. You'll forget all about this place. Promise me that.'

Paul has managed to hoist one of the suitcases into the boot and the other one onto the back seat of the car that used to belong to my mother, sold to him because I needed the money and couldn't bear the thought of anyone else driving it.

Already sagging under the weight of the two suitcases, it sags further as we climb in.

After my mother died, I cleaned the car in a frenzy as if the empty Rizla packets, Golden Virginia pouches, hardened orange peel and cracked cassette cases with the wrong cassettes inside were incriminating evidence. But the traces of Rive Gauche – the last birthday present I bought her – still clung effortlessly to everything.

Bleary from the pub last night, Paul talks himself through slotting the key into the ignition and crunching my mother's car into gear – she never crunched the gears.

In the early days, before Mark, it was driving the car that kept her happy, kept her alive. Most of her wages went on petrol and tobacco. Food, shelter, light and warmth weren't necessities to her like they are to most people. It's the only time I remember her at peace – behind the wheel, a cigarette between her lips, windows down, hair blowing.

'Where are we going?' I'd say, made anxious by the absence of any apparent destination.

'Does it matter?' she'd reply, much less snappish than usual.

We drove at random through country lanes and – after night fell – sleeping villages, my mother peering out at the illuminated houses we passed as though she was searching for something only half remembered.

The Greenline coach to London Victoria is already parked in the station forecourt when we arrive, trailing clouds of exhaust fumes behind us in the cold air.

'So,' Paul grins, sheepish.

'So,' I grin back.

Embarrassed suddenly, we eye each other up. Then I lean towards him and push my mouth into his cheek. Up close, he smells stale.

The first time I kissed Paul, I was thirteen. We were lying on my bed one empty afternoon, listening to the Cure above a summer storm. Unsurprised to find ourselves twisting towards each other – even though there had never been anything sexual between us. The kiss had more to do with a lazy sort of curiosity than desire. I was girl-soft. He was boy-smooth and smelt of good things. Like sherbet dips and pencil shavings. He put a hand against my cheek. It was the hand that wore the red leather Snoopy watch I'd always coveted. I could hear it ticking as he moved his face towards mine.

My first proper kiss. For a moment, I thought we understood each other more completely than either of us would ever be able to understand another person again. I thought this right up until Paul pulled back, his elbow pushed into my pillow, looking down at me and shaking his head.

'Nah,' he exhaled. 'Not my thing.'

My mother realized long before the rest of us did. When she told Angelina, they had a terrifying row, but that didn't stop Paul coming round. Just as I had my reasons for visiting his mother – the first aid kit, regular meals – Paul had his reasons for visiting mine. These reasons were the long, giggling dressing-up sessions that took place in my mother's bedroom, when they would wade and rifle through her dresses, high-heeled shoes, her scattered jewellery collection and any bits of make-up they could lay their hands on. Things I'd shown no interest in.

Paul, I know, still misses her.

He shakes the hair from his face, grabbing at my wrists and giving them a light squeeze. 'The Crawleys, Becky. You're going to work for the fucking Crawleys. I mean – what are the chances?'

Tugging a hand loose, I flick at his name badge. 'Give me six months. I'll have something worked out by then, and you can join me. We'll find somewhere to rent.'

He glances down at his uniform, which is for an electronics store in town. 'This is temporary. It isn't so bad. There's the 20 per cent staff discount.'

'Come on, London's always been the plan.'

We've been trading dreams since childhood, and he's the only person – apart from George – who knows that since I stopped playing piano at thirteen, I've been writing. Poetry and short stories mostly. But since winning the *County Times* Young Journalist of the Year award, I've been thinking about becoming a war correspondent – imagining myself writing reports while under fire, in shaking hotels with decor obscured by concrete dust.

'Maybe.'

He leaves the engine running as he hauls the suitcases from the car.

The coach driver watches us from the pavement while finishing a cigarette, then he jerks his head in the direction of the open luggage storage area and disappears up the steps of the coach.

Paul tails me to the door, standing with his shoulders hunched, shivering. He looks ill.

'Six months,' I urge, desperate suddenly to avoid this sense of ending. 'I'll phone with my new number, OK?'

'OK,' he says. Nothing more than an echo.

As we pull away it starts to rain. Slipping on my headphones, I wave at him from behind the streaked glass, but he doesn't wave back. We turn a corner and Paul disappears, along with my mother's car.

# Haversham

The summer I turned eight, my mother's car journeys started taking place at night. 'Let's go for a drive,' she would announce, waking me up and hauling me from my bed without explanation. The first time it happened, I thought she'd chosen our route at random, but we kept going back to the same village. Then we started pulling up outside the same house. I came to understand without her having to say anything that this house was the destination – had always been the destination – of our night drives.

It stood alone, a garden wrapped around it, just like all the other houses on the street: well-tended family homes with piles of bicycles in the front garden, children who had been allowed to stay up late shrieking somewhere close by, and often the smell of a barbecue through the open car windows.

'Who do you think lives there?' she would say.

It became a game, inventing the family who lived in the house – a game I was good at.

One night, we were parked in our usual spot when it started to rain, a torrential summer rain that made the windows of the car steam up immediately. I rubbed a peephole into the condensation as the door to the house opened and a child around my age appeared, illuminated by a porch light. Oblivious to the rain, she ran into the garden, arms flapping in the dressing gown she was wearing as if gesturing at the downpour to stop. Seconds later, a man followed her out of the house holding a coat over his head. Until, crouching beside a bicycle which had been left collapsed in the grass, she pulled a soft toy from the basket and started cradling it.

'It's Mr Hamilton and Amy,' I said above the sound of the rain banging on the car roof, turning – excited – to my mother (Hamilton was the name I'd given the family). As if they were two fictional characters brought, unexpectedly, to life.

'Open the window – I can't see.'

I started to turn the handle, but my mother, impatient, took wide sweeps at the fogged-up windscreen with her arm, accidentally switching on the headlights and catching the attention of Mr Hamilton. Pushing against me from behind, she thrust her head towards the open window. Sometimes, I'm convinced that she shouted into the rain. Other times, I'm equally convinced that she remained silent. Either way, Mr Hamilton scooped his daughter up into his arms, pulling the coat over them both, and fled – it really did feel as if he was fleeing – back towards the house.

We remained staring out of the open window, our faces wet. The next thing my mother said – or perhaps it was the first – I clearly remember.

'I could walk in there and destroy everything. The whole show.'

I waited, my breath slowing. I didn't for a moment doubt her – my mother wasn't a woman to make empty threats. Eyes fixed on the house, I tried to imagine the destruction. Would it explode? Go up in flames? Or simply crumple into the overgrown tangle of summer garden? And what about the people inside – did they have any idea of the danger they were in? Part of me wanted to find out, but another part of me – the bigger part – was terrified of her leaving the car, crossing the road, pushing open the front gate and following the path to the front door.

'It's a lie. A big, fucking lie. They don't know that, but we do, Becky,' she said, with a softness I wasn't used to. 'We have that on them. We have that, at least.'

By the time we returned to the estate, the lights in everybody's windows had gone out.

'Home,' I said, relieved.

Years later, when I was driving myself, I tried to find the house my mother threatened to destroy, but I couldn't remember the name of the village. If it ever had a name.

# Arriving

Blinking through clumps of waterlogged hair, I take in the stretch of marble dotted with side tables, lamps and flowers. Monstrous blooms that are reflected over and over again in the lobby's mirrored walls.

At the far end, near the lifts, a reception desk and uniformed concierge. Although he doesn't lift his head from the book he's reading, I can feel him watching me as I approach.

'You can't leave those there.'

A pair of eyes slide from the book to the two suitcases I've parked by the revolving door. Up close, he's not much older than me. Ignoring his comment, I say, 'I'm here to see the Crawleys.'

This seems to interest him. Enough to put down the copy of *Hollywood Wives* and take a better look at me. A smile ropes itself across his face.

'You must be the new nanny.' He sprawls back in the chair behind reception, counting out loud on his fingers. 'Nanny number four. Want to know what happened to the last one?'

'I know what happened.'

He repositions himself energetically in his chair, leaning across the desk whose surface is now covered in run-off from my hair. A series of miniature puddles.

'Number three got homesick. Apparently.' The smile widens, stretching from ear to ear before he collapses back in his chair again. 'Just take the lift straight up.'

I retrieve the suitcases one at a time, wheel them across the lobby and manoeuvre them into the juddering lift.

As the doors start to close, he calls out, 'You won't last a week.'

Standing in the carpeted hallway, I press on the doorbell and wait. I can't hear ringing on the other side. In fact, I can't hear anything at all. This is a padded world where sounds recede and diminish. A person could be murdered, I think, and nobody would notice.

At last, the door is opened by a woman in her late twenties. She has highlights and a Rolling Stones T-shirt stretched to its limits across the largest pair of breasts I've ever seen. Her face is a pretty but untidy smudge. Like she's been crying.

Beyond her shoulders, an expanse of cream and gold apartment stretches out indefinitely.

Pulling myself together and putting on my best Chilston House voice, I say, 'Excuse me, but is this the Crawley residence?'

'The Crawley residence?' she repeats, barking out a sudden laugh.

The voice is a surprise. Traces of Essex still in the vowels. Shaped, like my mother's, by wind-chewed marshes and low skies. It catches me out, but after a few seconds, I manage to regain my balance.

'Yeah, this is the Crawley residence.' She gives my soaking coat sleeve an unexpected squeeze. 'And thank fuck you're here.'

'Rebecca,' I finish for her. Before venturing, 'Mrs Crawley?'

'Call me Rosa.'

The next minute, both arms are thrown around me. Another blast of laughter, up close this time, as snuggled against her ample bosom, my visions of severe housekeepers and aloof, well-groomed wives vanish.

This isn't what I was expecting.

When I'm finally released, it's to find a waist-high child contemplating me with dark eyes only just visible beneath a pair of swimming goggles. This must be Violet Crawley. Half the reason I'm here. Her long hair hangs, uncombed, over shoulders that flinch suddenly as a baby starts to cry.

'Lulu's awake.'

The child says this to me rather than her mother.

'Fuck,' Rosa exhales.

But she seems to be more interested in my suitcases than the crying baby. I wonder if she might be drunk. Or even medicated. There's something uneven about her that reminds me of my mother when she was on Prozac.

'Did you bring those upstairs yourself?'

We all eye the enormous suitcases filling the corridor outside. Streaked, still, with dark patches from the rain.

'The little prick,' Rosa explodes, before I have time to answer. 'The little prick!'

She stalks off, barefoot, down the corridor towards the lifts.

'Do you want me to see to Lulu?' I call out after her.

'No,' she calls back, 'she'll cry herself out. And don't even think about moving those suitcases. Violet, why don't you show Becky around the apartment.'

The child watches me through the goggles she's wearing. I watch her back, briefly intent on each other before her eyes shift to the parked cases, almost the same height as her.

'You've got a lot of stuff.'

Is this a good or a bad thing?

'Kate only had one suitcase.'

Homesick Kate. Nanny number three. Feeling measured suddenly against my predecessor, I say, 'Do you miss her?'

Violet shrugs, considering me carefully. 'How far can you swim?'

'One thousand metres.'

'One thousand metres,' she repeats, her jaw going slack. 'Kate could hardly swim a length. She wore make-up to the swimming pool, and she wouldn't put her head underwater.'

I decide to risk an opinion. 'She sounds boring.'

Violet looks pleased. 'What's in them?' she demands, twisting back towards the suitcases.

'Guess.'

'Clothes?'

'Try lifting one.'

Curiosity animates her solemn little face as she slides across the parquet floor and attempts to lift one of the suitcases. She heaves her shoulders up towards her ears with the effort.

'I can't,' she gasps, making a show of shaking her arms and panting. 'It's too heavy. What's inside?'

'You're sure you want to know?'

'Tell me,' she demands, fists and jaw clenched as she starts to jump on the spot. Her crying sister is forgotten.

Lowering my voice, I whisper, 'Bodies.'

She lets out an excited yelp that seems to take her by surprise. Her face is alight now. Her eyes shine behind the goggles.

'The bodies of all the other children I've looked after.'

'You're lying,' she squeals, ecstatic.

'It's true. Take a look if you don't believe me.'

Violet flounders, coming to a complete standstill while darting a series of covert glances at the suitcases, whose lumpish bulges have taken on a far more sinister aspect. For a moment, I almost believe it myself.

'Go on,' I urge.

Running her tongue quickly across her upper lip, she advances. Cautiously. On tiptoe. Before coming to a stop. 'How did you fit all the bodies inside?'

'I cut them up,' I assert, gravely. 'Arms. Legs. Head.'

I mime the procedure, Violet following the movement of my hands.

A new determination settles over her.

Taking hold of a handle, she rocks one of the cases awkwardly backwards and forwards before aiming a kick at it and venturing the hopeful verdict, 'Doesn't feel like bodies.'

'Look inside.'

She extends a thin arm towards the shining zip then changes her mind.

'Open it!' she commands, rounding on me.

'You're sure?'

She nods.

Reaching around her, I pull on the zip.

She presses her face as close to the opening as she dares, then whispers, 'I can't see anything.'

'Put your hand inside.'

Caught somewhere between fear and excitement, she squeezes her eyes shut before pushing a small hand through the opening. A squeal, and the hand is withdrawn.

'You tricked me,' she announces happily, as the goggles are at last removed, leaving behind deep, red indents in the skin around her eyes. 'You're fun. Not like Kate. You won't get homesick, will you?'

'I can't.'

'Can't?' Violet echoes, her face wide open, waiting.

'I don't have a home. I don't have any parents either.'

'You're an orphan!' She stares at me with renewed fascination, as if looking for physical symptoms. 'Like Annie.'

Violet gives me a tour of the apartment as instructed by Rosa. I follow her through a series of vast rooms whose polished floors she slides across in stockinged feet while I tiptoe behind. Each one we pass through is full of the same heavy hush. The sound of the crying baby has as good as vanished.

It's hard not to be impressed and when Violet's back is turned, I give in to a gaping awe.

'Daddy's study,' she warns, suddenly censorious as we come to a halt outside a closed door. 'Nobody goes in there.' Adding, for good measure, 'It's locked.'

At the sound of her voice, there's a squawk on the other side, followed by frantic flutterings and scufflings.

'What *is* that?' I whisper.

'Winston, the parrot. It's why we go through so many cleaners. They're expected to muck out the cage and most of them refuse. Mummy fired the last cleaner yesterday.' She snaps the goggles back onto her face, sounding much older than five when she says, 'We've been alone since then.'

Perhaps it's her baby sister's arrival in the cream and gold apartment that has made Violet the sombre, watchful child she is. Or perhaps she's just made that way. But it's as if a little darkness has already crept into her childish world. It's something I recognize.

'Well, I'm here now,' I say, without thinking.

She grabs at my hand, a clutching, sticky-fingered grip. 'I know we're not meant to, but let's go and see Lulu.'

The door to the nursery is ajar and although the crying has stopped, lonely-sounding snuffles can be heard coming from inside. The thought of stepping into the shuttered room with its animal smells terrifies me. Despite the references and reassurances given to Jemima Pinkerton, I've never so much as held a baby before.

'Lulu,' Violet calls out in a singsong whisper, pushing open the door and padding into the room. Inside is a hectic world of primary colours.

The shape in the cot stirs.

I watch as Lulu hauls herself through the tumult of blankets and soft toys until she reaches the cot's bars and pulls herself upright. Once vertical, she lets out a series of excited screams. Her eyes never leave Violet who slides efficiently about the room, picking up toys from the floor and throwing them back into the cot.

As soon as these land behind bars, Lulu scoops them up enthusiastically and hurls them floorwards again while jabbing her manic little legs up and down.

'Lulu, stop it,' Violet scolds, enjoying the authority, twisting around to make sure I'm watching. 'Naughty,' she insists severely, looming over her baby sister, who starts to cry again.

'Shush. Lulu, shush,' Violet tries to soothe, as the sound of voices moving through the apartment reaches us. A series of high-pitched instructions from Rosa are followed by the rumbling of suitcases across wooden floors. 'Quick!'

Violet, panic-stricken, pulls me from Lulu's lair. Abandoning the sobbing baby, we run down the corridor hand in hand until we reach a bedroom, only minutes before Rosa and the uniformed concierge from downstairs appear.

Rosa is imperious, throwing her arms and voice about – 'Don't leave them there!' – putting on a far more impressive version of Mrs Crawley than the one I encountered on arrival. The spotty concierge, half her height and stuck, inescapably, at tit-level, is red-faced and struggling, his face tight with the effort of hauling the two suitcases across the threshold and into the room we are now all gathered in, his scuffed shoes scudding to a halt. The sight of them almost makes me feel sorry for him. Almost. Panting, he backs off, brushing at his trousers, wet from my suitcases.

Rosa's fuzz of highlighted blonde hair vibrates as she says, 'Heavy, aren't they! How on earth did you expect Rebecca to manage those herself?'

Only I did, I think. All the way from Victoria coach station. Hauling them for twenty-five minutes through driving rain. An image of myself lost and traffic-splashed is briefly conjured before I bury it, along with a whole host of other unwanted images. Girls I no longer want to be.

'Very sorry, Mrs Crawley.'

The concierge clasps his hands over his crotch and lowers his head.

'It's not me you should be apologizing to, it's Rebecca.'

Taking advantage of Rosa's outrage, he risks a quick glance at her breasts before swinging towards me. 'I'm sorry,' he manages.

'All right, you can go,' Rosa says, suddenly deflated.

The concierge reverses, stooping, from the room.

'I've been waiting to get back at him for months – Pitt's had that wanker spying on me, I just know it.' She waves her hand in the air. 'So, what do you think?'

I stare at her, trying to work out what it is I'm meant to have an opinion of. The concierge? Pitt, spying on her?

'This,' she says, impatient, sweeping an arm around the room.

And then it dawns on me.

'This is mine?'

I want to check, to be doubly sure.

'You like it?'

Overwhelmed suddenly, I give a quick nod before crossing to the window, aware of both mother and daughter watching me. Pressing my hands against the cold glass, I stare through the rain at the wobble of neon signs belonging to an Italian restaurant and pharmacy on the street below. London.

'So – you'll stay?'

There's anxiety in Rosa's voice.

Violet says, 'She has to. Rebecca doesn't have a home. Or a mummy. Or a daddy.'

Rosa is trying to keep up. 'So, your parents—'

'Dead.' I lower my eyes, hoping to mitigate the sheer scale of misfortune I trail in my wake. Unsure, yet, whether Rosa is the type of person who views misfortune as contagious and to be avoided at all costs or the type of person who feels drawn to the dark allure of it.

'Dead?' she echoes, as on cue an immaculately manicured pair of hands reach for mine, giving them a hard squeeze. 'Well, you've got us now. We should celebrate.' She raises her voice above Lulu, who has started wailing again. 'We need champagne!'

There is champagne in the cavernous fridge in the kitchen, though little else. Two glasses are taken from a cupboard and filled to overflowing. Rosa passes me one, shaking the excess drops from her hand, before bending over the other one and sucking the liquid down to a manageable level.

Violet follows this in silence. 'Daddy doesn't like you drinking before it gets dark.'

Ignoring her, Rosa turns to me and begins to run haphazardly through the children's routine. The mealtimes, playtimes, sleep times, bath times and bedtimes, in no particular order. As if she has trouble remembering it all. Or is simply making it up.

'I've been quite regimented,' she claims, wildly. 'I don't think I would have coped otherwise. After Kate, Amelia made lists for me.'

'Amelia?'

'The Valentines' nanny. They have the apartment above this one.'

'It was Amelia who found Kate,' says Violet.

Speaking loudly over her daughter, Rosa says, 'Violet has ballet on Wednesdays.'

'Tuesdays,' Violet puts in. 'And Thursdays.'

'You need to take them swimming on—'

'Monday.'

Violet and I look at each other; her eyes still wear the red rings left by her goggles. I think about risking a smile. Instead, I give my eyebrows a quick lift. The first gesture of complicity between us.

'But other than that . . .' Rosa turns towards the window as if worried that the outside world might disappear altogether. 'Every day's the same. As you know. It's what you're used to, I guess?'

'Of course. It's why I'm here,' I reassure her.

Reassurance, after all, is what Rosa is paying for.

'I want to show you something,' she announces suddenly.

She pushes herself unsteadily to her feet and grabs at the edge of the table for a moment, before lurching off down the darkening corridor leading to the bedrooms.

Eventually we reach a room Violet omitted from her guided tour earlier. Rosa flicks the switch, shedding light on the turbulence inside – I remember Violet telling me the cleaner was fired yesterday. The walls are dominated by a series of framed black-and-white photographs of breasts.

I can feel Rosa watching me, following my gaze.

'I was sixteen when my mum sent photos of me in my underwear to the *Mercury*.' Her tone is flat. 'They were running a glamour model competition. I caught the eye of a photographer called Birdie. Changed my life, that competition.'

She waits for the glimmer of recognition.

Then, with an eerie laugh, she throws back her head and strikes a pose. 'Rosa Dawson. *The* Page Three girl. It's how I met Pitt,' she says at last. 'My husband? Editor of the *Mercury*?'

She hesitates, about to add something else before changing her mind. 'There's a photograph of him on the dressing table. Take a look if you want.'

I turn to pick up a framed photograph from among the cosmetic debris and a guide to palmistry. Rosa as a young bride. Very young. Not much older than me. Flanked on either side by a man. One, tall and handsome – the groom? The other, much older – her father?

She leans in, unsteady.

'Gorgeous, isn't he?' A fingernail sweeps over the younger man.

Insanely, I think. Even more so than George. Although it's the sadness in the face that strikes me more than anything. 'That's Pitt?'

'No. Rawdon. Pitt's son from his first marriage – they don't get on. I'm the reason for that. There's a Mrs Crawley number one. A l-a-d-y.' She affects a drawl. 'I'm Mrs Crawley number two. Rawdon can't stand me. Used to send me a bouquet of dead flowers every week when we first got married. Completely creeped me out.' Rippling with a sudden shudder, she adds, 'And you should see some of the things people send me. The other guy – the *old* guy – that's who I'm married to.'

She pulls back. I can feel her gauging the effect of this on me.

'I was only twenty-one. It caused a huge scandal. Pitt's sister, Matilda – she runs the show – threatened to have him thrown off the paper. Sometimes I think that's the only reason he married me, to piss her off.' Rosa looks momentarily startled, as if this is something she has often thought, but never actually heard herself say out loud before.

Later, I'll make a careful record of this conversation in my diary under the heading *The Crawleys*. I'm forever taking notes, and always try to do as much background research as I can on everyone I meet.

'Sorry, I'm being unfiltered – I haven't had any company the same height as me in a while.'

Rosa is sitting scrunched up on the side of the unmade bed, hands pushed between her thighs. Eyes bright, teary.

This is all such familiar territory. Take away the backdrop of the Knightsbridge flat and I could almost be at home with my mother.

'God, I'm glad you're here, Rebecca. Look, why don't I go out and get us some lunch – I won't be long.' Another energetic hug. 'We're going to be such great friends.'

Then, after throwing something made of animal skin over the Rolling Stones T-shirt, she flees the apartment in a triumphant clatter of heels and keys.

Lulu hangs in the air, suspended by her armpits between me and Violet, who has just lifted her sister out of the cot in one swift movement. She must have done this before. Many times.

Left with no choice, I take a grappling hold of the rigid bundle, dropping her onto my shoulder, which she immediately starts to gnaw at. How hard can it be, looking after someone who weighs less than a bag of potatoes? I manage a smile and Violet, satisfied, slides out of the room towards the kitchen.

I follow, but Lulu, sensing the novice in me, starts to whimper before fast becoming a twisting bundle of rage. Soon her feet are caught up in a continual cycle of spasms.

'She seems unhappy,' I say, desperate.

Violet, laying the table in anticipation of the lunch Rosa has gone to buy, stares at me, her hands full of shining cutlery. 'Try the highchair.'

While I do this – the simple instruction far harder to follow than it sounds – Violet grabs a biscuit from a jar on the bench

and drops it onto the highchair's tray. At the sight of the biscuit, Lulu's rigid legs buckle, and she slips easily into the sticky
seat.

We wait, but there's no sign of Rosa.

Lulu seems content enough in her highchair as long as she
has a biscuit in her hand. Soporific, even. But as soon as she
finishes one, she throws her arm towards the jar on the bench,
unclenching her fist and waiting, palm up. If the palm isn't
replenished fast enough, she starts to bang her head against
the back of the highchair and scream.

The scribbled instructions Violet hands to me on an Elite
Models pad – misspelt and framed with felt tip hearts – tell me
that if Lulu finishes all her lunch, she's allowed two biscuits. At
the most. She's had ten so far and still no sign of Rosa.

Violet has been concentrating hard on drawing a mermaid
but looks up as I reach into the jar for the last remaining
biscuit, her neat little eyes watching me.

'What are you going to do when you run out?'

Before I have time to consider this, Lulu starts to vomit. A
textured cascade of brownish hues quickly fills the highchair's
tray, overflowing onto the kitchen floor. Lulu is too shocked
to cry. The penultimate biscuit is still clutched in her fist as
she sits stunned by the mess that has collected on the tray in
front of her. Then she pushes her free hand gingerly through
it and into her mouth.

'Oh, God. Lulu, stop. Stop!' I shout without thinking.
Appealing, frantic, to Violet: 'What should I do?'

She stares wide-eyed, first at her sister, then at me, before
slipping from the room and breaking into a run towards the
apartment's main door.

'Violet, wait. Wait!' I call after her. 'Where are you going?'

But she has already disappeared along the carpeted corridor
outside.

I can hear her receding wails. 'Amelia! Amelia!'

Back in the kitchen, Lulu has fistfuls of fawn-coloured vomit that she alternately pushes into her mouth then through her hair as she chatters happily to herself. The sleepsuit is covered. The highchair is covered. The floor is covered. Fallout from this will be found for months to come in the most improbable of places.

Despite the high ceilings, the smell persists. I restrict breathing to my mouth alone while wondering where on earth Rosa is.

After a mad scrabble under the sink, I find a pair of rubber gloves, presumably abandoned by the last cleaner. I pull them on and haul Lulu by her armpits into the air. It takes her a while to realize what's happening and it isn't until she lands on the kitchen floor that she starts screaming. Sliding her away from the vomit with my foot, I manage to grab hold of the kitchen roll and start mopping at the mess, a sodden pile of tissue growing steadily around me.

And it's then that a girl's voice cries out, buoyant, 'Hello!'

The next minute, she appears in the kitchen doorway with a boy of around two clamped to her hip. Violet and another child trail after her. All four of them survey the scene in silence. Even Lulu, sensing the gravity of the situation, has finally stopped screaming and eating her own vomit, although it continues to drip through the knuckles of her clenched fist.

This must be the nanny from upstairs.

Our eyes flicker over each other. Covert glances are exchanged until finally, grinning, she breaks the silence with, 'Oh Lulu, you really did eat ten biscuits, didn't you? How is that even possible?'

'I told you,' Violet says, turning towards her. 'And that includes the two biscuits Lulu's actually allowed.'

Although she must know that this information amounts to

a betrayal, Violet is clearly relieved to be able to share it with the other nanny, who would never have given Lulu more than two biscuits.

'We can't get away with anything, can we?' the girl says, smiling suddenly at me. 'Hi, by the way – I'm Amelia.'

# Amelia

The kitchen lights reflect off the metal running up both her ears and the stud in her nose. She's almost shamefaced about her own beauty, making a concerted effort to distract people from it. Her hair is short, she isn't wearing any make-up, and she looks as though she shares a boyfriend's wardrobe. On her feet, a pair of worn-out Doc Martens. None of these decoys work. I find myself taking another look. Peering more closely at her. Not just because she's beautiful, but because there's something familiar about her that I can't quite place. This is both unsettling and unexpected.

Prising the boy from her hip, she enters the kitchen, grabbing at tea towels, cloths and bowls – the Crawleys' apartment is clearly a familiar place to her. Once she has cleaned up as much of the mess as she can, she strips Lulu of her vomit-soaked clothes.

'Let's give the floor a mop while we're at it,' she commands.

This is more than efficiency.

Watching Amelia, it's hard to believe that there is anywhere else in the world she would rather be than here in this Knightsbridge kitchen clearing up a child's vomit. Her happiness is contagious.

Soon Violet and the two Valentine children are fighting over who gets to use the mop.

The afternoon becomes animated. Boisterous, even. Full of an energy that propels us from kitchen to bathroom where a warm, scented bath is run, and Lulu passed to me while Amelia scoops up Violet.

Finding herself suddenly airborne, Violet's innate decorum gives way to joy. The corridor is spacious but as Amelia swings her around, Violet's feet graze paintings until they hang at an angle, knocking furniture onto its side. Soon the whole apartment seems to be at a tilt as they collapse, laughing, to the floor. Amelia lies sprawled on her back as Violet kneels across her stomach, pinning her arms to the rug.

'Say you surrender!'

'You surrender.'

'No,' Violet giggles, breathless, 'you have to say, *I* surrender.'

'Oh. Right. *I* surrender.'

With a groan, Amelia flips Violet from her stomach and crawls into a sitting position. Her hair is splayed across her face and most of her clothes hang untucked as she bounces back into the bathroom and takes Lulu from me, plunging her into the bubbles.

'Aren't they just gorgeous at this age,' she exclaims, gently splashing at Lulu who is sucking on a yellow submarine.

I pass her a towel and watch, inert, as she somehow manages to lift the wet, wriggling Lulu out of the water and wrap her up in one smooth movement.

'Here. Sorry to take over.'

With an effort, I balance the child on my left hip, struggling to get a grip on Lulu's skin – still covered with bubbles – where the towel has slipped. There's something alarming about the child's nakedness. The way the damp flesh bulges and folds without purpose.

I can feel Amelia watching me.

'You haven't done this before, have you?' she says, suddenly.

'Rebecca doesn't like babies very much.'

Violet, who has been bouncing on her bed, is standing, dishevelled, in the doorway.

'Well, babies aren't everybody's thing.' Amelia shakes her head and looks away. When she turns to face me again, the expression on her face is decisive.

For an awful moment I think she might be about to call Rosa and tell her.

'But we're not going to say anything about Rebecca not liking babies, OK? It's going to be our secret. And anyway, she'll get the hang of it. You'll see.'

Violet considers me for a moment before nodding.

We watch as she tears back into her bedroom where the Valentine children are bouncing on the bed.

'Thank you.'

'That's OK.'

'I mean it.'

'It's no big deal,' she laughs, shaking the moment loose, so that it doesn't gather too much weight.

Laughter, I'll discover, is something Amelia's prone to. Here, in the early days of our friendship, anyway.

'So, what is your thing – if it isn't babies?'

'Journalism. I want to work for the newspapers.'

'Well, you're in the right place. You know Mr Crawley's editor of the *Mercury*?' She pauses, the laughter giving way to a narrow smile. 'Have you met him yet?'

'No.'

We watch the water drain from the bath, leaving the yellow submarine grounded on a sandbank of bubbles.

'Did you hear about Kate?'

'I heard that she got homesick.'

Amelia catches hold of one of Lulu's purple feet.

Since my mother's death I've been prone to violent day-dreams, and now – without warning – in the silence that follows, I imagine Kate, untidily draped in this very bath. The water, pitch red.

Amelia hesitates as if about to add something else before changing tack. 'I can't think of anything worse. Journalism, I mean. I've got really bad dyslexia – can barely spell my own name. I left school with four O levels, and I've got no idea what I want to do. Apart from this.' She picks up Lulu's sodden romper between thumb and finger. 'I'll just check to see if Rosa's got anything else that needs putting through the machine.'

In the Crawleys' en-suite, Amelia upends a large wicker basket onto the floor, adding to the devastation of towels piled in damp heaps, spilt lotions and liquids, discarded packaging and cotton wool pads smeared in graphic pinks. There's something frantic – resplendent almost – about the chaos that reminds me of my mother.

'Oh, Rosa,' Amelia mumbles, sad rather than irritated at the mess as she sorts the contents of the basket into lights and darks. 'Where *is* she?'

'She went out over an hour ago – to get lunch, she said.'

'Yeah, she does that,' Amelia smiles, shaking out the wet towels and hanging them back on the rail. 'Well, don't expect her back any time soon – I'll help you feed the kids. Look, something you should know about Rosa – she's been prescribed Prozac for her depression, but she's bad at sticking to the prescription. You need to keep an eye on her.'

Embracing the tumbling piles of clothes and underwear collected from the bathroom floor, Amelia says, 'I sort of helped out after Kate. Emergency measures.' It sounds like an apology. 'Rosa showed me your CV,' she carries on above the laundry. 'I know it's meant to be confidential, but after Kate . . . she just wanted me to take a quick look.' Amelia freezes for a moment with embarrassment. 'So, I couldn't help noticing that you went to Chilston House.'

*Hearse.* Of course. That's why I recognize her. Her face was all over the school prospectuses I used to consume in the waiting room outside the registrar's office during those long Saturday afternoons after piano practice while my mother was still cleaning. Willing myself into the photographs of cross-legged girls grouped on green lawns, sunlight in their hair.

'Rebecca, so did I! We must have been there at the same time. How old are you?'

'Eighteen.'

'Well, almost the same time. I'm twenty. Just. God— What's your surname?'

'Sharp.'

'Rebecca Sharp.' She shakes her head. 'Funny, I don't recognize you at all, and I'm usually good with faces. Different year groups, maybe that's why.'

I watch her flounder and give in to a frowning hesitation. The same hesitation that possessed Jemima Pinkerton when I became overly eager in her small, carpeted office. Instinct kicking in. The warning voice in their heads raising the red flag. It's important not to buckle here. To stand firm. Stay silent. Something I just about manage, until the moment passes and Amelia drops the laundry in a pile at her feet, giving me a hug I wasn't anticipating.

It catches me out. Catches unexpectedly at my throat. This hug that smells of strawberries.

Then, pulling back, 'Which house were you in?'

Those Saturdays, after piano practice, I would drift through the school buildings and grounds, an invisible trespasser absorbing as much as I could of school life and the codes that governed it. Drifting into boarding houses that smelt of poorly ventilated showers, rotting trainers, wet socks left on radiators – and hormones. Crazy. Confined. Through common rooms to see who was in the lead with house points, and which sports fixtures had been won – and the dormitories with their tidy rows of beds, the battered headboards covered in defaced stickers.

In the vast dining hall, I swept up uneaten bread rolls from lunch, and in the panelled library, which was always empty, I read books from cover to cover. Trailing groups of girls along carpeted corridors, I picked up school slang, so that when I overheard them arranging to meet on the Row, the Heights or in the Cave, I knew where these places were. All this and more I wrote down in my diary, which is why I'm able to answer, without hesitation, 'Camelia.'

I've been practising.

# Haversham

I used to have a paper round. I would cycle in the early-morning dark to the newsagent's beside the station, following the bouncing beam of my bicycle light. In the stock room, Mr Andrews would be stooped over packing the wide-strapped shoulder bag with my round. A quiet, preoccupied man, he would help to hang the bag over the bulky blue anorak I wore, checking that it wasn't too heavy. It always weighed the same, but if I had said as much it would have rendered this small, intimate ritual unnecessary, and it was something I had come to anticipate.

I sensed that Mr Andrews was grateful for my silence. His own daughter was in a home for severely disabled children. I don't know how I knew this because he never talked about her, and I have no idea whether he even visited. But it was her absence, I felt, that made our morning ritual as necessary to him as it was to me. Once the bag was fitted and Mr Andrews had said his usual, 'It'll soon be empty,' he would reach up at random for one of the jars of sweets from the dark shelves behind the counter, unscrew the lid in that slow, deliberate way of his, and put the morning's offering in the palm of my hand.

'See you back here for seven thirty, Becky,' he would say over the clanging of the bell, as he opened the shop door and I disappeared into the winter morning. I don't recall ever seeing him beyond the boundaries of the shop.

On Fridays, towards the end of the round, I would sit in a bus shelter and read the only remaining newspaper – always the *Mercury* – before delivering it to my final stop, a barber-shop. The pieces I enjoyed were the shorter ones that had been set adrift in the middle of the paper, as if whoever decided on these things was unsure where they should go. Random pieces with headlines like, 'Mother of four claims she heard voices in her head', 'Dad of two goes on killing rampage'. They were always accompanied by lopsided-looking family snap-shots from 'before' that revelled in the apparent ordinariness of these people's lives, leaving the reader to join the dots and fill in the gaps.

When I returned to the shop with the empty bag, there would be a small brown envelope waiting for me on the counter, my name written across it in shaky cursive. Inside this envelope was the collection of coins that made up my weekly salary. It forged a link in my young mind, one that I wasn't aware of at the time, between newsprint and money.

And then, the year I turned sixteen, I won the *County Times* Young Journalist of the Year competition. I was given the afternoon off school to attend the award ceremony, which was being held at the newspaper's offices, overlooking the park. After being presented with my £20 cheque and certifi-cate, I had my photograph taken with Mr Saunders, editor of the *County Times*, for the front page of that Friday's edition. He slung a comfortable arm around my waist. Up close, Mr Saunders smelt of pub carpet and meals nobody had enjoyed eating. But I ignored this because he had just told me that my prize-winning piece was standout. That's what he said: standout. I was a talented girl.

I'd written about John Haigh, acid bath murderer, who was famously apprehended and tried in our small town. Like me, he was a talented pianist, but what really drew me to Haigh were his abilities as a forger and fraudster. He had a talent for pretending to be people he was not. Killing, as it turned out, was simply something he was forced into in order to protect his alter egos.

I was prickling with pride as Mr Saunders' arm – the one held loosely around my waist – slipped away. This was followed by a sensation of warmth on my left buttock. I pictured a hand, hovering, but couldn't be sure. Only, at the same time, I was sure. I can't remember how I felt about this. Surprised, maybe. A little bit excited. Maybe. I turned to look at him, but he no longer seemed to be aware of me. Distracted, instead, by something happening elsewhere in the room. He started wheezing. Ever so slightly.

Then, still without looking at me, he said, 'You know what – we've got a vacancy at the moment for a Saturday girl. How about it?'

# Mr Crawley

Almost a month passes before I finally meet Pitt Crawley. Although I've managed to build a good profile of him from conversations with Violet who, unabridged in her enthusiasm, responds eagerly to all my questions, no matter how probing or inappropriate. From Violet I've also learned that her father loves cricket and racehorses, and a relatively innocent perusal of the sitting room's meticulously ordered vinyl collection has uncovered a passion for Hendrix. On dingy days we hole up for hours in the children's corner at South Kensington Library. Me with a pile of Pitt-specific reference books, Lulu sucking a board book to pulp on a beanbag, and Violet hunched over an age-inappropriate graphic novel.

Rosa, drunk and medicated, has likewise proven a lucrative source of information. Curled up on one of the apartment's many sofas, she has taken to sharing things about the state of her marriage that make her sob on my shoulder, leaving a wet slurry of make-up and grief on whatever top I'm wearing.

Useful things that I've been recording in my diary. Along with Pitt's movements, which I keep a close eye on.

This is how I know that by the time Lulu wakes at 6 a.m., Mr Crawley has already left the apartment. He returns late most nights. Well after midnight. A schedule that has had a negative impact on the opportunity for chance encounters in the apartment's long corridors and high-ceilinged rooms. It's hard to affect accidentally bumping into someone at 2 a.m.

And then one night something unexpected happens.

Mr Crawley and Rosa are out together at a charity gala. Violet, like her sister, is asleep at last, eyelids closed over that watchful gaze of hers. Finally, I'm free to roam the apartment alone for the first time since arriving. I start with a brief but frenzied foray through the Crawleys' bathroom. Having grown up without any sort of masculine clutter, I am particularly fascinated by Mr Crawley's toiletries: the shaving brush, which hasn't been washed properly and is still covered in a dusting of dried soap; the glass bottle full of an amber-coloured liquid that I've smelt traces of in the corners of rooms.

This is followed by an equally frenzied ransacking of the bedroom's cupboards and drawers. It's as if I'm searching for clues, but clues to what I have no idea.

In the dressing room with its wall of mirrors I watch myself rifle through Rosa's clothes, shoes and jewellery, trying on a dress designed by David and Elizabeth Emanuel, the same designers responsible for the Princess's wedding dress. Rosa's taller than she looks. The dress falls in fretful folds around my feet, as I try to balance in a pair of overlarge shoes. The jewellery looks fake on me. I feel like a child playing at dressing up and worry that other people's clothes – the donations; hand-me-downs; charity shop finds – are all I'll ever know.

Unzipping myself aggressively from the dress, I grab the jeans and T-shirt I stepped out of earlier. Then, before I can change my mind, I pad back down the corridor towards my room, scribble *Read this please!* across a scented Post-it note, and stick it on the copy of the *County Times* where my award-winning John Haigh piece was published. I retrace my steps until I'm outside Mr Crawley's study.

Crouching down, I begin to push the newspaper under the door and then on second thoughts try the handle. The door Violet told me was locked opens easily.

Light from the corridor illuminates bookshelves, a desk,

fireplace, chair and some framed photographs, just stopping short of the covered parrot cage in the corner. It smells bad in here. Like a fertilized field.

Picking the newspaper up from the floor, I position it on the desk instead, open at the page my piece appears on. The surface of the desk is disappointingly bare, and when I pull open the drawer, there doesn't turn out to be much in there either, apart from an A4 envelope. I give the envelope a shake, and four photographs fall out into the puddle of light from the desk lamp I've just switched on.

Grainy shots of a man and woman on horseback, emerging from woodland. The photos are virtually identical – they must have been taken within seconds of one another. The couple themselves are clearly unaware that they've been caught on camera. Picking up one of the photos and staring more closely at it, I immediately recognize the woman because she's one of the most famous women in the world. It's the Princess. The man, however, is unfamiliar – a question mark, in fact, has been drawn above his head.

Thinking back to what Rosa said about the concierge spying on her, I start checking the corners of the room for hidden cameras, catching sight of something bright, high up near the ceiling. A single, miniature eye. Avian. Blinking. The parrot isn't in his cage, he's on top of the bookshelves. Claws gripping the edge, feathered head tipped to one side, watching me.

Suddenly he raises his wings and starts jabbering.

Pushing the photos back into the envelope, I shut the study door behind me and run towards the Crawleys' room, just about managing to restore order as I hear the front door. Voices. I don't have time to make it to my room, so I cut blindly into the sitting room instead, dropping down at the piano I give Violet her lessons on. The first thing that comes to mind is Mozart's Sonata in C major. It's a showy and shallow performance because I'm out of practice – this is the first time I've played properly since I was thirteen. My fingers are stiff and reluctant at first, before remembering.

Violet's been nagging me to play for her, and although I admit to feeling a certain kind of itch sitting in front of the keyboard beside her while we have our lessons, I'm not sure that this alone would have been enough. Enough to see me sound the notes as I'm sounding them now; the shape, pattern and order imprinted somewhere deep inside, like a forgotten language. Enough for me to lose myself, almost completely, until I reach the end of the piece, light-headed. The furniture and objects in the room around me float, untethered by gravity.

In the heavy silence that follows, the sound of clapping comes as a shock.

Twisting around, I see an indistinct blur that takes some time to assume the separate forms of Mr and Mrs Crawley sprawled at opposite ends of a sofa. A bowtie hangs around Mr Crawley's neck and the collar of his white dress shirt is undone. Even seated, he somehow manages to give the illusion of great height. Perhaps because he's the sort of man who's happy to take up more space than he needs, something that makes him clumsy. He *is* clumsy. If I'm still awake when he returns home at night, I often hear things breaking in the kitchen. The next morning there will be traces of these breakages across the floor. Fragments and shards that have escaped his half-hearted efforts at cleaning up.

Rosa, who is possibly the taller of the two, looks insubstantial beside him. As if he has taken things from her faster than she has been able to replenish them, eaten right through to her reserves. She sits at a tilt, angled away from him.

'You're a dark horse, Rebecca.'

There's just a hint of recrimination in Rosa's voice as she

struggles to the front of the sofa, an off-centre look about her. She's been drinking.

'Yes, where on earth have you been hiding?' Mr Crawley murmurs, staring directly at me.

'This is Rebecca, Pitt.' Rosa drops a hand onto his knee. 'The new nanny.'

She rolls her eyes in my direction. A gesture of complicity I don't return.

'Rebecca. Of course.' His face is struck then by a hard-hitting smile that leaves wrinkles around his eyes. 'Who taught you to play like that?'

I feel the need suddenly to impress, to keep hold of his attention at any cost.

'My father. He used to play for the London Symphony Orchestra.'

'You dark, dark horse.' Rosa frowns, trying to place this new version of me, before turning towards Pitt and lowering her voice to a whisper. 'Rebecca really is an enigma. She never uses the telephone, and nobody ever calls for her. No mail. No boyfriend.'

The unexpected scrutiny comes as a surprise. It leaves me feeling exposed and unable to defend myself. Although from what, I'm not sure.

'Like something washed up,' Mr Crawley puts in suddenly.

'A castaway,' Rosa echoes, her hand on his knee still, warming – briefly, with what little focus she has left – to the game.

'Orphan,' I remind her. 'My parents died in a car accident. I was only eight when it happened. I don't remember much.'

This has the desired effect. Within seconds, Rosa is on her feet hugging me from behind as she tries to find her balance, hair tickling my neck, smelling of her evening.

'Rebecca, we're adopting you!'

'Rebecca's too old for adoption.' Mr Crawley maintains a persistent smile. 'And your mother – was she a musician as well?'

'No, she was a dancer. With the Bolshoi. The London Symphony Orchestra played for the Bolshoi during their UK tour of *Coppélia* in the Seventies. My mother was dancing in the corps de ballet, and my father was playing with the orchestra. That's how they met.'

I pause, expectant. Waiting for the next question.

Mr Crawley continues to smile his hard-to-read smile.

The part about the Bolshoi's UK tour is based on conversations I had with Cyril Byrd, whose first-hand account of one of their performances, although rambling and barely coherent, was the inspiration behind the idea of my mother being a ballerina.

'When was that?'

After a moment's hesitation, and in the desperate hope that Mr Crawley is no balletomane, I say, '1974.'

'So – she must have defected?' he persists, laughter now – I'm convinced – playing around his mouth.

But I rise to the challenge, plunging into an inspired account of my fictional parents' romance as a series of fraught assignations: deep, dark afternoons spent in hotel rooms. I go on to describe the defection that followed in detail: a melting pot of moments gleaned from various biographies I've read, including those of Nureyev and Baryshnikov.

I've been told that my recall for detail is impressive. Convincing, at least. But Mr Crawley doesn't look convinced, and Rosa has fallen into a stupefied silence. Perhaps I've overwhelmed them.

'I'm hungry,' Mr Crawley announces suddenly. 'Montefiore's, anyone?'

'It's almost midnight – they're closed.' Rosa continues to whisper, a hangover from their earlier game.

'The kitchens will still be open. I can get Gino to bring us something. Hungry, Rebecca?'

Using my shoulder for support, Rosa stands up.

'Rebecca's tired. We're all tired.'

Taking hold of my hand, she pulls me to my feet.

We exit together, Mr Crawley watching us. In the corridor outside, Rosa gives the hand she's still holding a final squeeze before letting go of it. She stands in her glittering dress, keeping an eye on me until I reach my bedroom.

From the doorway, I wave, and she waves back.

Unable to sleep, I lie on the bed in London's semi-dark, listening to my Walkman. Even with the curtains closed, the orange light seeping through outlines the Olympia SF portable typewriter positioned prominently on the desk. The rest of my belongings – clothes, shoes, jewellery box, make-up and cassettes – leave a meagre trail across the Crawleys' furniture, making the room feel sparse in a way it didn't before I unpacked. Witnesses to a bruising and untidy past that look out of place here.

I don't hear the bedroom door open. Mr Crawley appears suddenly in my line of vision.

Startled, I sit up, slipping off the headphones, cross-legged and watchful as he steps into the room.

'What's playing?'

'Springsteen.'

'The Boss. I met him once, backstage at Wembley.' He smiles. 'Come on, I ordered some food in from Montefiore's. You look hungry.'

'Rosa changed her mind?'

'Rosa's sleeping.' His eyes slide towards me. 'She takes stuff to help her do that.'

The disloyalty to his wife triggers a fluttering sense of

triumph in me as he presses down on one of the Olympia's keys and says, 'We haven't had a nanny show up with a type-writer before.'

And after the weeks spent looking for it, here's my open-ing. The one I've been waiting for. But the apartment's buzzer sounds then, and he goes to answer it.

As soon as he's gone, I stumble out of the pyjama bottoms I'm wearing and pull my jeans back on. The old T-shirt I sleep in is exchanged for a low-cut red top. My face I leave make-up free – I don't want to look like I'm making too much of an effort.

Mr Crawley is not alone in the kitchen; there's a man in a white tunic with *Montefiore's* sewn across the breast pocket pushing a trolley loaded with plates and dishes, like in a hotel. Not that I've ever been in a hotel. Rainwater runs down the stainless-steel domes covering the food. It runs down the man's face and into his beard. He has to blink it out of his eyes.

'I took the liberty of ordering ragù alla Bolognese, pasticcio di maccheroni and Ciacci.'

The man from Montefiore's bows his head in Mr Crawley's direction, acknowledging what sounds to me like a perfect Italian accent.

Later, I will make a meticulous record of the names of these dishes, practising the pronunciation until I get it just right. It doesn't take long. Learning languages has always come naturally.

'Montefiore's specializes in regional dishes from Emilia-Romagna.'

This means nothing to me. Growing up, we didn't really do food. I put it down to a lack of routine. Beyond the con-fines of school and work, minding clocks was something my mother avoided, which is why we didn't keep regular habits.

Or eat regular meals. It could be cheese on toast at midnight or spaghetti hoops at dawn. Popcorn anytime. A bucket of fried chicken from KFC if it was payday. A packet of jelly babies if the cupboards were bare and the electricity off.

And for some reason, I can't shake the feeling that Mr Crawley knows all this.

Two places have been set at the breakfast bar.

He pulls a stool out and pats it, only just removing his hand in time as I slide self-consciously onto the seat. If he's noticed that I've changed out of my pyjamas, he doesn't mention it. He's changed too; his dinner suit has been swapped for jeans and a cricket sweater. Well-worn, both of them.

We're drinking wine. The man from Montefiore's poured two glasses before he left, the empty trolley making its distant but rattling progress towards the front door.

'So, what do you think of the ragù alla Bolognese?'

My initial confusion over the cutlery now mastered, I can turn my attention to the food, aware of him watching me as I take my first mouthful.

'I've never tasted anything like it before.'

It's true. I had no idea eating could feel like this. And whether it's the food or simply the attention from Mr Crawley – who continues to chew violently, enjoying my reaction – I don't know, but for a moment, tears threaten.

'You've got an appetite. I like that in a woman.'

His voice is simultaneously insistent and hollow. The words forgotten as soon as they're spoken.

'So, what's with the typewriter?'

I tell him about my dreams in a careless rush, unaware until now how lonely I've become, how hungry for intimacy I am – not the sort on offer from Rosa, but the sort I've only ever experienced before with Mr Crisp when we used to talk about music. Or those Saturday afternoons with George in the

*County Times* offices. Moments in my life when I've felt seen, in the way I feel seen now by Mr Crawley.

'A war correspondent?' he laughs, glancing at my red top. 'You're too pretty for landmines.'

Nobody has ever called me pretty before. And although I'm flattered, I'm also worried that Pitt's not taking me seriously.

I tell him about the course at the London School of Printing that I'm saving for.

I tell him about my job on the *County Times*.

'Which, thanks to the Crawley Corporation, I lost. You took over our paper.' I sound more upset about this than I mean to, more upset than I was aware of feeling at the time. Forcing a smile, I conclude, 'In fact, you owe me a job.'

This, I risk – because he called me pretty.

'You have a job,' he points out. 'You're already on payroll.'

His smile hangs differently for a split second, our eyes meeting above it.

During the pause that follows, I track the course of a slick of oil across his chin. I'm out of my depth and in an effort not to show it, try turning the conversation to the *Mercury*. By the time we finish our pasta supper, dawn already fingering the night sky, I know the names of all his editors: Les O'Dowd, Malcolm Skinner, Tony Turner. He talks about a young showbiz reporter he has his eye on as well.

'Took him on as a favour to Amelia, actually – after she helped out with Kate.'

I hold his gaze, wanting to ask how exactly Amelia helped out, what it was that homesick Kate needed help with – because this sounds like a sizeable favour.

'But he's good. Hungry.' Pitt jabs a fork towards me, still bright-eyed despite the late hour. 'I see that in you as well, Rebecca.'

Deciding that now's the time to press home my advantage, I mention my award-winning piece on John Haigh.

'I've left a copy on your desk.'

'And how did you manage that? It's in the study.'

'I know.'

'Which I keep locked.'

'It wasn't locked.'

If he's surprised by this, he doesn't show it. 'But you went in anyway?'

'I wanted to get your attention.'

'You have my attention.'

In the silence that follows, Pitt pushes his plate to one side and picks up the glass of wine. Despite the laughter playing around his face, it's a serious voice that says, 'What a constant surprise you are, Rebecca. I'm going to have to keep an eye on you, aren't I?'

'Yes. Yes, you are.'

Smiling, he gets abruptly to his feet, holding on to the breakfast bar for balance. 'Come with me.'

Clumsy with drink, I follow him through the sleeping apartment until we reach his study. Light seeps from beneath the door – I must have forgotten to switch off the desk lamp earlier. He glances at me, eyebrows raised, before pushing it open.

The room looks nothing like it did earlier.

The copy of the *County Times* has been completely shredded. Angry strips of newsprint are caught on every surface, and as the door opens these are given temporary uplift and the air is full of them. Along with something else: the photographs and remains of the brown envelope. I must have forgotten to put them back in the drawer earlier.

'Oh, Winston!'

The parrot is back on top of the bookshelf and jerks its

head about the room as if unable or unwilling to make the connection between itself and the mess.

Pitt's face, so serious only seconds before, shifts again as he surveys the carnage. 'You really were snooping, weren't you? Those photographs were worth a fortune.'

'But you have copies?'

'No, unfortunately not.' He turns to look at me, the smile spreading slowly to all four corners of his face. 'Well, Rebecca, you have my attention now.'

# Haversham

The first time my father died, I was eight years old. At school, in a classroom pinned to a July afternoon, hot and still. The window had been opened by Miss Taylor, using a long wooden pole with a metal hook at the end. She had trouble wielding it, the effort causing her tongue to flick untidily out of her mouth.

Miss Taylor was young for a teacher. She had bright eyes and leaned in close when she helped us with our work. That afternoon she was so close I could smell her make-up. Her hair fell across my drawing of a house – we were doing a project on our family tree, starting with a picture of 'home'. It was the usual childish arrangement comprising four windows and a door and, although the execution was wanting – I was no artist – the house was, in my mind, a close copy of the house we parked outside on our night drives. Its symmetry disrupted by two mutant figures – one tall, one short.

'So, this is you.' Miss Taylor's finger pointed to the shorter figure. 'And this is?'

'My mum.'

'I see.' She straightened up and moved on.

I rubbed at my hands, which were stained from the felt tips I'd been using, unable to shake the feeling that there was something my drawing lacked. Something fundamental missing.

Then a girl called Louise, sitting beside me, said, 'Becky doesn't have a dad.'

Louise was feared rather than liked. She was a thief and

a covert pincher of flesh. She knew how to get her way and was rarely caught out. Often, at playtime, I would hang on the fringes of her group, my eyes avidly following the games she organized, Louise herself studiously ignoring me. I was never invited to join in.

I heard the 'oh' that escaped from Miss Taylor, but nothing more. The distinct absence of any reprimand for Louise made me feel unsafe. Laughter broke out across the hot classroom and with it a welcome sense of disruption.

Louise jabbed a purple pen towards my drawing. 'And she doesn't live in a house. She lives in a flat.'

'Oh,' Miss Taylor said again, sounding lost.

'My mum says your mum's a slut.'

This was said so quietly it was little more than a whisper, but everybody heard. There were gasps. The scuffle of children rearranging themselves on chairs. Excited eyes.

Louise, shy but triumphant, kept her head tucked down, not looking at anybody.

From Miss Taylor, a breathy, 'Louise – you will leave this classroom immediately and stand outside.'

But nobody moved. The afternoon slowed. Although Miss Taylor was still in the classroom with us, it felt suddenly as if there was no teacher present. That word, spoken by Louise, had reordered our universe. None of us had any idea what might happen next.

I stood up, making Louise flinch.

Perhaps Miss Taylor anticipated some sort of physical assault as well because I felt her hand on my arm then, restraining me.

'My father's dead,' I blurted. In the frenzy of the moment, I almost believed it myself.

The class fell silent. The only sound was the mower on the playing field outside. Miss Taylor let go of me, placing an arm around my shoulders instead.

'He died in a car crash.'

I have no idea what inspired this, only that a violent death seemed preferable, suddenly, to an unexplained absence.

Miss Taylor pulled me towards her, pressing my head against her undulating cardigan. I was led to the reading chair in the book corner. From this elevated position, I watched as Louise continued to dart glances at me. Doubtful. Suspicious, even.

During the afternoon break, I played marbles with a boy called Kenneth. Crouched over a drain beside the bike shed, intent on the game, I failed to notice Louise and Imogen – one of her lieutenants – approach. I don't remember what she said to me, if she even said anything at all. Before I knew it, I was on my feet, hands grabbing at any part of her they could. Hair, arms, dress. Imogen, pinned with shock to the spot, screamed as I struck out at the wildly struggling Louise.

Louise was sent home while I was kept in the isolation room for the rest of the afternoon, like a rabid animal. The school phoned my mother. This had never happened before; up until then I was one of those quiet and compliant children. Unremarkable. Invisible.

When my mother arrived, Miss Taylor marched me down empty corridors to the head's office. Mrs Davis sat on one side of the desk, my mother in an orange plastic chair on the other. I was made to stand in the corner by the door. It was strange, seeing her at my school in her Chilston House cleaning overalls. She looked tired and kept fiddling with things in her pockets as Mrs Davis spoke.

Mrs Davis broke off. 'Mrs Sharp.'

'Miss,' my mother corrected her. It was something she always insisted on. She pulled her green and gold tobacco tin from her overall pocket.

'You can't smoke in here.'

She slumped back in the chair, arms folded. 'Fuck's sake. Seriously?'

Mrs Davis and Miss Taylor shot each other a glance.

I could feel myself flush. Fear mixed with relief. My mother was setting herself against them and siding with me.

Miss Taylor stepped in then and told us about Louise being so traumatized she needed to be sent home. She failed to mention what had happened in the classroom that afternoon, before I attacked Louise. At first, I thought this was an accidental omission, but as Miss Taylor continued to avoid looking at me, I realized that there was nothing accidental about it. Shocked, I tried to interrupt, but Mrs Davis held up a hand to silence me.

'She's lying,' I blurted, shock giving way to anger. I risked a glance at my mother, who winked at me over her folded arms.

Both Miss Taylor and Mrs Davis saw.

Mrs Davis rearranged herself in her chair and began speaking in her assembly voice: the situation was grave, she insisted; I faced expulsion.

'But—' I tried again.

Talking over me, she began to advise my mother on how to raise children. Miss Taylor leaned forward to join in, pointing out that I sometimes fell asleep at my desk. She emphasized the importance of routine.

My mother made no pretence of listening. It was as if she was barely in the room at all. At first, I thought it marked defiance, this withdrawal. But as I watched her shoulders spasm, I realized that it was taking her all the energy she had right then not to burst into tears. We were being attacked in some fundamental way, and I wasn't even allowed to stand up for myself. Neither of us were. It was the injustice that made my eyes sting, not any sense of remorse. Because somehow, with a child's instinct, I knew that Louise's mother hadn't been called into school as my mother had.

The tears started to fall – my mother's, not mine – and Mrs Davis at last relented. She pushed some leaflets from social services across the desk, along with a list of helpline numbers. She spoke slowly, as if my mother were a child. We were on their radar now, she said.

Later that night, I asked about my father for the first time.

My mother's face went blank. She gave me that long-distance stare of hers and suddenly I knew that it wasn't a question I wanted an answer to. But before I had a chance to take it back, she grabbed the car keys and disappeared through the front door at breakneck speed. I followed, sobbing and barefoot. Stumbling down the cement steps leading from our flat to the street below, I begged her to take me with her wherever she was going, my fists banging on the windows as the car slid away.

I rang Angelina's doorbell. Angelina had hot chocolate in her cupboard and milk in her fridge, and that night she washed my bare feet and bundled me, still heaving with disbelief, against her jumper.

I held on to her. And though she didn't say anything, I could tell that she was angry.

When my mother finally returned, I heard them yelling at each other.

I never asked after my father again.

# Pitt

Spring arrives. The city thaws, and I can feel myself starting to flourish inside the bell jar of Pitt's continuing interest. I discover the pleasure of dressing rather than clothing myself, and that I have a good eye. A pair of velvet jodhpurs are just one of many treasures uncovered in an unpromising corner of the Notting Hill Oxfam shop. I change my hair, wearing it down instead of caught up in a clip. I change.

There have been no further impromptu suppers and Pitt and I only ever meet in passing, but the smiles exchanged in dark corridors at unsociable hours, and in the crowded weekend kitchen, feel like acts of growing insurgency. Rosa feels it too. She goes out less and I often catch her watching me. A new and awkward silence lies between us. Cold-edged.

So, it comes as a surprise when she announces that she's going to spend a week away from us at a clinic that does things to noses. It's her nose, Rosa has decided, that's to blame for her disintegrating marriage; her flailing career; the antipathy she feels towards her children, herself. If she can fix her nose, everything else will fix itself. The plan is that her mother, Mrs Dawson – the woman who launched Rosa's career as a glamour model at the age of sixteen – will come to stay. In the event, however, Mrs Dawson chooses a ladies' golf tournament in Portugal over time with her grandchildren.

Leaving Pitt and I alone together.

The first day of Rosa's absence, Pitt comes home earlier

than usual. Early enough to share an impromptu supper from
Montefiore's.

By Thursday, he's home so early the children are still awake.
He says it's quiet at the newspaper.

'Daddy!' Violet screams, momentarily stunned to see him
in daylight.

Pitt, bearing Harvey Nichols food hall bags, allows himself to become caught up in his children's excitement as he's
immediately hugged and leapt on, his legs clung to.

He carries the bags through to the kitchen where he and
Violet sort through them. Together, they make a pasta sauce.
Violet, in her child-size apron, hanging with solemn concen-
tration over bubbling pans.

Bath time becomes wild. The bathroom itself, flooded and
treacherous. Afterwards, Violet streaks through the apartment,
wet and naked, chased by her roaring father. By the time he
catches her and scoops her up in the air, she's unhinged with
joy. Lulu trails after them, stumbling in their wake.

'You're good for me, Rebecca,' he pants, the writhing Violet
wrapped around his neck.

Some small, childish part of me blooms with inappropriate
pride.

As far as I know, I've never been good for anyone.


Later, when the children are in bed, a storm breaks. The rain
is so loud that even inside the apartment all we can hear is the
rush of it, stripping trees of spring's young leaves, breaking
umbrellas and flooding pavements. We watch through the long
French windows from one of the sofas in the den. The distress
out there is hypnotic; so hypnotic that neither of us seems to
notice when Pitt puts a hand on my ankle, clasping it lightly.

Neither of us notices Rosa, either, who appears suddenly
and without warning.

Standing in the doorway, rain-battered and with a dressing obscuring half her face, she looks like a recently released hostage.

Eventually – it feels like eventually although it can't be more than a few seconds – Pitt pulls away from me and stands up.

'We weren't expecting you until the weekend. What happened?'

Rosa remains transfixed by the two cocktail glasses on the coffee table. 'I checked out.'

The voice is thick, fluish.

'They let you do that?'

'It's a clinic, Pitt. Not a fucking prison.'

'You should have phoned. Did you phone?'

He stares accusingly at the telephone on the glass console table behind her, as if it is to blame.

She shakes her head, her eyes – above the dressing – falling heavily onto me.

'Baby, you should have phoned, I could have sent Douglas. You're soaking. Tell me you didn't walk?'

'Walk?' she yelps. 'Why the fuck would I walk? I got a taxi.' She pulls at her top, her hands grabbing at it. Then, pouting and sniffing, she says, 'This is from running into the lobby. It's mad out there. I missed you.'

The confession makes her look momentarily haggard. But I believe her. She believes herself. Even Pitt wavers.

'I just don't understand why you didn't phone. Baby—' He breaks off. 'Where are your bags?'

'My bags? I don't know. Somewhere. Downstairs maybe?'

He turns towards me, one of his arms encircling Rosa despite the water forming a barrier between them both. 'Rebecca, could you go down and get Mrs Crawley's bags?'

I stand up, unsteady, as he turns back to his wife who is trying to wipe the water from her bruised face, smearing the make-up she has somehow managed to apply. The black blur of liner and mascara give her a fragile, broken air.

The last thing I hear Pitt say is, 'Let's get you something to drink.'

The next time Rosa and I speak, it's to be told that I'm being given the weekends off with immediate effect. From now on, the Crawleys will spend them exclusively en famille at their Oxfordshire retreat. Even though Rosa hates the Georgian vicarage – it's where Pitt lived during his first marriage.

She breaks the news in a rush of foundation, fake fur and Calvin Klein Eternity, as she flees the apartment for a Monday lunch with friends.

'Shit, Rebecca, I thought you'd be pleased,' she says, losing patience with my silence and digging around in her handbag for the keys to her Range Rover. 'I'm doing you a favour. I don't get weekends off. Maybe we can swap places, for fuck's sake.'

She smiles at me then, and for the first time I feel just a tiny bit afraid of Rosa. 'You'd like that, wouldn't you?'

# The Sedleys

When I tell Amelia about the new weekend arrangements, she doesn't look surprised.

'You already knew.'

She blushes and tries to shake her head. Amelia is a terrible liar.

'You've been talking to Rosa about me?'

'No, Rebecca. No. I would never say anything about you behind your back. Rosa came to me.'

'So, what did she say?'

'Nothing much. I don't think things are going well with her and Pitt.' She glances at me, in the same slanting way Rosa does these days.

We're sitting on the edge of the sandpit in the playground. The girls – Violet and the older Valentine child, Eva – are hanging upside down from a climbing frame in their summer dresses, long hair brushing the tarmac, laughing like crazy at a private joke.

Lulu hums to herself, beady eyes on James's yellow digger, which she covets. It would never occur to Rosa to buy her daughter a digger. Soon, growing impatient, she'll make a grab for it. James will cry. Lulu will catch my eye – an unspoken secret between us is that we both enjoy making the over-loved James cry. I'll make a show of reprimanding her because this is what the situation demands. But later, as we rise in the lift towards the apartment, I'll tickle Lulu and snuffle at the hot creases in her neck and let her know that I'm not angry with her at all.

'What am I going to do the whole weekend on my own?'

Amelia pushes her hands into the sand, uncomfortable for a moment, before leaning in to me and issuing the invitation I've been waiting for.

'Come home with me. This weekend.'

For propriety's sake, I try to hold out. 'I don't know.'

She gives me a nudge. 'Come on, what else are you doing? I know you don't have plans.' She peers at me from beneath her thick, black fringe and smiles a sly, un-Amelia-like smile that takes me by surprise. 'You never have plans. And anyway, there's a whole crowd of us going to a club off the King's Road Saturday night. You're coming with us, Rebecca,' she finishes, imperious.

Home turns out to be a three-storey townhouse overlooking Clapham Common. We cross the gravel drive, passing an old coach house where – I'll later discover – the Sedleys' Welsh housekeeper, Babs, lives. Parked next to the front door at an angle is a Porsche 911 Targa belonging to Mr Sedley. Amelia leads the way in silence. Presuming in her careless, good-natured way that there's nothing exceptional about any of this.

I try hard not to stare as we pad through the mansion's many rooms, overcrowded with comfortable-looking furniture whose upholstery is faded and, on closer inspection, covered in dog hairs. Ash from recent fires is banked in empty grates. The vases on mantelpieces and sideboards are full of wilting flowers that drop pollen onto the carpet, the carpets themselves patched with indeterminate stains. Polished surfaces are marked with cup rings and cracked bowls from Edwardian washstands, filled with dusty pot pourri, while abandoned books and magazines lie open, curling in the afternoon sunlight.

I never knew disorder could feel so plentiful.

Somewhere close by, Bryan Adams is playing.

We follow the music to the kitchen, where an older woman is coughing up phlegm in the sink and a fragile blonde is scolding a spaniel. She looks like she's just woken up, even though it's nearly noon.

Amelia launches herself at the blonde, hugging her so hard I worry that I'm going to hear her crack.

'This is Rebecca, Mum.'

'Darling,' she murmurs vaguely into the air around her, as if unable to remember which one of us is her daughter, before dusting my cheeks with a couple of kisses.

'Thank you for having me, Mrs Sedley.'

The words come out at a gallop. I sound too grateful, and worry – despite the perfume I'm wearing – that up close she will be able to smell unwashed dishes, rotting window frames and overflowing bins on me. Tell-tale traces of my secret past, because Mrs Sedley is one of those women who always smell good.

'Liv, please.'

'Rebecca was at Chilston House.'

'Really?'

The eyes that sweep over me are not so fragile, I decide, as the rest of Liv Sedley. And this single, softly spoken word sounds unexpectedly hostile. It's enough to cast doubt suddenly, and now I sense mother and daughter taking a closer look. Even the phlegmatic older woman – a housekeeper? – flicks her head up and peers at me over her cigarette.

Until Amelia decides to step in and show her support. 'Yes,' she responds roundly, although her mother's 'Really?' wasn't a question so much as a statement. 'And this weekend we need to spoil her rotten because Rebecca doesn't have a home – or family of her own.'

'Both my parents died in a car crash.'

Liv stares at me for a moment before pressing a hand against her eyes, overwhelmed.

'It was a long time ago,' Amelia soothes. 'But Mum, you'll never believe this – Rebecca's mother was Russian, a ballet dancer with the Bolshoi.'

I don't remember telling Amelia this. Rosa? During one of their heart-to-hearts?

At last, the hand is lifted from Liv's eyes. She scoops up the spaniel foraging around her feet and gives its ears a few distracted strokes.

Pleased at the rousing impact this information has on her mother, Amelia carries on. 'And Becky's father was a famous pianist.'

'How wonderful,' Liv breathes, coming to life, as if able to see the point of me at last.

When I get to know her better, I'll come to understand that Liv is someone who likes people to be either useful or interesting. Preferably both.

'Do you play, Rebecca?'

'You should hear her, Mum.'

Again, I don't recall ever having played the piano for Amelia.

Liv's hand resumes its rhythmic stroking of the dog's ears. 'Would you play for us?'

'Tread carefully, Rebecca. Mum's a patron of . . . something,' Amelia shrugs. 'Anyway, she has these horrible soirées where impoverished concert pianists in threadbare tails are forced to play until their fingers bleed in return for some supper.'

'Play for us tonight,' Liv insists. 'John would be thrilled.'

'He would not. Classical music bores Dad shitless.'

'Amelia.'

'It's true. He'll be asleep on the sofa in seconds. And no offence, Rebecca, but so will I. Unless you can play Queen?' She grins and turns her attention to the older woman, wrapping her arms around the hunched frame from behind and holding on as the woman shuffles from sink to bench.

She remains gruff and withdrawn in the face of Amelia's affection, preoccupied by the immense fish laid out on a board in front of her, flat and grey with orange spots. Ash from her cigarette falls onto it and becomes immediately camouflaged as she runs a knife along the length of the belly with unblinking efficiency.

'Babs is an extraordinary cook,' Liv says, floating deftly into the lull. 'We call her the Escoffier of Blaenau Ffestiniog.'

Liv turns out to be right. Babs is an extraordinary cook. Or perhaps it's the champagne that makes it all taste so good. Either way, I've never experienced an evening like it, but then families – in particular the happy sort – aren't a place I've spent much time in.

Afterwards, we lie sprawled across Amelia's bed beneath a Madonna poster I'm convinced must have been on her wall at school. Madonna, white-haired and red-lipped, during her Marie Antoinette phase. It's a Herb Ritts shot from an old *Vanity Fair* article, but I don't bother sharing this with Amelia because she won't care.

'God, my parents are embarrassing.' She lunges for a pillow, pushing her face into it. 'I should have warned you. All that stuff about how they first met – *please*,' she groans, rolling onto her back and catching my eye. 'Sorry you had to hear that.'

I'm not. In fact, resentment aside, I'm completely enamoured – a little in love, actually – with both Sedleys.

'They always put on a show for strangers.'

Strangers. The reminder that I'm not – and will never

be – part of the family hurts far more than it's meant to; it's just Amelia being careless.

To hide the hurt, I get to my feet and start scanning the silver-framed photos lining all available surfaces in the room.

Amelia on snow-ridden mountains, beaches and yachts. There's even one of her underwater in diving gear, flanked by stingrays. Her face, masked, her dark hair floating upwards. Every childhood memory has been recorded, every smiling achievement captured.

My own photographic archive is a lot less impressive – a small Polaroid-sized album containing seven photographs that I have no intention of showing anyone. I was an unphotogenic child and distrustful of the camera. In most of the shots, I'm out of focus. Nothing more than a moody blur. Apart from the day of the Royal Wedding, I have no memory of my mother using a camera, let alone a Polaroid one, but I can't think who else would have taken these photographs. There's only one of me as a baby, sitting in a washing-up bowl full of bubbles. I'm even smiling – a tearaway, toothless smile.

I caught my mother once, sitting on the edge of my bed, legs crossed, a cigarette held aloft as she squinted down at the album open in her lap. I watched her carefully from the bedroom doorway, holding my breath and trying to make my presence as unobtrusive as I could until, jerking her head up suddenly, she said, 'You must have been farting. Here. In this one.'

I got as close to her as I dared. Just close enough to see the photo in her hand.

Laughing, she said, 'Yep. Farting. For sure. Only explanation for that smile.'

She continued to laugh, slamming the album shut and getting to her feet. My main possessions were books, second-hand ones bought with my paper round money and arranged alphabetically, by author. She moved towards them with affected disinterest, but I could tell they unnerved her.

'You need to live a little, Becky,' she said.

All families, no matter how small, have their myths. We were no exception. One of my mother's favourites was this: they gave her the wrong baby in hospital. I was a changeling. A succubus. It left me haunted by the idea that my real parents must be out there somewhere. And in the intervening years, I've been able to imagine them any which way I choose. My parents didn't create me, I created them.

'Seriously,' my mother would insist, licking at the Rizla paper expertly rolled around its line of Golden Virginia tobacco. 'It's the only explanation.'

In the room behind me, Amelia is emptying the contents of her wardrobe onto the bed; a tumble of clothes that I suspect have been chosen by Liv on mother–daughter shopping trips.

I pull out an expanse of black velvet and hold it against me.

'God, I wore that to the Leavers' Ball.'

The dress has been dismissed, but the softness of it tugs at me so I hold on to it. Amelia turns back to the kaleidoscope of fabric on the bed, picking stuff up at random before dropping it on the floor by her feet.

'Saddest night of my life.' She slumps onto the side of the bed, defeated, before adding, 'And the happiest.'

'How come?'

'I was stood up by a boy I was seeing at the time. He went to Tavistock – two years above me. He was already working at the *County Times* when we met at the Bear.'

My body feels the hot shock of recognition even as my mind rejects it – too much of a coincidence. And anyway, George is no more of an alumnus of Tavistock than I am of Chilston House.

I move over to the window, still holding the dress against me, turning towards the sound of distant traffic and laughing voices coming from the dark common in order to hide the smile I can feel playing at my face.

Amelia's eyes trail the dress, wary, as she tells me how this boy managed to break into the boarding house much later that night through a fire exit that had been left open by a cleaner taking a cigarette break. There were excuses and apologies – a story came in at the eleventh hour that he was forced to cover. Still drunk from the saddest night of her life, she didn't hesitate to break bounds for him, despite the heavy rain. Under cover of darkness, they slipped and stumbled across the playing fields to where he'd parked his car. The back seat is where sad became happy, and the sex they had pretty much wiped the first eighteen years of life from Amelia's hard drive, fatally resetting her. It would be 3 a.m. before she made it back to the dorm, shivering and dripping over the carpet. She drifted sleepless through those last days of school and has been drifting sleepless ever since.

Again, I recognize George. Just as I recognized him in the showbiz reporter Pitt mentioned, the one he said Amelia put in a word for. Although this time, there's no surprise, only a growing numbness at the inevitability of it all. So that when I at last hear her say the name George, I feel nothing more than a sense of confirmation.

She's never had the dress dry cleaned. It still has his semen stains on it. She alternates between grinning and looking like she might just burst into tears as she tells me this.

I need to look disgusted and hurl the dress back across the gap between us. This is what the moment demands. Instead, I ask if George is coming to the club tonight.

'Maybe. I don't know. I'm worried that I've been putting too much pressure on him lately. He doesn't like that. It's so hard.' Her eyes go glassy as she stares at me, desperate for reassurance. 'Rebecca?' she probes into the continuing silence, a flicker of something in her voice.

For a full three seconds, I toy with the idea of telling her about George and me. The temptation is strong and the sense of danger tangible in the air around us. But then Amelia turns away, and starts to tear through the clothes on the bed once more, keeping up a constant mantra of, 'No, he won't like that,' or, 'He's seen me in that already,' oblivious to the fact that it doesn't much matter what clothes she wears: Amelia looks good in everything. A fact she herself remains unaware of. The only thing that matters is the prism of George. George, who I haven't seen since the night my mother died.

# Haversham

I wasn't beautiful. I grew up knowing this about myself. Girls do.

Unlike my mother, who *was* beautiful.

It's why we never got invited anywhere. Women were afraid of her. Men stared, and lost sight of themselves.

'Like I want their dough-faced, overweight husbands,' she would say. Shrugging them all off, each and every one of them.

'You're not much to look at, Becky.' She didn't mean to be cruel. Cruelty was something she couldn't abide, she was just a truthful person. Perhaps she thought that my plainness would spare me some of the trauma her beauty had caused her. 'But you've got a good head on your shoulders.' Here, she would make herself a roll-up with tidy, perfectly manicured fingers (they were always perfect, despite the bleach and the Jeyes Fluid). Light it. Suck in, exhale. And as she exhaled, she would mutter softly, 'Fuck knows where you get that from.' Giving the crown of my head a quick scrub with the palm of her hand. Looking momentarily satisfied.

And then at fifteen, things changed. I noticed it with the boys who hung out in large, scuffling groups on the way home from school. Men on the street. It's as if one day I simply stopped being invisible. Maybe, as I grew older and gained a silhouette, I made it to pretty. Maybe. But I sensed that it wasn't to do with how I looked. It was something else. A newfound energy that drew people in.

Perhaps it was this energy that attracted George.

I noticed him before he noticed me. I was sixteen and desperate to fall in love. It happened the first time I laid eyes on him across the hot, carpeted offices of the *County Times*.

In his faded flannels and outsize cricket jumper, he looked unlike anybody else who worked on the newspaper. His face was only ever partially visible beneath a floppy fringe. He spoke with a disaffected drawl, like something out of the Merchant Ivory films I adored.

It would be years before I discovered that the look he cultivated was nothing more than a front.

I only worked Saturdays to start with because I was still at school, and rarely saw him unless he was covering a fête or a local dance school show, the sort of work he hated, given to him whenever Mr Saunders, the editor, was after revenge and wanted to pull rank. They argued a lot. Almost every time George passed through the offices.

We enjoyed the rows that flared up inside Mr Saunders' cubicle. The pointless way the door was shut and the blinds pulled down, when within seconds the glass would start vibrating with word after shouted word. Like the time George tried to run an exposé on local resident Derek Palmer, whose video rental business was trading in pirated VHS.

George's voice, yelling, 'Bins? Fucking wheelie bins on the front page when I've given you Derek Palmer on a plate?'

Mr Saunders' voice, functioning at a normal volume and rounded with conviction, 'Wheelie bins are a big issue – when the council introduces them, they're expecting people to wheel their own bins out on collection day. Our neighbour, Val – she's eighty! Barely leaves the house and can't walk unaided. How's she going to wheel a bin almost the same height as her onto the street once a week?'

Saunders wasn't finished. The voice rose, becoming high-pitched with passion. 'We're local press. Bins. Street lighting.

Parking. Dog fouling. The price of a pint. The price of petrol. One-way systems. Stray cats. Tramps. Vandals. It's who we are; what we stand for. It's what our readers want – along with coupons and the TV guide.'

People had stopped even pretending to work, and although this speech felt conclusive, nobody moved. We waited until the glass finally stopped rattling. But Saunders had been known to change direction before, and this was what happened now as he returned unexpectedly to Derek Palmer.

'You hounded Derek.'

'*Derek?* Wait – you know him?'

'You made it impossible for him. And now there's that poor girl who found him hanging from a climbing frame by his belt.' Saunders' voice hit a crescendo. 'In the play park, for Christ's sake, George.'

'Nobody hangs themselves because of pirated movies – they're only the tip of the iceberg.'

The office door flew open and remained ajar, juddering.

George stalked out.

Everyone's eyes trailed him, bodies swinging gently from side to side in their chairs. None of us had taken a breath in what felt like ages. The room was almost out of oxygen. He passed the photocopier I was hovering beside and flashed me a smile I returned without thinking, happy for it to split me in two. It was the first time he'd ever acknowledged me, and I allowed myself to feel singled out. Chosen.

Mr Saunders started to follow him into the main office, then stopped.

'We're not running the story – any story – on Derek Palmer.'

George came to an abrupt halt by the double doors leading into reception, a misplaced grin on his face.

'So, I'll take it to someone who will.'

He was halfway through the doors and then suddenly turned around, making a beeline for me. 'It's Becky, right?'

The office was silent. He knew my name.

'Fancy a drink?'

George put a half-pint of cider on the table in front of me. The Bear was where I usually met Paul after work on a Saturday, and I was meant to be meeting him tonight, but I was too preoccupied by George to check whether he was already there.

'Still at school?'

George's eyes balanced on the rim of the raised glass as he looked at me.

I nodded. I didn't want to let him know I was at Haversham High. I was almost certain he went to Tavistock, the boys' private school, and if he was at Tavistock, he was bound to know girls at Chilston House, so claiming I went to Chilston myself was too risky.

Instead, I asked him about Derek Palmer.

'Yeah, well, I'm not surprised Saunders won't run with it. He and Palmer were probably Masonic pals. Creeps, all of them. I bet he's tried it on with you – Saunders, I mean.'

He lifted his glass towards me and took another long sip. For a moment, I worried that this was a story he was trying to work up – some sort of revenge on Saunders – and that he wasn't interested in me after all.

'Tell me about Palmer – what it is you've got on him,' I persisted.

'You really want to know?'

'I really want to know.'

'It's pretty heavy-duty. Not worried that you'll lose sleep over it?'

'I don't sleep.'

'Me neither.'

He gave a twitch of a grin and took a few silent sips of his pint. Then, leaning forward, he told me that uncovering a good story was like opening a set of Russian dolls.

'You know there's a crack in there somewhere. And when you find it, you twist it open – only to find another story inside. So, you open that one up, and another and another – until you get to the one nobody wants you to find; the one hidden inside all the others. Seamless. Flawless. The truth of the matter.'

He stopped abruptly and flicked his head up. Twisting around, I realized that Paul was standing behind me. For the first time in my life, I wasn't pleased to see him.

'Boyfriend?' George smiled as Paul lowered himself onto one of the velvet stools, unable to take his eyes off him.

'Childhood friends.'

Then, just as I was about to ask him where he was planning on taking the Derek Palmer story, Paul said, 'We've met before. It was years ago. At a party. We were both working as waiters.'

I watched as George's face clouded over, and then I heard myself say something that must have been preying on my subconscious mind for some time. Because I recognized him too, I realized. Like Paul, I'd been at the same party.

'You saved my mother's life.'

# George

We wait in one of the dimly lit alcoves with a view of the bar and dance floor, presided over by a gloating Buddha. Amelia is in a twisting frenzy, trying to locate George in the crowded club. It will become a place I frequent regularly in later years, hosting countless liaisons in the cavernous intimacy of its lacquered red and yellow rooms. But I'm not a regular yet. This is my first time here and I've never been anywhere like it before – the closest I've come is a black box of a nightclub with sticky floors beside Brighton Pier.

And then I see him.

For a moment, I'm overwhelmed by an old and crippling shyness.

Amelia leaps to her feet, arms thrown high, waving and yelling. Unable to push through the tightly packed bodies separating them, she bounces wildly on the spot while I remain still. Watching.

'He's here,' she says, her teeth chattering.

And even in a club crowded with beautiful people from the big screen, small screen and every glossy magazine on the market, women follow George with their eyes. Their bodies incline towards him. Men too.

He can't have failed to notice this.

He arrives at the centre of a glittering crowd. Although it's Rawdon Crawley, Pitt's son, I recognize first – along with a girl in a gold sequin dress, cowboy hat and boots. The pair were photographed together in this month's *Tatler*, which Liv Sedley buys religiously and passes on to her daughter, who passes them unread on to me. The accompanying caption referred to her as 'The Honourable Elizabeth "Lizzie" Saltire, wild-child granddaughter of hellraiser Earl of Dexter'.

Breaking away from the group, Lizzie's face flickers briefly with its old schoolgirl shine as she sees Amelia and starts yelling, 'Emmy! Emmy!'

Lizzie Saltire was head girl of Chilston House while Amelia was there and featured large in the school prospectuses.

The two girls hug hard, their light and dark heads pressed together.

George, who has ignored Amelia until now, leans, boozy, into this loud and emotional reunion.

Amelia stretches her face airily towards him in an attempt at restraint, but almost immediately relents, throwing herself at him and clinging on. She wraps her wrists around his neck, fitting her body along the length of his. They look good together. This is something that hurts. A lot.

'You're late.' She gives him a slow, smiling reprimand.

'I know,' he smiles back, making no effort to apologize.

'I was beginning to think you weren't coming.'

'I almost didn't. I was invited to a party.'

'*You* weren't invited anywhere. *I* was invited to a party, and I considered taking you with me. Then I changed my mind.' Lizzie's words hang in the air, disinherited, as if she can no longer be bothered with them once they've left her mouth. It's something I'm soon able to mimic, flawlessly. 'We could still go.'

She scans the club, looking for Rawdon Crawley, who I watched peel away from the group into the club's red dark during her reunion with Amelia.

'Do I know you?'

A pair of eyes heavy with liner settle on me, but before I have a chance to respond, Amelia says, 'Rebecca was at Chilston.'

Lizzie continues to stare but says nothing.

George, who hasn't yet looked in my direction, does so now. For a wavering second alarm contracts his face, before the eyes widen once more and the lips stretch towards a grin. And it's then, as I feel my own face settling into the same grin, that I realize: George is as eager as me to keep what we left behind in Haversham a secret. There are almost as many dark spots on him as there are on me. Dark spots that both of us have gone to great lengths to hide, in order to make ourselves tarnish-free. This is what we have on each other.

Lizzie and George sit down along with the rest of the crowd they arrived with, an infectious boisterousness gripping our cramped table. For a while, I remain on the fringes, eyes mostly on George, watching as everybody shouts clumsily at each other, knocking things over and falling off the few chairs they've managed to appropriate.

But then it dawns on me – I'm at the party. I was invited, and I'm here.

For the first time ever, I feel like I'm at the centre of something. Not outside looking in.

'Dobs!' George roars suddenly, Amelia toppling from his lap as he jumps to his feet. 'Dobs!' he roars again. 'You weren't seriously thinking of skulking off without saying hello, were you?'

This is not the voice I remember, the slow but uneven drawl a work in progress. His vowels are now long and rounded, the consonants clipped. Technically flawless. I'm impressed. But it's in the delivery that he has really pulled it off. The imperious carelessness. The sure knowledge that however little the words mean to him they will always mean far more to his listeners.

As if reading my mind, he flicks me a quick look. I half expect him to raise an eyebrow and say, 'See?'

A couple of tables away a tall man in a suit moves his arm in an attempted wave, but the gesture brings chaos in its wake. Bottles and glasses tumble, and within seconds he's surrounded by waiters, cloths and confusion. Yet despite being in the middle of all this, he seems removed from it. His head is turned in the direction of our group, although he makes no attempt to approach.

'You *were* thinking of skulking off. That's bollocks,' George yells, retrieving his reluctant friend and hauling him back to our table where he looms over everybody, red-faced. Although it's Amelia, trying to reposition herself on George's lap, who holds his attention.

Noticing this, George says, 'Emmy, you remember Dobs, don't you?'

'D-D-Dobbin. William,' the man introduces himself, before blurting messily, 'G-G-George's flatmate.' He thrusts a hand towards her, knocking over the empty champagne bottle. 'W-w-we met at a New Year's Eve p-p-party,' he insists, his stutter becoming more pronounced at her lack of interest.

Amelia stares down at the hand held in the air between them.

'You w-w-wore a r-r-red dress.'

She laughs dismissively. 'I don't remember.'

For a moment he looks straight at her. 'I do.'

Later, we move collectively towards the dance floor where couples are sweating tightly together beneath the club's low lighting.

Amelia only wants to dance with George.

But George dances mostly with Lizzie, who would rather be dancing with Rawdon Crawley – who's dancing with a model.

Amelia has to pretend not to notice. Then she has to pretend not to care by dancing with strangers, clumsy, laughing and a little wild. A little sad. Her hair all over the place.

Breathless, I return to the table in the alcove where I sit alone for a while, watching her, before George slides onto the shadowy banquette beside me – our abandoned chairs have already been stolen.

'You've changed, Becky.'

He says it without looking at me.

'People do. And the name's Rebecca now.'

Although I manage to match his carelessness of tone, I'm intensely focused on the parts of him I can see in the low light: his right thigh and the wrist resting across it; the covering of black hairs; the raised veins along his lower arms.

'No, actually. Most people, they don't change at all. But you, *Becky* . . . I almost didn't recognize you.'

He looks at me then.

Grabbing clumsily at the cigarettes he pushes onto the table between us, I turn to him for a light. Bent over the flame, I clock his bitten nails. The only tell-tale sign of the old George.

I pull away, exhaling. 'You recognized me.'

He eases himself into a laugh, shaking his head slowly from side to side. 'So, how do you know Amelia? And don't tell me you went to the same school.'

Our eyes follow her, on the dance floor still, under the wash of red light.

'She's a nanny; I'm a nanny. For your boss, actually – Pitt Crawley. The nanny thing's a stopgap. I'll be on the *Mercury* soon.'

He laughs and reaches for the second-to-last cigarette in the packet. 'So, you didn't say anything about us?'

'You know I didn't.' Conversation with George has always felt like this. A series of threats, exchanged.

'You're good at this, Becky.'

'Rebecca. We're both good at this.'

Tipping his head back, he exhales. 'Emmy thinks I went to Tavistock.'

'You told her that?'

'No, she just kind of presumed and I went along with it.'

'She doesn't care where you went to school, George. She's in love with you.'

This sounds more disloyal than it's meant to.

He frowns and we fall silent, both of us scanning the dance floor again.

'Hey.' Amelia is suddenly there, propping herself against the table because there's nowhere to sit. She reaches at random for a glass with wine still in it. 'You two seem to be getting along.'

There's a lilt of worry in her voice that she's too drunk to conceal.

I'm drunk myself, at that stage when things alternate between high definition and foggy. Too drunk to assuage Amelia's worry. The opposite in fact. I glance at George, who grins back. An air of menace falls over our mess of a table.

'Royally,' he says.

'What's that?' Amelia tips her head back and finishes the wine, which stains the corners of her mouth.

'We're get-ting on roy-al-ly,' George enunciates slowly, as if English is Amelia's second language.

'Right.'

She nods hazily and reaches for the cigarette pack. But her fingers aren't compliant, and the gesture turns into a small struggle until, at last, George holds the packet steady. We watch her pull out the cigarette she doesn't want. Amelia isn't a smoker.

'That's the last one,' I say without thinking.

'You have to watch Rebecca,' Amelia laughs. 'She's a very careful person. Far more careful than she looks. You should see her bookshelves – they're so organized, it's creepy.'

Sober, Amelia would never be so unbridled. If it wasn't for George, I'd be curious to see how far I could push her.

'The sort of person who measures things,' George cuts in. 'Keeps a tally.'

'Exactly,' Amelia says, while attempting to slide back onto his lap. 'I mean, even her notebooks are colour-coded and arranged in groups. I used to think they were diaries, but now I'm not so sure.'

Unable to hold her gaze, I pan out over the dance floor and pick out Lizzie Saltire on the fringes of the sweating dancers. At a distance, beneath the lights, she comes up lacklustre. I hear George say, 'Inventories maybe. Things owed. Unpaid debts,' and am about to respond when I see who she's dancing with – it's him, the man from Pitt's photographs.

'Who's that Lizzie's with?'

George swings his head around. 'No idea, but he'll definitely be *somebody*. Lizzie knows everyone. She's very well connected.' Too late, he asks, 'Why – d'you know him?' But I'm already on my feet. I follow Lizzie into the club's toilets: a stretch of cubicles, sinks and mirrors dotted with orchids. It's busy in here, like another club altogether. I stand at a sink washing my hands and wait until finally she emerges from one of the cubicles. There's a ladder in her tights, streaking up her right thigh.

'Lizzie?'

She swings an unfocused pair of eyes towards me, steadying herself by holding on to one of the sinks. Before saying, for the second time that evening, 'Do I know you?'

'Rebecca. Amelia's friend.'

She begs a cigarette from the woman standing next to us, haphazardly studying her reflection as she lights it. Without the support of the sink, she slides against me, our shoulders touching. Her skin is surprisingly cold.

'Who's that guy you were with just now?'

'Which guy? I'm always with a guy.'

'Guy in a navy blazer?'

'Oh, him,' she groans, pulling herself upright and piling her hair on top of her head. The cigarette is still caught perilously between her fingers.

Then, in an unsteady whisper, 'He's in the Horse Guards, I think. We call him Polo. Rumour has it he's giving the Princess "riding lessons".'

She twists her head from side to side, pouting at her reflection. 'Do you think I'm pretty?'

And it's then, staring at her reflection as instructed, that the veil drops, and I realize exactly who she is. Why she's familiar, and why the sense of familiarity – skin-pricking – has nothing to do with *Tatler* or school prospectuses.

'No, I don't think you're pretty. I think you're beautiful,' I insist, my voice catching, waiting for her to recognize me back. Almost craving it, despite the retributions that must surely follow.

She drops her arms as if they weigh too much suddenly, her hair falling over her shoulders again in perfect waves.

'You know, I swear I don't recognize you from school.'

# The Vicarage

All week summer grows, the city becoming high-strung with it. Skies are suddenly blue and down at street level the pavements shine. Then the heat arrives and nothing stirs, inside or out. The nights are the worst. Dark and sticking. Even breathing makes me sweat. Sleep, which I've always struggled with, comes in short stretches. I have vivid dreams. Dreams of falling that I wake from suddenly, a jolt of arms and legs.

The heat unsettles Violet and Lulu. If we go to the park, we have to go in the early morning while there's still shade. Lulu refuses to nap and both of them are hysterical with exhaustion by bedtime, hurling themselves from tantrum to tantrum while their parents hurl themselves from row to row. By the end of the week, the flat is full of shouting, screaming, slamming doors and the angry slap of bare feet. No chance of catching Pitt alone, so that I can tell him about the man in the photos.

Saturday morning, things reach a crescendo.

Pitt and Rosa have been arguing since they woke up. They're still arguing, with all of us jammed into the sweltering kitchen unable to escape. Violet concentrates on her breakfast, eating it mechanically while I feed Lulu and try hard to pretend that Rosa isn't repetitively crossing my line of vision, loose-limbed and shrieking. Pitt is virtually static in comparison, leaning against the bar, sullen and unresponsive.

Rosa's mother, Mrs Dawson, has had a stroke. It happened at the beginning of the week on a golf course in Bognor Regis.

Yesterday Mrs Dawson was out of intensive care and able to receive visitors, but this morning the hospital rang to say that her condition had deteriorated.

Rosa wants to leave for Bognor Regis immediately. Pitt thinks it's too hot to spend the weekend in a hospital. He wants to take the children to the vicarage, as planned.

'Let's give her time to improve. Her condition needs to stabilize before we take the girls to see her.'

I start to move around the kitchen, clearing breakfast things away.

'What if she doesn't improve?' Rosa is suddenly deflated. She no longer sounds angry, just scared. 'This might be the last time we get to see her. Violet, Grandma Dawson is very unwell. You want to see her, don't you?'

Her voice falls away.

The children are already fractious. On top of the heat, the tail-end of their parents' argument hangs heavy in the morning air. Violet has refused to get dressed. The hot weather has made her eczema flare up and clothes – any clothes – make her itch. She sits in her chair naked as she eats, impassive to her mother's appeal.

'Baby – you'll never cope with your mother *and* the children.'

Rosa straightens up at this. Her edges become sharper suddenly. 'I'll take Rebecca with me.'

For the past few minutes, I've been standing with the bread knife in my hand, no longer even pretending to tidy away. I don't dare look at either of them.

Violet's mouth stops chewing. 'But I want Rebecca to come with us to the vicarage.'

'Nobody's going to the vicarage,' Rosa is shrieking again. 'We're going to see Grandma Dawson before she dies.'

'I hate Grandma Dawson,' Violet explodes, sitting with her arms folded, traces of jam on her chest where it has run off her toast. 'She won't let us touch anything and we're not allowed to sit on the furniture or walk on her white carpet. I want to go to the vicarage.'

'Violet!' Rosa rounds on Pitt. 'Are you just going to stand there and let her speak like that?'

'She's got a point.'

Violet grins at her father and made bold by his support adds, 'Pleeeaaassse.'

'Look, why don't Violet, Rebecca and I go to the vicarage,' Pitt shrugs, resting a paternal hand on Violet's head while managing to avoid looking at either me or Rosa. 'And you take Lulu to see your mother.'

An hour later, Rosa, beaten, makes a loud and clattering departure, Lulu slung over her shoulder.

Once the door to the apartment slams shut, Pitt turns to me, sunlight bouncing off a triumphant smile. Violet dances naked in front of us.

A hard-to-ignore stench of slaughter hangs in the hot morning air.

The chauffeur, Douglas, drives us, so there's no chance to talk in the car. Pitt then disappears as soon as we arrive, saying that he has phone calls to make, promising to join us for lunch. I don't know what I was expecting, but after the London apartment, the Crawleys' Oxfordshire vicarage comes as a surprise. Such a surprise, in fact, that on first sight it's hard to make any connection between the two. Apart from Pitt himself, of course, who somehow manages to look at home in both places.

The vicarage feels unexpectedly gloomy, arrested rather than neglected, the whole place trying to balance shamefaced ruin with a barely-preserved dignity.

There are few traces of Rosa here – no wonder she hates it. The first Mrs Crawley, however, is everywhere still. She's in the wallpaper, a repeating trellis design dotted with cornucopia. This, along with the upholstery, is tatty and watermarked but somehow all the grander for it. She's in the furniture as well, which is dark and inherited. Even her old housekeeper's apartment – a woman called Mrs Briggs, who died of cancer two years ago – has been left intact.

Despite what I've gleaned from conversations with Rosa about the acrimoniousness of the divorce, I half expect to find photos of the first Mrs Crawley among the frames crowding the piano in the sitting room. But these are mostly – another surprise – of a much younger Rawdon Crawley.

'I want to show you the river, and my horse!' Violet pulls hard on my arm, hopping and impatient.

Ignoring her, I remain focused on the photographs, studying them at close range, my face stopping just short of the glass. Rawdon on horseback, and in school uniform. The wide-eyed boyishness vanishing along with the smile as the years progress.

Sixteen would appear to be where Rawdon stops – there are no photographs of him any older than this. It makes me feel sad, looking at them. His clearly wasn't a childhood that stands up well to being chronicled and I wonder, briefly, why Pitt keeps the photos on display. What is it exactly that he's attempting to preserve here in this mausoleum of his first marriage?

Later, before supper, I'll conduct my own tour of the house, and will come across a room still littered with boyish debris: badger skulls, rugby trophies and sun-faded Athena posters. Along with a fossilized apple core, perfectly preserved, which I'll find balanced on the edge of a desk as if it has only just been discarded by a vanishing teenager whose return the room has been waiting for ever since.

Eventually, I allow myself to be dragged away from the photos and led to the stables, dusted in patches of sunlight and thick with animal smells. Alongside Violet's own pony, there are two black stallions with rolling, tearaway eyes. Ever since I was lifted onto the back of one at the fair as a child – I'll never forget the animal shifting unpredictably beneath me – I've been terrified of horses, and these are huge: snorting, stamping beasts. Hanging back, I watch as Violet approaches her pony and presses her face into its flanks.

'Whose are those?'

'The one with the white mark on his head is Gawain,' she mumbles. 'He's Rawdie's horse. The other one, Shambles, belongs to Daddy.'

'Rawdon keeps a horse here?'

'Sometimes he comes at the weekend.'

'Is he coming this weekend?'

She shrugs.

'And your dad rides?'

'They both do. Sometimes they go riding together.'

'But – I thought they didn't get on?'

Violet twists her head slowly around, the horse taking a few sidesteps as the pressure in its flank shifts. Violet has a way of looking at me sometimes when I ask questions – like she's trying to weigh up how worthwhile they are. She does this now, finally deigning to answer. 'They don't. Apart from here.'

In the end, Pitt doesn't appear until after lunch, but when he does it's immediately apparent that his mood has shifted. Less preoccupied, close to raucous even, he proposes a game of cricket.

Led by Violet, we burst out of the house into the wilting

garden laden with bat, balls and wicket stumps. Violet is squealing with excitement and completely incapable of understanding the rules Pitt explains to her. We play with old tennis balls that keep getting hit into the river the garden runs down to. Shoes and socks are discarded so that Violet and I can splash through the shallows. We run back across the pitch barefoot and take up our positions once more, the dry grass pricking at the soles of our feet.

Once she has the bat in her hands, Violet becomes a taut and engaged cricketer, hitting every one of Pitt's bowls. The more her father praises her, the more seriously she takes the game. When she's finally bowled out, she begrudgingly concedes the bat to Pitt and, crouching at a distance, becomes a preoccupied fielder instead.

I can hear her singing to herself behind me as I focus on Pitt, who stands sweat-streaked and panting over the bat. The shirt he's wearing – I've only ever seen him in shirts – is wet and sticking to him.

It's my turn to bowl.

Running, I let go of the sodden ball. Over-arm. Teeth clenched. There's a wet thud as bat makes contact with ball.

Then Pitt breaks into a streaking run across the lawn towards me.

'Violet!' I yelp, completely caught up in the game now.

Without thinking, I tear after the ball as it continues its trajectory towards the river. I hear the hollow sound of her feet across the lawn behind me.

Then a dog appears from nowhere, small and wiry. It gets there before either of us, stretching its mouth wide over the ball and disappearing again. Turning, I give chase, the sun low in the sky, blinding. I don't remember the collision, only the jab of elbows and knees. The bruising tumble into the grass and, after the shock, laughter – mine and then Pitt's.

A hand reaches out for me. 'Rebecca? You OK?'

I manage to get into a kneeling position, still stunned.

I'm only vaguely aware of Pitt beside me in the grass, his hand running down the length of my arm.

And then the dog reappears.

'Rex!' Violet shouts. Followed by an even more excited, 'Sophie!'

Pitt lets go of my arm.

Retrieving our shoes, I follow him and Violet towards the terrace where introductions are made, our long shadows stretching across the lawn and afternoon.

Violet has her arms around the girl's waist and is holding on tight. The girl, who is wearing jodhpurs and an old T-shirt, smells of horse.

Sophie, Pitt tells me – still panting – used to live here with her mum, Mrs Briggs, in the apartment upstairs. She grew up in the vicarage, like Rawdon. It's the first time I've ever heard him mention his son's name.

'She used to be his *girlfriend*,' Violet puts in, her face stretching itself into a shy smile.

Sophie doesn't react to this.

'Childhood sweethearts,' Pitt goads, 'isn't that right, Soph? Rawdon's the only reason you stay on.'

'I stay on because of the horses,' she corrects him.

He lets out a laugh, pleased. Again, Sophie fails to react, and the air remains charged with hostility although this doesn't seem to bother Pitt. The childhood sweethearts jibe, I realize, is an old one.

Sophie says, 'I made supper – it's in the fridge.' She shakes the hair from her face, eyes trailing me. 'I wasn't sure how many of you there would be.'

'Just us.'

Pitt's voice is loud, but Sophie's eyes remain on me until I find myself having to look away.

'Well, I just thought I'd check in, make sure you have everything you need.'

'All good, Soph.'

'Sorry not to see Rosa. Give her my best.'

Later, through the open windows, we hear her footsteps cross the gravel drive and a car door slam. I saw the car earlier, its back window obscured by protest stickers: CND, Greenham Common, PETA. The sound of her engine fills the evening for a moment and then she's gone.

We eat the supper she made in the kitchen, presided over by an Aga that rises like the hull of a shipwreck on a deserted stretch of beach. Now that Sophie's gone, there's a raw sense of anticipation, making conversation stilted and the already tired Violet fractious. The more she senses that she isn't wanted, the more insistent she becomes on staying, terrified of missing out.

Until she's finally persuaded into bed, leaving Pitt and me alone.

The TV room is hung with the same tattered florals and chintzes as the rest of the house. There are oil paintings on the walls, dingy and nondescript – livestock, landscapes, the odd portrait: women and men with sad eyes, who have grown accustomed to no longer being looked at. Night falls and, for the first time all week, I'm close to cold in the strappy dress I'm wearing. It's one of Amelia's, given to me last weekend.

'Have you always had this place?'

From the sofa where he's spread, Pitt stares. There is nothing playful about the way he does this. I can feel the weight of his eyes.

'This place? No – I bought it when Rawdon was born.

Somewhere for us to spend the holidays when he wasn't at school.'

His tone is evasive, reluctant even. This is something he doesn't want to talk about, so I'm surprised when he adds, 'At the start of each term, when it was time for him to go back to school, he would hide so that we couldn't find him. Always a different place. Attic, cellar, cupboards, potting shed, stables – anywhere he could slide, crawl, climb or squeeze his way into.' Lifting his eyes to the window, Pitt says, 'Once he took himself off into the woods.'

I find myself looking out of the window as well, through the remains of dusk until the dried-out fields become just about visible, running towards a dark line of trees. We stay like that for some time, as if straining to catch sight of a streaking blur of schoolboy.

'We searched for hours, until in the end we had to send Sophie to find him.'

'So, they *were* childhood sweethearts?'

'No, that's just a family joke, but they were both only children, and close. Brother and sister close.'

'And did she? Find him?'

Pitt smiles one of his ambivalent smiles. 'Yes. But only under duress. She knew all his hiding places.'

He closes the subject by asking me to choose some music.

I cross the room to the bookshelves, fingers trailing the mould-spotted spines of books on naval history, until they come to rest on a vinyl collection identical to the one in the London flat. I pull out *Electric Ladyland*, dropping the record onto the turntable and lowering the arm. There's a brief crackle as the needle finds its groove. I push up the volume.

'Come and sit down.'

He slides his hand across the sofa, into the pool of light from a side lamp.

I do as he asks, sitting close enough to enable his knee to push against my thigh and for it not to feel deliberate.

'I wanted to talk to you about the photographs in your office.'

'You haven't been snooping around in there again, have you?'

He sounds only half amused. Uninterested in the photographs, his attention is taken up by our legs, pressed together on the sofa.

'The photographs of the Princess and her mystery man. They were on horses.'

He smiles. 'Oh. *Those* photographs.'

'You're trying to find out who he is, aren't you?'

'And?'

I try to shake the feeling I often get speaking to him – that he already knows what I'm about to say. 'Well, I know who he is.'

Pitt moves his head from side to side, smiling still.

'What, you don't believe me? I saw him at a nightclub last weekend.'

'Oh, I believe you, Rebecca.' A hand rests on my left leg. The smile persists. 'The thing is, the mystery's been solved. We know who he is.'

I can hear the thump of my heart. So violent now that it's making the thin summer dress I'm wearing shudder.

'You're bluffing.'

'William Armstrong. Household Cavalry. Although most people know him as Polo. Features are running a fluff piece on him in Monday's edition. Along with a photo of the Princess presenting him with a polo trophy. He was playing today in a match with the Prince. Maybe there's something going on between them, maybe there isn't. Flirting, yes, but anything more than that? Who knows? Not enough for us to risk our necks. Yet . . .' he soothes, sliding the hand up my leg. Numb,

I watch it span my skin. The hand looks strangely detached from him. 'But good work. The sort of work that could have landed you a job on the *Mercury*. If only you'd let me know sooner—'

Once, in a blind fury, I opened all the cupboards in our tiny kitchen and hauled what little crockery we had onto the floor. I watched the shards bounce across the filthy tiles until I was surrounded, and the cupboards were bare, and I could breathe again.

I can feel the same blind fury taking over now and am close to tears with the effort of controlling it.

'I tried, but there was never a right moment.' Nonplussed, his hand continues its creeping progress thigh-wards. 'How did you find out?'

'Oh, I know all about the nightclub,' he murmurs, his sweating face shining, 'think about it – who else was there with you?'

'George,' I murmur back, not needing to think about it.

Pitt sends a laugh towards the peeling ceiling.

'See – told you he was good.' There's admiration in his voice as he twists his head towards me. 'What the fuck were you thinking telling George? You should know better – you worked with him at the *County Times*.'

Too stunned to respond, I remain rigid on the sofa as he leans in, leans over. Whispering in my ear with his hot mouth, 'You won't make that mistake again.'

I can feel the heat of him, his intent. Lying alongside the shock, it's like being doubly suffocated. Suddenly unable to bear it, I push a hand into his chest.

'Look, I'll find you something on the *Mercury*, don't worry. I'll have to,' he chuckles, wet in my ear still, 'Rosa wants you gone.'

'Gone?'

He nods, and then I realize. It's all been decided. Last week's rows were part of a war that was being fought behind the scenes. Why didn't I see it coming? Why do I never see it coming? But before I get a chance to speak again, two things happen. I catch movement out of the corner of my eye – Violet? – and at the same time the front door slams.

'Shit. Rosa,' Pitt wheezes above the record, which is still playing.

In the lull that follows, we struggle to our feet, putting as much distance as possible between us and the sofa with its ghetto of squashed cushions.

'Shit,' Pitt says again, rubbing at his face and hair.

'I think Violet saw us . . . She was in the doorway.'

He stares at me, his eyes crazy. 'Saw what? Nothing happened . . . Wait here. I'm going to try and steer Rosa towards the kitchen.'

But when I peer around the doorway in the direction of the front hall, it isn't Rosa I see Violet hurl herself at, laughing. It's Rawdon Crawley. Her body slams against him. She hangs from his neck until he's forced to put his motorcycle helmet down on a table and haul her up in his arms, wrapping her legs around his waist.

'You weigh a tonne, Vi. What have they been feeding you?'

She tilts her head, coquettish, to one side. 'Lulu.'

He feigns shock. 'You ate your sister?'

Violet nods, excited, as Rawdon pulls her mouth open and calls out, 'Lulu? Lulu, are you in there?' Then, ignoring Pitt and turning to me, he says, 'So, what is this? Some cannibal convention?'

Immediately, I feel as if a danger I was aware of but chose to ignore has passed, the latent sense of shame I should have felt on the sofa catching up with me. Fast. I can feel it blossoming across my face and throat.

'Rebecca's not a cannibal,' Violet screams, delighted.

'No? I wouldn't be so sure—'

Up close, I can see what it is that makes Lizzie Saltire thread her arm through his and keep him as close to her as she can. And now I know something else about him that I never would have found out from *Tatler*: he likes children.

We continue to watch each other, my shoulder against the doorframe

Then he smiles. Nothing more than a grin. Quick. Boyish. With Pitt, I often had the sensation of standing alongside myself watching a whole different version of me. With Rawdon, I feel like there's only space for one version. And even though I haven't spoken so much as a single word, have barely moved in fact, I sense that I've managed to catch him out in some fundamental way; that I've surprised him, and that being surprised isn't something he's used to.

Clutching her koala bear in one hand, Violet lands a thump on his chest with the other. 'Rebecca's my nanny.'

'Which does little to explain why you aren't tucked up in bed fast asleep.'

'I was asleep. *They* woke me up with their music.'

The collective pronoun sounds stark spoken in her accusing child's voice as she slithers to the ground, grinding her chin into the bear's head while watching me steadily. The bear is wearing one of Lulu's old cardigans. Violet loves it with that frantic love children reserve for inanimate objects, able to keep up a one-sided stream of patter with it for hours on end.

'Oh,' Rawdon says at last, looking from me to Pitt. He picks up his motorcycle helmet and for a moment, I panic, thinking he might have changed his mind and be about to leave. But instead, he turns to Pitt. 'Rosa rang – she said you guys were here. I thought I'd come down and join you for a ride tomorrow.'

Violet starts to jump on the spot.

'If you're going for a ride, that is.'

'That's the plan,' Pitt concedes with an effort.

He looks much older suddenly, and shapeless in a way I hadn't previously noticed. There's a new wariness about him as well, as if his son's presence has put him on the alert. Like a sleeping sentry, woken with a kick and left groping around in the dark for his abandoned spear.

'Oh, and Rosa's mum's doing fine,' Rawdon adds, his eyes sweeping over all of us. 'In case anybody was worried. Well – nice to meet you, Rebecca.'

I remain in the hallway, unsure, even though it feels like I've been dismissed.

Watching as they disappear towards the kitchen discussing tomorrow's plans for an early-morning ride.

# Haversham

My mother was addicted to falling in love. Falling in love, she once said, was a rush. Gravity-defying. Technicolour. Staying in love, however, was a different matter. But that wasn't something she worried about because the world was full of men. Why stick to one? This was her mantra.

After our neighbour Angelina got me my first library card, I would scour the shelves for love stories to take home.

I adored Jane Austen, but my mother preferred the wild-eyed Brontës. *Wuthering Heights* she read eight times, the book propped open in her lap, ankles crossed, slippered feet balanced among the debris on the kitchen table. The hand that turned the pages was forever clasping a cigarette from which she would take slow, preoccupied drags, brushing away the ash that fell off the end.

Heathcliff was a man she understood, a man she could get to grips with. Deep, dark and tormented. But then she'd always had a preference for tragedy, the crash and burn endings. She had an unnatural fascination with Myra Hindley and Ian Brady's romance. Bonnie and Clyde too – lovers in arms.

I think what my mother objected to in Austen's novels was that they all led to marriage. Happy endings. The spectre of ordinary life and the road to servitude: cooking and cleaning and washing and ironing. These things, she claimed, terrified her. They could turn a woman invisible until she became nothing more than background noise in her own life.

Worst of all, they spelled the death of love.

Which was why my mother was so insistent about keeping love ahead of her. Something big and impossible for the future. Until Mr Crisp, who changed everything.

The first time I saw him in our flat was the first time I'd ever seen a man in our house. I must have been around twelve. It was a year before I was due to sit the music scholarship exam and although I had piano practice with him on a weekly basis, I didn't recognize him. He was out of context. I couldn't contemplate him having an existence beyond the music rooms at Chilston House, yet here he was, standing in our teetering lounge in a squash kit. Stranger still, his hair was wet, and somehow I knew that this was connected to the fact that my mother was wearing her dressing gown in the afternoon.

For an awful moment, I thought I'd done something wrong and that he was here to reprimand me. But all he said was, 'See you, Becky,' before disappearing down the corridor towards the front door, trailed by my mother. I was sure that I heard the wet suck of heavy kissing. Then the front door, shutting.

When my mother reappeared, she lit a cigarette and stood by the window, watching him drive away. Back to Chilston House and the cottage he lived in on school grounds with his wife and new baby.

'Tell me about him,' she said, anchored to the window even though Mr Crisp was long gone.

'What d'you mean?'

'I mean,' she carried on, emphasizing the word and turning to me now, her face and voice coming back into focus, 'what sort of things do you two talk about? What's he interested in? What makes him tick?'

Her face was open, excited. And although it wasn't a face she'd worn in a long time, and it should have made me glad, it didn't. The opposite, in fact. I could feel my mood darkening by the second.

'What makes him *tick*?' I laughed.

But she only nodded. 'Yeah, you know – like, what music is he into? What does he listen to? Classical, I guess?'

I was becoming increasingly hostile to her enthusiasm. The sly, flickering curiosity she was showing in classical music for the first time ever, even though I'd been playing piano for over five years now. With a jolt, I realized that this was a part of my life I didn't want to share with her. I didn't want her trampling around in the conversations I had with Mr Crisp, or the feelings I experienced when playing and listening to music. These were private things, my things, and I wanted them to remain that way.

'Stuff,' I said at last, to the floor, jabbing the toe of my shoe into the carpet's worn pile.

'What stuff?'

I lifted my head up then and stared at her in her dressing gown. 'You wouldn't understand.'

That did it. The eyes narrowed and the light that had been there only seconds before left her face, shutting it down. I've done that, I thought with something like pride. Something like triumph. For the first time ever, I had the upper hand.

'I'm not stupid, Becky.'

Then suddenly she sagged, her arm wrapping itself around her stomach as she leaned over and started to cry.

Mr Crisp came every Thursday after that.

There would be a gift, usually an electrical appliance. He had a thing about electrical goods. Over time, we acquired a freezer, microwave and video player. Over time, Mr Crisp became Mark. Occasionally, he drove my mother to a hotel at Gatwick Airport and she would come back beaming over a stash of miniatures lifted from the bathroom. But mostly, he'd rent a video for me to watch with the volume up high and they'd stay in the flat, even though it was a pigsty. He said that to her once and it made her cry. She made an effort for a while, but all those years getting paid to clean had burnt her out. Afterwards, I'd hear Mark in the shower, singing. He'd reappear looking the same as he had when he arrived, only more cheerful, his hair wet.

Around this time, my mother got a new job at Chilston House. In the mornings, she left the flat in a skirt and blouse and shoes with high heels instead of the blue overalls she used to wear. She put on make-up, and she smelt good. The new job was in the registrar's office. It was a job she claimed she never would have got if it hadn't been for Mark. Something I'm sure Caroline was aware of – to this day I don't know how my mother squared it with her.

Our lives changed. The worries that in the past stretched them thin eased. The salary that came with the new job meant that we no longer had to make up our days as we went along. Instead, we were able to think ahead, make plans for the weekends and holidays; a luxury life hadn't afforded us to date. I felt pricked all over with a newfound joy while a latent curiosity in the world at large unfurled inside my mother. She spoke about night school and qualifications, channelling her exuberance into the future rather than trying to force it all into the present moment.

Towards the end of her first year working in the registrar's office, we were invited to the bursar's summer party. This was an annual event for all school staff and their families, held in the bursar's garden. I'd never been to a grown-up party before. Parties were something that happened to other people. But when the invitation from Mr and Mrs Hunter arrived in the post, it had both our names on it.

Still, I wasn't sure if we would go. Mark would be there, but so would Mark's wife. And baby. They'd had an argument about it the previous Thursday; Mark had asked my mother not to come, promised he'd make it up to her. A weekend away, he said. Somewhere hot. My mother said she didn't have a passport. Brighton, then, he'd tried. 'I don't want to go to fucking Brighton. I want to go to the fucking party,' she insisted, sullen. The more he didn't want her to go, the more she wanted it.

They fought after that, and Mark left without showering, his hair dry.

The day of the party, we drove in silence to Chilston House. Up until then, I'd been excited about it, but as we turned through the gates there was something about the thick, empty afternoon that made my stomach cramp. We drove with all the windows down, but still our dresses stuck to our legs and our hair curled at the back of our necks. The heat was making my mother tetchy. As we parked opposite the bursar's house, we were able to smell the meat haze from the barbecue through the open windows.

My mother turned off the engine but kept her hands on the steering wheel, staring at the house as though it was much further away than it was. Something the horizon might swallow up at any moment. A mirage.

'You're sure you want to do this?'

'No.'

'Me neither,' I said. Then, suddenly decisive, 'Come on.'

Clutching the crumpled invitation in my hands, we got out of the car, my mother unsteady in her new sandals.

Everything in the Hunters' garden was the colour it should be. The grass was green. The water was blue. The sun, yellow. The house backed onto the prep school swimming pool, and it echoed with the sound of children as they swarmed over inflatables. We hovered for a moment on the fringes of this flawless world, worried about spoiling it in some indeterminate way.

My mother was awkward and frazzled from the car journey. Grabbing at the invitation, she kept folding it into an ever-decreasing square.

Perhaps we wouldn't stay after all, she said. Nobody had seen us arrive. If we were to leave now, who would have known that we were ever there?

But I didn't want to leave, I realized suddenly, taking in the house and garden stretched out around us, aware of a quivering sense of possibility.

My eyes were adjusting to the tidily arranged groups filling the garden – the women gathered at tables near the pool's edges where they shrieked as they got splashed by children taking running jumps into the blue water. They were drinking wine and laughing among themselves. They wore sunglasses and what my mother referred to with a sniff as sensible clothes: shorts and pastel-coloured T-shirts and flat shoes. They all looked pretty much the same. Uniform. Although some of them wore dresses, none of them were like my mother's sherbet lemon sheath with plunging neckline. She'd coupled it with high-heeled sandals and an ankle bracelet.

They stared at her.

I saw Mark standing with a group of men around the barbecue. He was wearing an apron and had a pair of tongs in his hand. Children were running in circles around them, their wet feet slapping on the patio. There was another group of younger staff spread out on the lawn, hunkered over beers. And moving through everybody with trays of drinks, boys and girls from a local catering firm. I looked out for Paul. He had a weekend job with the company and was meant to be working here today, but there was no sign of him.

My mother's gaze was fixed on Mark at the barbecue. She was waiting for him to notice her, but I could tell he already had and was just doing a good job of ignoring her.

One of the pastel-coloured women in sunglasses approached then. Smiling, she put her hand out towards my mother. 'Hello. Mary Hunter.'

A soft, unhurried voice. A soft, unhurried woman.

'We were invited.' My mother, nervous now, thrust out the crumpled invitation.

'Of course,' our host soothed, waving the invitation away so that my mother had no choice but to keep hold of it.

Her eyes, beneath the sunglasses, ran over my mother's dress. Women like Mary Hunter were always interested in what my mother wore. She moved an arm across the hot afternoon and everybody in it – it was a graceful gesture, like the raising of stage curtains – before leading us towards the barbecue.

I had the impression she wasn't sure what else to do with us.

The women stared as our small procession passed. Some of them leaned confidentially together, whispering. My mother drew herself up, which made her wobble, and the men's eyes trailed her uneven approach, but she was used to that. Enjoyed it. She was a beautiful woman. Still. Despite her earlier misgivings in front of the bathroom mirror.

'I've got wrinkles, Becky. Here. Look at my eyes.'

I shrugged at her reflection. I hadn't noticed. She was barely thirty.

'Wrinkles. I'm getting old,' she insisted, genuinely scared. 'And I can't do shit about it. You can't fight the clock.'

'Well,' I said after a while as she stood biting her nails, preoccupied, 'you'll always be younger than Mark's wife.'

Our eyes met in the mirror. A laughing moment of camaraderie.

'All right, boss,' my mother said loudly, cheerfully, her eyes bouncing off an immense man standing to the left of Mark, before coming to rest on Mark himself. His apron was black and had the words *natural born griller* written across it.

She shook out her hair and did something with her shoulders, but Mark only smiled vaguely at her before sliding away across the lawn. She watched him go. She watched for too long.

'Jess and her friends are indoors if you want to go and join them.'

It took me a while to realize that Mary Hunter was speaking to me. Who on earth was Jess? Their daughter, I guessed. Somebody the same age as me, that's what she meant. She was being kind.

'Go on.' My mother flapped an elbow against my back, her voice loud. She accepted a drink passed to her by a boy in a black waistcoat. He was so handsome that it made me blush. She was going to get drunk, I realized, worried. 'Enjoy yourself. Scoot.'

Reluctant, I made my way slowly across the garden towards the house, glancing back every now and then at the circle of men gathering around my increasingly buoyant mother. I had no intention of seeking out the Hunters' daughter and her friends. It was a quiet vantage point I was after. Somewhere I could keep an eye on things. But first, I needed a glass of water.

I stepped into the house and was crossing the conservatory when someone grabbed my arm.

'What the fuck are you doing here?' Mr Crisp hissed.

He was angry. His face was restless with it. I'd never seen Mr Crisp angry before. I'd never heard him swear before either. It made him look different.

'We were invited.'

It was what my mother had said earlier, to Mary Hunter.

'She promised she wouldn't come.' He was whispering aggressively and watching the garden beyond my shoulders, through the open doors.

My arm was pulled up at an angle and beginning to hurt. 'Let me go.'

He stared at me for a moment, confused. 'Sorry. Look, Becky, sorry. But we had an arrangement.'

He let go of my arm and I stood rubbing it, suddenly aware that I was angry myself.

'She said she'd stay away from the party, and we agreed I'd make it up to her.'

I didn't want to think about Mark making things up to my mother.

'I just don't want things to get complicated,' he appealed to me.

'I'd say they got complicated when you first started seeing her.'

'Yeah,' he agreed, laughing. It was a surprised laugh. 'Yeah,' he said again, 'I'd say so as well.' He continued to grin down at me. 'Keep an eye on her for me, will you, Becky?'

I felt hot and suddenly tearful. I shouted at his retreating back, 'She's not my responsibility!'

Without waiting to gauge his reaction, I disappeared into the depths of the Hunters' enormous house. The place was an unexpected warzone of shouting, slamming doors and stampeding feet. In one of the rooms I passed, a group of teenage boys were crowded around an Atari, the screen full of pixelated meteors, falling and exploding. The surrounding corridors were a hazardous clutter of shoes, bats, rackets and balls. Endless sporting piles. I was used to mess, but this was different. The mess of plenty. Life lived at high volume and full tilt.

I drifted upstairs, towards the sound of Iron Maiden playing on a stereo, and found myself in a room at the end of a corridor, overlooking the garden. The open doorway framed a sanctuary, and as there didn't seem to be anybody around, I stepped inside. Immediately I was overwhelmed by pastel pinks in every shade and hue stretching as far as the eye could see. Walls, carpet, curtains, duvet – I half expected the leaves on the trees filling the window to have turned pink.

The iron bedstead had fairy lights threaded through it, partly obscured by cushions and soft toys. What dreams did a person have in a bed like that? There was a velvet armchair strewn with discarded clothes, and next to it a dressing table and mirror hung with necklaces. Catching sight of my reflection – hovering and ghostly – I felt a strange urge to sound the alarm, let them know there was an intruder in their midst who meant them harm.

Crossing to the window, I scanned the garden below in search of my mother.

And then a voice behind me said, 'Jess?'

It was a low, strung-out voice and, spinning around, I saw that it belonged to a boy in black jeans and an Alice Cooper T-shirt; as much of an interloper as me among the room's pastel pinks, bringing a smell with him that reminded me of the old shower block at school where girls went to smoke weed.

His eyes were hollow as they carried out a slow, deliberate appraisal of me.

I stared back.

'You're not Jess,' he said after a while, grinning and pleased with himself.

There were shouts of laughter then from the corridor outside, and the next minute two girls a little older than me came crashing into the room.

'Jess!' the boy yelled with a burst of enthusiasm, as one of them grabbed him by the elbow and hauled him over to the window. I don't think she even saw me.

'You have to see this! That woman in the yellow dress, she just fell in the pool. Hil-ar-ious.'

I joined them at the window. Down in the garden, most people were now standing around the pool where there was a woman floundering in the water. Her arms hauled at the blue surface as if trying to find something solid to hold on to. And then she sank under.

'Oh my god – look at her!'

'She can't swim,' I said, far too quietly. Unable to make myself heard. And then again, louder this time, 'She can't swim!'

All three of them turned to stare at me.

I felt myself move, and without really being aware of it, I was soon at the bottom of the stairs. The next thing I knew, I was crossing the lawn towards the pool, when someone in a white shirt and black waistcoat went streaking past me and jumped straight in. A boy from the catering staff.

My mother was in shallow water but too terrified to realize it. Even after he'd hauled her to her feet, she continued to claw at the surface of the pool. He had to pull her towards the steps, the pair of them making waves that sent the few children remaining in the water bobbing, wide-eyed, on their inflatables. Struggling out of his grip onto the lawn, she knelt, retching, on all fours, the soaking dress clinging to her. The boy's sodden uniform clung to him too. He was bent over, hands on knees, water running off him. It wasn't until he stood up that I recognized him – it was the boy who'd made me blush earlier. A boy I would see again when I started work at the *County Times*: George.

Mr Crisp appeared then. My mother thrust an arm out blindly towards his legs, but as a woman in a suit – too hot for the day – peeled away from the crowd, he took a step back suddenly, pulling at the ties of the apron he still wore as if worried he looked ridiculous. At first, I thought the woman must be his wife, but then I recognized her from the school prospectus. This was the headmistress of Chilston House, Miss Pinkerton.

She stood over my mother, her foot and my mother's hand almost touching in the grass, Miss Pinkerton's shadow acting as an inadvertent screen. Not for my mother's sake, I realized – she didn't so much as bend towards her and made no effort to check and see if my mother was OK. But for the sake of everyone else gathered in the Hunters' garden.

Mary Hunter arrived. Alongside her, Paul, in his waiter's uniform, with towels. He crouched down in the grass beside my shuddering mother in the shade cast by Miss Pinkerton's towering figure. I hadn't moved. I was standing among the women as they tried to distract their children by encouraging them back into the water. The pace of the afternoon started to pick up again. More drinks were poured. Conversations restarted. Although eyes kept drifting back to where my mother now sat alone, wrapped in a towel on the lawn. Paul was fussing over the other waiter, the handsome lifesaver. Helping to wring him dry.

I remained buried among strangers, watching her at a distance.

During the journey home, still wrapped in Mary Hunter's towel, I heard how she had threatened to jump in the pool because of the way Mark was ignoring her. Knowing she couldn't swim, he hadn't taken the threat seriously.

Until she jumped.

# LOVER
1994

# Polo

A telephone starts ringing somewhere close by. My body slides automatically out of bed. The distance between bed and floor is much shorter than it should be, until I realize that I must have spent the night on the sofa. For a moment, I'm disorientated. Something that makes my progress clumsy and bruising as I stumble through the seasonless dawn into furniture I fail to anticipate, following the telephone's persistent ringing across a high-ceilinged room with thin curtains.

The telephone is one of those old-fashioned handsets with a dial, and it isn't until I see this that I remember where I am – the Queen's Court flat I share with Amelia. The lounge, to be more precise.

I came home late last night to find Lizzie Saltire asleep in my bed, but there was nothing I could do about it. At least nothing that wouldn't spell the end of our current living arrangements, and these are far too convenient to forsake.

If it wasn't for the peppercorn rent Amelia charges me, I wouldn't be anywhere close to this postcode. On my salary, I ought to be in Pinner. Or Uxbridge. A flat share with strangers somewhere on London's dingy fringes. And perhaps I would have been in Pinner by now if it wasn't for the fact that I work with George at the *Mercury*. Seeing him most days, I'm ideally placed to report back on his every mood and movement, almost 28 per cent of which I share with Amelia.

I've become an asset to her. Part of our peppercorn rent arrangement, along with answering the phone, which has become almost exclusively my job, even though it rarely rings for me; usually either Amelia or Lizzie. Whether Lizzie's staying with us or not, this is the number she gives out. The pad Amelia bought, with its logo of a pigeon-toed teddy bear clutching a comforter, is full of addresses left by people summoning Lizzie to parties.

Sometimes when Amelia's out, I answer in her voice. I did this once when Mrs Sedley called and successfully sustained a fifteen-minute conversation about the job the tree surgeons had done on the Sedleys' walnut tree. I'm a talented mimic, but towards the end of the call there was a quiver of doubt in Mrs Sedley's voice.

'Are you sure you're all right, darling?' she said suddenly.

I was stung on two accounts. It had been a long time since anybody asked me if I was all right, but it was the 'darling' that really caught me out. I had trouble responding. 'Of course, why wouldn't I be?' An eerie pause followed. 'Mums,' I carried on, having heard Amelia call Mrs Sedley this before, 'I'm fine, just been out a lot, that's all. Tired.'

'Late nights?' Mrs Sedley probed, sounding pleased. She was very taken with the idea of her daughter being a 'girl about town', and scanned the pages of *Tatler* religiously every month, looking for Amelia's face among the photos of the Right Honourable crew moving through the London season together, rubbing shoulders with royals: Ascot, Wimbledon, Henley, and the parties. The parties.

This is more Lizzie's set than Amelia's, although Amelia – unlike me – is always welcome. I'm only ever allowed in on a tourist visa. Tolerated and made to feel it. Not that it matters; the important thing is to be seen at the parties because I have my own agenda – William Armstrong and Rawdon Crawley.

Rawdon has been made editor of the Crawleys' other newspaper, a broadsheet – the *Courier*. He and Lizzie are still photographed together but don't seem to be romantically linked.

Picking up the receiver, I recognize the voice immediately. Drunk as it is.

'Polo,' I say.

For once, the call isn't for Amelia. Or Lizzie.

Since that night almost five years ago when I first saw William Armstrong at the club, we've become close. Absent fathers played an important role in establishing trust during the early stages of our acquaintance, which I've been steadily cultivating – especially now I've made it to Features. Drunk, Polo is indiscreet; indiscreet enough for me to believe that there must be some element of truth in the rumours that have perpetuated over the years about him and the Princess. The wildest of these – mine and everybody else's golden fleece – being that he has love letters from her.

'I've decided. I'm ready to meet your people, Rebecca. Talk to them . . . see what they can offer.'

The voice wavers somewhere between assertion and disbelief. Over the past few months, he has been giving me bits and pieces about his supposed affair with the Princess; bits and pieces I've paid for in cash, meeting him at an NCP car park near Victoria for the drop. But this is the phone call I've been waiting for. Briefly, I wonder what has prompted it. Why now?

'When you say you're ready to meet . . .'

'I mean I'm ready to go public,' he clarifies.

'That's great,' I reassure him, my voice loud with excitement. 'Really great.'

'You think so? God.' This comes out as a long pant. 'I don't know.'

Putting my hand over the receiver, I walk as far as the coiled cord will allow. Across the hallway, the door to Amelia's room is shut, but the door to my room is open and through it I can see Lizzie lying untidily on top of the duvet, hair falling across her face. From this angle, her legs look broken, as if she's been dropped onto the bed from a great height. I'm certain she's asleep still.

I turn back into the lounge, pulling the door shut. Easing myself onto the sofa, I'm careful not to dislodge a half-eaten bowl of spaghetti that has been left to balance on one of its arms. It's a miracle it managed to stay there all night. Amelia made the Bolognese sauce yesterday for a supper she was meant to be having with George. By the time I left, there was still no sign of him. It's becoming a pattern – Amelia's attempts at orchestrated intimacy and George's failure to show.

At some point, she must have rung Lizzie.

There are bottles, mostly empty – wine and spirits – banked on the coffee table.

'Polo, we've been through this, it's time the world heard your story. This is the right decision.'

It's important to use the imperative with Polo, who, despite being a military man, can be critically indecisive. A side effect of the undiagnosed PTSD I'm convinced he's suffering from, not as a result of the Gulf War – where he played a major part in the Liberation of Kuwait – but because of his doomed affair with the Princess.

'Where are you phoning from?'

'My flat.' A wet crackle as he licks his lips, a nervous habit of his. 'So, you'll fix the meeting?'

'Of course.' Too much enthusiasm sets Polo on edge, makes him nervy. I add, 'Although I'll need to see some hard evidence before taking this to Pitt.'

The phone cord just about manages the stretch as I cross the room to the bay window and peer through the curtains. The dawn world is clenched and grey.

A drawn-out, 'Goooood.' Then: 'Thing is, Rebecca, I'm a little short. In a bit of a fix right now, actually. Any chance of an advance?'

Polo's flat is less than a ten-minute cycle ride from Queen's Court. 'Why don't we kill two birds with one stone – you show me what you've got, and I'll see what I can do by way of an advance?'

I drop the phone with a rattle, breathing hard. It takes me a while to realize that Amelia's talking. Her voice is impatient from having to repeat herself.

'Was that the phone?'

I turn around to find Amelia awake and watching me. 'Work.'

She starts to shake out the cushions on the sofa, keeping hold of one and hugging it to her. 'That's early – for work to be phoning.'

A lot of our conversations are like this these days, with Amelia preoccupied and suspicious, as if I'm only telling her half the truth. Or, worse, outright lying. Punishment, always, for George failing to show, Amelia's instinct having long ago uncovered a connection between us that her conscious self refuses to acknowledge.

'Something came in on the night desk that they want me to cover.'

Uninterested suddenly in pursuing this any further, she changes tack. 'Why are you wearing my kimono?'

The kimono is blue, made of silk, and was a gift from Mr Sedley to his daughter. It came home with him from Tokyo after one of many business trips and was in a bundle of clothes Amelia bequeathed me when she relocated the contents of her Clapham wardrobe here to Queen's Court. This took three trips, something that seemed to please all the Sedleys enormously and was still spoken of at family gatherings. When I came across the blue kimono in the bundle, I carried it back to Amelia thinking it had got caught up with the other clothes by mistake.

'Keep it, I never wear it.'

'You're sure?' I said, holding up the kimono she had barely glanced at.

'George doesn't like me in blue,' she smiled. As if George not liking her in blue gave her some mystical sense of purpose that threw the rest of her life into relief.

Now, however, she's giving the kimono her full attention. This is quite an achievement given how hungover she is. I stand on guard, waiting. Sad – and Amelia is very sad right now, far sadder even than she is hungover – she becomes cruel. Perhaps we all do.

'You know, I wish you'd stop taking my stuff. You only have to ask. I'm a pretty generous person.'

Slowly taking off the kimono, I pass it to her, my arms and shoulders suddenly cold. I don't remind her that she gave it to me.

She scrunches it up in her arms along with the cushion, drifting towards the sofa and collapsing onto it. 'George never showed last night. Try to find out what kept him, will you? Maybe something came up at work.'

Lizzie appears then, shuffling into the lounge, hesitant in the semi-dark. This is unusual. While Amelia is gainfully employed at a Montessori nursery close by, Lizzie's working life is far more random. Stints here (*Vogue*). Stints there (Savills). Under normal circumstances, she rarely surfaces before around three in the afternoon. A side lamp is switched on.

'Too bright,' Amelia yells.

'Fuck, sorry.'

The light goes out again, reducing us to nothing more than outlines. Lizzie is by the TV trying to light a cigarette in the gloom. Amelia lies along the sofa, the kimono bundled against her.

Lizzie and I realized early on that we don't like each other. So, we keep our distance. Amicable but watchful. Wary, even. Given Amelia's mood this morning, however, I'm almost pleased to see her as we squint at each other through the grey light.

I wonder how long she's planning on staying. There have been times over the past few years when Lizzie has crashed with us for weeks at a stretch, sleeping in my bed and wearing Amelia's clothes. Crashing, I've discovered, is an informal arrangement that gives Lizzie guest rather than tenant status. It's an important distinction to make. As a guest, Lizzie doesn't pay for her accommodation. She doesn't shop for food – her own or anybody else's – and she doesn't clean. Or wash up. Or do the laundry. Her predicament, I've come to realize, doesn't seem that dissimilar to my own (a critical lack of funds), she just has a different vocabulary for it. Along with a title.

I still haven't succeeded in getting to the bottom of her living arrangements.

Sometimes she has a place to go. Often, she doesn't.

She never seems to have any money and is constantly either breaking up or breaking down. Whenever she arrives on our doorstep – always unannounced – it is as an invalid in need of sanctuary. Care. When this happens, Lizzie and Amelia end up having long, tearful conversations on the sofa. Conversations I only ever manage to overhear tantalizing fragments of. But they nearly all seem to involve the same society hostess. Tissues and ice cream and hot water bottles are used as props in these intimate scenes. Scenes starring a very different Lizzie from the gleaming, shimmering, party-faced one that continues to appear on the pages of *Tatler*. Page after page, month after month.

'Emmy's pretty upset. George isn't returning her calls and she really needs to speak to him. It's important.'

It's always important. I remain in the bay window, tracking the end of Lizzie's cigarette as she crosses to the sofa, bundling against Amelia. Their silhouettes merge. I think of the tales I could tell about George; tales that would make the brittle Amelia break. This knowledge of the power I have over her is the only thing – other than the shadow of Pinner – keeping me compliant. One day.

'I'll speak to him,' I manage lightly at last, 'I'm heading into work now.'

I shower and dress in under fifteen minutes, then pound downstairs to the neglected communal hallway where I wrestle with my bicycle. Despite the day's grey beginnings, the sun is now rising, an already frayed spread of orange and pink. The overhead strip lighting looks sickly against this natural kaleidoscope.

As I carry my bike down the small flight of steps leading from the block's entrance hall to street level, Amelia appears between the curtains at the window, looking out.

I wave, but she doesn't wave back.

Polo's flat is immaculate and musky. More like a country house squeezed into three cramped rooms than a London bachelor pad. How all this overbearing mahogany furniture could have possibly fitted through the flat's tiny front door still perplexes me, when Polo himself has to twist his shoulders sideways in order to slide through it.

The walls are papered in Regency stripes, though almost every inch of them is obscured by framed medals, oil paintings of horses and photographs of family dogs, past and present. On my first visit all those years ago, Polo ran through their names. Breeds. Character traits. There are only two pictures of human beings in the entire collection. One, a black-and-white photograph of his mother, Joyce, as a young woman. The other, a line drawing of a naked woman.

'The Princess?' I once asked.

Polo reared back, startled by the direct question, his face stretched and frozen. Eyes wide. Then, licking at his lips, 'God, no.' He shook his head. 'No,' he said again, sounding sad.

Polo is a man weirdly out of sync with the world around him. The only electronic device in the flat is a TV and there's nothing to play music on. There is a reason for this. Polo's father was a Royal Marine who walked out on his beloved mother, Joyce. The dentist's daughter from Barnstaple had her dreams destroyed by the departing Royal Marine, and life, which had briefly looked so promising, closed in on her. But rather than becoming embittered by his absence, plucky Joyce came up with the brilliant idea of turning Polo into her one-time husband. Meaning that Polo effectively became his own father. A young man with old-fashioned ideas about himself and the world, groomed throughout childhood to view women as damsels in distress.

First, Joyce, whose Devon cottage became his and the Princess's secret love nest. Then, the Princess, whose state of mind I can only wonder at given her willingness to spend weekend after weekend holed up in Budleigh Salterton with Polo and Joyce.

Once I'd won his trust, he told me how he'd first met her.

A summer's day and twenty-eight-year-old Polo, in the Household Cavalry at the time, was at a meeting inside Buckingham Palace. Something to do with wedding plans for one of the younger princes. After the meeting, he made his way down a flight of steps where a group of women stood, giggling. One of them was barefoot and as he passed, she turned to him and said, 'Nice uniform.'

It was the Princess.

Two weeks later, an invitation to a cocktail party arrived via one of the Princess's friends.

The Princess was afraid of horses, and it was at this party that she asked him to help her overcome that fear. Riding lessons followed. An opportunity for both of them to look good in jodhpurs. Things moved fast from there. The pair were swept up in a heady combination of the Princess's unhappiness and Polo's cavalier need to turn every relationship into a search and rescue operation.

This is my take on his version of events anyway.

But since the Princess's recent abandonment, Polo has been nursing singed wings. And is always short of money.

Today, after being buzzed up, I walk in on an argument between him and the cleaner, who is refusing to switch on the hoover until Polo pays her. Apparently, he is over a month in arrears.

She stands with her arms folded, her face a symmetry of hard lines.

Polo has his hands deep in his cardigan pockets and stares glumly at the hoover on the floor between them both.

This is why he sounded so desperate on the phone.

Breaking the impasse, I hand the woman the cash she's owed, and we watch as she meticulously counts it before folding the notes into her jeans pocket. Polo towers over her, chin jutting and shoulders back, gripped by a latent and misplaced sense of moral outrage. Without looking at him, she starts to push the hoover across the little accessible floor space there is while simultaneously spraying an air freshener about the place, exclaiming aggressively to herself.

Despite this, the smell of rotten food persists.

'So, what have you got for me?'

# Haversham

The day of the Royal Wedding, we wore new dresses. They were made especially by Mrs Baig, who lived in the flat above. My mother's dress was green with sleeves that looked as though they had been inflated with a bicycle pump. Mine was yellow, a sundress with ties at the shoulders that swung out when I spun around. Entirely new. Most of my other clothes were donations from neighbours whose children had outgrown them, but I was the first person to wear the yellow sundress. The night before the wedding, I hung it from a hanger on the bedroom door, where I kept catching at it and burying my face in the brand-new-smelling fabric.

We took photographs of ourselves in the new dresses with a Polaroid camera and propped the prints on the table, against the empty fruit bowl. Angelina and Paul were meant to be coming round to watch the wedding on our TV, but they were running late and coverage of the build-up to the ceremony, which was taking place at 11 a.m., had already started. Impatient, my mother went ahead and opened the bottle of champagne that had been sitting in the fridge for two weeks. Her head held back, face scrunched in anticipation, she let out a squeal as the cork popped, bouncing off the glass in the kitchen door. The kitchen still smelt of toast from breakfast and I stood with my hands over my ears, worried that something was going to get broken.

'First time I ever opened *real* champagne,' she laughed, amazed, looking unsure where to go from here.

This wasn't the mother I was used to, anxious and careworn. Here was an entirely new version. It felt like I was getting a glimpse of a rare beast, and suddenly the day was full of a sense of possibility that left me feeling jittery.

She handed me a Pink Panther tumbler with about five centimetres of champagne in the bottom, watching as I took my first sip.

'D'you like it?'

I didn't, but I couldn't bear to put so much as a single dent in her excitement that day. So, I nodded and tried not to screw up my face, making an effort to swallow as she drank half her glass in one go.

She was so excited that she hadn't taken her pills that morning. She kept them lined up in little orange pots on the bedside table – to help her sleep at night because she had bad dreams, she said. But the pills didn't only help her sleep at night; sometimes she slept all day as well, reduced to nothing more than a hump under the duvet. On those hollow days I would get myself breakfast and call out, 'I'm going to school now.' Then I'd wait. Just in case. Hoping to hear water running in the bathroom; her hurried tread crossing the hallway; the jangle of keys grabbed from the rack near the front door. The whole noise-filled rush of us trying to leave on time for once, which we never managed. On hollow days, I left the flat in silence and I was always on time. Retrieving my brown Raleigh bicycle from the drainpipe at the bottom of the stairwell where I kept it locked up. Cycling to school fast, in knee-high socks that kept sliding down my legs.

But today wasn't a hollow day. Today, 29 July 1981, was a special day. A girl was getting married to a prince and becoming a princess. The royal nuptials had emptied the streets, filling them instead with an end-of-world silence. Cars remained on drives and people stayed indoors in front of their TV sets. My mother was shiny and alert in her new dress and red sandals that she would wear later, to the street party. A committee of women from the estate were responsible for organizing this. My mother hadn't been invited to join the committee. Neither had Angelina. Or Mrs Baig.

Angelina and Paul eventually turned up at 10 a.m. with a bottle of Asti Spumante that Angelina said she was given for Christmas. Paul slid shyly onto the carpet beside me, happy to be close in a way most boys weren't at our age. My mother and Angelina finished the champagne before the bride had even arrived at St Paul's Cathedral. They finished it while she was still driving around the streets of London in her carriage, nothing more than a wave and a face behind glass. And they were already getting rowdy.

Lying on our stomachs across the carpet, our faces pressed up against the screen, we told them to be quiet – Paul was, if anything, even more engrossed in the wedding than I was. But they wouldn't be quiet. We exchanged glances, the worried glances of children who know that the adults looking after them are – possibly – no longer in control.

'Shush!' I commanded, twisting my head over my shoulder.

They stood hunched and giggling in the lounge doorway, trying to catch the white froth running down the sides of Angelina's bottle. There were splashes of it on the carpet, and down the front of my mother's new green dress. But she didn't seem to care.

'The dress!' Paul shouted suddenly.

All eyes shifted to the TV and at last the longed-for silence descended. The only sound was the commentator's voice. The bride was attempting to emerge from her carriage, which was full of wedding dress. Her face was lost amongst it. She stood on the red carpet without moving, surrounded by this bridal mess, helpless before the roaring crowds. I held my breath. For a moment, I had the feeling that she might be about to change her mind, simply step out of the dress and disappear into the crowd, never to be seen again. But suddenly there were people on the red carpet, trying to unravel her. Then, hung on the arm of a lumbering man who must have been her father, she was climbing away from everybody towards the cathedral entrance, her train spread out behind her filling the entire flight of steps.

I exhaled.

And then my mother's voice came cutting through the afternoon.

'Like a lamb to the slaughter, poor sod.'

Behind me, there was a burst of hard laughter.

'Shut up!'

I didn't want to hear about lambs and slaughter. I wanted kings and queens and princes and princesses and rings and vows of eternal love. I wanted this July day to remain intact. Hopeful. A girl in a white dress marrying a prince.

But the laughter carried on. Raucous now.

My mother and Angelina were bent over double in the doorway, Asti Spumante spilling onto their sandals.

No longer able to follow what was happening on screen, I scrambled unsteadily to my feet.

'What do you know about weddings anyway?'

The red-faced words flew out of my mouth.

The laughter stopped.

My mother's face, which had been so bright, became empty. 'Becky.'

It was the voice she used when she was ill. Or upset. The collapsing voice.

'It's TRUE!'

For some reason I was shouting, my throat straining with the effort, full of a new and frightening fury that threatened to break over the day. My childhood. The Prince and Princess exchanging vows inside St Paul's Cathedral. At last, I understood. My mother had never got married, and this was what made us different. Different was a struggle, exposing. Different was why I didn't have a dad and never got invited to class parties. It was why I didn't have the right things in my PE kit and, after the incident at school with Louise, why a woman called Sylvia, unsmiling and with unwashed hair, had the right to spend hours at a time in our flat inspecting every corner of our lives.

At the thought of Sylvia, I started crying. Chest and shoulders heaving, I sobbed louder than I'd ever sobbed before, while my mother remained fixed in the doorway, holding on to her drink, the distance between us unnavigable.

Instead, it was Angelina who crossed the lounge towards me. Fast, untidy strides. Her face was set hard, and for an awful moment I thought she was going to hit me. I don't know why. Perhaps my mother thought the same thing.

'Ange,' she said, moving at last and catching hold of one of Angelina's arms.

Angelina pulled her arm away without looking at my mother, her eyes still on me.

'Ange,' my mother said again, her face contracting with alarm.

'Don't you ever speak to your mother like that again. You don't know anything.' Her words stung. 'She's one of the bravest women I know. One of the bravest. We are all of us very brave women.'

She gave a shudder as she stopped speaking, the fury leaving her as suddenly as it had descended. I realized, shocked, that she was trying not to cry.

The room had become very still. Nobody moved. Nobody spoke. Coming from the TV behind us, the deep tones of the commentator as the Prince pushed a ring onto the girl's finger, turning her into a princess. But I discovered in that moment that I no longer believed in fairy tales.

# The *Mercury*

Pitt's office has the spartan feel of a bachelor flat. The shelves behind the desk are empty apart from a hookah pipe and calendar with its page turned to a photograph of naked women in hard hats, rock climbing. It's the first time I've been in here, the first time in years that I've stood in the same room as him.

He doesn't look up from whatever it is he's doing when I step in front of his desk, or when I ask after Rosa and the girls. When I tell him about Polo being ready to go public – the letters – I'm forced to address the crown of his head.

The letters, even by his standards, are big. But despite this, his face remains empty. It's soul-flattening. I thought I was ahead this time, but maybe I'm not. I've taken the special relationship with Polo for granted, when he's probably juggling a whole host of special relationships. What if I'm not the only person he's talking to about the letters? What if Pitt thinks I'm bluffing?

At last, he looks up, a grin lifting the eyes and mouth. 'I've missed you, Rebecca.'

'No, you haven't.'

'I have now.'

I feel like we're getting into our stride with each other again, but then he changes direction. Another Pitt tactic I'd forgotten about. 'So – how have things been?'

'How have things been?' I try not to sound as caught out as I feel. 'You mean since you left me for dead in the admin pool?'

Throwing his pen down on the desk, he leans back in the chair, crossing his arms and staring happily at me.

'I'm with Features now.'

'Under Turner. And George.'

'They don't know that Polo's ready to talk. I wanted to bring it straight to you.'

'Clever girl.' He picks up the pen again, clicking the end rhythmically for a while without speaking. Then at last, he says, 'OK, let's do this. I'll call a meeting.'

By late afternoon there are six men sitting around the table in Meeting Room 1 on the executive floor, whose wraparound windows give onto a grey, wind-blown sky full of seagulls up from the Thames Estuary. I fix briefly on the seagulls as I do the maths in my head. The number of stairs between the admin pool and here, divided by sixty months. We're talking advances of around one tread a month. It has been slow but dogged progress.

I switch my focus back to Pitt's head of news, Les O'Dowd.

Les is sitting beneath the sort of energy-saving strip lighting that would be hard pushed to do anyone justice, but that makes the knotty Ulsterman look homicidal. Next to him, Andy Packer, the *Mercury*'s deputy editor. Mild, in comparison to Les. So mild, in fact, that it's as if his operating switch has been turned permanently to 'off'. A well-pressed, well-cared-for man who speaks rarely and quietly, hardly ever spilling beyond his boundaries – unlike Les. Andy is the *Mercury*'s spirit level. Malcolm Skinner, the paper's royal correspondent, is also in the room. He wears red braces over a white shirt that he will have had made at Turnbull & Asser – tailors to the royal family. Tony Turner, features editor, is present. As is George, recently promoted to deputy features editor.

I'm the only woman in the room.

The *Mercury* and the *Courier* – both owned by the Crawley Corporation – are housed in the same converted Wapping factory that used to manufacture parts for Jaguar, Rover and Concord. They moved out here from the City just before I joined the *Mercury*, when the corporation poured millions into building new full-colour computerized presses. So, unlike the six men sitting around the table who grew up on Fleet Street, I've only ever known Wapping. It's my natural habitat whereas they're reluctant frontiersmen, haunted by a world left behind. This is what I tell myself as the dressing down from O'Dowd continues. In terms of hierarchy, it should be Andy who does this, but O'Dowd has the floor. O'Dowd who, for some reason, is only ever referred to by his surname. It was to be expected – someone as junior as me bringing something as big as this to the table, going over people's heads and blatantly ignoring all protocol. But still, the ferocity of it takes me by surprise. Something Pitt is clearly enjoying.

'How the fuck did *you* get onto William Armstrong?' O'Dowd explodes, on his feet suddenly. 'What fucking fertilizer did they grow you with?'

The chair he was sitting on tips over, making a silent landing in deep carpet. At home, O'Dowd has a squall of daughters he loses sleep over. At work, he's a foul-mouthed psychopath.

Standing with arms folded across a rigid midriff, in the short-sleeve shirt he wears all year round, O'Dowd has the build of an athlete. As a boy, he trained at Belfast's Willowfield Temperance Athletics Club (I've done my research) and has twice completed the London Marathon. But the long-distance running has done nothing to dispel his infamous and apocalyptic fury. He used to deposit grenades on the desks of reporters who didn't deliver. And legend has it that he once took a hammer to an automatic barrier in the underground car park when it refused to accept his pass. There's meant to be CCTV footage of the attack in the company safe.

It's the first time since starting at the *Mercury* that I've been addressed directly by O'Dowd, whose gaze is pathological, hard to meet. I remember some of the other things I've heard about him – that he personally oversaw the procurement of a video recording device that Carl Sutcliffe was able to get past Broadmoor's metal detectors in order to tape a visit with his brother, Peter Sutcliffe, the Yorkshire Ripper.

When O'Dowd's done running his eyes up and down me, I feel rubbed out.

'I've been working Polo for almost five years.' My voice sounds strange, the words half submerged and gulped at, as though I'm on a long-distance call. 'Since 1989.'

I try to catch George's eye. He's pissed off that I went straight to Pitt with this, but I've learned that anything I take to George gets swallowed whole, printed under his name without so much as a by-line credit to me. They're all pissed off. Tony, Malcolm, O'Dowd. Andy doesn't take sides, but even so, I have no allies in the room.

'Polo?'

'Armstrong,' I correct myself. 'Only nobody calls him that.'

'Working him? *Working* him?' O'Dowd wipes at his mouth. 'Where from? The beauty pages in the magazine? Fat, wrinkles and hair loss? Which is plain English for "you shouldn't fucking be here".'

'I'm with Features,' I remind him, glancing at Turner, who runs a hand down the length of his tie and stares, cross-eyed, at my breasts.

In his spare time, he likes to fly model gliders on wasteland near Biggin Hill Airport with his three sons. This is what he told me, drunk, at last year's Christmas party. A hand was laid on my thigh as we spoke. There were a lot of us sitting bunched up on a banquette, and I have no idea if the hand on my thigh actually belonged to Turner. Who was staring, preoccupied and strangely mournful, into the haze on the dance floor. He went on to tell me that he loved his family so much, he'd be happy to die for them. As if this was one of the most appropriate manifestations of love a man could have for his family. He confessed to being kept awake at night by both the world AIDS epidemic and the threat of nuclear war. He'd remortgaged the family home, he said, in order to build a nuclear shelter in the back garden, accessed via a concealed button on the sundial he'd given his wife to mark their wedding anniversary. I wasn't sure how much of an invitation this was. But again, for good measure, I said that I'd love to be given a tour one day.

I was made features assistant in the New Year.

O'Dowd swings towards Turner for confirmation. 'This twat's with you?'

'Yeah, Rebecca's with me.'

'Did you know she was onto Armstrong?'

Turner, ashamed, shakes his head.

O'Dowd grabs at the buff folder in front of him, executes a lithe twist of his torso and swings it into the bulky assortment of features on Turner's face.

Turner, slow even at an instinctive level, stares at him for almost two whole shock-ridden seconds before finally wrapping a defensive arm around his head in case O'Dowd isn't done yet.

I'm also worried that O'Dowd isn't done yet, and wonder when – if – Pitt, or even Andy, is going to step in. For the first time, it occurs to me that he might not. Perhaps he didn't believe me about the letters after all and called this meeting in order to throw me to the dogs publicly.

'And you didn't think there was anything out of line about these expenses she's been filing?'

He flaps the folder in front of the cringing Turner for a while before tossing it across the table. O'Dowd's face and throat are lacerated with veins, and his tight white fists push down onto the table's surface hard enough to leave dents in the wood.

It's then that Malcolm, the paper's royal correspondent, speaks at last, contemplating me through the lenses of his steel-rimmed spectacles.

'These rumours about Armstrong and the Princess have been circulating for years now.'

Whenever the Princess wants some positive publicity – which these days automatically amounts to giving her husband, the Prince, negative publicity – it's Malcolm she calls, telling him, in her soft clipped voice prone to laughter, where to send the photographers. He's been there since the beginning. They have a long-standing relationship and a direct line to each other. In O'Dowd's book (almost everyone's book, in fact), this gives Malcolm – who wears a trilby, drives an Austin 7, has a passion for Ealing comedies and still lives with his mother in Croydon – licence to do as he pleases.

The Princess makes him virtually untouchable.

'I blame Rawdon for publishing that "Di's Dashing Desert Pal" piece.' He glances at Pitt as he drops Rawdon's name into the conversation, before adding helpfully, 'After the Liberation of Kuwait.'

O'Dowd is breathing hard. 'I *know* about the fucking Liberation of Kuwait.'

Malcolm blinks.

I say, 'Polo was on the front line in the Liberation, Commander of the Fourth Armoured Brigade.'

'Becky, you don't need to sell us Polo – we're already sold on him. But,' Pitt adds, 'I could get off on that.'

For a brief second O'Dowd – the room at large – is stumped.

He doesn't know where to go with this. Andy raises his head and stares at nothing in particular.

'The Princess did get off on it,' I say.

'The Princess personally assured me' – Malcolm pauses for effect, then raises his voice so that its high-pitched falsetto cuts in – 'that there's nothing in the rumours. The man's been flirting with the media for years. She's upset about it, of course, says that her trust has been betrayed by him. They used to be friends. She even sent him little care packages when he was on tour – shampoo bottles filled with whisky, to get round Saudi regulations.'

'Along with magazines,' I jump in. 'And not just *Horse & Hound* either. She sent him *Penthouse* and *Mayfair*.'

Malcolm's mouth remains open in a tight little 'O' as he holds on to the arms of his chair.

Pitt's smiling at me. Has been smiling at me throughout O'Dowd's uninterrupted rant and Malcolm's attack. 'Come on, Rebecca. Put us out of our fucking misery,' he invites at last. 'Tell them what else she sent Armstrong in those *little care* packages.'

For some reason, the sound of Pitt saying my name startles everybody. He's kept the real reason for the meeting secret, to avoid any leaks, which is what gives me my punchline now.

Letting my gaze land on each and every one of them in turn, I say, 'Love letters. Blueys. In Kuwait he sometimes received two a day.'

There were also letters addressed care of his mother, to the Budleigh Salterton cottage, but these I refrain from mentioning. I don't want to bombard them with too many images. I've managed to get them to Kuwait; better to leave them there for a while before forcing them to consider Budleigh Salterton.

'Before you ask, yes, she's seen them,' Pitt puts in, on side suddenly.

This is true. I was shown them this morning after the cleaner left, Polo opening the safe in his flat to reveal his precious collection.

'Obviously, they haven't been authenticated.'

I wasn't allowed to read any of them either. Or even touch them. Polo stood behind me, shining a torch into the safe so that I could see for myself. It smelt of perfume – the Princess's, I guess.

A suspended silence follows before I say, 'After the Liberation of Kuwait, the Princess promised Armstrong a trip to the opera when he got home – Pavarotti at Covent Garden. Followed by supper at Claridge's. But when he returned to the UK, there was too much heat around him and the Princess panicked. He was kept under wraps at Highgrove, until it was time for him to return to Germany, where he was based at the time with his regiment.'

Malcolm bangs on the table and gets to his feet. For a second, I worry that he might simply walk out of the meeting. 'All categorically untrue.'

I can't resist it. 'They had sex in the loo. At Highgrove.'

'All categorically untrue,' Malcolm says again, struggling to be heard over the whelps and howls that have broken out, his pinprick eyes sliding around the room. But not even O'Dowd comes to the rescue this time.

Pitt's smile broadens at the chaos, and without thinking, I make instinctively for Malcolm's recently vacated seat.

Too late, he makes a crazy dash for it, as if we're at a children's party playing musical chairs. The seat is warm still.

Turner says, 'You haven't had a scoop in over eighteen months, Malcolm.'

He's been waiting to say this for a long time. He loathes Malcolm.

'How the fuck did you get all this out of the poor cunt?' O'Dowd sounds almost human as he says this.

'Rebecca can be very persuasive.' George has finally decided to risk speaking on my behalf, now that he can see which way the wind's blowing.

'Very,' Pitt agrees. 'And right now, she's doing your job for you.' He jerks his head in Turner's direction. 'And yours.'

Turner lets out a weird laugh he doesn't know what to do with once it has flown from his mouth.

Ignoring him, I stay focused on Pitt.

'I think all these little splashes Armstrong has given me have been about more than the money. It's like a way of communicating with her – I think he's still in love. That gives us leverage.'

Pitt leans in. 'Maybe.' His eyes are shining. 'But why's he going public now?'

'Here's what I'm thinking: Armstrong's in Germany. He calls the Princess, but she's changed mobile phones and not given him the new number. The only way he can get through to her is by calling the Kensington Palace switchboard, but his calls are never put through – this is the man, don't forget, who she had sex with. In the loo. At Highgrove.'

Malcolm groans.

'Armstrong falls to pieces. He thought he was on the homestretch and now he's being frozen out. He's twice fined for disobeying orders that autumn and fails his promotional exams for a third time, which means he doesn't make it from acting major to major. This is the man, don't forget, who destroyed forty enemy tanks and took a thousand prisoners during the Liberation of Kuwait. So, he begins to suspect somebody somewhere has been given a directive to fail him, as a warning not to go near the Princess again. The army dismisses him after that, which is effectively the end of his military career. He gets a forty-thousand-pound severance package and fuck all of a pension. Forty thousand is like forty pounds to Armstrong. He's been free falling ever since. Now he's short of cash and hurting bad and ready to sell himself, the Princess and the letters.'

Pitt gets to his feet and crosses to the window where he comes to a halt. We all watch his back as he stands, staring mutely out. When he turns around again, his face has fallen into an excited arrangement of folds and creases.

To nobody in particular, he says, 'How can we be sure he isn't talking to anybody else?'

'We can't, which is why we need to move fast. Tomorrow.'

There's a new sense of urgency in the room. We all feel it.

'Fix the meeting.'

Suddenly everybody's standing, shouting. Things are speeding up, the men closing in on each other. A tight, strategic pack that threatens to exclude both me and Malcolm. Not now. Not after getting this far. This close.

'We should record it – the meeting – without Polo's knowledge,' I shout. 'Insurance. In case.'

At this, Pitt throws an arm around my shoulders and pulls me close. A quick succession of hard hugs follow. 'Rebecca, Rebecca, Rebecca,' he mumbles with each rhythmic squeeze before letting go.

'Features leads,' Turner cuts in.

Andy, hands in pockets, moving in slow motion compared to everybody else, says at last, 'We should get a suite booked. A hotel. Somewhere central.'

O'Dowd jabs a finger at me. 'You. Fuck off and book us a hotel suite.'

I don't move. The dismissal at this stage is unbearable. 'Armstrong's *my* contact.'

O'Dowd squares up to me; we're about the same height.

I risk taking my eyes off him, turning to Pitt. 'He'll only talk if I'm there. I need to be in the room. Either I broker this or I call it off. I can do that. Polo's pathologically paranoid.'

'You're already in the room, Rebecca,' Pitt soothes.

The mirror reflects a bank of urinals – there are no female toilets on the executive floor. Closing the gap between me and my reflection, I press my forehead against the glass and hold my hands under the tap until the water runs warm. Hearing the door open, I straighten up and watch as Malcolm appears in the mirror.

'Pitt doesn't like me,' he announces abruptly.

'Malcolm, nobody likes you.'

There's a brief silence.

'That's true – but I thought you were different.' His eyes flicker towards my reflection, then away. 'So, why do I feel like you've screwed me over?'

I turn off the tap, pull a handful of blue towels from the dispenser and carefully dry my hands.

Anybody else would have said 'fucked me over', but Malcolm is the only person in the building who doesn't swear. Doesn't drink. Is notorious, in fact, for the things he doesn't do rather than the things he does.

'I thought we had an arrangement.'

He sounds puzzled rather than angry.

When I first crawled out of the admin pool and made it to an office with windows, I floated between News and Features, belonging to neither. I used to do copy tasting and put quite a few things Malcolm's way. This, on the understanding that he would put a word in for me when the time came. He was a big deal back then. Only the time never seemed to come, and as Turner pointed out, the past eighteen months have been a desert for Malcolm. These days he barely leaves his glass cubicle in the corner of the newsroom.

Still, he's been in the game for decades and has a personal line to the Princess. I don't want to make an enemy out of him.

'You were meant to keep me updated. No surprises, remember?'

Balancing on the edge of the sink, the wet paper towel still in my hands, I say, 'And I've tried, Malcolm. I've really tried. But all my updates involve Polo, who you insist is a fraudster.'

'He *is* a fraudster.'

For Malcolm, the Princess will always be the blushing kindergarten teacher; the Sloaney flirt who grew adept at dodging him and his photographer in her little Volkswagen, tearing through tree-lined streets while laughing behind the wheel. Like all the other royal reporters in the early eighties, Malcolm fell in love with the girl. He sensed, as they all somehow instinctively sensed, that she was going to be the making of him. And she was. I've heard the stories. In the Coleherne Court days, before the royal engagement was announced, she once brought him and his photographer mugs of hot cocoa. Standing in the street in her pyjamas and passing them through the windows of the parked car where the two men were about to spend the night.

Once upon a time, she was the girl who was going to marry a prince and restore order to the world; the girl who rode a butler's bicycle around the courtyard of Clarence House the night before her wedding, ringing the bell and yelling at the top of her voice with excitement.

Maybe we all need to hold on to the idea that there's somebody out there worth dying for. In Malcolm's case, this is the Princess, and he cannot bear to tear her down.

'The Princess personally assured me.'

'Of course she did. What else can she do? She's trying to protect her reputation and knows you're the man to do it. Which is why Polo – whether he was the Princess's lover or not – isn't the problem, Malcolm. The problem is you. Not wanting to believe something is true doesn't make it any less true.'

He blinks gauntly at me. 'Does he really have letters from her?'

'Yes, which is why it's only a matter of time. If we don't run this, someone else will. So, let's make the first explosion a controlled one.'

He winces. 'This is going to destroy her.'

'No, it's going to save her. Don't you see? She's one of the most famous women in the world. Young. Beautiful. But her husband is just about the only man on the planet not in love with her. She's lonely. She needs company. I mean, it's not hard to imagine and more importantly – who's going to blame her? The opposite, in fact. Yes, we're going to pull her down from her pedestal. But in doing so, we make her human. We make her one of us, Malcolm.'

'That's your take on all this?'

'That's my take.'

'Very persuasive. But one hell of a gamble – what if it backfires?'

Without thinking, I lay my hands on his shoulders, which stiffen on contact.

'People have outgrown the fairy-tale Princess. They want a real woman. Sad, heartbroken, confused, hopeful, messy . . . People are going to love her even more for it.'

He's about to respond when we're interrupted by the door opening again.

'Nice move,' George says, padding over to one of the urinals. Shaking himself off, he adds, 'Didn't see that one coming.'

'None of us did. Don't take it personally.'

Ignoring Malcolm, he washes his hands at the sink opposite while inspecting himself in the mirror. Then he says to me, 'Well, you've had your revenge.'

'You think that's what this is about?'

'Maybe. Partly.'

'I bring in the scoop of the century and you think it's nothing but revenge? That's some fucking ego.'

I throw the balled-up remains of the paper towel at him, but it doesn't even hit the mid-point between us on the tiled floor. We're focused on each other now in a way we haven't been since Haversham. It's impossible to hide the intensity between us from Malcolm's pin-eyed curiosity. We're beyond caring. A small part of me wonders whether this is all the past five years have been about after all: a bid to get George's attention back. Feel his gaze on me.

'You used to believe in the bigger picture. And that's what this is. Surely you see that. You of all people must see that.' I try not to stare at his lips, pushing my eyes away, towards the empty soap dispenser. 'It's what we used to talk about – not letting them get away with it; bringing the whole show crashing down.'

And suddenly there I am, sitting up front in our old Allegro. My mother beside me, hands gripping the steering wheel even though the engine's switched off, a heavy stillness taking root in the car. Through the windscreen, a house with illuminated windows surrounded by a dusk-ridden garden commands all our attention.

I barely register George's voice as he says, 'OK, but that's quite an assignment you've set yourself. At least let me talk to O'Dowd about organizing the recording.'

The flat's buzzer sounds, distant but impatient, while I'm in the bath. It's dark outside and only now do I notice how cold the water's become. Hauling myself upright, I grab a damp towel, clutching it around me as I cross the hallway towards the beige handset attached to the wall by the front door.

'Fuck's sake, Em, lemme in,' Lizzie's voice blasts down the intercom.

I buzz her in, slipping the chain from the door before heading to the bedroom in search of some clothing. Over the past week, my room has become Lizzie's domain. I've stolen in a couple of times to retrieve things from drawers and wardrobes but been too preoccupied to really appreciate the chaos. Switching on the light reveals the true extent of it. Piles of clothes, shoes, make-up, cups, plates, glasses, cigarette butts. Flies buzz above the bed.

I'm still standing in the doorway taking it all in when she pushes past.

'Took your fucking time answering the door, Rebecca.'

'I was in the bath.'

She doesn't apologize, automatically making her way over to the mirror above the desk in the corner. She pushes the hair back from her face and peers intensely at her reflection for a moment. Everything about her is days old. Hair, make-up, dress. Not that looking dull and smelling stale make her any less beautiful. The next minute she peels the dress off, followed by her underwear, stalking frantically about the room. Summer's tan lines are visible and I stare at her, surprised at how her nakedness has managed to steal the white-hot rage I felt for her only moments before. She gropes at the piles of clothing on the floor for a while before yanking open my chest of drawers and rifling through my stuff, holding up top after top and pulling a face. 'Ugh.'

Finally, she finds something, wincing as she pulls it on along with a pair of jeans and the cowboy boots she lives in.

Then she hauls her suitcase out from under the bed, swooping indiscriminately on the piles surrounding her and throwing them into it. Her movements are clumsy, and she has to kneel on the case to get the zip closed. Another out of town party, clearly.

'Where's Em?' Lizzie demands suddenly.

'I don't know, she was out when I got back.' I can't resist it. 'With George, maybe.'

She twists around so that she's sitting on the suitcase. Legs splayed. Breathless after the exertion of packing. 'Has she told you yet?'

'Told me what?'

She gets to her feet, tugging on the suitcase, and smiles. 'Talk to her.'

Down at street level a car sounds its horn.

'I should go.' She pulls at the top. 'I'll try to remember to return this.'

'No, you won't.'

The smile widens into something genuine. 'Well, I'd be doing you a favour. I'm getting a rash already. What is this, polyester?'

The horn sounds again.

'Shit.' Suddenly flustered, she bangs the suitcase out of the bedroom and along the hallway towards the door. 'No idea when I'll be back. A friend in Devon's having a party.'

'You can tell me about Amelia, you know,' I try one last time, genuinely curious. 'I'm good with secrets.'

'Your own, maybe. I'm not sure that I'd trust you with anyone else's.'

'Well, you can trust me with yours.'

This stops her in her tracks. One hand on the door handle, she stares at me as if I've said something profoundly inappropriate.

'You've got nothing on me.'

'Maybe not, but I've got a whole lot on Lady Jane Southdown, who's having a party in Devon this weekend. That's where you're headed, I guess?

Both of us jump when the intercom sounds.

'So fucking go, I'll get a cab,' she yells into the receiver, before struggling to push herself and her case out of the door.

I move through the dark flat to the bay window. The battered BMW belonging to Lizzie's new on/off boyfriend is parked outside our block. After a while Lizzie appears. The new on/off boyfriend – not her type at all; tweedy and flaccid – takes her case and loads it into the boot of the car. They're arguing. Both of them look jerky and highly strung from up here. Watching them, I feel a corresponding jerk of panic. Something instinctive and half-formed takes shape in my mind: Lizzie, the boyfriend, the rushed exodus to Devon, and the relief on her face when I mentioned Lady Jane Southdown rather than the fear I'd been anticipating.

# The Rathbone

The Rathbone in Knightsbridge is all soft carpet, potted palms and shining surfaces. A discreet oasis. So discreet that from the street outside it takes me a while to realize that the red-brick building – in a row of similar-looking apartment blocks – is in fact a hotel. The meeting is at 4 p.m., but I'm there for 9 a.m. so that I can help set up the room with George's contact. He's already there when I arrive. I can hear him in the bathroom, finishing a series of racking coughs as I push open the door.

The man's bent double, his spine poking through the T-shirt he's wearing, an empty vase on the floor by his feet and a sink full of lilies. I don't know when exactly I recognize him, but it's definitely before he straightens up and becomes visible in the mirror.

I'm not even surprised.

To Paul's credit, he's equally unsurprised to see me.

We continue to watch each other in silence.

Beneath the John Lennon frames, the skin around his eyes falls away to hollows. The drugs he started using in school stripped him of all appetite long ago, but it's only now I realize just how dangerously thin he is: emaciated knees juddering inside black jeans; hands and arms a mess of bruises and track marks; part of his left arm in bandages – later, he will tell me he has septicaemia.

The truth is, he's hard to look at. There's a lot of him missing and I feel somehow responsible.

Breaking the silence at last, he says, 'You never phoned.'

Another bout of coughing follows this accusation. Wiping at his mouth, he checks the back of his hand and straightens up again.

'I phoned, but you weren't there. The woman I spoke to said you hadn't left a number. Or a forwarding address.' I pause, then add the only safe thing I can think to say. 'How's your mum?'

Because I've missed Angelina. I've missed her a lot, I realize suddenly.

'Remarried. To a total cunt. We fell out about him big time. We're not speaking any more.'

He gives me a quick, sad smile. All of Paul's smiles, I'll learn, are like this now. 'George didn't tell you about me, did he?'

'No. And I'm guessing he didn't say anything to you about me either?'

This is familiar territory. In Haversham, George was all Paul and I talked about, keeping each other's obsession stoked. Every encounter, no matter how incidental, would lead to an in-depth post-mortem. If we all arranged to meet and he failed to show at the Bear, we went into mourning together. George's absence or presence dictated our every mood. We behaved badly towards each other in our attempts to get George to ourselves. Whenever Paul, triumphant, announced that they'd met up without telling me, I suffered a jealousy like no other, one that it would take me weeks to crawl out from under.

'So, how did you get here?'

'By accident. A guy I was working with at the electrical store was into surveillance – phone tapping mostly – from his garden shed. Cousins were ex-coppers working for a private investigator who's a big deal. The *Mercury* was already using him.'

Paul holds up his arm, the one with the bandage wrapped around it. 'I have a problem that needs funding, and addicts, it transpires, are ideally suited to this kind of work. Plus – I'm good at it.'

I've heard the rumours of 'ghost' expense accounts – tens of thousands being paid to tracers, blaggers, PIs – people like Paul. I wonder how long he's been on payroll, how long we've been working for the same newspaper.

'So, when did George first get in touch?'

'Years ago. He contacted the agency – didn't know I was working for them though.'

He rearranges the lilies in the empty vase and carries it through to the main room, positioning it on a console table.

'How many years ago? Around five?'

'Yeah, I guess.'

I can tell from the way he says it that five years ago is more than he can get his head around right now.

'But – why all the secrecy? Why didn't you reach out?'

'Look, Becky, I asked him not to say anything. I didn't want you knowing about me.'

'What's there to know?'

'This.' He tries to shrug his shoulders, but it looks like a shudder passing through his body. 'And that suited George – because he didn't want you knowing about me either.' His face slips towards another sad smile. 'I'm an asset to him.'

Coming from the corridor outside, I pick up the sounds of the lift; the rattling of a room service trolley; voices.

'They could probably do with some water,' I say after a while, nodding at the already wilting lilies.

'I put a device in the vase – it's why there isn't any water in it.'

There's something detached, methodical about the way he speaks.

'Has anybody ever asked you to listen in to Armstrong's phone calls?'

Paul shakes the fringe from his eyes. 'What makes you think Armstrong's calls are being listened to?'

'The Princess told him all her lines were tapped. That's why she uses mobile phones and why she likes to keep changing them. Now Polo's convinced he can hear these muted clicking sounds whenever he's on the phone. He used to think it was somebody on the Prince's staff. Or the Palace. Or MI5. But it's you, isn't it?'

Paul walks over to one of the room's long windows, pulling carefully at a corner of curtain and giving the outside world an anxious glance.

'Who asked you to look into him?'

'Nobody. Recently.'

He appears even more ill at a distance, standing in the wash of morning light coming through the window.

'Recently – so you've been asked in the past?'

'It was just standard digging. Bank statements. Medical records. School reports.'

'School reports?'

'It's important to profile.' Paul pauses, eyeing me again.

'When were you asked to do that?'

'Hard to say – me and time, we have a complicated relationship.'

'George. Five years ago,' I fill in for him. 'You're the one who worked out who Armstrong was, aren't you?'

'Yeah, maybe,' he concedes.

Since Polo first contacted me to say that he was ready to discuss selling the letters, I've been unable to sleep much. Or to shake the feeling that at any moment all this could be taken away from me. Now, I feel young and stupid and out of my depth suddenly. 'Everyone's onto him, aren't they?'

'Yes, but Becky – he's talking to you. And you did it the old-fashioned way. Charm.'

'There's nothing old-fashioned about me.'

'Tell Polo he should start using a scrambler. It'll stop his calls being crashed.'

The rest of the morning and early afternoon is spent phoning Polo's flat, only streets away, every hour on the hour. I get a rush of relief each time he picks up.

At 3 p.m., he assures me again that everything is OK, but as we speak, I'm certain I detect the distracted tone of a man contemplating bigger things. Things like jumping from a fifth-floor window. Or in front of a rush-hour tube. I know from experience that when anxious, Polo can become maudlin. Suicidal thoughts are something he has confessed to before when speaking about the unexpected twists and turns his life has taken. Sometimes, the thoughts overwhelm him and he can't see any way out, feels like disappearing on himself.

That's how he put it – disappearing on himself.

He had an army friend who disappeared on himself after Kuwait. In a wood with a shotgun. That's the kind of thing he imagines. Autumn woodland. A well-greased sixteen-bore shotgun. His body buried afterwards by falling leaves. Something masculine, he concluded, sounding almost cheerful.

The green digits on the radio clock beside the bed read 15:06. I make a note to call every fifteen minutes from now on, and then the phone starts ringing again. One of the hotel receptionists. My group has arrived, could I please come downstairs as soon as possible.

I can hear them before the lift doors open. Loud. Too loud. The noise levels are making the two receptionists anxious, and the older one, in her fifties with dyed hair pulled back in a chignon, is keen to clear us out of the lobby. She emerges birdlike and jittery from behind the desk, a pair of half-glasses hanging from a chain around her neck. She has trouble corralling us, but eventually we're loaded into a lift where I'm squashed in among too many suits in need of dry cleaning.

The lift rises.

Pitt wanted to form a delegation, to impress Polo. To impress *on* Polo the magnitude of this scoop for the *Mercury*. I tried telling Pitt that Polo is a timid beast – that he frightens easily and that the idea of a delegation could spook him into retreat – but Pitt wouldn't listen.

Turner is on a roll, riffing on the subject of my relationship with Polo. How did I get so close so fast? I do what's expected of me: laugh it off gamely, suggestive but non-committal in a way that gets everybody roaring. It's exhausting but necessary. Malcolm – here for no other reason than to defend the Princess's honour – stands at a tilt in the corner looking sick. O'Dowd remains stony-faced. George stares out across all our heads.

We reach the floor that our suite is on. More soft carpet, a stretch of corridor and then the series of rooms that Paul's spent the morning rigging with recording devices. Turner crashes in first, making a very audible trip to the bathroom. O'Dowd positions himself, cross-armed, by the window. Malcolm sits down on one of the sofas and picks up a copy of *Country Life*.

Turner emerges from the bathroom zipping himself back up, and then makes his way towards the tray of drinks I was told to organize for the meeting. He pours out five fingers of whisky and tips his head back, gulping it down. He pours himself another. In addition to the whisky, there are two bottles of champagne on ice.

This isn't nerves, it's adrenaline. But Turner's outstripping all of us. 'Like a fucking sauna in here.'

He pulls off his suit jacket and tries to roll up his sleeves, but he's too thick-fingered with drink and adrenaline to undo the cuffs. We're all feeling it. The inability to sit or stand still.

Turner's clumsiness makes him aggressive, and he ends up ripping off a button, dropping unexpectedly to the floor and almost losing his balance in an effort to retrieve it. The aggression vanishes as he crawls around, breathless, on the carpet. In fact, he looks far more at home on all fours than he does standing.

He finds the tiny white button and gets back to his feet.

'Here.' He holds the palm of his hand towards me, his stomach still shuddering with the aftershock of motion. 'Sew this back on, will you. There'll be one of them kits somewhere, places like this always have them.'

I could just say no, but I feel outnumbered suddenly in this stuffy hotel room.

So he stands and I sew, trying not to touch the skin on his wrist, which looks like it has been preserved in formaldehyde, willing myself not to prick him while trying to work out whether it's carelessness or something more strategic that has provoked the request – it's hard to tell.

The radio clock flickers to 16:12 as he lifts his cuff to inspect my handiwork.

'Thought your man was military. Strict about timekeeping,' O'Dowd says. 'Where is the cunt?'

'He'll show.'

'Fucking hope so.'

And although it's the sound we've all been waiting for, when the phone starts ringing, it takes us by surprise.

O'Dowd's the only one to make any sort of movement.

I glance at Pitt. Too tense for triumph.

'Yes. Right. Send him up.' O'Dowd throws the handset back onto the desk, then reverts to prowling about the stretch of carpet between sofa and window. 'Cunt just showed. We're on.'

Polo is at his raffish best, preened and polished in Turnbull & Asser blue, chinos, suede loafers and a tweed jacket. Every bit the gentleman who tolerates London for business or pleasure but who prefers the muddy obscurity of his country seat. It's a look he swears was created for him by the Princess when she used to buy his clothes. It's a look he will probably sport for the rest of his life, even though the Princess no longer dresses him, and his only claim to a country seat is Joyce's Budleigh Salterton cottage. His military gait, however – the one I imagine he retained even crumpled in the boot of the car that used to drive him to assignations with the Princess at Kensington Palace – makes quite an impression.

'Rebecca!'

In private, Polo has a tendency to meander and lose sight of himself. But Polo in public is an altogether different beast. The press has already started to refer to him as dashing. Later, when the campaign to discredit him begins in earnest, he will become a cad, cast as a black marketeer from a previous generation, making money out of others' misery. But today in the Rathbone he's still dashing, and true to form he acknowledges me now by catching my hand gallantly and kissing it.

Perfect.

Without realizing it – or perhaps he does – he's playing to the gallery.

Over his bent head I join in the bullish looks Pitt, Turner, George and O'Dowd exchange. Excluding Malcolm. The quick raft of gestures as Turner blasts out, 'A redhead! I forgot he was a redhead!'

Polo releases my hand and pulls himself up straight,

suddenly aware of the intense scrutiny he's under. Although I warned him in advance that there would be six of us in the meeting, he seems taken aback by the other men in the room, appraising them now with startled black eyes. Polo likes to place people, to know where he stands in relation to them. His approach to life is hierarchical. He's in better shape than all of them, apart from O'Dowd, but he looks somehow diminished by the onslaught of Turner.

Whatever he was expecting the betrayal of a princess to look like, he's not sure this should be it.

For the first time, I have a sense of the impending carnage. I can see that Polo does too and feel a sharp stab of protective-ness towards him. He glances at me, licking his lips, and for a moment there's so much tension in the room that I'm once more terrified he's about to bolt. Turner, possibly thinking the same thing, positions himself between Polo and the door. I take hold of his hand again and guide him towards the sofa where Pitt's sitting, introducing them to each other. I then perch on the arm of the sofa and balance a hand on Polo's shoulder. In case.

'Why don't we talk money?' Pitt suggests.

'Yeah,' Turner nods, his eyes on Polo, 'let's talk about the money. Heads up.'

'Once we've seen the letters and had them authenticated, there'll be an advance against signature on the contract, which will of course be for exclusive rights.'

'Of course,' Polo echoes, straining forward in anticipation of hearing numbers. I'm not convinced he understands a word Pitt's saying and Pitt knows it. He's baiting him, I realize. A showman who understands his audience perfectly. He can see the raw hunger on Polo's face. All of us can.

'We're in discussion with Editorial at the moment, but the plan is to serialize the ten letters you're interested in selling – two a week across five weeks, in Saturday's paper – alongside the revelations about your affair.'

Polo looks winded by this.

Pitt flicks me a sharp look.

I squeeze Polo's shoulder. 'Selected extracts from the letters.'

'Extracts,' he agrees, wary. 'Yes.'

Pitt considers him for a moment. 'Do you have them on you now?'

We all stare at him. Or more specifically, his jacket, trouser pockets – any place on his person that could conceal the letters. I'm not sure, if he was to change his mind and make a run for it, that we wouldn't just set on him anyway. The potential for violence has become tangible in the hot afternoon.

'You do have them, don't you?' Pitt persists.

Polo inadvertently pats at his blazer and all eyes in the room are now fixed on his hand, which I know is kept well-manicured. Slowly, he draws out a slightly crumpled bluey. He stares down at it as if surprised to see it clasped in his hand, before passing it shyly to Pitt. I'm certain that Pitt grunts as he takes hold of the letter – carefully, with his fingertips. O'Dowd, Turner and George move in on him. O'Dowd from behind, stooping tightly over man and letter, Turner crushing him sideways. There are more grunts as hungry eyes graze the letter. Noses inadvertently sniff at it and fingers manhandle it, leaving their prints across the inky declarations that were meant for no one's eyes but Polo's. Malcolm, to his credit, stays well out of it, holding a hand over his face as if unwilling to let his curiosity loose, worried it might add to the already primal atmosphere in the room.

It's a terrible, terrible violation, no doubt about it. And I feel the full force of it, but violation of what? The Princess, for all her blushing shyness, has refused to play the Establishment's games, opting time and time again for honesty. If I want these letters to expose anything, it's this. Yes, they're going to lay her bare – but hasn't she always been willing to do that herself? Isn't it the institution itself that these will hold up to public scrutiny? The truth behind the scenes? And what will the public do, once they know? What will their demands be? I feel something else now. A hot excitement.

His eyes never leaving the letter, Polo at last puts his hand out and Pitt, reluctantly, passes it back to him. Everybody tracks its return journey to the obscurity of Polo's tailored blazer.

'Like I said,' Pitt continues calmly, his voice almost devoid of emotion, 'we would need to get the letters authenticated, and the contract drawn up. But . . . you stand to make ten million out of this, Mr Armstrong. A million for each letter published.'

Ten. Million.

The thrill of it passes through all of us.

Only Polo – worryingly – fails to react. Until finally, he whispers, 'I did love her, you know. And she loved me.'

He concentrates hard on his fingers, which are rubbing at the fabric covering the arms of the sofa he's sitting on. 'We were in love.'

Pitt stares sadly at him. 'We'd also like to run a few pieces about the affair in the lead-up to publication, whet the public's appetite.' He raises his hands into the air, preacher-style. 'Bring them to their knees with expectation.'

'So,' Turner wheezes, 'what have you got for us?'

Legs crossed, Polo responds in the quiet, slightly hesitant way I've become used to. He starts by telling us how he first met the Princess. He looks trapped, and his eyes slide around the room as if expecting the cavalry to rescue him at the eleventh hour. I imagine them emerging from the en-suite, swords raised, an advancing wall of red and pounding hooves. Only there is no cavalry and so he has no choice but to lay his soul bare, unaware that he has lost Turner.

After lots of lip licking and unfinished sentences, Pitt lays a hand on Polo's chino-clad thigh and says softly, 'Sweetheart, we don't want a fucking Barbara Cartland novel.'

Polo flinches, his eyes on Pitt's hand.

O'Dowd tucks his chin down as if about to launch himself into a running tackle. 'Are you premenstrual or something?'

'No,' Polo blurts, trying to hold O'Dowd's gaze. 'God, no.'

O'Dowd snorts and Pitt gives Polo's leg a squeeze.

They're going to eviscerate him, I think, me as well if he doesn't give them something soon. 'Tell them about the loo,' I say, gently. 'At Highgrove.'

Pitt raises his head, lifting his hand from Polo's thigh and jabbing a finger at me. 'That's more fucking like it. Flesh and blood headlines.'

'God,' Malcolm groans.

Polo turns warily towards Pitt. 'I . . . I . . . Is that the sort of thing you want?'

'We've just put ten million on the table, that's exactly the sort of thing we want.'

At the mention of the ten million, Polo starts to nod automatically in agreement. But I can tell he's suddenly aware that it means giving up everything: the July day when a twenty-five-year-old Princess stood barefoot on a flight of stairs and flirted with him; the illicit trysts at Highgrove, poolside under a blunt English sun; the dreams of elopement, of running away to Italy and starting a family together – it's what bound them to each other, him and the Princess, the desire to raise a happy, healthy family away from the spectres of divorce and abandonment. Why it didn't occur to him that it would come to this, I have no idea. Because we're about to strip him of it all. As efficiently as the army stripped him of his rank, and the Princess from her phone contacts.

'You've had sex, more than once, with the future Queen of England. That's the story.'

'Offence, actually,' Malcolm murmurs, 'punishable under the 1351 Treason Act.'

Polo uncrosses his legs and sits up, becoming suddenly intent on Malcolm. 'Really?' He sounds genuinely worried. This is just the sort of information that feeds his paranoia. According to Polo, there are forces at play that would like to see him dead. Before getting into his car, he always checks the wiring and has shown me the ion mobility spectrometer he runs underneath it as well. All his mail goes to a PO Box. 'Punishable how?'

Malcolm starts to expand on this, more animated than I've ever seen him.

'Bollocks.'

O'Dowd, who has crossed the room at least a thousand times in the past thirty minutes, loses patience with Malcolm then, slapping him hard on the back of the head and setting Malcolm's spectacles at a slant.

Pitt continues to watch Polo. 'Rebecca's going to be writing the piece for Saturday's paper. I know you two have a special relationship.'

Slowly, I stand, wondering when he decided. It's what I was hoping for but was almost certain he'd give it to George – or even Turner.

Polo remains silent, his attention still on Malcolm. 'The thing is – I'm going to need something up front. Now that you've seen the letter.'

'Which we need to get authenticated along with the other nine,' Pitt soothes. 'But first – a celebration.'

Polo recommences with the lip licking. Pitt yells for champagne.

'So, the first payment.'

'How does five hundred thousand sound? We can wire it to

you as soon as you've had your interview with Rebecca and the letters have been authenticated. We'll get something drawn up for you to sign as well. That exclusive rights agreement we've been talking about.'

Polo nods vacantly.

Turner stands with difficulty and opens both bottles, a couple of controlled pops that see everybody released from the tensions of the afternoon. Glasses are handed around and I stand wrapped in Turner's half-embrace. He's part aftershave, part sweat, and I try not to spill my champagne when he twists me around to face the rest of the room.

'A toast,' he says loudly, over my head, 'to Rebecca!'

After everyone's left, I stand by the open window, relieved to be alone. I step out of the shoes I bought especially for the meeting today. They were purchased on my first ever credit card, along with the suit. The card came with a £500 credit limit. Only a few weeks ago this seemed like a vast sum, but today's outfit has already taken me to the edge of that.

I move over to the bed and, lying down on top of the cover, roll back towards the open window. The indistinct voices rising from street level untether me from the day's events and I can feel myself sliding towards sleep. How am I ever going to find the energy to leave this room?

It takes me a while to realize that there's somebody at the door.

'Becky! Come on, open up. I know you're in there. They said you hadn't checked out yet.'

On the floor between bed and window is a pillow. My black skirt lies across it, along with one of the heels I abandoned earlier, toppled on its side. A suit jacket hangs, misshapen, over one of the sofas at the other end of the room. Mine, I think, but I'm not entirely sure. It could be his. Definitely his trousers and tie on the coffee table. No sign of my white blouse, although I can feel something balled up beside our feet in the sunset-lit bed.

Discarded bits of ourselves everywhere.

The air is thick with us, despite the open window. We didn't bother to close the curtains framing them. Fussy, my mother would have called them, with their pelmets, pleats and swags. I can almost hear her saying it. Fussy. A lot of bother. Always dismissive of bother, my mother. Life, which was short, was for living. And by living, I now realize she meant this.

Time, stopped.

All sense of purpose, lost.

'I should think about going,' I say at last, sitting up. Although there's no need to go anywhere.

George knows this and makes no effort to move. I can feel him watching me.

Propping himself up on his elbow at last, he says, 'We work well together, don't we?'

'Yeah,' I concede, pushing him hard on the shoulder where he has a scar. The legacy of a childhood accident involving a bicycle. 'Yeah, we do.'

He makes a show of collapsing back onto the pillow, where he lies staring up at the chandelier.

'We always have. I knew we would – I knew it the first time I saw you.'

'God, I was into you.'

'I know,' he says, pleased, twisting his head on the pillow so that I can feel his breath on my arm. The orange sunlight weighs down on his features without illuminating them. 'But we're not those people any more.'

'We'll always be those people.'

'You don't believe that.' He looks momentarily lost. 'Becky, we were wretched.'

The word hangs strangely in the late afternoon. A stark reminder that we have this on each other – our shared past.

'Look at us now. We know how to get what we want out of people and we're not afraid of that.'

He sits up and kisses my shoulder before rolling out of bed. Pulling loosely at his cock, he kicks his clothes across the carpet into a pile and disappears into the bathroom, where he pees in the dark.

'When were you going to tell me about Paul?'

He flushes, then washes his hands and face, dropping the towel on the floor after he's dried himself.

Standing naked in the doorway, he says, 'Paul doesn't matter. You're about to write the biggest scoop in the world. It's going to be huge. You're going to be huge.'

I grab at the ball caught up by my feet – it is my shirt after all – and slide off the bed, pulling it on. Slowly doing up the buttons and crossing the room towards him.

'So, you're not mad at me – even if I didn't give you the heads up?'

'It's really something, what you did – bringing in Armstrong and the letters.'

He pulls me towards him, and we start to kiss. Hard, selfish kissing. It was the same when we had sex. We were frantic. Careless. Leaving bruises on each other's bodies from buckles and watches. I can feel the dull ache of them now and think we might make our way back to the bed. Or the sofa, where we started.

But George steps away then. A thin smile caught in his face. 'Becky, did you and Armstrong . . .'

'What do you think?'

'We've put bets on it.'

'Who's "we"?'

'Just about everybody, actually.'

I turn away and retrieve my clothes with an angry efficiency, feeling robbed somehow of all my earlier triumph. 'What are the odds?'

'Fifty to one that you did.'

'Which way did you bet? Don't answer.'

We get dressed in silence.

When we are fully clothed, the unmade bed becomes somehow improbable.

Momentarily embarrassed, I straighten my suit jacket, brush out the skirt and then cross the room to where a mirror hangs above the console table with its vase of now wilted lilies – has Paul's recording device been running all this time?

'Aren't you meant to be seeing Amelia tonight? You know I'm supposed to report back on your every move, right? It's part of an arrangement we have. Reduced rent in exchange for information.'

'So, tell her.'

'Seriously?'

I can see all of him, standing by the door on the other side of the room. From this angle, he barely takes up a quarter of the mirror's surface.

'Seriously.' He crosses the room, grabbing my wrists and spinning me around to face him. 'You make people reckless. You make *me* reckless.'

'I don't mean to.'

He lets go of me, looking unhappy suddenly.

'Yeah, you do.'

# Haversham

When my mother started seeing Mark, Paul stopped coming around to our flat. That summer – the summer I turned thirteen – we drifted apart. For a while, the only time we ran into each other was when passing on the communal stairwell, and the most these accidental encounters yielded was a cautious nod. Which is why I was surprised when he rang on our door one afternoon.

He wanted my help with something. That's what he said, and it was a command rather than a request.

'OK.'

He nodded, pleased, although he clearly hadn't anticipated anything other than my acquiescence. He remained standing on the mat by the front door, eyes sliding past me and into our house.

'So . . . are you going to invite me in?'

Without waiting for a response, he stepped inside the flat, staring about him. It wasn't until then that I noticed the rucksack he was wearing. For a moment, I was worried that he was going to ask me to help him burgle my own home. I think I had this idea because of the conversations I overheard between Angelina and my mother on Friday nights. Paul was becoming troublesome, stealing money and other things from Angelina. She was worried about his friends, and almost certain he had started to take drugs.

Snatching sideways glances at him as he stood in the lounge watching the TV screen – *Top Hat* was playing – I looked for giveaway signs of the Paul who made his mother cry. We heard her, through the wall.

'You're still watching this stuff?'

I tried to decipher his tone. Nostalgia? Disapproval? Paul and I used to love the old Fred Astaire and Ginger Rogers movies. I still did. Their choreographed, monochrome world made me feel safe.

I picked up the remote control from the sofa and pointed it in an exaggerated way at the TV, switching it off.

'Ready to go?'

After a second's hesitation, eyes on the rucksack still, I said, 'Ready.'

I followed him down the stairwell, across the forecourt and around the back of the block of flats until we reached the garages, two symmetrical rows running parallel to the railway line. Each flat had access to one, although nobody used them for anything other than storage. The paint was peeling on most of the metal doors and quite a few of them were buckled with dents. Debris collected in the corners and crevices – broken glass, needles, cans, glue gone solid. During daylight hours children rode bicycles and scooters here. It was where I used to come on my roller skates, although I made no attempt to join in the other children's games, and they never invited me to play with them.

But this afternoon, there wasn't anybody around.

Paul told me that the plan was to break into Mr Cutler's garage – I had no idea why. Mr Cutler, now retired, used to be in the navy. I saw him sometimes, his moustache stained yellow from the pipe he smoked while gardening. In the winter he wore a cap and large, padded gloves.

Among the children on the estate, he had a reputation for kindness. He always let us retrieve the tennis balls and footballs that went over his fence. Unlike Mr Riley, who punctured the footballs that landed in his borders, before returning them.

Paul showed me the padlock hanging from the door, rattling it. Mr Cutler's garage was the only one with a padlock.

'Why does he keep it locked?'

I wasn't at all curious about Mr Cutler's locked garage; I was stalling for time. The thought of breaking into it made me anxious. By nature, I was law-abiding. Sticking to the rules, I'd discovered, helped me to remain virtually invisible, and while invisible I saw things and heard things that others didn't.

Paul raised his eyebrows, impatient. 'Because he doesn't want anybody going in there.' He let the padlock fall back into place. 'I'm going to saw through it.'

He undid the rucksack and pulled out a hacksaw. 'Some tool, right?'

He held the hacksaw in the air between us then pressed his thumb hard against it, aware of me watching him. When he pulled his thumb away there were indents from the saw's metal teeth in his skin.

Now my anxiety was turning to fear. 'Isn't there a key?'

'Look, I thought you might be interested in helping me out, Becky. But if you're not, you can leave.'

It would have been safer to go, but a new voice inside me said that if I did, I would regret it.

'Keep a lookout.'

Turning his back on me, he started to saw at the padlock until it clattered to the ground among the shards of broken glass.

Grinning and triumphant, he handed me the hacksaw and hauled open the garage door.

We stepped inside.

The air was close and warm. The walls were lined with floor-to-ceiling shelving, stacked with labelled boxes. They were all so meticulously and systematically ordered that I immediately felt like a trespasser.

Paul pulled at one of the boxes, flinging the lid to the floor. But the box failed to yield whatever it was he was looking for. So, he reached for the next one and the next, becoming increasingly frenzied. He'd forgotten all about me, and I half thought about running away until he let out a triumphant, 'Ha!'

He'd found a box full of magazines which he started to flick through, pushing random spreads in front of my eyes as I gripped the hacksaw to my chest.

Men and women's bodies in indescribable poses. Page after page of them.

I couldn't think of anything to say, feeling clouded, suddenly, by the growing awareness that this summer afternoon was taking root somewhere inside me. It was as if too many doors had been opened onto too many rooms at once. And even though the box of magazines was inside Mr Cutler's garage, I stood there wondering who they belonged to.

'This is heavy shit, but not what I'm looking for.' His voice was hard suddenly with disappointment. 'Reckon they're nothing more than a smokescreen.'

A smokescreen? What could be worse than these magazines?

'Doesn't matter,' Paul concluded, his voice lifting again. 'We'll use them anyway.'

He dropped his rucksack, reaching inside and pulling out a couple of carrier bags. A stash of A4 envelopes and a pack of pens fell onto the dusty garage floor.

'Mr Cutler does disgusting things to children, Becky.'

Paul dropped his head and I had a horrible feeling he might be crying. But then he flicked it up again. Eyes distant.

'Here.'

He divided the envelopes into two piles and passed me a pen, a new sense of urgency taking over. I watched as he started to stuff the envelopes with Mr Cutler's magazines, slow to realize that I was meant to be doing the same thing. We only stopped when we ran out of envelopes. Then he started to scrawl across each one, *A gift from Mr Cutler*, nodding at me to do the same.

I wrote in thick marker pen, *A gift from Mr Cutler*, as instructed, on envelope after envelope. When we had finished, we filled the carrier bags with the envelopes and stepped back outside into the sun-stricken forecourt. I knew by then what was expected of me, so when he said, 'You take Blunden House, I'll take Shelley Court,' I simply set off in the direction of our block and, starting on the fourth floor, posted the envelopes through people's doors.

# Scooped

There's no answer at Polo's Knightsbridge flat. I ring the buzzer at 8 a.m. – something we arranged yesterday. I'm meant to be interviewing him then taking the letters to the *Mercury* to get them authenticated. Once the letters are authenticated, we've agreed to release Polo the first £500,000 of his fee. When he doesn't pick up, I use a payphone outside a greengrocer's on the corner, thinking maybe he's overslept.

Given his institutionalized life – boarding school followed by the military – my rational self knows this is unlikely. But it's still preferable to the other thought I'm trying hard to dismiss as I continue to call the flat, letting the phone ring out until the answer machine kicks in. I do this twenty times before the clench of anxiety gives way to a stampeding panic. I make my way back to Polo's block, the world around me suddenly off kilter. Unsure what else to do, I wait on the steps to his building, growing a shadow as the sun climbs.

At 9 o'clock the cleaner arrives on a gleaming new moped, sunlight bouncing sharply off her helmet.

'Hey,' I smile, hoping she remembers me as the bearer of cash on previous occasions. 'I was meant to be meeting Mr Armstrong at 8 o'clock?'

She stares up at the windows of Polo's flat. 'He gone?'

'Gone? I don't know. Did he tell you he was going somewhere?'

Her face remains unresponsive inside the helmet as she parks the moped and climbs the steps past me. I offer her money to disclose his location, but she refuses. Either because she doesn't know or because her silence has been bought. Disturbing to think that Polo, who until now has been unable to afford the shockingly small cash-in-hand sum she demands for cleaning his flat, is suddenly liquid enough not only to pay for her silence, but to no longer have any need of £500,000.

She punches a code into the pad beside the main entrance and doesn't stop me from following her into the lobby, or the rattling cage of a lift. We enter the flat together. It smells shuttered. Vacant.

I hover in the entrance hall as the cleaner makes her way into the kitchen, pushing the clutter of bills and flyers around a brass dish – I guess this is where Polo usually leaves her cash, only there is no cash. After this, I watch as she makes for the walnut bureau by the window in the main room, rifling through the scant paperwork piled on the desk, which I know – from previous visits to the flat – comprises mostly crested invitations to past military and official functions; bills with sums underlined, defaced by towering exclamation marks and dates when Polo has made phone calls to query the unbelievable cost of his life. But nothing else.

'He gone,' she says again.

I stare beyond her, through the window at Polo's view of the world: a symmetrical row of red-brick mansion flats and a patchy line of sky. I'm meant to be in a cab right now, with Polo and the letters, heading towards the *Mercury* offices. I booked out the entire fifth floor of the building saying it was a kiss-and-tell interview with a footballer as a smokescreen, so that we could mock up the layout of tomorrow's paper in secret. Trish, Pitt's PA, is the only other person in on this, and it was her who booked the forensic specialist, to authenticate the letters.

But Polo has, to all intents and purposes, vanished into thin air.

I leave his flat and walk back to the phone box on the corner, shock and disbelief catching up with me inside its hot grubbiness. The windows are obscured by sex workers' calling cards. Toeing the cigarette butts banked on the cement floor, I phone Paul. It isn't until I hear his voice that I realize how angry I am.

'I need you to find someone for me.'

'He's gone?'

'He's gone.'

I'm sitting on a stool in the cleaner's storeroom, which doubles as a locker room for the *Mercury*'s female staff, eyes shut, head tipped back against the wall, surrounded by the comforting smell of Jeyes Fluid. Impossible to wash off, the smell of Jeyes. Even after a bath and despite the gloves she wore, my mother's hands would be raw with it. It gets through the gloves, she would say, worried about her nails, splaying her fingers for me to inspect the damage.

I often come in here to sit among the cleaners. An invisible fleet of mostly Latinas from Colombia via Elephant and Castle, their lockers hung with crucifixes and photographs of their children.

Usually, I catch them at the beginning of their shift, smoking and laughing and trading stories in rapid Spanish, tired feet raised off the floor, balanced on the edge of the table. There's a small stove that they heat stuff on, and sometimes I'm invited to share their breakfast, sitting with them to talk about the weddings, baptisms, First Communions and Quinceaños that fill their lives.

Opening my eyes, I see Pitt's PA standing in front of her locker.

Trish is in her fifties and has worked at the *Mercury* most of her adult life. There are those on the staff – Malcolm among them – who remember her as a swinging slip of a girl in Mary Quant, with geometric hair and knee-high boots.

She was hired during an editorial reign when the preference had been for Jane Birkin lookalikes.

It's daunting, trying to imagine Trish as a waif.

The gamine girl rumoured to have once spent a night in a suite at the Ritz with Pitt Crawley has long since disappeared. Today's Trish holds catalogue clothing parties and wears comfort-fit slip-ons.

She's one of those women who doesn't like other women, holding particularly strong opinions on married women in the workplace. Opinions she's always keen to share. The young and the unmarried she puts up with, as long as they treat the office as a nuptial hunting ground. But once a mate has been found and marriage accomplished, a woman's place is at home – not depriving young men with mouths to feed of work.

According to Trish, every married woman who works is responsible for aiding and abetting a family's starvation somewhere. There are roars of approval when she holds forth on this topic at the Lighterman, thighs spread across stained upholstery in one of the pub's booths. She has her formidable back slapped and round after round bought for her, drinking up to eight pints of Guinness straight with no visible effect before getting a company cab home to Hammersmith.

She adores men, Pitt in particular. Over the years she has cultivated a despotic allegiance to him. On the rare occasion that she uses her holiday allowance, she sends faxes reminding Pitt of meetings, dental appointments, deadlines, her existence. Sent when drunk on piña coladas (Trish's drink of choice after stout), often from a cruise ship, these crazed scrawls are always signed off with a skyscraper of a 'T' followed by a string of Xs replacing the rest of the letters in her name. They collect in one long shiny roll on the floor beneath the fax machine, where they remain until one of the cleaners bins them.

Opening her locker, she pulls out a bottle of vodka and a bag of Fox's Glacier Mints. Stuck to the inside of the door are photographs of her six terriers, named after the Mitford sisters – Nancy, Pamela, Diana, Unity, Jessica and Deborah.

Trish fixes her glassy doll's eyes on me, powdered today in absinthe green. 'I've been in the business for almost forty years – never seen anything like it before.'

'Never seen anything like what before?'

Banging the bottle of vodka down on the table, she picks up a couple of cups, glances inside them, pulls a face then fills both, pushing one towards me. She sits down, balancing swollen-looking feet on the chair, then takes a mint out of the bag, unwrapping it and putting it in her mouth.

'You,' she blurts with a triumphant suck, adding, even more unexpectedly, 'the way you scooped Armstrong and his letters. Incredible.'

My shock at her praise must be showing because she allows a smile to settle on her puckered face.

'Only I didn't – Armstrong's gone AWOL.'

'He's bolted?'

'To France, apparently. With the letters. It gets worse.'

Balancing herself on her elbows, Trish leans towards me, making ferocious sucking sounds.

'I just found out that he's been working on a book about the affair with the friend of someone I know. They've got a column in the *Courier*. The book's being published in October along with extracts from the letters. But here's the sting – they're serializing the first few chapters of the book in the *Courier*, starting tomorrow. We've been played.'

Trish gets to her feet, putting the vodka back in her locker. 'You've got to tell Pitt.'

'I know – why d'you think I'm holed up in here?'

'But first, you have to find a fix. You're finished if you take a problem to Pitt without a fix.'

'My contact in the print room just confirmed a bigger than usual run for tomorrow's *Courier*. Much bigger.' O'Dowd jerks his head in my direction without looking at me. 'She's right.'

Nobody speaks.

It's a big deal, having a contact in the print room. Housed on the building's ground floor, this area – with its vast, clattering yellow and black machines – is strictly off limits to editorial staff. Pre-1987, when printing was still done using hot presses, the only place editorial and printing staff would meet was the composing room. But even then, editors were forbidden to touch the composing stone.

Turner, holed up in a corner, keeps tilting his eyes towards the ceiling, anxious. He's trying to work out on whose head the blame will fall, because it can't stay suspended up there for ever. Gravity will out.

George has collapsed in a chair beside him. He looks busted up.

O'Dowd, perched on the edge of Pitt's desk, bounces a paperweight in his hand.

Outside, on the newsroom wall, there's a poster of Jack Nicholson in *The Shining*. Beside this is a head-shaped indent marking the spot where O'Dowd once charged the wall.

Pitt stands behind the desk. Distant. Distracted.

'Armstrong must have had this in the pipeline all along. The book.' Pitt looks directly at me, before repositioning a pen on the desk in front of him with an eerie calm. 'He used our offer for the tell-all plus letters as leverage with the *Courier* to get them to raise their fee. That was the only point of the meeting for him.'

'He isn't giving them the letters – well, none of them in their entirety, anyway.'

Pitt nods, still intent on the pen. 'They're probably fake, that's why. We've been played.'

O'Dowd continues to bounce the paperweight in his hand. 'So – who the fuck is this Lizzie cunt?'

'There were rumours for a while that she was dating Rawdon, but that didn't come to anything.' I hesitate, glancing at Pitt who doesn't react to this. 'Although they're still friends. Clearly. She and Armstrong move in the same social circle – it was Lizzie who led me to him in the first place, and it's her friend who's got the column in the *Courier*'s weekend magazine – society gossip. But I had no idea that this columnist and Polo were writing a book together.'

Glancing around the sullen-faced room, nobody – apart from Pitt – will look at me. It takes longer than it should to realize that even though I'm telling the truth, they don't necessarily believe me. I'm treading water right now in a hinterland of doubt.

'Fucking Rawdon,' Pitt whispers at last. 'Of all the people to scoop us on Armstrong. Fucking Rawdon.'

Without warning, he grabs the paperweight in O'Dowd's hand and throws it into the glass separating his office from the newsroom.

George instinctively protects his head as the paperweight bounces off the glass, fracturing it, and onto the floor.

Pitt remains angled towards me, expectant – as if the paperweight had nothing to do with him. 'What's the plan, Rebecca?'

'The plan is – we fuck up their scoop.'

'I need details.'

'I'm going to steal a copy of tomorrow's *Courier* from the

presses so that we can hijack Polo's extract by crashing it, word for word, into tomorrow's *Mercury*. Along with bonus material they don't have – that I've been sitting on for years. We'll type it in, then send it down to the print room in time for the last run.'

O'Dowd lets out a bark of a laugh. 'You'll never get past security to the presses.'

The glass wall separating the office from the rest of the newsroom finally gives way then, splintering and collapsing with a low-pitched squeal, exposing the back bench, picture desk, cramped News and Features departments, scurrying sub-editors – all of them framed and gawping at us through the empty window.

Pitt and I remain locked on to each other. Neither of us has moved.

I swing away from him, seeking out the digital stop clock at the back of the newsroom. The one that counts us down to the daily deadline. I'm just about able to make out the green digits: 02:19:00. Two hours and nineteen minutes to go. They flicker, landing on a wobbly 02:18:00.

Nobody speaks.

Until I hear myself say, 'Tubbs needs to increase our print run.'

Pitt nods, distracted. 'And how much would you tell Tubbs to increase our print run by – if I were to give you permission to do that?'

'Five hundred thousand,' I say, without hesitation. I've learned this about myself. When I'm put on the spot, I don't hesitate.

'That's a big increase, you'll give Tubbs heart failure.' He jerks his head towards the low-hanging ceiling tiles. 'Upstairs will come crashing down on us for pulling a stunt like this.'

'Either we do it, or Rawdon wins.'

Shaking his head and sounding the closest to tired I've heard him sound, Pitt says, 'You're sure?'

'I'm sure.'

'Wait.' O'Dowd thrusts himself into the centre of the room, a tense apparition. 'This is fucking mad. What if she doesn't pull it off?'

Pitt contemplates him for a moment before stepping through the gap where the window used to be, crunching over shards of glass. 'Tubbs,' he yells to the sub-editor standing at the back of the room beneath the countdown clock. 'I need you to tell production we're increasing the print run for a special edition of the *Mercury* tomorrow.' He pauses before adding, 'Five hundred thousand. We want to increase it by five hundred thousand.'

I wait in the toilets – as close to the printing presses as I can get, so that I'm able to hear when they start up. My make-up's been washed off and my hair hidden beneath a loose blue cap. The cap and overalls I'm wearing belong to one of the cleaners, Carmen, and smell of another woman's body. Another woman's life. I helped get her husband a job on security and she handed them over – along with her pass – without question. Beside me, a blue bucket and mop. I figure that if I'm stopped, I can say there's been a spillage I've been asked to sort by maintenance.

A rumbling starts up then, growing in scale by the second, so that I feel it through the soles of my feet. The three cubicle doors shake and rattle on their hinges. It's time.

Inside the print room itself, the noise is immense; a mechanical churning that's immediately disorientating as I move between the vast black and yellow machines, pushing the cleaning bucket on its castors, until I catch sight of him suddenly – a multitude of Polos in full regimental uniform on the *Courier*'s front page. His left arm is bent around a helmet, a forgotten smile on his face. As if he's posing for a painting rather than a photograph. Beside him, there's a picture of the Princess in a high-collared white evening dress, her kohl-rimmed eyes searching for the exit. The layout – it really is brilliant – screams star-crossed lovers. Anna and Vronsky.

I gravitate towards the conveyor belt, still pushing the bucket, transfixed by the newspapers running away from me at high speed. Then, balancing the mop against the side of the bucket, two things happen at once – I finally manage to grab messily at one of the newspapers, and a shout rings out above the sound of the machines.

Everything after this becomes hurried.

Abandoning my props, I break into a run across the print room's concrete floor, the newspaper pinned against my stomach. But it isn't until I push through a set of double doors with my shoulders and find myself hurtling breathless along the corridor past the toilets I hid in earlier that I feel it. A thief's exhilaration. The thump of it keeps pace with me as I tear up two flights of steps and through another set of doors, checking to see if I'm being followed. There's nobody behind me.

I keep moving towards a final set of doors. The production department's reception area is on the other side of these.

Through the windows, the same city as before, lit up now. The same sofas and low-slung coffee table. The receptionist replaced by a night security guard in dark uniform reading a magazine – *The Deep-Sea Angler* – held close to his face, mouth slightly open. He raises his head as I pass; the eyes are faraway and in Carmen's blue cleaning overalls I'm as good as invisible, despite the speed I'm moving at. Almost there. Beyond the last set of doors, I can see night pressing down on the glass ceiling of the building's floodlit atrium.

And it's then that the phone on reception starts its urgent ringing, the doors behind me still shuddering to a close.

The security guard is already on his feet by the time he

answers the phone, *The Deep-Sea Angler* and accompanying daydreams abandoned. Eyes locking on to me now, he makes the connection between whatever's being conveyed to him on the phone and my speed. As I streak past, I see his free hand starting to work itself into a gesture.

Keeping my arm clamped tightly around my stomach, I crash through the doors leading onto the balcony that hugs the atrium's perimeter. The cleaner's blue hat flies from my head, my hair suddenly loose, streaming out behind me.

There's a stab of momentary panic that almost sees me drop the newspaper and snatch at the disappearing hat instead, strange and airborne as it makes its way over the edge of the balcony, into the void.

But I manage to keep on running.

I don't look back.

These are my horizons. The words on the screen in front of me and the digits on the clock beyond – 00:06:11; 00:06:10. Which is why, at first, I mistake the new sense of commotion in the room for nothing more than excitement as we approach the final print deadline.

'Rebecca – we're good to go.'

Pitt's voice, and it sounds like a warning. An accompanying hand falls heavy on my shoulder, making me feel briefly lopsided.

I stay focused on the screen in front of me. We've gone for a different layout to the *Courier*. A photograph of Polo and the Princess at an actual polo match. They're standing together on a piebald summer field, an outsize silver trophy between them. Polo, fresh from his horse, the speed of the game held captive in his face and body, is straining towards the blushing Princess as if about to abduct her. The Princess struggles to shake his right hand while bearing the weight of the trophy in her left.

Her long white skirt matches his white trousers. It's early days, but they're already falling towards each other. The promise of intimacy, the inevitability of it all, is so obvious that I wonder how any of us could have missed it at the time.

And then a new voice.

'I've just had the oddest phone call from security. Apparently there's been a theft.'

Resentful at the interruption, I finally force myself to look up from the screen.

Rawdon Crawley has managed to break through the crowd surrounding the desk. His head temporarily blocks my view of the clock. He's dressed to ride a motorbike – like he was the last time I saw him this close.

He breaks off to catch his breath – he must have been running.

I watch as he takes in the bank of men, his eyes coming to rest on his father, before dropping and making their way, confused, over the cleaner's uniform I'm still wearing.

'You—'

Ignoring this, I say, 'I didn't steal anything. Polo was meant to be the *Mercury*'s scoop – I've been working him for almost five years.'

'*Five years?*' Rawdon laughs unexpectedly, as if we have all the time in the world. Echoes of his laughter are caught up by the men surrounding my desk. 'How old are you?'

'Twenty-three.'

'Twenty-three,' he repeats.

We continue to watch each other. Then, gesturing at Carmen's overalls, he says, 'And this? Who put you up to this?'

His eyes flicker towards his father again, standing beside me, his hand gripping my shoulder.

'Nobody.' Before I can help it, my mouth twists into a proud mess of a smile. 'This is all me.'

He smiles back.

'Rebecca,' Pitt urges. He gives my shoulder a hard squeeze.

'Re-bec-ca, Re-bec-ca,' is taken up by the rest of the room. Clapping soon accompanies the chanting. Rawdon makes a movement then, but instead of stepping towards the desk, which is what I was anticipating, he steps away from it, turns and leaves. Far more shocked by his departure than his arrival, I half expect Pitt to call his son back.

The clock, visible once more, reads 00:00:54. Reaching for the mouse on the mat in front of me, I line up the cursor with the send button, and give it a decisive tap.

It's after midnight, the cab pushing through empty streets, the river to our left somewhere. We're drunk from the champagne that was opened after we made the deadline, loud and galloping with the shock of it all as the full extent of what we've managed to pull off tonight catches up with us.

'You're fucking extreme,' George yells, sliding across the back seat as the cab turns a corner and we swing south over the river, both sides of the glittering city visible. 'This is going down in newspaper history. You're a fucking legend, Becky.'

He gives my shoulder a hard shunt before skewering himself more firmly into the corner of the back seat, and saying to the cab driver, 'Just here.'

We slow down. The man leans over the wheel and peers through the rain-streaked windscreen, unconvinced.

'I grew up around here. Wouldn't recognize it now. That used to be the Sarson's factory. That was Jacob's. Lipton's was across the way there.'

He continues to list an empire's brands, now nothing more than names trailing derelict warehouses that are being bought by property developers and converted into luxury apartments. Like the one we pull up in front of – a former jam factory where men, women and children once stood, suffocating in the fumes of strawberries.

It's the first time I've seen where George lives. The flat he shares with Dobbin.

Grabbing at my wrists, he gives them a light shake. 'Come up, and tomorrow morning we'll buy a copy of the paper together – how romantic is that?'

I catch the cabbie's eyes as he watches us in the rear-view mirror.

'Come up,' George says again.

Even drunk as I am, I can hear something in his voice which has never been there before. A pleading.

'Is Dobbin home?'

'I don't care.'

'I'll only come up if he isn't there. Dobbin doesn't like me.'

'You're right,' he laughs, made inexplicably pleased by this fact, as if released from something suddenly.

The driver, impatient, slides open the internal window. He's wearing a copper bracelet to ward off arthritis, and it clinks against the glass. 'Are we going or staying?'

George slips forward, imperious. 'How about we get out here, I sign the chit saying you've completed the booking to SW3, and you throw in a couple of those joints I know you've got stashed in the glove compartment?'

The man's eyes switch between George and me.

'Your daughter?' I say, nodding at the photograph stuck to the dashboard. It's of a girl with a gap-toothed smile and a glossy ponytail, in school uniform: a green gingham dress and matching green cardigan.

'Yeah.' He shifts in his seat, giving the photograph an un-complicated smile.

Then he opens the glove compartment and passes the two joints to me rather than George.

We cross a white lobby dotted with dusty yuccas, in the corner a bowl of cat food. I'm wavering and unsteady; my shoes are too loud.

We move inside the lift and, as soon as the doors shut, take hold of each other, stumbling against the carpeted wall. Our clumsiness makes me feel much drunker than before. George's hands are over my ears as he grips my head. He doesn't let go when the doors open on his floor and instead walks me backwards out of the lift in an awkward dance that feels like it might end in a fall.

We come to a stop outside the door to his flat.

He steps inside and I'm about to follow when he comes to a sudden standstill.

The hall lights are on and there's the sound of a cat whining.

Then Amelia's hopeful voice calling out, 'George?'

'Hey,' he calls down the hallway, letting go of me. 'What on earth are you doing here?'

'I haven't been able to get hold of you, so I thought I'd drop by. You don't mind?' Amelia carries on, fragile-sounding. 'Luckily Dobs was home. And look, I found a cat downstairs. She followed me up.'

George fills the doorway and doesn't move. 'Dobs is allergic to cats.'

'Dobs, is that right? George says you're allergic to cats, why didn't you say?'

I can't make out what Dobbin says in response to this, but when George turns around, he's holding the cat in his hands. He drops it onto the floor, and it lands at my feet with its back arched and fur bristling.

We stare at each other as the cat shakes itself out, mewling, and starts to rub itself against my legs.

Then George turns away, and I watch as his fingers slip from sight and the door slams shut between us.

I'm halfway across the lobby when I hear the lift doors open behind me. There's nowhere to hide. I think about running, but by the time I turn around, Dobbin is bearing down on me carrying a bin bag full of rubbish. With improbable speed, and none of his habitual clumsiness, he takes hold of my elbow, steering me out through the building's entrance and propelling us along the empty street towards the river.

'We should talk.'

'Are you going to drown me?'

'S-s-sit.'

We've reached a flight of steps. At low tide, they will lead down to a narrow shoreline. But it's high tide now, the water deep and dark-smelling with only a couple of wet steps visible. Dropping the bag of rubbish onto one of them, he sits himself down in a tangle of long arms and legs.

'S-s-sit,' he says again, fishing a box of cigarettes out of his shirt pocket and offering me one.

I lower myself onto the step beside him, water lapping just below our feet.

We light up. The truth is, I'm afraid. Dobbin has always had this effect on me. He's someone who knows himself. Like Amelia, I think suddenly.

'Amelia's pregnant. She d-d-didn't tell you?'

He turns to face me.

Shocked, I avoid his gaze and exhale into the damp night, staring, preoccupied, at the buildings on the opposite side of the river, illuminated scratches against the dark sky. 'How pregnant?'

'Does it matter? Around eight weeks.'

The rain has eased, and two moons have appeared: one in the sky, the other in the river. We watch in silence as a police boat passes. It isn't until the water settles in the boat's wake and the second moon makes a shaky reappearance that I ask him if George knew.

'Not until tonight, no. It changes everything,' he says. 'E-E-Emmy's pregnancy. That's what I want to t-t-talk to you about. You need to stay away; let them work it out.'

'Why?'

'To g-g-give them a chance.'

'What you're saying is that the success of their relationship rests on my head. Have you got any idea how fucking ridiculous that sounds?'

'The thing is . . . George does l-l-love Amelia. She's his p-p-point of return. The p-p-place he goes back to. Home. You must see that.'

I take a grasping hold of my knees, rocking lightly backwards and forwards on the wet step as I finish the cigarette, throwing it into the river. 'And is George definitely the father?'

This shocks him. He lifts his head, looking about him as if he feels suddenly unsafe.

'It's a joke. Oh, Dobbin, you've got it bad, haven't you?'

He scrambles messily to his feet, grabbing the bin bag. I can tell he's torn between loathing me and the lure of confession. 'I should g-g-go. I told them I was taking out the r-r-rubbish.'

'You don't like me very much, do you?'

He stares down at me in a way that makes me feel like a distant point on the horizon, viewed through a telescope. 'You'd be an OK person if you weren't so af-f-fraid all the time. Constantly looking over your shoulder.'

Now it's my turn to be shocked. 'Afraid? I'm not afraid.'

'You're the m-m-most frightened person I know.'

# Holiday Inn Express

Even though the Lighterman is as good as empty tonight, George is sitting in a dark corner at the back of the pub surrounded by oak panelling and green tasselled lampshades. Rearing over him is a bear standing on its hind legs with teeth bared and head thrust out, perpetually in search of whatever it was that tricked it into leaving the deep sanctuary of the forest.

George doesn't look up as I slide myself into the chair opposite. His gaze remains fixed on the beer mat he's twisting morosely in his hand.

'How was your weekend?'

'The Sedleys held me hostage,' he blurts, head flicking up then immediately down again. Eye contact between us is a random, bouncing affair. 'The entire weekend. Can you believe it?'

He's putting a lot of effort into looking outraged.

But it isn't outrage he feels, I can tell. He's too scared for that.

'Liv chaired the whole thing like a fucking COBRA meeting.'

I watch him in silence as he makes an uncoordinated attempt at reaching for the half-drunk pint in front of him but knocks it over instead.

'Shit. *Shit.*'

He mops ineffectually at the spilt beer with his beer mat, before giving up and sweeping the liquid onto the floor instead. 'I didn't stand a chance.'

'What happened?'

I realize, as I ask the question, that I'm not really interested in the answer. He told me earlier about the pregnancy. Over the phone. Very George. And for reasons that are still unclear to me, I decided against telling him about the encounter with Dobbin. Pretending, instead, that I was hearing the news for the first time. This wasn't hard. I felt all the hurt I failed to feel when Dobbin told me by the river that night. Which is why the sudden lack of interest surprises me. It's as if George has somehow faded. Even now, sitting across the table from me, he's becoming more see-through by the second.

'Didn't Amelia—'

'I haven't seen Amelia. She must have stayed in Clapham last night.'

Keeping hold of the soggy beer mat, he collapses back in his chair and takes a few nervous sweeps at his unwashed hair. 'We're getting married. Apparently.' He looks dazed. Like he's hearing it properly for the first time.

'Why did you agree to that?'

But he either can't or won't answer. Instead, he takes in the empty pub, fixing on the door as if half expecting someone to walk through it.

Neither of us can think of anything to say.

'So – you must want this baby as well if you're going for marriage, the whole thing?'

He stares at me, his face blank in the Lighterman twilight, before taking hold of my hands across the table and giving them a gloomy shake. 'You're angry.'

'Why am I here?' I say at last.

'Maybe we should cool off for a bit.'

He swallows his words. Hangdog.

'Do you want me to agree with you, or disagree with you?'

Tilting over the table, he pulls his hands away and runs a finger down the side of my face. 'We could just leave. Tonight.'

'And go where?'

'Anywhere. Away.'

'George, why would I want to run away now – after the Polo scoop? For the first time in my life, I'm exactly where I want to be.' I pause. 'Who I want to be.'

'You really mean that.'

For a moment, he sounds bitter. His bitterness is a new obstacle between us, far more insurmountable suddenly than Amelia. It makes me feel distant from him – sorry for him, even, in a way I've never felt before.

'Pitt's invited me to Matilda Crawley's party this weekend.'

Without commenting, he pushes his hand through the spilt beer towards me. He takes hold of one of my hands in his and inspects it so intently that it starts to feel unfamiliar.

'I'm getting married.' He sounds sick as he says this. 'We should celebrate.'

We end up in a Holiday Inn Express overlooking a roundabout. He's far too afraid of Dobbin now to risk going back to the flat. We have no idea what we're doing. The place is all wrong and we're confused. Fraught. Unable to decide whether we're clawing our way towards something, or away from it. Nothing feels right, but we tell ourselves that this is the last time, so it doesn't matter. A sense of leave-taking – of imminent departure – hangs over everything, but this makes us sad rather than passionate.

And neither of us feels like fucking.

Instead, we drink our way through the vodka we brought up to the room with us. We drink until my nose bleeds and George is left scrunched up in the cracked shower tray, sobbing. I'm relieved when it's over. Maybe we both are.

# Matilda Crawley

Arriving alone by cab, I cross the gravel drive leading to a Georgian house framed in wisteria, and the sounds of music and people. Waistcoated girls and boys stand around with trays of champagne. I'm handed a glass and directed around the side of the house into a garden, where I come to a standstill.

The party is held every year at Matilda Crawley's Highgate home, but this is the first time I've been invited. The original plan was for George and me to come together, but then Amelia caught wind of the party and asked to come.

There are already a lot of people here, their faces shining in the setting sun.

Faces I know.

Faces I recognize.

Faces I don't, but that I soon will.

Politicians, actors, chiefs of police, models, film producers, footballers, racing car drivers, robbers, boxers, bankers, shipping magnates, spies, entrepreneurs, gurus, gamblers, tech giants . . . nobody is invited without a reason. Before the millennium is out, I will splash every single one of them. But tonight, I'm still close to invisible. A girl from nowhere.

In the distance, above the dusky treetops, all of London. Bloated-looking under the heat haze spread thick over the city. Hyde Park was sun-scorched when the cab that brought me north passed through it, the smell of confined animals strong as we circled Regent's Park.

Storms have been forecast.

A long stretch of green lawn, miraculously unaffected by the city-wide drought, flows directly onto Hampstead Heath, close to the bathing ponds, where Matilda Crawley swims every morning of the year without exception. Groups of people fill the garden, although the largest and noisiest of these is the one around Rawdon Crawley. His is one of the faces I recognize immediately. Everywhere that he isn't becomes suddenly less significant.

I feel the tug of it now, the sense of promise, and yet still I hesitate. Toeing the edge, deciding whether to jump in.

Until a voice close by says, 'Perfect, isn't it?'

George drops a heavy arm around my shoulders. His face, a blur hanging over me as I look up at him. It's clear he's already very drunk and a long way from himself.

Mumbling into my hair, he says, 'Amelia's here.' It sounds like a warning. Then he lets go of me, stumbling backwards. 'Didn't you hear? We're officially a couple now. Engaged to be married. This is the kind of thing engaged couples do. They come to parties together. They leave together. Forever more,' he finishes loudly.

He's jittery, unable to shake out the dents the previous weekend with the Sedleys has made in him.

I scan the garden. 'Where is she – I can't see her.'

'Oh, she's here somewhere, but you know Emmy and parties.' His face suddenly grows dark. 'She hates them.'

Then I spot her, kneeling in the grass beneath a tree with a group of children. Dobbin is crouching beside her, the whole arrangement like a slightly out of joint family portrait. Strangely private. A Gainsborough, I think.

Amelia looks straight at us as she gets to her feet, and I realize then she must have been watching us for some time.

'So, why did she come?'

'To keep an eye on me. Let's give her a wave,' George says.

He waves, a crazy grin on his face, grabbing at my hand and flapping it in the air. I try to pull away but he keeps a tight, painful hold. His eyes are on Amelia, who makes no effort to wave back.

We're brought up short by someone wildly shouting my name – the actress Lily Kent. I've been leaving messages with her PR team for over a month now.

'Rebecca!' she yells across the crowded lawn, streaking unsteadily towards us. 'Rebecca Sharp!'

I got to know Lily a couple of years ago when she first hit the headlines with a BBC costume drama she was in. Though she was an unknown at the time, Features decided to run a piece on her. I had just joined the department and got to interview Lily, but only because nobody else was interested in doing it. We met in the downstairs bar at the Gate Theatre where she was playing Marie in a production of *Woyzeck*. The director had made her shave off all her hair, and I barely recognized her without her Regency curls. We drank and smoked a lot. I liked her. She was down to earth with a filthy sense of humour. The piece I wrote was enthusiastic – Lily Kent was somebody to watch; a prodigious new talent; versatile; an English rose with brains.

She phoned to thank me.

After the BBC drama, Lily's career started to run. She has since landed a role in a blockbuster film, and rumour has it she's dating Hollywood star Ed Soames, which is why I've been trying to get hold of her. He's probably here somewhere. Everybody is here.

'Rawdon's been telling me – telling everybody in fact – about how you screwed him over with that scoop about the guy who's been having an affair with the Princess.' She nudges me hard as she mentions Rawdon's name, laughing her smoker's laugh.

'He has?'

I look in the direction I last saw Rawdon Crawley, but there's no sign of him.

Lily links arms with me.

For a brief moment, I think George isn't going to let go, but he does. Lily leads me towards a marquee where there's a bar. Waves of grinning and eager people pass us as we make our way, clumsy in heels, across the grass. Lily is bitching about the assistant she says has failed to pass on any of my messages and promises to give me her direct number, all the while trading new and ever more filthy gossip.

'Rebecca, here you are, there's somebody I'd like to meet you.'

Pitt's voice. Pitt, behind me.

Matilda Crawley is standing at the bottom of a flight of stone steps, the illuminated house behind her, holding court to a group of men. All of them are laughing as they incline towards her. Pitt and I draw closer, and her eyes rest on us for a moment before she turns her attention back to the men. I recognize Turner and possibly Malcolm in the shadows of an outer circle. The flat-faced man hovering behind her, with the looks of a monochrome film star and an umbrella hanging ready from one of his arms, has to be Wenham, her PA.

Wherever Matilda Crawley goes, Wenham follows. In a previous life, he used to speculate in precious metals for Barclays Capital. Gold, mostly. He spent a lot of time in South America. The only other things I've been able to find out about him are that he has a mother living in Preston, who he adores, and that he plays the harpsichord beautifully. He also has a reputation for saying outrageous things in a broad Lancashire accent that sends Matilda Crawley into paroxysms. Wenham himself, I will discover, isn't prone to laughter. But he does have an eerie giggle reminiscent of mating foxes.

Matilda Crawley's name features in *Forbes* and on *The Sunday Times* Rich List, but almost nothing is known about her before she bought the failing *Mercury* in the sixties. The Crawleys themselves are an old northern family. Lancashire Catholics. Descendants of the Pilgrimage of Grace. Matilda has never been married. There are no known lovers, and she is rarely seen in public with anybody other than Wenham, and occasionally Rawdon, who is widely accepted as heir apparent to the Crawley empire.

The group peel apart as we approach. Close up, Matilda is a small woman with short hair, dark like her nephew's. Rawdon is standing beside her, half obscuring his aunt.

People, I've been told, are surprised when they meet Matilda Crawley for the first time. I'm surprised too, and a little disappointed. I might have mistaken her for an ageing City PA, or the dowdy headmistress of a girls' grammar, but what I would never have mistaken her for is a media mogul. Although she's standing at the centre of the group, there's something withdrawn about her, as if she's only just arrived at her own party. Perhaps she has. Either way, the truth is she falls short of expectation. Something she must have become used to seeing in people's eyes.

Pitt's hand is on my back, pushing me lightly forwards, until I stand facing his sister.

'Rebecca,' she says, warmly. She's holding a folded newspaper in her hands and slips it to Wenham. A quick glance confirms that it's last weekend's *Mercury* with the photo of Polo and the Princess splashed across the front page – my scooped 'scoop'. Since then, there has been no summons from Matilda's office, and no contact from Rawdon. The silence, on both accounts, is daunting, leaving me wondering whether the only reason I received an invitation to tonight's party was so that I could be publicly humiliated. Put in the stocks. Fired in front of everyone.

She takes hold of my shoulders, kissing me on each cheek. Up close, she smells overpoweringly of lemons. It's a mannish smell, more cologne than perfume.

Her hands slip away as she focuses on Pitt. 'Your circulation figures, which have been as limp as a dead man's dick, are up.' She swings round to face Rawdon. 'As are yours. Where would we all be without the Princess?'

There has been a lot of talk about the awful father–son rivalry masterminded by Matilda Crawley when she appointed Rawdon editor of the *Courier*.

Cutting in without thinking, I say, 'The *Mercury*'s were up by six hundred and eighty thousand after last weekend's special edition.'

I'm not sure whose benefit this is for – Matilda's or Rawdon's.

Turning slowly back to me, she repeats, 'Six hundred and eighty thousand. That's right.'

Matilda Crawley speaks quietly, barely opening her mouth as the words are pushed out through thin lips. It's a voice, I'll later discover, that saw her turned away from countless boardrooms and banking halls when she first came south to buy the failing *Mercury*. Yet after she bought it, Matilda succeeded in turning the *Mercury* into Britain's fastest-selling daily in under eighteen months.

'Six hundred and eighty thousand,' Pitt echoes, grinning wolfishly at Rawdon.

'You can't rely on theft to boost circulation.'

'We didn't steal anything – it was meant to be our scoop,' I say defensively.

'Well, that's the thing about sources.' Rawdon eases himself into the conversation, if that's what this is. 'They can be unpredictable.'

He doesn't sound angry. If anything, I think I detect traces of admiration in his voice. This isn't what I was expecting. Matilda Crawley pulls at the newspaper she passed to Wenham. Tapping my shoulder with it, her tone ambivalent, she says, 'Well, you've had your revenge, Rebecca. And Armstrong's going to have the whole world knocking on his door after this. His street value will go through the ceiling.'

'Actually, we've only just started,' I cut in again. 'And no, it won't. Because next week we're going to run a shredding piece on how he attempted to sell the Princess's heart to the highest bidder and flog us her letters. Letters we decided to tell Buckingham Palace about rather than publish.'

Matilda Crawley stares at me as distant thunder rolls out across the Heath and a hard rain starts to fall.

On a whim, I risk a smile.

She laughs beneath the umbrella Wenham has opened and is now holding over her.

'Do you swim, Rebecca? You look like a swimmer.'

Wenham blinks against the torrent. He's already drenched, we all are, but nobody dares to move while Matilda Crawley's still speaking.

'Meet me at the ladies' pond tomorrow,' she carries on above the rising sounds of chaos. The garden is suddenly full of shrieking and people running through the wet night to take cover, piling into the marquee or through the open terrace doors into the house. 'I'll be there for seven. Whatever the weather. Don't be late.'

She turns to go, and Wenham leads her up the steps into the house. It isn't until then that anybody moves and when they do, they all move at once.

Rawdon and I are left standing alone, gasping at each other through the downpour.

'Come on.'

He grabs my hand and we start running in the same direction as everyone else, the evening suddenly falling wide open.

'Have you ever ridden a motorbike?' he shouts above the rain.

He pulls me around the side of the house to the gravel drive at the front where he lets go of my hand, and I try not to mind. There's a motorbike parked beneath a tree, the dense covering of leaves offering us some shelter as he grabs a spare helmet out of the compartment under the saddle and passes it to me. Pushing it on – the helmet smells of someone else's perfume – I see the strings of shining bulbs threaded through the branches above our heads and realize that it's now dark.

Rawdon gets on the bike, gesturing for me to sit behind him.

I haul a cold pair of legs barely covered by the sodden dress I'm wearing across the seat and loop my arms around his jacket as he starts the engine. It isn't until he's reversing the bike that I become aware of a man's voice yelling. At first, I think it must be Pitt.

But it's George, lopsided and furious, although he must realize that he doesn't have the right to fury. Surely not, even drunk as he is.

As the bike shifts into gear, I hear my name being called, and over the yelling, Rawdon's voice crackling through the intercom connecting our two helmeted heads.

'Hold on,' he says.

For a moment, it feels like I have a choice.

Then we're gone, accelerating into the storm-stripped night. Leaving George behind.

I don't know what I was expecting, but it isn't this: a murky series of basement rooms somewhere in Earl's Court, with furniture that looks like it must have come from a Seventies porn set. On the walls, a random collection of Victorian oils hung in gilt frames; Highland cattle fixed to wild crags.

Soaking wet, I follow him inside.

It smells neglected: empty wine bottles; half-eaten take-aways; overflowing bins; clothes put through a cycle in the washing machine and then forgotten; sliding piles of unopened mail. I remember what I've heard about Rawdon Crawley – that he didn't want the promotion to editor of the *Courier* because it would anchor him to the office. Long hours. That he isn't a man looking to be anchored to anything.

He throws his helmet at the sofa. It's an almost aggressive movement, as if we're at the tail end of an ongoing argument.

'This is your place?'

'Yeah,' he laughs, in response to the tone of my voice, neither offended nor embarrassed, just disinterested. 'I don't usually bring people back here.'

'From a hygiene point alone, I can see why.'

We continue to watch each other, keeping our distance, the cluttered coffee table between us like a barricade. Protective of ourselves in each other's company, as if unsure of the damage we might unwittingly inflict on each other. And suddenly I worry that he's changed his mind and is about to ask me to leave.

Outside, the rain continues to bounce around in a dank square of courtyard, the sound of overflowing drains and gut-ters filling the room.

'You must be cold,' he says finally, his eyes moving lightly over the dress I'm wearing.

He disappears down the corridor and reappears holding a towel.

I start to rub ineffectually at my wet clothes, arms, legs and hair. 'You're not angry with me – for lifting the *Courier*'s scoop.'

'Is that a question?'

'Observation.'

'D'you want feedback?'

'A reaction would be good.' I wrap the stale-smelling towel around my shoulders. 'Just so that I know where I stand right now.'

'You know where you stand. I already told you – I don't usually bring people—'

'Women—'

'Women back here. You're the first.'

I'm unsure how badly I need this to be true.

Rawdon shakes his hair – which is already beginning to dry into messy clumps – out of his face. 'And no, I'm not angry. I'm in awe. On many accounts. But most of all, because you have my father's admiration. It isn't something I've ever managed. He's impressed by you.'

'The *Mercury*'s my life.'

He lets out a laugh then checks himself. 'Shit. You really mean that.'

'I really mean that.'

He crosses the room to a cabinet, kneeling untidily in front of it and pulling out a bottle of whisky and a couple of glasses. He places these at an angle among the debris on the coffee table before dropping onto the sofa. I sit down beside him as he pours us a glass each.

'Tell me something about yourself.'

It feels like a question he asked me a long time ago, one that he's still waiting for the answer to.

'Something I should know before we go any further.'

'How far are we going?'

I start to put the sentences together in my head. I know this story. I've told it enough times. But now, the well-rehearsed 'facts' elude me, sound ridiculous before I've even said them. This isn't like talking to his father. This isn't like talking to anyone I've ever known because it isn't information Rawdon's looking for. He's looking for me.

'I've never been on an aeroplane before.'

I say it without thinking, unprepared for the sense of release that comes. And I carry on. Haversham. My mother's death. I twist towards him so that I'm kneeling on the sofa, suddenly full of an overwhelming urge to get back on his motorbike and drive there now through the pouring rain. I want to show him the school I went to; the newsagent's belonging to Mr Andrews; the offices where I used to work for the *County Times*; the flat I grew up in. I want to show him all of it, share the weight.

He pulls me to my feet and leads us to the bathroom, a tiled cell that soon fills with steam. We peel off each other's clothes. My dress. His T-shirt and jeans.

Lying in water that's too hot, his cock pushing against the small of my back, he tells me things in return.

School was hell. The MPs and other Establishment figures that the *Mercury* pursued with such unrelenting doggedness – into the back seats of Ford Cortinas, between the polyester sheets of obscure seaside hotels, among the bushes of Hampstead Heath and behind the net curtains of semi-detached suburban dwellings housing specialist brothels – always turned out to be somebody's father. One misty October morning the day before Rawdon turned thirteen, the Health Minister threw himself onto railway lines at Balham. He was having an affair and had caught wind of the fact that the *Mercury* were about to expose it.

'The awful thing is, I used to bully his son something terrible. We were in the same year at school.' Rawdon's arm is resting against the top of my chest. His grip tightens as he says, 'Which is probably why I begged my father not to run it. Begged. And all the time I was begging, he had this smile on his face . . . like he could finally see me for who I really was, and all his suspicions – long-harboured – had just been confirmed. I don't think I've ever come back from that smile.'

Neither of our childhoods, it transpires, were straightforward places. Not having to pretend otherwise is, I'm convinced, what drew us together that first night.

'My father's a dangerous man. Don't be fooled into thinking otherwise.' He pauses, about to add something else before changing his mind. 'But you already know that.'

He untangles himself from me, stepping out of the bath and starting to dry himself.

'So, what's going on between you and George Osborne?'

For a moment it feels as though everything hangs in the balance. But while I'd be happy for George to find out about Rawdon, I don't want Rawdon – I realize suddenly – knowing about George. George's currency has always lain in his secrecy, and I'm not sure that I'm ready to devalue that yet.

Dropping the towel he's been drying himself with onto the floor, Rawdon picks up another one and holds it open for me.

'George Osborne?' I pull myself out of the water, self-conscious suddenly, and step into it. I turn away from him as he pulls the towel around me. 'We work together.'

He twists me towards him again.

I wait for further questions, but he starts kissing me instead. Slowly at first, his lips soft. Until things start to feel more urgent. Rawdon lifts me up, staggering clumsily through the piles of towels, out into the corridor and back towards the blue room we were in earlier. We hit cluttered surfaces – coffee table, sofa – pushing things onto the floor and laughing at the sound of them breaking, enjoying this small-scale carnage.

His recklessness reminds me of the way he drove, like he was trying to lose sight of something only he could see in his wing mirrors. It's a recklessness I easily match, although ever since Rawdon said George's name, George has become a presence I'm unable to make disappear. It's as if I'm performing for him. And part of me worries that my unguardedness with Rawdon is nothing more than a lover's dare.

# Swimmer

I watch as Matilda enters the pond, climbing neatly down a ladder at the side of the jetty and slipping into the brown water. Her hair is tucked into a swimming cap whose progress I track as she barrels efficiently towards the far side, steering a course through the water lilies and scattering ducks. Then she turns, treading water.

'Rebecca, come on!'

Her voice, like those of the other swimmers, is flat-sounding in the lazy mist covering the pond's surface, subduing the world so that it feels short of colour. As if it has undergone some sort of bloodletting.

This first swim feels like an initiation. A test I know I need to pass. The jetty is already dotted with wet footprints leading to and from the water. Many of these footprints, I'll later discover, belong to the women running this country, both publicly and behind closed doors. In the changing block with its single shower, rumours are verified, information exchanged, deals brokered, assurances given and promises made.

Most of these women are wearing the same purposeful, dark-coloured swimsuits as Matilda, hair tucked beneath caps. Their uniformity makes me feel self-conscious. It's an old feeling. The costume I grabbed earlier this morning from the bottom of a drawer, after Rawdon dropped me at the Queen's Court flat, is chlorine-bleached. A patchy purple. My hair hangs loose down my back, and my movements are full of the night before.

Making a note to buy a new Speedo swimsuit, cap and

goggles, I lower myself down the ladder, forcing my body to make contact with the water. The cold comes as a shock. Nothing could have prepared me for the burn of it. My head immediately numbs with pressure. Until, scrambling through the water towards Matilda, I become suddenly, crazily jubilant, yelping and splashing.

We complete four laps, and then Matilda swims back to the steps. I follow, clawing my way up after her.

Back on dry land, silted pond water running off us, we make our way towards the changing block. Matilda is silent and preoccupied. She remains silent and preoccupied as we dress, pulling clothes over damp skin, eyeing each other warily. Once in her tracksuit, she sits panting, staring down at her bare feet. A pair of trainers wait on the slatted bench beside her, but she makes no move to put them on.

Instead, she says, 'My brother tells me you used to be their nanny.'

I'm much slower than usual this morning, so it takes me longer than it should to realize that she's referring to Pitt.

And then, before I get a chance to respond: 'How long did you last?'

'Six months.'

She stares at me for a moment, eyes narrow. 'You started work at the *Mercury* immediately after that?'

'Yes. I did admin, a bit of copy tasting.'

'And then, five years later, you bring in Armstrong and his letters.'

'Yes.'

She continues to stare at me, sunlight moving on the changing room walls and across her face.

'You and Rawdon left the party together last night.'

How does she know this? Wenham? Rawdon? Matilda, I'll learn, never asks direct questions, she simply makes statements that serve as invitations to responses, so I'm unclear as to how much she wants me to elaborate, or even what's required of me here. She bends down with difficulty, drying her feet and fighting to get first her socks then her shoes on. Breathless, she pauses.

I offer to help.

She starts to wave me away, out of breath still, then changes her mind.

Kneeling, I take hold of her ankle and start feeding her tiny feet into the trainers. Crouched on the floor, I notice things I wouldn't otherwise have noticed – the telephone number written in biro across the wall just above the bench; the balled-up lilac sock, forgotten on the floor. Unfathomable details from other people's lives.

I can feel her watching me with renewed focus.

'I'm curious – how far do I have to push you before you say no?'

Unsure what territory we've strayed into, I stare up at her and hope that I'm not holding her ankle too tightly. 'I don't know.'

'Everybody has a ceiling. Limits. A line they won't cross. We're none of us bottomless.'

There's a hint of reproach in her voice.

'In my experience, most people have no idea where they end.' I drop my head again and concentrate on pushing the right foot into the other trainer. Tying the laces. 'So, they just carry on. Until they run out.'

'Your point being that you're not like everybody else.'

'I didn't mean that. I'm a nobody, I—'

'Oh, Rebecca, I think we both know that's not true.'

It's a bright day. I can hear voices from outside, bodies splashing in water.

She gets to her feet, and I pass her towel up to her. Leaving the changing room, we push through the gate with its *Men Not Allowed Beyond This Point* sign and turn in the direction of Parliament Hill rather than Highgate.

'I know everything that goes on in this family. Everything.'

We continue to walk under trees heavy with summer.

'Rawdon's my weak spot. I'm irrational about him – probably because he's the only other human being I've ever loved. It doesn't come naturally to me, love. I think you're the same.'

We're at the top of Parliament Hill. She gestures towards a bench with a view across the city, pooled in the valley below. I sit down, thinking she needs to rest, but she remains standing.

'Why lie about yourself, Rebecca, when the truth is so much more extraordinary? You've been underestimated your entire life, haven't you? We have that in common too.'

She clutches at one of my shoulders, giving it a squeeze and, shocked, I realize that she's leaving.

She walks away from the bench in the direction we've just come from. I start to get up, ready to follow, but am pulled back down.

A man's hand on my wrist.

A flickering panic that remains even after I've twisted towards him and recognized Wenham. Wordlessly, he places a folder on my knees, brushing away some debris from nearby trees that has blown onto it.

The folder has my name written across it: REBECCA SHARP.

I don't need to open it. I know what's inside.

We sit, without speaking, for some time.

Wenham's air of formality feels out of place here on top of the hill. And it seems to me that everyone who passes us looks uncomfortable. After a while, I become convinced that people are giving the bench a wider berth than necessary. Couples pull each other close, tucking themselves together and increasing their speed; mothers slide their eyes from side to side, to make sure that dawdling toddlers are within sight. Even the dawdling toddlers themselves, preoccupied by sticks and feathers and puddles from last night's rain, veer suddenly – still humming – away from the bench.

It's as if some dark, unseen force is emanating from us.

This is an unsettling thought. Strangely exhilarating, also.

I say, 'Matilda had you look into me? Run some background checks?'

'No, actually.' Wenham sounds pleased. 'It was Pitt. When you became their nanny. And he says to tell you that it was *Spartacus* the Bolshoi performed on their 1974 UK tour, not *Coppélia*.'

# WIFE
# 1999

# A Row

We've had parties before, but those were in Rawdon's Earl's Court basement – entire weekends given over to loud, long gatherings that ended with people hanging on to each other, crying and singing. Or pissing in the courtyard garden, over ferns growing out of the walls. Parties where people fell out of love, and into furniture, and everything got broken.

Tonight's party is different. There's a guest list, a dress code and chamber music. I've memorized the names of everybody coming, how many children they have, grandchildren, their names and ages. I run through them now in a low murmur as I pad backwards and forwards across the bedroom's thick carpet. There are caterers moving through the downstairs rooms. Nobody will piss in the garden, and nothing will get broken because tonight we're celebrating the *Mercury* winning Newspaper of the Year, a newspaper I'm now deputy editor of.

It's also our first party as a married couple.

'Who are you talking to?'

Rawdon has appeared without warning in the bedroom doorway – it's possible that he's been there for some time. An air of inertia hangs over him that makes me feel worried about the time suddenly. His carelessness with time, his neglect of it – he's even more of a saboteur than my mother – has this effect on me, forcing me into being the sole guardian of it in our relationship.

This is Rawdon at his most manipulative.

The more anxious I get, the more detached he becomes.

He's doing it now, staring about him through heavy-lidded eyes, head tipped back against the doorframe. Arms folded. He's in one of those moods and has been since our row last Sunday.

I check my watch – a Cartier he bought me for my birthday – in case time has played any tricks on me while I haven't been looking.

It's 6 p.m. and I can feel the pre-party noises from downstairs and the garden outside pull at me.

'Just running over the guest list again.'

'Really? It's pretty much the same as the guest list from our wedding. Imported wholesale.'

He laughs, an unkind laugh, half-heartedly attempting to push the conversation into more argumentative territory.

'Same faces,' he yawns.

I don't have the stamina for this right now, not after last weekend's row. It wasn't our first, but it grew unexpectedly in magnitude. What started out as anger about the Lizzie Saltire piece grew into jibes about tonight's party before turning into a soul-breaking barrage of grievances that must have been building for some time without us really being aware of it. Grievances that hang between us still because they can't be unspoken or unheard. The most we can hope for is that over time, they'll fade from sight and sound. I no longer feel like a newly-wed.

'Tonight's a big night. For us. The newspaper.'

He makes a squawking noise that immediately hits my nerves. 'Other way round, you mean. Surely. The newspaper, then us.'

'I want it to go . . .' I search for a word that isn't going to provoke him and land, weakly, on 'well'.

'What other direction could it possibly go in? The only potential area for error is me.'

He grins unhappily through the raft of early evening sunlight falling into the room, an admission of sadness rather than a threat.

With an effort, he shunts himself from doorframe to window, looking down at the activity in the garden for a while before lifting his head and shifting his gaze towards a more distant point.

'How's it going down there?'

'Fine. I guess.'

He's bored, but then Rawdon's often bored. His posture – every physical movement he makes, no matter how minuscule – is heavy with it. As if he might just give up and stop moving altogether at any moment.

This is the juncture we often reach, and it can go two ways from here. I can cajole him back to life. Or I can leave him out in the cold, in the hinterlands of his boredom – a place where he becomes irascible, unkind. It came as a surprise, Rawdon's unkindness. But worst of all is his unpredictability, and I can't have it tonight. The Prime Minister and his wife are coming to the party. As is the Commissioner of the Met. I need him on side. We have to stand united. Aligned. Married. King and Queen of the newsprint world. Media royalty.

I cross the room towards the window where he's now standing, inert.

The Highland cattle are watching us. They're pretty much the only things to have made it here to our Notting Hill home from the Earl's Court flat.

When the house came on the market and I told him we should buy it, he laughed in that surprised way of his, as if the fact that I might want to live on a cherry-tree-lined crescent overlooking private gardens wasn't something he had anticipated.

It troubles him, the things I want.

Think of the parties, I said. Think of the parties we could have.

Over the course of the next year, the house was emptied, gutted. Walls moved, French windows installed, the garden landscaped. Interior designer Marc Chang – son of a fisherman from Hull and a Chinese immigrant – was brought on board. He had a ridiculous waiting list, but Lily Kent saw to it that we were moved to the top almost overnight after she had an abortion I agreed to report as a miscarriage in the *Mercury*. I've kept the medical records for insurance in a room at the office that has become legendary: the darkroom.

I stand close. The closest I've dared to get all week since Sunday, when the Lizzie Saltire story broke.

### ROMP AND CIRCUMSTANCE
*The Earl of Dexter's granddaughter involved in shadowy party scene where girls took money for sex . . . petro-dollar fever . . . Lady Jane Southdown began recruiting girls she knew socially . . . English rose would do anything for the right price . . . weekend parties where sex was on the menu . . . well-bred country girl becomes part-time hooker . . . making up to £10,000 . . .*

The front-page splash was accompanied by a photograph of Lizzie without make-up, wearing an old jumper, pyjama bottoms and slippers. She had a carton of milk from the corner shop in her hand and her face was caught in a slow spasm of shock.

There, undone on an early-morning London pavement, was a Lizzie I hadn't seen in a long time. I recognized her immediately. She'd been there all along and I'd made the terrible mistake of forgetting. It *was* terrible of me. I admitted that much to myself. A lurid flash of conscience lit up everything for a moment before it went dark once more.

I knew the piece was coming, of course, but Rawdon didn't, because he was skiing with old school friends when we ran it.

'Fuck's sake, Becky – the front page? You told me it was a puff piece buried somewhere in the twenties. I gave Lizzie the heads up on this . . . this . . . whatever it is. She trusted me.'

The horror on his face that morning was vivid.

'It's news, Rawdon. Not a personal attack.'

'But it is, Becky – everything with you is personal, and you are relentless. Absolutely fucking relentless. You're obsessed. This isn't journalism, it's revenge for Lizzie setting the *Courier* up with Polo. Still.'

It was the last thing Rawdon said before storming out of the house.

I later found out that he went round to Lizzie's, where he spent the rest of the day holed up doing hopefully nothing more than taking cocaine.

I press my stomach against his buttocks, breasts into his back. He doesn't respond, but he doesn't move away either. A thin breeze catches at us through the open window. Shutting my eyes, I kiss his back between the shoulder blades.

He makes a blind grab for my left hand, which is curled into an anxious fist, and lifts it to his mouth. Soft. No longer quite so careless. No longer quite so bored. Sucking, pointedly, on two of my fingers. First one, then the other.

It's going to be all right.

I exhale as if I've been holding my breath for an entire week. The tension finally leaves my body. I've missed him. My hands creep to his shoulders and I move my mouth energetically across the fabric of his shirt.

We rarely see each other during the week, keeping the hours we do. Even though we work together and share a driver, broker the same friendships, go to the same parties and eat in the same restaurants, the only contact between us occurs when our eyes accidentally meet across the plates and glasses and candles and flower arrangements – each momentarily surprised to see the other so animated talking to strangers. The truth is, most weeks we leave nothing more than a meagre trail of co-habitation in our wake.

But the distance between us this week has been different, pushing us into new and unchartered territory. I knew Rawdon would react to the Lizzie piece, but I didn't expect him to remain this angry and preoccupied. It has left me feeling unanchored and I need Rawdon to anchor me. It's something I realized early on, in the beginning when we were warily taking hold of each other. Trying to work out where our differences lay and whether these were the sort of differences that would pull us together and keep us together, or push us apart.

Rawdon's a good person. Without him, I've discovered that I'm frightened of myself.

Down in the garden, a girl and a boy from the catering company pass a joint backwards and forwards behind one of the large bushes growing against the house. They're giggling and into each other. For a moment, they have my full attention as I hover between irritation and envy, able to smell the tail end of the joint drifting upwards. I should go down there, speak to their manager and have them sent packing, but I know that this would have a catastrophic impact on the tentative reunion currently taking place between Rawdon and me. Still, I can't resist bringing them to his attention.

'Those kids down there are smoking.'

Pushing the window up as far as it will go, he leans out in a way that makes me want to grab at his belt and hold on. Just in case.

The girl and boy, hearing the rattle of the sash, turn around.

Squinting in unison against the sinking sun, the anxiety drops away from their faces as soon as they see Rawdon. They wave. He waves back.

'Yeah,' he smiles, pulling his head slowly back inside.

And then I realize. 'You were down there with them? Smoking?'

This is what has slowed him down.

'Yeah,' he says again. 'They've got good stuff.' He sounds impressed, mulling on this for a moment. 'Anyway – isn't that what we'd be doing, if we were them, in our garden?'

His smile widens.

Rawdon often concludes conversations like this, with an attack of empathy, saying something so simple and truthful it's impossible to disagree with him.

And it always has the same effect on me. I find it as frustrating as I do beguiling. It gives him the upper hand although I'm never entirely sure why.

He turns away from the window and traces his fingers over my face, the earlier sadness replaced by a new sense of urgency. 'Let's run away together.'

He means it.

He'd be happy to leave this very moment in nothing but the clothes we're wearing.

'I tried it once,' I say. 'Running away. It was after an argument with my mother. I can't have been more than ten.'

He pulls himself up, attentive.

I tell him how I packed an old, unused suitcase from the airing cupboard with stationery, mostly. A treasured hole punch and stapler. Some Sellotape. Paperclips. As many books as I could carry. Once the suitcase was packed, I crossed the playing field separating our block of flats from the main road and waited at the bus stop. The day was slow and empty-feeling. There were two buses an hour and both went to Haversham railway station. While I sat there, the same bus passed six times. The last four times, it didn't stop. And then I realized – it wasn't the bus I was waiting for.

I stop there. I always keep a part of every story for myself, plying Rawdon with so many details that he's lulled into a false sense of security and thinks there's nothing left to tell. That he has all of me. Here's the part I keep to myself:

I wanted to be missed.

I was running away in order to be found.

It would be another eight years before I finally made it to the railway station.

And by then there was nobody left to come looking for me.

We end up in the bathroom where he closes the toilet seat with a bang, pushing his jeans down around his ankles and dropping onto it. He pulls me across him with an efficiency that unleashes a newfound energy in us both. Straddling him, my feet straining to reach the floor so that I'm able to move in the way I need to, I forget about the party. He looks happy. Then I stop worrying about how either of us looks.

This is us at our best.

By the time our first guests arrive, we're a united front once more, complicit in the endeavour that is this party. We complement each other. Me, taut with expectation. Rawdon relaxed in comparison. He not only plays his part, he plays it well.

Soon, I lose myself in the jostle of faces and rising roar of the party, a sound that I recognize for what it is: a collective admission that the evening is a success.

Such a success that I make the mistake of thinking it doesn't matter when Rawdon becomes very drunk. Or when he steals away to share more joints in the corner of the garden with the same girl as before, made bold by his attention. After catching sight of their bent heads behind a shrub, I beat a silent retreat towards the house. The sun has left the small, green space. Only the odd shaft makes its way between the houses surrounding us, highlighting the familiar and unfamiliar at random. Which is why it takes me a while to recognize George standing alone, toeing the edge of the lawn. Why it takes a little longer again to realize that he must have been watching me.

'How's it going?'

'Good, I think.'

I know it's going well and feel expansive, suddenly, with this knowledge.

'Marriage, I mean. How's marriage working out for you?'

The light's turning duskier by the second. We can still see each other clearly, but the shadows are shifting and lengthening, falling at unexpected angles that makes gestures, expressions – words, even – open to misinterpretation.

George needs to be handled with caution. Like me, he has the ability to weaponize even the smallest scrap of information. He's turned the *Courier*, where he's now deputy editor, around completely. I know – we both know – that Rawdon would be lost without him. George has always hankered after the professional respectability the Crawleys' broadsheet affords him. Keen to leave the tabloid world, the *Courier* was always his goal.

'Where's Amelia?'

Amelia, like Rosa, has managed to avoid me all night.

'Here somewhere,' he says brightly, before changing direction. 'How's the police investigation going? I saw you talking to John Newton earlier.'

'Horses. We were talking about horses.'

'Right.' George pauses long enough in the darkening garden to give a sliding smile. 'I heard that they've found more than enough evidence to build a case and that arrests are imminent?'

Several months ago, Malcolm wrote something in one of his weekly royal diary columns, published under the pseudonym Eliza Styles, Malcolm's alter ego. A small piece about one of the Princes getting injured in a rugby match at school and needing to see the royal doctor. But there was a problem: the information had been obtained from Malcolm listening in to the Prince's voicemail. This in itself would have been fine. Only in the end, the Prince decided that he didn't need to see the royal doctor after all – the injuries turned out not to be serious – and he cancelled. Malcolm wasn't aware of this. If he had got his information from a regular palace source, he would have run the whole story in his column, and nobody would have given it a second glance.

As it was, he only ran half of it. And the half he ran was enough to alert police to the fact that the royal family's phones were being hacked. This information was passed on to Special Operations branch and the *Mercury* was now being investigated for malpractice.

'Did I say that John Newton's giving me a retired police horse?'

George's smile widens. 'You didn't, no. Does the riding help?'

'With what?'

He jerks his head towards the corner of the garden. 'I guess Rawdon was pretty pissed off about the Lizzie piece?'

'I guess Amelia was pretty pissed off as well?'

This time, we exchange the same complicit smile. But he's even harder to read than usual in the faltering light, and at the first opportunity I move away from him until there's a safe distance between us.

*

It isn't until later, after everybody has gone home and we stumble, laughing, through the empty house, that I realize Rawdon's anger has returned.

I walk straight into it.

One minute, I'm steadying myself against the bedroom wall and stepping out of my shoes. The next, I'm stranded, bewildered and barefoot near the en-suite we made love in earlier, as he tears the evening to shreds.

He goes through the guest list, the house, the food, rolling the shreds into tiny paper pellets fit for nothing but spitting through straws.

'I thought you had a good time tonight. I was watching you.'

'Keeping an eye on me.' He tugs hard on his bowtie but fails to undo it. 'So, how did I do? Did I behave myself? Marks out of ten?'

I push myself away from the wall towards the bed, sitting down carefully on the edge of it. Exhausted, suddenly.

He paces around the bedroom.

'You did enjoy yourself,' I persist.

'*Enjoy* myself. You sound like my fucking nanny. Becky, nobody over the age of five enjoys themselves.'

I feel briefly helpless. 'But I saw you talking to Lily.'

'Fuck, if having a conversation with Lily is the definition of enjoyment . . .' He rolls his eyes then glances at me, suspicious, as if he might be missing the point. 'She's afraid of you.'

'She told you that?'

'She didn't have to. We spoke about Lizzie, who's afraid of you as well. So afraid she didn't show tonight.'

'Lizzie wasn't invited.'

'Yeah, she was. I invited her and she promised to come.'

'Why would she do that?'

'Because she's my friend, and I wanted to support her publicly. I was worried that if I couldn't get her to come to our party tonight, she might never go out again. Have you got any idea what it's been like for her – and her family – this week?'

As he talks, I can feel his anger giving way to the undercurrent of sadness that is always there, tugging at him.

'Look, I get that you're mad about Lizzie, I do – but it's a story that someone was going to break. If it hadn't been us, it would have been another newspaper. You know how this works.'

He drops warily onto the end of the bed. 'Lizzie said something about you and my father. Something Amelia told her.'

'Amelia?'

'About the time when you were working for them as a nanny.'

'Again? We've been over this and over this, Rawdon.'

'I know,' he concedes, still wary.

'That's what's cutting you up?'

'Fucking yes,' he yelps, jumping to his feet again. 'Have you got any idea how that makes me feel?'

'And you've got no issue with the timing of Lizzie's revelation? Because I would have some serious questions about her motivation, Rawdon. Serious. Come on!'

A fury breaks over me then, although it's the thought of Amelia that provokes it. Amelia and Lizzie locked on the sofa together in the Queen's Court flat, laughing about me. Wrongs that cannot be undone. I start hurling things at Rawdon. Anything to hand. We're alive to each other now in a way we haven't been for weeks.

Hours later, I wake up still dressed for the party, stiff and disorientated as the night before comes back to me, piecemeal. I'm able to make out a lamp lying on its side between the bed and the door in the dawn light, before falling back asleep. When I next wake, it's morning proper. The lamp is still lying on its side, the shade crushed. Did I throw it at him, or did he throw it at me? There's no sign of Rawdon, but there's blood on the pillow next to me. Slow with shock, I check myself over but there are no obvious injuries.

I find him in the kitchen trying to make tea. There's blood on his dress shirt. He looks up when I appear and tells me that he's wounded somewhere but seems pleased about this, just stopping short of a smile.

Without knowing how or why, it feels like we've entered a new stage in our relationship with this letting of blood. And Rawdon is much calmer. But then he's often like this following a row.

'Shit,' I say after a while. 'We're meant to be having lunch with the Osbornes today. We could always cancel?'

Rawdon looks outraged.

'No way. I promised Gina I'd see her vegetable garden.'

He's looking forward to lunch with the Osbornes far more than he was the party last night, I realize. And he always keeps his promises. Especially to children.


According to Amelia, the Osbornes' South London terraced house is in Deptford; according to George, it's in Greenwich. A respectable postcode, at least. Something she likes to joke with him about – his need for respectability; his caring what other people think. Either way, the entire house occupies around the same number of square metres as the kitchen in the Sedleys' Clapham mansion, which had to be sold – along with the SW3 flat – after the family's fortunes went down with Barings Bank.

It's something that bothers Amelia far less than it does George, who was unhooked, almost overnight, from everything he had married into, making him dangerously resentful. Only Amelia doesn't seem to notice this. It amazes me, the things she either fails to see or chooses to ignore. The latter, surely. Her mission is helped by the distractions of motherhood. Perhaps this is how she copes, buried deep in her unfathomable life with the children – Gina, four and Jon, two – who she adores to the exclusion of all others, even George, fattening them to the point of obesity with her energetic love.

She appears now at the front door, Jon clamped to her hip. Over the past five years, I've never once seen Amelia either not pregnant or without a child in her arms. It suits her.

Rawdon makes a fuss of the boy before he and Amelia hug, holding on to each other like the survivors of something.

I hang back, waving at her around the bulk of Rawdon. We make no move to kiss or embrace. Amelia understands, at an instinctive level – although she's afraid of probing further and discovering things that would destroy her – that I'm a threat. I don't mean her harm, but I wouldn't go out of my way to keep her from harm either. We outgrew our earlier friendship long ago. The current arrangement – made easier by my recent marriage to Rawdon – is that we tolerate each other. With a bit of effort, we could probably get back to liking each other. But neither of us has made the effort to do this, settling instead on a shuttered curiosity. And today not even that's present – because of last weekend's splash on Lizzie, and the fact I now know Amelia's been spreading rumours handed down from Rosa about Pitt and me. We're in new and far more hostile territory than we've ever been, wary of each other.

As Rawdon bundles into the house after Amelia, George emerges from the hallway's gloom, and we slide cheek against cheek. First one then the other, curved in knowing smiles. We can't help ourselves. George was made deputy editor of the *Courier* around the same time I was made deputy at the *Mercury*. An astute move on Matilda's part – the intimacy of rivalry is something we both enjoy. I wonder if Matilda foresaw this as well.

George's hand remains, warm on my back, as we squeeze our way through the crush of family life – highchairs, pushchairs, piles of shoes – into the series of tiny rooms with grubby walls. Toys crowd every surface and there's too much furniture. Flatpack, mostly, that I can't imagine George constructing – perhaps he didn't; perhaps it was Amelia. Just as it was Amelia who, with Gina's help, has planted the shade-ridden square of garden with the tomatoes and runner beans we've crossed London to see today.

It's ridiculous, us being here at all after last night's party. I tried to reschedule weeks ago, but Rawdon wouldn't hear of it, making the crazy claim that he would rather cancel the party than let Gina down, a claim that was wildly out of proportion to the occasion.

We make it to the kitchen/diner where we stand in a cluster, George looking about him, at a loss in his own home. Usually, we meet up in the country, at the gamekeeper's cottage given to us by Pitt as a wedding present. Or at the barn Dobbin bought close by in the Chilterns, something he did shortly after the Osbornes moved to Deptford/Greenwich. Dobbin is Gina and Jon's godfather, and he takes his godfatherly duties very seriously. I'm certain that the only reason he bought the barn was so that Amelia and the children would have a place to escape to. George as well, of course, but it's Amelia who remains Dobbin's primary concern. I know that it's Dobbin rather than George who accompanies her to visit John Sedley, who has lost his mind and been taken into care. According to George, it's a desperate place somewhere on the Kent coast, with ramps and stairlifts and communal spaces where time dies. He went once.

'I'd offer you a seat, but I don't know, is there even room on the floor?'

He laughs angrily before lunging for the tray of spirits and starting to pour drinks for everyone, holding the bottle a long way from the glasses, which he fills haphazardly to the brim.

'Smells good,' Rawdon announces over George's discontent.

Nobody says anything. Since when did Rawdon give a fuck about food?

George gulps at his drink and remains watchful, on the alert for anything that could be construed as condescension. Mockery.

He doesn't need to worry. In their Deptford/Greenwich terrace, Rawdon is happy. Happier than I've seen him in a long time. Especially when Gina comes tearing in from the garden. With a roar, he lifts the child through the air, dropping her, squealing and euphoric, over his shoulder in a fireman's lift.

He catches my eye. His face is wide open; he wants me to see his happiness. I feel like I'm being presented with a simple solution to something.

Amelia beams, content amidst the chaos, while George scowls, seemingly resentful of the whole bursting, blossoming lot of them. His wife. The children.

Tugging Rawdon by the hand, Gina leads him into the small walled garden, a scrap of patio obscured by some garden furniture and a sandpit. Jon's tricycle is there, along with a bucket full of naked dolls, some balding lawn and the oblong of vegetable patch that so much seems to hang on.

Rawdon and Amelia become completely absorbed as Gina and Jon proudly demonstrate how they keep the wobbly row of struggling plants watered, each with their own small watering can. I don't think Amelia ever expected to like Rawdon. But they bonded almost immediately over Gina and Jon. Now the only reason we still meet socially at all is because of Rawdon and Amelia's friendship.

Bored, George and I leave them to it and drift back into the house, where neither of us does anything helpful towards the preparation of lunch. Instead, we fall onto the sofa, our arms touching, and lean greedily over a second round of drinks.

The silence between us is laced with expectation in a way it hasn't been for a long time, everything made suddenly vivid by it – the voices in the garden, the heat of his body along my right-hand side. Then the children, Rawdon and Amelia come crashing back indoors, interrupting us.

I get to my feet.

George groans, his head falling back against the sofa. I watch as his eyes roam the ceiling for a moment before he pulls himself upright once more.

We have lunch, and afterwards go for a walk in Greenwich Park.

Rawdon sets off at a gallop through the chestnut trees at the top of the hill near the observatory. He chases Gina until she's quite literally sick with excitement, all over his jumper. Amelia tries to calm the overwrought child, who is already laughing again through her tears as she watches Rawdon remove his jumper and drop it into a nearby bin. She breaks free of her mother and runs after him, wiping at her face while her feet pummel the pavement.

'She'll sleep well tonight,' Amelia says, watching the streaking figures of Rawdon and Gina as they disappear over the hill and down the other side. Then, without looking at me, caught up in her daughter's excitement still: 'When are you two going to get around to having children? Why wait when Rawdon's so good at it.'

Her voice sounds more urgent than I think she means it to.

'Oh.' For some reason the question embarrasses me. 'I don't think we're ready.'

'Nobody ever is.'

She gives George a shy smile, searching his face for a moment. But whatever it is she sees there makes her look away, and she seeks out Rawdon and Gina again. George finally peels away from us, giving chase.

'No, I mean, I don't know if I'll ever be ready. I just can't imagine it somehow.'

We walk on towards the park gates, Amelia silent as she pushes Jon in his buggy. We're awkward at unexpectedly finding ourselves alone in each other's company.

'Listen,' I say after a while, 'I'd appreciate it if you could stop spreading rumours about me and Pitt.'

She brings the buggy to a stop outside a crowded cafe by the gates.

'Who—'

'Apparently Rosa told you, you told Lizzie and then Lizzie told Rawdon. Not a great moment. As you can imagine.'

Amelia falls silent again, pushing the buggy rhythmically backwards and forwards.

'Firstly, because they're untrue. Nothing more than malice on Rosa's part now that divorce is looking likely. I'm surprised,' I probe, trying to reach her eyes, 'I never had you down as the gossiping type.'

But Amelia keeps her head twisted away, focusing on Jon and the buggy, and this starts to madden me.

'Secondly, if Lizzie persists in spreading these rumours, I'll make her life hell.'

This is unnecessary; it's not the way to handle Amelia and not what the moment demands. I'm not even sure why I do it. To counterbalance the vague yet persistent sense I have that Amelia is in the lead. Still. Despite everything.

'Her life's already hell because of you,' Amelia mumbles,

trying to sound defiant and failing. Then, finally meeting my eyes, she adds, 'And the awful thing is, I'm glad. At last we've seen the real Rebecca Sharp. Poor Rawdon.'

By the time we get back to the house, Gina is exhausted and uncooperative. George loses his temper with her, and Amelia responds by losing her temper with George. Jon, unsettled, starts to cry and the Osbornes close in on themselves. I can't bear the thought of all of us cramming ourselves into the over-flowing house once more.

'Amelia,' I say, catching at her arm as she attempts to remove Gina's shoes, Gina herself prone on the hallway floor. 'I think we'll probably head home.'

'Oh. OK.'

Distracted, she swings from me to Rawdon, who shrugs before surging forward to tickle Gina one last time. But she's too exhausted now to respond, rubbing her face against the hall carpet.

'Rawdon,' I insist, beginning to lose my patience.

What can he possibly be getting out of any of this?

And it's then that the phone starts to ring somewhere in the house.

'Just a minute, I'll be right back,' Amelia says, carefully climbing over her daughter's prostrate body. 'It's probably Mum. Don't go without saying goodbye.'

Rawdon gives a mock salute before dropping to his knees beside Gina and whispering something in her ear.

It takes Amelia a long time to reappear. By the time she does, Rawdon is sitting cross-legged with his back against the hallway wall, Gina in his lap.

'What is it?' he says.

She doesn't come any closer. Holding on to the doorway to

the living room, she's staring at him as if waiting for him to dispute something she's just said.

Gina stops playing with Rawdon's hands and looks up, her face already crumpling as if sensing her mother's upset.

Gently disentangling himself from her, Rawdon clambers to his feet and takes hold of Amelia's arms.

'Lizzie's dead. Oh, Rawdon. She's dead.'

Later, I watch Lizzie's father on the TV in the bedroom. He's blanched-out and strangely distracted, as though speaking about his daughter's demise is something he's been put up to. Some sort of dark dare. Hollow cheeks shaking, he admonishes us, the press, for Lizzie's death, for the senseless hounding that drove his beautiful girl over the edge. It looks like an overdose, although the family has ordered an inquest. He plucks every now and then at the skin on his neck, and it takes me a while to make out the orange baling string – this is what it looks like anyway – keeping his trousers up. There are dogs in the background, and no sign of Lizzie's mother.

Lizzie was found yesterday – the day of our party – lying face down on the bedroom carpet in a flat belonging to a friend after suffocating on her own vomit. The flat was on the market. Lizzie was discovered by the estate agent and a young couple doing a viewing.

It's thought that Lizzie died on Wednesday, which means that for three days and three nights, she wasn't missed.

# A Funeral

I wake up to find myself lying among velvet cushions on the sofa with the ticklish upholstery, wearing a shirt but no under-wear. My legs are bare and cold. Sitting up, I grab a twisted pair of knickers from the coffee table as a naked George crosses the room, bare feet slapping against the floor. He reaches the windows, stretching up into the acres of curtain and tugging them open.

This wasn't meant to happen. Ever again. It started with lunch at the Ivy, at George's suggestion. A reaction on both our parts – his invitation and my acceptance of it – to Lizzie Saltire's funeral, which took place this afternoon in a honey-coloured Oxfordshire village. A funeral to which all Crawley-owned press were expressly not invited. An echo of the Princess's funeral two years ago.

Amelia was there. As was Rawdon (the only Crawley to be invited, as a friend of the family). And surprisingly Dobbin – who helped look after Lizzie during her two most recent bouts of rehab as a favour to Amelia and a way of legitimately spend-ing time with her. All three of them, I realize, were in fact busily burying Lizzie as we lay in a bruising tangle of elbows and knees on the rug in the living room.

Now she's underground and here I am, at home in the afternoon.

'This wasn't meant to happen,' I say out loud, thinking about the moment in the cab after lunch when George said to me, 'Hotel?' Thinking about the careless nod I gave, on the fringes of drunk. There was a sensuality to letting go; a sensuality I haven't felt in a long time. Then on Regent Street, I changed my mind. I didn't want to go to a hotel.

The cab drove to our Notting Hill house instead.

Careless.

George is the last thing I should have let happen.

Careless.

'I know,' he grins, triumphant.

I'd forgotten how much he likes to play the victor.

Eyes panning the room, he gives himself a few lazy strokes before padding up to the Damien Hirst, shaking his head. 'Shit, Becky. I might steal this.'

He might, I think. Money has become a problem for the disgruntled George, who spends far more than he earns.

Here in Notting Hill, however, where things are a lot less cramped and a lot less cluttered than his own home, George doesn't sulk.

Here, he stretches and preens, as if waking from a long hibernation.

He's retrieving clothing from the floor and – somehow – the fireplace, a console table and the corridor outside. He walks back into the room and stands in front of me, clutching everything he was wearing when we stepped out of the taxi and into the house. Distracted, he starts to get dressed.

I start to get dressed myself, becoming increasingly aware of the time. Mehti, our driver, is due at 7 p.m. and won't be late. He's driving me to the Oxfordshire cottage, as he does most Fridays. Only usually, he drives me straight from Wapping. I had to phone him to rearrange after lunch.

The Osbornes are spending the weekend close by in Dobbin's barn.

'What time are they expecting you?' I ask.

'I don't know. I've got to get back to Wapping first. Collect the car.'

'Forget the car,' I say, feeling momentarily reckless and then immediately regretting it. 'Mehti will be here any minute. Come with me.'

It sounds like a challenge.

We run our eyes over each other again, melancholy pulling at the fringes of the evening despite the sunshine. The outside world is suddenly audible.

'You're happy for the driver to see us leave the house together?' George probes, sounding half curious, half hopeful.

I have no idea. And anyway, it's too late.

Here's the car pulling up outside the house.

Catching roughly at my arm before I open the front door, he says, 'I don't want to lose you again, Becky.'

He doesn't believe the words he says. I don't believe them. He's just trying them on for size. This isn't the kind of declaration George is used to making. He's out of practice and it shows. Perhaps it's all he's got to offer me as repayment for the risks I've taken this afternoon – continue to take.

'I was never yours to lose. And anyway, you chose Amelia, remember?'

Squinting against the bright evening, I can see Mehti standing beneath a cherry tree, already holding the car door open.

'Mrs Crawley,' he says in the loud, excited voice he always uses to address me, eyes shifting to George as he tries to read the situation.

'Mr Osborne is coming with us.'

I slide into the back seat and the well-engineered door is shut behind me with a soft thud. George is shown around to the other side of the car.

'I should phone Emmy,' he murmurs, anxious, as he folds himself in next to me. 'Let her know I'm going to be early.'

It stings, hearing George say his wife's name. It shouldn't, but it does. A careless revelation of intimacy between them that I've taken for granted doesn't exist. It occurs to me now that I might be wrong about this. That George's feelings for his wife might be more complicated than he himself realizes. In that 'Emmy' there is an entire domestic world that holds its own against whatever it is that has happened between us this afternoon.

This thought keeps me occupied until we pass the spot on the M4 just outside Reading that Rawdon pointed out to me when we first started dating.

Pitt's driver was taking him back to school for the start of another term. Unable to bear the thought, Rawdon opened the door and threw himself out. He rolled straight onto a verge and landed with his arms caught under him, breaking a wrist. I don't know what makes me remember this now, but as we pass the spot, I find myself staring anxiously out of the window, as if expecting to see a child lying face down on the verge, thin white legs emerging from grey school shorts. A rumpled blazer. The pale face raised in triumph for a moment before the pain of the broken wrist starts to register.

Mehti parks between the Osbornes' Volvo estate and Dobbin's convertible, which has its roof down.

A voice screams, 'Daddy!' as soon as we climb out of the car.

George and I, standing on the drive, tilt our heads skywards as his daughter, Gina, appears high in the branches of an oak tree. Last summer, Rawdon decided to build a treehouse. I've never seen him as animated as he was when discussing the surprisingly detailed and technically competent plans he drew up. He was particularly proud of the hinged trapdoor, which has a rope ladder hanging from it connecting the treehouse to the earth below. The ladder, he explained, could be pulled up through the trapdoor, making unauthorized access virtually impossible.

'Keeps the enemy at bay,' he concluded.

'Who's the enemy?' I asked.

From the beginning, the cottage has meant different things to both of us. But lately for Rawdon, it has become a sanctuary. Somewhere to escape to. A bolthole where he can shut doors, draw curtains, light the stove and hunker down. Every Sunday he wakes up early and heads outside whatever the weather, putting on unwashed jeans and a filthy old wax jacket. Oblivious to the rain that turns his greying hair black once more, he chops firewood and erects fences to keep out the deer. He builds huge bonfires. And he does it all in a quiet sort of rapture that I would never have suspected him capable of when we first met.

He appears now next to Gina on the platform of the tree-house, wearing the trousers and shirt he must have worn to the funeral: a sombre-looking, outsize playmate. I can tell from the way he's waving that he has been drinking.

Dobbin's also in the treehouse. It isn't clear why he's still here. It's never particularly clear, but we've all silently come to accept – the children included – that wherever Amelia is, Dobbin is too.

'Come up!' Gina yells.

'There isn't enough room,' George yells back. 'You come down.'

Gina wrenches open the trapdoor.

'C-c-careful,' Dobbin admonishes her. 'L-l-let me go first.'

They make their way down the rope ladder, Dobbin reaching the ground and holding it steady for Gina, who jumps off the last rung onto the gravel drive, bounding immediately towards George.

'Steady on,' George warns his daughter, holding his hands out in front of him to deflect her passionate assault.

But Gina persists. Ignoring the restraining hands, she holds on tightly to her father's legs as George pats her dark head and we try not to look at each other. Seeing George with his children always makes me feel strange. Eventually, Gina steps back and starts to gabble excitedly about the treehouse, pulling on her father's arm.

'Uncle Rawdie's going to put a telescope up there, so we can spy on the people on the moon.'

George responds with patient, half-interested smiles, looking about him for a way out of all this, while Dobbin holds on to the bottom of the rope ladder in order to aid Rawdon's clumsy descent. As he stumbles to the ground, Gina gives up on her unresponsive father and goes tearing back to him. Rawdon catches her up effortlessly.

'Becky offered me a lift,' George appeals suddenly to him.

We're standing unnecessarily far apart, George and I.

Gina slides down onto the gravel drive, Rawdon looking momentarily lost as the weight of her leaves his body.

'Well, hello, George *old chum*,' he says at last, as if seeing him for the first time. Rawdon would never demean himself with an all-out attack or confrontation. These linguistic nudges are far more effective. They not only remind George that he's been rumbled, but they get under his skin – because he genuinely admires Rawdon.

Then Amelia appears at the side of the house in a black dress, trying to juggle Jon along with an improbable number of bags.

Dobbin moves to help. An awkward tussle follows as toys fall and collect around their feet.

Jon starts to cry, arms thrust out, straining towards the primary-coloured debris littering the drive.

'Becky offered me a lift,' George calls out to his wife as Jon's hysterical, snot-filled wails continue to crescendo.

Ignoring him, Amelia unpeels Jon from her hip, struggling to strap the turbulent mass of toddler into his car seat. Nobody – not even Dobbin – makes a move to help. Once she has her youngest clipped into place, she turns to face us. A sense of expectancy settles over the evening.

There are things that the situation now demands of us all. George must cross the distance separating him from his family. Amelia and I need to hug and touch cheeks even if neither of us feels like it. Dobbin and Rawdon need to load the Volvo's boot with the bags and toys they have managed to collect up between them.

At the very least, George and I must ask about the funeral.

But nobody speaks. Nobody moves.

'How was the service?' I manage at last.

Rawdon, Dobbin and Amelia glance at each other and say nothing. I think Amelia might speak. Despite looking shot to pieces, she seems poised, ready to. I stare at her.

But in the end, all she says is, 'We should go.'

'Don't leave. Stay!' Rawdon commands. He sounds panicked. 'Have another drink.'

'George, I'm ready to go.'

Amelia gets into the Volvo's passenger seat without looking at him.

Dobbin grabs the final toy from the drive, passing it to the sobbing Jon and ruffling his hair.

Gina, sensing that all is not well, has clambered unprompted into the back seat of the car. Even Rawdon's promise that a telescope will be in the treehouse the next time she comes elicits nothing more than a mute nod.

George, now occupying the driver's seat, winds down the

window. He tries blearily to think of something to say before giving up and putting the car into gear.

Dobbin gives the roof of the Osbornes' Volvo a final pat as it slides away and then gets into his own car. He leaves Rawdon and me alone, waving in the twilight. Rawdon stands at a tilt, arms folded. I've seen him fall asleep like this before. But he isn't going to fall asleep standing tonight. He's too angry.

In the kitchen there are empty beer and wine bottles. A lot for three people.

Briefly hungry, I open the fridge. There's nothing close to edible inside, only Rawdon's collection of hot sauces and more wine.

As I pour myself a glass, he lurches across the floor space between us and grabs at the cigarettes, making a show of lighting one before exhaling extravagantly.

'Are we going to talk?' he says at last, alcohol and rage making him breathless.

'We can talk, but what is there to say?'

I'm still waiting to catch up with myself, stranded between the afternoon with George that has already passed and the evening with Rawdon that is yet to come. Infidelity, I'll learn, does this. It traps you in a nowhere space. Perhaps, also, there's a part of me that's offended because Rawdon doesn't seem to sense the afternoon spent behind closed curtains with George. His lack of perception makes me angry. He doesn't know me, I tell myself. Not in the way George does, anyway.

'Seriously?' Rawdon laughs. Every now and then his left eye quivers. 'I buried my best friend today. The funeral was awful. Awful,' he repeats, his voice dropping away.

I watch him stalk over to the French windows. Outside, the trees swing in the wind and rain now streaks the glass. When did the storm start?

'Well, funerals tend to be.'

'Yeah,' he agrees, throwing his stub at the sink and then pulling another beer from the fridge, avoiding looking at me – he knows I'm talking about my mother's cremation when I was seventeen. 'Yeah, you're right.' He opens it and raises the bottle to his mouth, watching me along the length of it. 'There was the novelty aspect, at least. It isn't every day you get to see parents bury their own children. It was pretty fucking unnatural actually.'

'It's a tragedy,' I agree.

'Fuck. How do you do that?' He moves his arm through the air. A wild, sweeping movement. 'Make it all vanish? Total absolution.'

'I'm not looking for absolution, Rawdon. Lizzie died of an overdose. No matter how much you blame me, nothing's going to change that fact.'

'No? What about the relentless hounding? *Your* relentless hounding, Becky? It was enough to send anyone over the edge, but Lizzie was more fragile than most people. You wouldn't think it – the way she came across, that was just to put people off the scent.'

A sadness slips across his face. 'Something happened to her when she was a kid.'

'You know about that?'

He stares at me for what feels like a long time, and then he starts to sob, dropping a hand over his face. 'Jesus, Becky, you knew?' he mumbles messily through the tears and spread fingers. 'You knew about that?'

He doesn't ask me how I know, and as I watch him cry, the familiar kitchen starts to look and feel wrong. There is sunshine suddenly, flickering and leaf-dappled. Trapped smells that belong in a wooden bird hide on a summer afternoon, not here in an Oxfordshire cottage after dark where I no longer feel safe.

Unsteady, I pull out a bar stool.

A few minutes later, Rawdon drops down beside me, swollen-eyed, the bottle of beer caught between his legs.

The tears have had a cathartic effect on him, and when he speaks again, he sounds deflated. All anger gone.

'I'm thinking of resigning from the paper.'

I laugh, out of shock more than anything. It's a long time since Rawdon's had this effect on me. 'Why? Because of Lizzie?'

'Because of a lot of things – and, yes, because of Lizzie. I've been getting these panic attacks. In the morning, before work. Some mornings, I can barely get my shirt done up my hands are shaking so much.'

He stares expectantly at me, hoping I might have noticed his shaking hands – I haven't.

'Matilda will never let you resign,' I say, feeling the need to emphasize this and almost believing it.

'But if she does, the editorship of the *Courier* will be up for grabs.'

'Are you asking me to help persuade her?'

'Would you?'

# The Investigation

Matilda sits on the opposite side of the oval table in Meeting Room 1, her back to the aggressively blue sky filling the windows. For Pitt and me, facing her, the sunlight is inescapable. Blinded, we shift pointlessly in the chairs we were told to take. My clothes have gone limp and are sticking to me. Pitt's arm, lying across the surface of the table, looks like something left behind by a grave robber, shirtsleeve rolled back to the elbow and hand curled in a loose fist.

But it's an effort, I can tell, this affected slouch. The veins in his arm tell a different story, betraying an alertness his body is otherwise concealing. There's something else in the room as well, something I've never been aware of before in Pitt, and that's fear. He's afraid of his sister. It makes him restless. Soon, the hand uncurls, and the fingers start tapping on the table's surface.

Matilda continues to stare expectantly at us both, even though she was the one who called the meeting.

'Nice watch,' Pitt says into the silence, without looking at me.

The Cartier – Rawdon's gift to me – sends crazy darts of sunlight about the room as I lift my hand to shield my eyes, ignoring him. Pitt has seen the watch before, and I know exactly what his face is doing. Also, I have no intention of aligning myself with him. My focus is on Matilda, who only ever calls meetings to humiliate someone. Pitt and I have no choice but to sit out the heat and tension in the room while waiting for her opening gambit.

'You know that Rawdon wants to resign?' she says at last. And then, before either of us gets a chance to respond, she turns to me and adds, 'Did you put the idea in his head?'

'No. Of course not. When he told me, I said you'd never let him do it.'

She stares at me for a moment, eyes peering out from the shaded face. Then she nods and asks how I think things are going at the *Mercury*. Not the *Courier*, but the *Mercury*.

Beside me, Pitt shifts and starts to speak, but Matilda raises her hand. He slumps back in his chair, fingers drumming on the table again.

I say, 'Circulation's down.'

Pitt lets out a sound. Nothing more than air escaping his lungs.

Matilda nods again, in her brother's direction this time. 'He's running the paper into the ground.'

'Losing O'Dowd was a blow.'

O'Dowd had a breakdown following his recent divorce and has since disappeared to a gamekeeper's cottage in the Scottish Highlands. We haven't heard from him, and nobody knows if it's a short- or long-term thing.

'Yes, but the *Mercury*'s become tired,' Matilda persists. 'Don't you think it's become tired?'

This time, Pitt makes no effort to intercede. He's sitting as far back in his chair as he can, beyond my peripheral vision. But I can feel him watching me.

'Outdated, maybe.' I hesitate, searching for the right word. Worried that I might be walking into a trap. 'Ragged.'

'Ragged,' she repeats.

The sun in my eyes means it's too bright for me to make out her face, but I can tell from the tone of her voice that she's smiling.

'So, what do we need to do in order to make the *Mercury* less ragged?' She lands heavily on the word, emphasizing it.

'You need to bring more female readers on board.'

This is something that has been clear to me for a long time, but it's not what anybody else wants to hear.

'Is a lack of female readers a problem?'

Pitt lets out another round of inarticulate sounds and shifts position again, more forcibly this time.

'Circulation figures would suggest that it's a problem. And the *Mercury*'s never going to become the campaigning newspaper I know it has the potential to be without them.'

Matilda doesn't comment on this. Instead, she gets to her feet and crosses the room to a sideboard where there's a tray with bottles of water and glasses.

'Rebecca, I'm going to accept Rawdon's resignation.'

I wonder if she's told Rawdon this yet. After he came back from the meeting with her last week, he disappeared into the basement and listened to R.E.M. on his record player for hours on end. At the time, I thought it was his way of dealing with her refusal. Now, I'm not so sure.

She pours herself a glass, the sound of the water making me even more thirsty than I am already. Pitt and I watch her drink.

'I'm making George editor of the *Courier*.'

It isn't until Matilda says this that I realize how much I'd taken it for granted that I'd be given the editorship. The Crawleys' broadsheet has never interested me as much as the *Mercury*, but I was working on the premise that it would be a good dress rehearsal.

'Ha.' Pitt's single jab of laughter seems to release the tension in him.

He gets to his feet, lumbers across the room to where Matilda's standing and pours himself three glasses of water in quick, gulping succession.

I can tell from Pitt's face, his entire stance – the arms hanging, one hand still clutching an empty water glass – that he's as shocked as me. Suspicious as well. Both of us. It's a suspicion that puts me on edge.

'You're angry,' Matilda says.

'Furious, actually.' Ignoring Pitt, I address Matilda directly. 'Everything I just said about the *Mercury* is even more true of the *Courier*. Despite a brief uplift, circulation's divebombed again. It's decades out of date. And you know I'm the only person in the company capable of turning it around,' I insist, getting to my feet at last and retreating from the blinding sunlight, the room full of red spots when I move my head.

'Oh, I do.'

'So, let me do something about it. Give me the *Courier* and I'll make the shareholders happy. After the last few quarters, you owe them.'

Matilda holds a palm up in the air as if hailing me from the other side of the room.

I can feel Pitt grinning at me above the glass, which he raises to his mouth, forgetting that it's empty.

'I can't do anything from the sidelines when I have no steer, no input on editorial direction.'

'Pitt,' Matilda interrupts, 'you can go now.'

Pitt places his empty glass back on the tray, shunting himself away from the sideboard and stalking slowly across the room towards the door, which he closes behind him, leaving Matilda and me alone with the sting of his silent retreat.

The room feels much quieter suddenly. The sound of Matilda pouring another glass of water, distorting. For a moment, I think she might be about to dismiss me as well.

'The last thing we need right now is either of our newspapers in the spotlight. Our priority is to keep a low profile and get through to the other side of this court case.'

'Court case? But – I thought the consensus was that the police investigation wouldn't come to anything?'

She carries the glass across the room to where I'm standing, handing it to me and leaning back against a chair.

'The police have indicated that they won't widen the investigation to include other *Mercury* staff unless they get any direct evidence. Which they won't. Because I'm fairly certain Malcolm was operating alone. Not that Malcolm sees it that way – apparently, he's making the most outlandish threats.'

She doesn't sound angry about this. Just disconnected from it all.

'Malcolm's confused,' I counteract. 'His mother has terminal cancer and he's had to take time off to nurse her.'

Matilda's face flickers, but whatever emotion it is she's experiencing, it doesn't settle. Her features remain blank. 'Confused. Precisely.'

'Let me try talking to him.'

'You think you can do that?'

'I think I'm the only person who can, and I think you know it. You've always known it.'

Matilda breathes out a sigh.

The atmosphere in the room remains paralysed. There's almost no sense of movement now.

'Rebecca, I don't know. Is Malcolm the kind of responsibility you want at this stage in your career? You're at a real turning point right now. Far better to stay below the radar. Remain invisible.'

'I've been invisible my whole life.'

'But if you fail—'

'I don't fail.'

'It isn't the kind of failure you'd be able to come back from. I mean – there's no return ticket.'

The powder on her face has become pockmarked in the

room's heat. In order to stop staring, I try drinking the glass
of water she gave me, but I can't keep my hand steady and
water splashes over my knuckles.

'If anyone's going to approach Malcolm, I think it has to be
the *Mercury*'s editor. Given the gravity of the situation.'

'So, make me editor and solve all your problems.'

Matilda hesitates before reaching out for the door to the
meeting room, taking a tight hold of the handle.

'I'll sort Malcolm *and* send circulation through the ceiling.'

She opens the door. 'That's an offer I'll consider carefully,
Rebecca.'

# Rogue Reporter

Malcolm's Croydon home is a hopeful inter-war semi. The original features remain intact – right down to the stained-glass rising sun above the front door, something that stands it apart from the rest of the houses on this never-ending suburban street, which have mostly been converted to flats. I continue to press on the doorbell, worried that he might be out – I didn't give him any advance warning. That way, he wouldn't have time to think about recording our meeting.

Eventually, a corner of net curtain is lifted, and Malcolm's face appears. Dim. Ghostly.

Despite Pitt's attempts at communication, he looks surprised to see me. So surprised that for a moment I think he might not answer the door.

But he does, although it takes him some time to get past his own security. Since the Princess's death in a high-speed car chase two years ago, the world has become a different place for Malcolm. A much darker place. The truth is, he fell to pieces after the tragedy and has never quite managed to put himself back together again.

This is what I tell myself, anyway: he's already broken.

He stands in the partially open doorway wearing the clothes I'm used to seeing him in at work, even though he's been at home for the past week.

'I wondered who they'd send.' The eyes blink rapidly. 'So, you drew the short straw.'

'Malcolm, can I come in?'

I step into a heavily patterned hallway. Patterned carpet. Patterned walls hung with a row of Palm Sunday crosses. I follow Malcolm through the hush of illness that has taken root in the house, towards the kitchen. The air in here is only marginally less antiseptic-smelling than the hallway.

'Can I get you something to drink?'

I watch in silence as Malcolm loads a tray with three glasses of orange squash – dropping a straw from the box by the sink into one of them – and a plate of ginger snaps. Everything is put away and the kitchen surface wiped down with a J-cloth before the tray is picked up and carried into the lounge.

This room is as immaculate as the rest of the house. Not a thing out of place, apart from the hospital bed hung with equipment and the woman dying in it. Malcolm's mother has cancer, something aggressive and treatment-defying. Her face is obscured by an oxygen mask and the eyes above it are shut. Malcolm ushers me away from her, towards the dining table where parts from an Airfix Harrier Jump Jet model have been laid out. The smell of glue is strong.

He returns to his mother, leaning over her and smoothing the dyed auburn hair across the pillow before kissing her forehead.

'She's asleep,' he announces in a relieved whisper, joining me at the table.

Lowering my voice to a matching whisper, I say, 'Can we speak somewhere private?'

'Oh, I don't have any secrets from mother.'

Malcolm reaches for one of the glasses of squash, drinking it methodically. When he's finished – the corners of his mouth stained orange – he starts poking at the model to see if the glue's set. On the mantelpiece behind his shoulders there's a wooden carving of the word JESUS.

'She likes to see me busy with my models. It relaxes her.'

I slide my hands across the table, brushing his fingertips, still occupied with the model. 'I don't know how you're coping with all this, Malcolm. The stress you're under . . .'

He stares at me, but without any real focus. He's too tuned in to his mother, the intimacy between them impenetrable. Suffocating. The hiss of her breathing apparatus continues to fill the silence.

'Your juice,' he encourages me, pulling his hands away. 'And we've got biscuits, don't forget.'

I reach obediently for one of the ginger snaps and take a bite. 'Things must be so confusing right now. I mean, it's no wonder you went off-piste.'

'Your juice,' he interrupts again, pushing the glass in front of me.

I take a sip, but the sweetness makes me immediately nauseous.

'It happens. We all make mistakes. People think that we're defined by our successes, but we're not. We're defined by our mistakes. Our mistakes make us human. Matilda understands that. It's why she's happy for you to take as much time as you need.'

'Matilda?'

I glance at his mother, worried that the eyes – flickering above the oxygen mask – are about to open.

He follows my gaze, distracted.

'On full pay.' I watch as Malcolm picks up a pair of yellow-handled pliers. 'So that your mind's clear when it comes to taking the stand in court.'

The pliers are dropped back onto the table and for the first time, he loses his poise. 'Court? The investigation hasn't even finished yet.'

'Yes, but the police have seized a lot of evidence. The paper trail is vast, as is the electronic one. There *will* be arrests,

Malcolm. And then it will go to trial . . . I'm not the source of this information, merely the mouthpiece.'

At this, there's the faint clang of rings against the bars of the hospital bed as his mother wakes up, hauling at the mask on her face.

Malcolm is there in seconds, gently chastising her.

She struggles to speak, the effort of it making the blue veins on her forehead visible. Malcolm leans in close and she manages to grab hold of a handful of his shirt – mother and son clasped, briefly, in a fraught embrace – before he lowers her back onto the pillow and refits the oxygen mask. Her breathing is more laboured than before.

'You want me to plead guilty.'

He sits down carefully on the side of the bed, his face shapeless with shock as he stares around the room with its single sofa and electric organ. He once told me that his mother liked to play hymns. Hymns they would both sing along to on Sunday afternoons.

'But if I plead guilty, I'll get sentenced.'

'A reduced sentence.'

'Prison.'

'Nobody wants that, Malcolm. But given the circumstances, it's your best option. Your only option.'

When this fails to elicit any response, I allow my eyes to run over his prostrate mother. 'Look, I want to see you get through to the other side of this. You were kind to me – when I first started on the paper. You were the only person who really noticed me, and that meant a lot. I don't forget. You know that.'

'People aren't interested in kindness. It's seen as a sign of weakness, an invitation to trample.' He pauses, lost in his own thoughts.

'What we want is to put this behind us and get you back on the paper as soon as possible. How does chief reporter sound?'

'Chief reporter?'

'Chief reporter,' I assure him.

'On whose authority?'

'Mine.'

The clock on the mantelpiece strikes the hour and the shadow of a smile crosses Malcolm's face.

'You didn't draw the short straw coming here, did you, Rebecca,' he says, understanding at last. 'You volunteered.'

# MOTHER
## 2000

# Ella

I'm kneeling on the floor of the toilet cubicle, head hanging over the bowl, shoulders juddering. It's the third time I've been sick this morning. At 5 a.m., in our Notting Hill bathroom, I barely made it from shower to basin, water running off me and collecting in treacherous puddles on the bathroom floor.

At 6 a.m., Mehti had to pull over on Lower Thames Street where I made it to a black and red City of London Corporation bin. And now here, in Wapping, surrounded by pink tiles and Jeyes Fluid, unable to keep down so much as a glass of water. My palms press into either side of the cubicle as I get slowly to my feet, legs shaking, and flush the chain.

'All right, boss?'

The voice is O'Dowd's, and it comes from the other side of the cubicle door. One of the first things I did when I became editor of the *Mercury* was to bring O'Dowd back from the Scottish Highlands where he'd been growing fat and drunk on loneliness – I didn't recognize him when he showed up in the newsroom again. Despite his aggression – or maybe because of it – he's one of the best news editors I've worked with. I couldn't imagine running the paper without him.

No longer the marathon runner, these days O'Dowd grows short of breath standing still. He's short of breath now. 'Something just came in.'

I stand with my eyes shut, waiting for the last of the nausea to pass. I've learned not to ask for details on sources. 'Can't it fucking wait?'

'Not this.'

I brush down the suit I'm wearing. McQueen. Splatter-free, I note, relieved. I open the door but remain in the cubicle, staring out at O'Dowd.

'Missing child,' he pants through a smile.

'Over a hundred thousand children go missing in this country every year.'

A woman walks into the toilets, the sight of O'Dowd making little impact. There is no such thing as privacy at the *Mercury*.

'Fuck off,' he growls.

Giving him the finger, she turns and leaves, the door banging shut behind her.

'Ella Walsh. Thirteen years old.' He tips towards me, on the cusp of triumphant and keen to gauge my reaction. 'Took the dog for a walk with her sister after school and hasn't been seen since.'

'So, what do we know?'

'Details are just coming through now, and I've run some background. Nice girl. Nice family – mum, dad, sister. Went missing from a nice place.'

It's there – the familiar flicker of excitement – despite the persistent and disorientating taste of vomit in my mouth.

I can hear the mirrored heart-thump of it catching at O'Dowd's voice as well, the laboured breathing. Right now, he's all lit up in a way he hasn't been for months, and staring crazily at me. 'Thirteen years old,' he repeats. 'Cuts you up, a thing like that.'

His voice is distant-sounding as his head swings away, the eyes unable to pick out whatever it is he's searching for beyond the pink tiled walls.

'Ginger tea helps,' he says after a while. 'Well, it helped Sal. She used to get it really bad, especially with Hayley.'

His face empties. Over a cliff edge. Drunk, he talks mostly

about his daughters, who live with his ex-wife and her new husband.

'I ate bad fish last night, O'Dowd.'

Stepping past him, I wash my hands and face at the sink, ignoring the well-used bar of Imperial Leather with its network of blackened cracks. I'm certain it's been at this sink since I started at the paper in 1989.

'It's going to be hard getting access. We've been able to get through to the dad's secretary though.'

I dry my hands. 'Where are they?'

'A place called Hav-something.'

'Haversham?'

We glance at each other in the mirror. He looks impressed. 'How did you know?'

'I didn't.' And then I add, 'Lucky guess – Haversham's my hometown.'

I rarely give away personal information that's true. On the few occasions when I do, people are far more prone to doubt than when I lie. I can see the suspicion now on O'Dowd's face.

Maybe it's the way I tell the truth.

Or maybe it's the truth itself that has this effect on me.

Later, at the trial, witness testimonies will state that I was someone who never spoke about the past. Someone who appeared to have no past. And an accent that slipped, when drunk.

I try the only number O'Dowd was able to get hold of – Mr Walsh's secretary. The girl who picks up sounds young and panicked. Cagey. From the way she says his name, 'Mr Walsh', I'm guessing that she's a little in love with him. I imagine her choosing what she's going to wear to work in the morning with him in mind. This could be useful.

The name of the company is Printworks. Their premises are

on Foundry Lane Industrial Estate. I know it and tell her this. Tell her that my first job was on the *County Times*.

It keeps her on the line. I can hear the background buzz of people in the Printworks office, and the squeak of her chair as she swings from side to side.

'The phone hasn't stopped ringing,' she confides after a long pause, her voice dropping to a whisper.

'How long did you say you'd been working for Mr Walsh?'

'I didn't.' Another pause, colder than the first. 'Two years.'

'You must know him pretty well by now.'

'I guess.'

'And you must like working for him?'

'I guess. Yeah,' she adds with more enthusiasm. 'Yeah, I do. He's nice. Funny,' she carries on, warming to this.

'A funny guy, who's nice – there aren't many of those.'

She laughs.

'Make sure you hold on to him.'

Laughter turns to a fizzing giggle that falls out of range. She must be checking to see if there's anyone around to overhear the conversation.

'He's not mine to hold on to,' she whispers, guiltily.

'Maybe not, but I'm sure he appreciates you.'

'Yeah. I guess so. I mean, I get like twenty pounds of M&S vouchers at Christmas.'

'Seriously?'

'Yeah,' she breathes, pleased. 'Like I said, he's a nice guy. Why does bad stuff always happen to nice people, never the shitty ones? And Haversham of all places. I mean, *nothing* ever happens here.'

'Well, it has now. You're on the map.'

'He didn't come in today,' she says, falling out of range again. I imagine her looking towards his office, still swinging, distracted, from side to side. 'I haven't heard anything from him, so I don't know what's going on. Whether I should phone or . . . I don't know. I'm just having trouble coping with all this.'

'I feel bad, adding to your stresses. Sorry, what did you say your name was?'

'Suzie. Oh. Should I have told you that? See,' she whines, 'nobody's really telling me anything. I don't know what I'm meant to be saying. Or not saying.'

'Look, Suzie, I've taken up enough of your time and you've been really helpful. Could you give me a number I can get hold of Mr Walsh on?'

'Oh. No. I should go.'

'Suzie, wait. Wait – I'm sorry, I didn't mean to put you on the spot. It's just that my newspaper wants to launch a campaign – a nationwide missing persons campaign for Ella. You probably know this already, but the first seventy-two hours are the most critical. It's important to generate as much public awareness as possible, because that's the way police get the leads they need. Those leads slow down after the first seventy-two hours and people's memories start to fade. What I'm trying to say is – time is of the essence.' I break off here. 'I guess you've met Ella?'

'She's been in a couple of times. She seems smart,' Suzie concludes, hopeful.

As if being smart might just get Ella out of whatever scrape she's in right now.

'Well, we're going to be working with the police to help bring Ella home safely and as soon as we can.'

'Shit.' For the first time, she sounds close to tears. 'I can't believe this is happening. It's all so *real*.'

Her breathing goes funny then, and I worry that she might be asthmatic.

'Suzie, can you put me through to someone else? Is there an office manager or anyone I can talk to?'

'The office is pretty empty – we've been printing missing

person posters and most people are out putting them up across town. But I think Vivian's here. She runs things with Mr Walsh. But Mr Walsh is like the overall boss.'

'OK, that's really helpful – can you put me through to her?'

'I'll try her line now.'

'Suzie, do you use an inhaler? If you do, I want you to use it now. I want to know that you're OK.'

'OK,' she echoes, gasping.

# **Small Town**

I haven't been back to Haversham since I left at the age of eighteen with two suitcases and a ticket to London. I was expecting the town to feel even smaller than I remember, but in fact it's grown. Prospered. It starts to rain. Fat, greasy drops on the windscreen as I drive for what seems like ages, through a never-ending landscape of housing developments and roundabouts, eventually reaching a new estate on the edge of town. Turning into it, I pass dozens of identical executive homes with double garages and generous stretches of tarmac drive surrounded by fields. It's from one of these fields that Ella Walsh disappeared on Wednesday. I try to pick out the one whose crop has been flattened, destroyed by the hundreds of volunteers armed with sticks and organized by police into long rustling lines that moved through the field yesterday, in search of the missing girl. But the fields look intact as I pass, in fact everything is as it should be – apart from the missing person posters that start to appear on lampposts, fences and car windows, like Ariadne's thread, operating in reverse – guiding me into rather than out of the labyrinth. At its heart, number six Harvesters Close.

By the time I arrive the sky has cleared, and the rain-soaked gardens are drying out under a late-afternoon sun. Harvesters Close looks like a place where good lives are lived. O'Dowd's word sticks – it's nice. Ordinarily, I guess, a sun like this would have brought people out of their houses to wash cars, to plant perennials on bended knees. Ordinarily, there would be children playing. Paddling pools and bicycles. Footballs and roller skates.

But there are no children out playing today.

Ella's disappearance has catapulted the residents of Harvesters Close into a parallel world, one where reporters stand banked behind garden hedges and block driveways, and nothing is as it should be. It will be some years, I think, before children play out in this street again.

There are police officers carrying out door-to-door interviews across the new housing estate, talking to people about what they might or might not have seen.

Anything that can help them to establish a trail.

Anything that can help them to establish why it is that thirteen-year-old Ella Walsh hasn't yet made the journey home.

I step out of the car and push my way through the reporters – Shane Macalister I recognize from our own staff, although it takes him a while to recognize me back. Ignoring the shouted comments, I cross a small garden towards the Walshes' front porch – pots full of geraniums, a 'welcome' doormat and four pairs of wellingtons. I ring the doorbell.

Despite the recent rain, the air is close and I'm sweating. There are tiny black bugs – thunder bugs, my mother used to call them – stuck to my arms.

I continue to press on the bell, but nobody appears.

Earlier, I tried phoning the number Paul gave me, but there was no answer. Other numbers as well. We've got everybody working on Ella. The only thing we don't yet have is any photos of her.

The heckles and comments from behind grow louder. Word's getting around. They know who I am now.

Giving up on the bell, I start rapping on the glass panel in the front door instead.

I pull on the jacket I'm wearing, straightening it, and glance down at myself. I decided on plain trousers and flat shoes. A T-shirt.

Pushing open the letterbox, I call through, 'Hello, my name's Rebecca Sharp – I've come to help you. Can we talk about Ella?'

I keep the letterbox open with my hand.

Glancing through this tiny portal into the Walshes' world, I'm able to make out carpet and a pair of children's trainers on a mat. I can smell cake. Later, Jack Walsh will tell me that his wife, Lisa, spent most of Wednesday baking. He'll tell me that she has a small business making birthday cakes for children's parties. I'll see for myself the kitchen full of uneaten fairy cakes.

The afternoon is punctured then by a series of rising howls. Dogs. Close by.

A few minutes later two bloodhounds bound onto the porch, jumping up and sniffing at me. A roar of laughter goes up from the pack of reporters as I attempt to call off the dogs, but they only fall back when a man's voice yells at them. With a whine they sit flanking me, panting and expectant as their owner appears.

'I tried the doorbell, but it isn't working.'

'I took the batteries out.' The man's eyes flicker briefly over the reporters, calling out his name, unsure what to make of it all. 'You with them?'

'Mr Walsh' – this has to be Ella's father – 'my name's Rebecca. Rebecca Sharp. I'm editor of the *Mercury*.'

He gives no indication as to whether this is a good or bad thing. And in any case, before he has time to respond, the front door opens.

A woman appears, arms folded across her narrow frame and flat eyes fixed on me. From a room behind her comes the sound of a TV, high-pitched and animated.

'Sorry, Mr Walsh, but if she's who I think she is, she can't come in. No media allowed.'

Family liaison. A relatively new role in the police force, so she won't have much experience.

'Doesn't matter who she is,' Mr Walsh interrupts, pushing past the woman, a sweat patch like a Rorschach test across his T-shirt. 'This is my fucking house.'

The dogs leap after him, brushing against the FLO, who is clearly terrified of them. Taking advantage of her terror and the general commotion, I step inside without waiting to be invited.

# 6 Harvesters Close

A dark-haired girl appears carrying a puppy over her shoulder; a miniature version of the two older dogs still prowling around the hallway, taking thrusting sniffs at me. But it isn't the puppy I'm interested in; it's the girl who holds my attention. She's pretty. More than pretty – the promise of real beauty is taking hold. Although it's something she's clearly only just becoming aware of herself and is trying out for size; something that makes her newly shy.

There's an unnatural stillness to her as well that's at odds with her eyes. The eyes belong to a much more vibrant girl. Demanding. Happy. Healthy. Normal.

I've seen it before, this stillness, in other siblings of missing children. The stillness of the one left behind.

She goes straight to my heart.

'Ella?'

She gulps quietly at her sister's name. Nothing more than a hopeful wobble in another unbearable afternoon. The question is for her father – standing guard over a pile of missing person posters that he's just put on the hall table, his hand spread over them – but it's me she keeps her eyes on.

'Not yet, Dinkie.'

Jack Walsh sounds exhausted and does nothing to hide the fact as he crosses the hallway and stands beside his remaining daughter, throwing an arm about her shoulders – there isn't much difference in height – and pulling her against him. Holding on. He pushes his face into her hair, but his eyes are

restless, seeking out the pile of posters again. After planting a
kiss on her head, he steps away.

Dinkie's wearing pyjamas. Probably the same ones she went
to bed in on Wednesday, the night Ella disappeared. Since
then, I'm guessing no hair has been washed, no baths run, no
laundry done.

Ordinary life has been rudely and unexpectedly interrupted.

Now it's all about Ella, who is everywhere she isn't.

'That's an unusual name,' I say, crossing the carpeted hallway towards the girl.

I have no idea how old she is, I realize. Everyone's focus
has been on Ella. Dinkie was referenced simply as the sister. I
didn't think to ask for any details, and this was an oversight.
Up close, she seems older than eleven, which is the age I first
took her to be. It's as if the shock of Ella's disappearance has
made her retreat, fall back to a safer age. A time when there
weren't strangers in her house. Or pictures of her sister on
every lamppost for miles around.

She glances at her father, then at the FLO lurking by the
front door, and then back at me.

I smile, patient.

Barely moving her mouth, she says, 'It's because I was so
small when I was born. Almost too small.'

She sounds pleased about this. Pleased to be talking about
herself when all anybody's been talking about for the past
forty-eight hours is Ella.

Dinkie, I already know, was the last person to see Ella. Over
the past few days, she will have had extensive interviews,
alone, with the FLO currently filling the doorway to the TV
room, and been asked the sort of questions that will make
sleeping impossible. She will have seen her sister's bedroom
ransacked by police officers. Her parents are either medicated

or in a state of animal trauma. Everyone around her is strung out, dissolving before her eyes.

There are no adults left in her world.

We are still a long way from trust, but curiosity is taking root. As we speak, she starts to uncurl, becoming less rigid.

'Are you going to ask me questions about Ella?'

She glances again at the FLO, frightened. The woman looks almost as frightened herself. Like the Walshes, she's probably new to all this. And training – although extensive – has no doubt fallen a long way short of reality's mark. However, she's only in this world for a fixed period of time each day. At the end of her shift, she has another world to go home to. One without missing children. Whereas this is now the only world the Walshes will ever exist in. Jack Walsh – I can tell from his posture – knows this.

The frightened FLO knows this.

But Dinkie, who is the only one among us with youth on her side, is holding out. She believes it's still possible for life to go back to normal. She believes it's her right. Ella's right. Her family's right. And the effort of believing this so fiercely is making her frantic.

I run the puppy's ears through my hands, Dinkie's eyes on my nail varnish.

'The police came this morning and took all of Ella's stuff. Her private stuff. Stuff she wouldn't want anybody seeing,' she says, under the impression that I'm someone who can do something about this. There's anger in her voice.

'Well, they're just trying to do everything they can to find Ella.'

'That's right,' the FLO echoes.

Dinkie doesn't look convinced. Turning her attention back to the puppy, she says, 'Her name's Ginger – she's the reason Ella and I argued the other night.'

Dinkie's clearly keen to tell her version of events, and she won't stop talking despite the FLO's constant attempts to interrupt. I push the information she tells me into different front-page layouts, until she gets to the part where she saw Ella for the last time.

'We walked together until we got to the field but then Ella wanted to take Ginger off the lead even though Dad told us not to because she hasn't been properly trained yet. That's when we started arguing, so I turned around and came home. I just didn't want to get into trouble,' she confesses, her voice small.

I imagine her in this moment, sullen and sweating as she made her way back to 6 Harvesters Close.

'When I got home, I went upstairs, listened to some music and stuff, and forgot all about Ginger and the argument and . . .' She breaks off here, upset. I can feel the weight of the FLO's focus on us. 'Ella. I forgot all about Ella.'

'It's OK,' Jack Walsh says, absently, a hand on his daughter's head still.

She changes tack, a newfound energy in her voice suddenly as she says, 'D'you want to hold Ginger? Here.'

Before I have time to hesitate, she pours the puppy into my arms. 'She likes you.'

I feel as if a verdict's been passed.

In the lounge, the curtains are still drawn. The light that filters through touches at random on the spines of videos and a carriage clock engraved with something commemorative. There's a sofa large enough to accommodate the entire Walsh family and stray items of clothing hanging from the radiator behind it. A coffee table whose surface is obscured by more missing person posters.

Jack Walsh stands at a loss in the centre of the room.

Dinkie has finally been persuaded into the other room where the TV is still playing. The FLO, Maxine, has offered to make tea. I can hear her in the kitchen.

'Lisa yelled for Ella three times when dinner was ready.' He nods, as if trying to reassure himself of something. 'In the end, we started without her. Dinkie told us about their argument, but we only half listened. You know – kids.' He pauses. 'Have you—'

'No.'

He nods again, processing this. 'We waited. And we waited some more, and then I got angry. I went running upstairs two at a time because she's been tricky lately. You know,' he urges again. 'Teenagers.'

When he says 'tricky', I hear different things in his voice. Things he either doesn't think to or can't articulate. Blossoming. Hormonal. Confused. The truth is, Jack's afraid of his daughter, the potential of her. Fear made him angry that night. It isn't information I've asked for, but after two days of police questioning, this is clearly what Jack feels his purpose in life has become: to answer questions about Ella. And he's more than willing to split himself open and let everything he holds dear be trampled over, in case there's anything useful he might have overlooked. Useful enough to save his daughter.

'I just kept calling out her name even though her room was empty.'

I imagine him looking under the bed and in the wardrobe. Improbable places for a thirteen-year-old to hide. But perhaps he looked anyway. Hide and seek. An angry father searching for his errant daughter. Anger slipping into irritation slipping into worry slipping into panic.

'We tried her mobile, but she didn't pick up.'

'I bet she loves her mobile,' I put in here.

'Yeah,' he agrees, stepping sideways into a different conversation. A normal one. Relieved. 'We just want her to have everything the other girls at school have. I mean, we can't give her *everything*, but a phone – we can run to that.'

'So, when she didn't pick up?'

He stares at me for a moment, trying to bring himself up to speed. He has been asked to go over this a lot in the past forty-eight hours, and copies of the family's police statements have already made their way to our newsroom. But there are things I can capture by talking to him, here in Ella's home, that I'll never be able to get from statements or anything else we manage to harvest.

'Lisa rang around friends' houses. Dinkie and I went to the field, walked around it, through it. When we got back, Ella still wasn't home. The light was going then. I drove through the estate, stopping when I saw anyone to ask if they'd seen her. Then I drove through Haversham. I went on to her school.'

'Which school?'

'Chilston House,' he says, his dark, swollen face lifting.

Something snaps in me then. Suddenly I'm a stray child lost in a long afternoon, tiptoeing through other people's lives.

'Ella's got friends who board, and I thought maybe she'd gone to see them. But she wasn't at school, and it was suddenly dark, and then I had to stop the car. I had a panic attack or something. Like – I was trying to wake up and couldn't. I'd left my mobile at home, so I found a phone box and called Lisa to see if she had any news. But she didn't. Nobody had seen Ella. And now – Ella's nowhere. She's . . .'

His voice falters, threatening to break.

Difficult. Tricky. Blossoming.

So very unique.

His. All his own. He made her.

The succession of sentences each has the same lift in inton-ation at the end. As if he's hoping I might dispute them, alter the terrible truth.

'Lisa's upstairs. The doctor gave her something to knock her out. We had to call him at 4 a.m. She hadn't slept since Ella disappeared.'

He collapses onto the sofa, cut in half by a line of sunlight, an arm slung across his face. The dogs reposition themselves close to him. He gives the skin around one of their necks a hard fondle before leaning forward and taking a cigarette from the pack on the coffee table.

Once it's lit, he shuts his eyes.

I know that Jack Walsh has been up all night along with around fifty police officers, colleagues from the fire station where he volunteers and over eighty neighbours, walking through moonlit fields with his bloodhounds. Each hour that passed another hour that failed to yield his daughter.

The terror of returning home without her.

Pulling carefully at one of the missing person posters, I say, 'Can I?'

The eyes blink open, then shut again.

Unprepared for the shock of the photograph on the poster, at first I think it's Dinkie I'm looking at. That the Walshes, in their trauma, have posted pictures of the wrong daughter everywhere. Then I realize. 'Identical twins?'

Jack stares at me for a moment then lifts an arm in the air, gesturing towards the sideboard before letting it drop back into his lap. 'There are photos over there of the girls together.'

I approach the group of framed photographs. Two sisters sit in matching summer dresses, eyes bright above wide, easy smiles. Matching eyes, matching smiles, matching sisters.

'Last night, when I got back from the search, there was some-one in the kitchen. I saw her from behind – the lights weren't on – and I thought it was Ella come home. I thought, of course. What were we thinking? I watched her standing at the sink, drinking a glass of water, one foot balanced on top of the other. It made me laugh out loud, you know? The relief. The sheer bloody ordinariness of it. Like a miracle. I stood in the doorway not daring to move – and then she turned around.'

Jack hangs his head down.

I shift my eyes back to the photo. Dinkie is taller than Ella but only fractionally so. The first signs of a growing self-consciousness, a reticence, tighten the edges of Ella's smile – absent from Dinkie's. Another more recent photograph shows the slightly older pair against a backdrop of books in a uniform I recognize. The red Chilston House blazer. The eyes have become serious, the smiles cautious. Ella alone will easily hold the front page, but the fact that she's one half of a twin . . .

These are my thoughts, but not ones I can share with Jack Walsh, whose eyes are open, watching me.

He stares at the photos I've been looking at as if they too might disappear, before making a lunge for the bookshelves, almost losing his balance, and then passing me a family album.

After this he falls back onto the sofa.

Carefully, I sit down in an armchair opposite and start to turn the pages. A family shot taken on holiday somewhere. The Walshes under big blue skies, tanned and smiling, holding each other close on a rocky promontory with an ocean behind them and below, in the distance, a walled coastal city.

The small, neat blonde in the photograph must be Lisa Walsh. She's the sort of woman who looks like she takes care of herself and expects, in return, to be taken care of. I imagine her at the town's new leisure centre after dropping the girls at school. Trim and hectic in lycra. She's around the same age as me and her face is vaguely familiar. There's a chance we were at school together.

In the photograph, Jack Walsh has an arm around his wife, proud of her. The girls have arranged themselves loosely in front of their smiling parents, tipping their heads back in order to make their own smiles visible beneath the matching sun hats they're wearing.

A photogenic family.

For the briefest of moments, I feel like an interloper in a land of plenty, before continuing to turn the album's pages, fighting to conceal the awful excitement as I find the photo I've been looking for – the one that's going to launch our campaign. This is it. Here she is. Our Ella. Smiling. Open. Caught off guard in the garden one day, standing behind long grass and plucking distractedly at the hazy fronds.

I imagine the photograph cropped to a headshot, reproduced over and over again.

Ella, happily being thirteen. Until she was so rudely interrupted.

Because Ella, I know, will sell millions of miles of newsprint. We're going to have a hard time satisfying reader appetite. Even after we've filled news, features, leaders, commentary, analysis and opinion. The hot pages. The cold pages. People are going to fall for Ella. Take her to heart. Root for her. Pray for her. Candles and lanterns will be lit. Night after night, these flickering shoals will fill the skies above Haversham – Chilston House. I'll see to that.

'Let us help you, Jack,' I say. 'Let us help Ella.'

He watches me before looking away. Fixing his gaze on the empty hallway, he exhales.

For a moment, everything hangs in the balance. If he's going to ask me to leave, he'll do it now.

If I were a decent person, I'd offer to leave anyway. There are things happening here in this house that no stranger should be party to.

But I'm not a decent person.

And I grew up hungry.

He looks at his watch. 'It's been almost forty-eight hours.'

Keeping very still – I don't want to startle him – I say gently, 'Over three and a half million people read the *Mercury* every single day. Six days a week. If you give us the green light, we'll make sure that Ella goes straight to the heart of each and every one of them. Into their homes. Into their lives. Day after day. Until Ella becomes more recognizable to them than their own children. We will be tireless in our efforts to bring her home, Jack. Relentless. When I set my mind to something, I'm a fanatic. And when it comes to Ella, I'm your fanatic. Use me, Jack. Use what my paper has to offer.'

As Jack's silence continues, I worry that I've pushed too hard.

'I'll have to speak to Lisa,' he says at last.

But his face, as he swings back towards me, is wearing something it wasn't before. Belief. Hope. I put those things there.

'Of course.'

Through the ceiling above our heads there's the sound of somebody moving around. Footsteps that make the lamp-shade judder.

The woman who shuffles into the lounge is not the woman in the photograph. This woman has been bruised by the events of the past forty-eight hours; her eyes hang wide and low over swollen cheeks. She occupies all the space there is in the lounge at number 6 Harvesters Close and yet she isn't here at all.

She looks from me to Jack, seeing neither of us, pulling the sleeves of the grey sweatshirt she's wearing over her hands and constantly glancing at the mobile in her hand.

Jack stands up and crosses the space between them as she presses the heels of her hands into her eyes. She stays like that, even after he takes hold of her, sliding his chin over her head.

'Shush,' he says, and, 'Come on.' And, 'There now.' And, 'She'll come home.'

He keeps on saying things like this, murmuring promises while holding on to his silent wife, helpless in the face of her agony. The limitlessness of it. He's a provider. This is his role in the family, but right now the one thing his wife wants – her daughter, home – is the one thing he can't give her. The FLO appears with a tray of tea and puts it down on the coffee table, then hovers beside Lisa Walsh as if anticipating the need to restrain her in some way.

After a while, Lisa pulls away from Jack and glares through the late-afternoon sunlight at me.

'Who are you?'

'Rebecca. Rebecca Sharp. A friend – from the papers.'

'A friend,' she repeats, nodding aggressively before making a lunge for the pack of cigarettes on the coffee table. After several attempts she manages to light one, and exhales towards the ceiling. Her free arm, the one that isn't holding the cigarette, is wrapped tightly around her abdomen.

Jack sinks his hands into his trouser pockets. 'Lisa, Rebecca's from Haversham.'

Forcing myself to meet her gaze, I say, 'I think we were at school together. Haversham High.'

She nods in the same aggressive way as before, running the hand holding the cigarette around the back of her neck. 'D'you remember Miss Baron?'

This isn't a conversation, it's a test.

'Miss Baron. Home economics. God,' I breathe. 'Those handbags.'

'Lipstick,' Lisa counteracts, face still tight. Wary.

'Farmhouse eggs.'

This catches her off guard.

'Farmhouse eggs,' she repeats, amazed, her face relaxing.

She tries a laugh then reins herself in, her lips hardening into a line. 'Haversham High was a shithole. Vowed I'd never send my girls there. They go to Chilston House.' She gives a defiant shake of the head before becoming suddenly out of breath.

Jack rubs her back.

And in that moment, I understand Lisa Walsh.

Like me, Lisa has managed to haul herself out, to overcome. She has five bedrooms. A double garage. A dark, alluring husband. But when it comes down to it, these achievements are nothing more than trappings because now Ella's gone.

She glances at the clock as if hoping to discover that some trick has been played. 'Ella can't not be here. She can't not be here.'

The FLO closes in, ready to lead Lisa away. Back to bed; more medication, if necessary.

At the same time, Dinkie appears in the doorway.

'I'm hungry,' she announces loudly to nobody in particular, above the sound of the TV. Frightened eyes come to rest on her mother, as the puppy threads itself in an irate way through her legs, nose to the carpet, intermittently whining.

Jack walks me to the fields they've been searching. Dinkie insists on coming with us. We walk for some time before reaching the edge of the estate. Tarmac pavements and fences eventually give way to scrubby grass dotted with hawthorn bushes, the occasional magnificent oak and wild roses.

Dinkie enjoys being listened to, and I can be a very attentive listener. She keeps thrusting her arm out as she talks, pointing to the exact spot where events happened. There's the hedge where she and Ella had their first disagreement about whether to let the puppy off its lead. Here's where the argument became a row and nasty things were said.

As we reach the edge of the first field, Jack tells me there are plans to build here. I can feel what he has just said catching up with him. The implication of it. Soon, the field Ella disappeared from will itself disappear without a trace beneath yet more tarmac and concrete. Time, already against us, has just added another hurdle.

I stare out across the flattened crop, imagining Ginger, unleashed, running helter-skelter about the grass at the edge before turning and disappearing into the still-standing wheat, Ella following. And for a moment I can see her, visible from the waist up only, blazing a clear trail after the puppy until she reaches the middle of the field. Here she stops, calling out and looking around her. After this, she breaks into a run again, but in what direction? Towards the stile set in a hedge marking the boundary of the field? Onto the road beyond?

I lose sight of her then.

'Ginger found her way home, didn't she – and Ella will too,' Dinkie says, catching at Jack's hand and tugging on it. Trying to force some sort of reaction out of him.

But Jack, stupefied, has his eyes fixed on the field still.

Dinkie gives up on him and turns her attention back to me, unexpectedly slipping her hand in mine. It's hot and full of life. Her life. I can feel it, drumming through our palms as they press together.

'Ginger was home, so we thought Ella must be home,' Jack says. 'When I went up to her bedroom after she didn't come down to dinner, I was angry and forgot to knock. I just flung open the door, so hard that it banged back on its hinges. There's a dent on her bedroom wall.' He pauses. There are tears, a whole joined-up stream of them, making their way out of the corner of his eye.

'The thing is, I'm even angrier with her now than I was then, and I don't know why.' He starts to sob.

Dinkie, startled at her father's tears, looks like she might cry herself.

'We're going to bring Ella home,' I say, starting to swing Dinkie's arm gently backwards and forwards.

It's a terrible promise, one I have no right to make, but I can't help myself.

And for the first few weeks of the *Mercury*'s campaign, I really believe that our coverage of thirteen-year-old Ella Walsh's disappearance from a Sussex field might just keep the child alive. Might just bring her home. Safe.

It doesn't.

But missing children, it turns out, are good for us, and for the briefest of dark moments, I worry that I've willed it.

# Infidelity

Trish is kneeling on the floor among plastic panels and disembowelled machine parts, mending the photocopier. A set of screwdrivers are spread out on a roll across her thighs. She reaches for a small circuit board and starts to rewire it while telling me about a child her dog, Unity, saved from drowning near Kew Bridge.

It's the most animated Trish becomes – talking about her dogs.

Once she's finished, she crawls towards the photocopier and starts to refit the circuit board. She's surprisingly adept when it comes to repairing office machinery. Surprisingly adept, full stop. Something Pitt either took for granted or purposefully kept under wraps.

'Write it up,' I say, kneeling beside her and taking hold of the other side of the machine's front panel that she's trying to click back into place.

She laughs and stares at me for a moment, unblinking.

'I'm serious. No more than eight hundred words.'

Trish pushes the tools she's been using into a pile on the carpet. 'It's just something that happened.'

'We've got space on page sixteen – we need to plug it with something. What about a Star Pets column?'

Trish has become very still. 'A column?'

O'Dowd appears in the doorway then. His eyes – shifting from the photocopier, to Trish, to me – are balls of panic. His face, under the office lighting, is marbled with sweat.

He must have news about Ella.

Disappearing children are a thorny issue for O'Dowd. He's ripped up about Ella and hasn't seen his own daughters for at least three years. Not since they disappeared down the rabbit hole of his wife's second marriage and he has become too fat to follow. He's meant to see them once a month, but they always pull out at the last minute. Torn up with rage and more love than he knows how to handle, he buys gifts – misjudged; reckless; overpriced – that are returned, unopened.

O'Dowd has grown even fatter on all this unopened love. And in his angry mind, the line between Ella and his daughters is becoming blurred. He steps into the office, shutting the door behind him.

'Good news? Or bad?'

It has been twelve days since Ella disappeared.

People are beginning to fear the worst.

In the last fortnight, Ella has gone from being nowhere to everywhere. Family videos that captured her with jolts and crackles have been released into the public sphere. The photograph of her teetering girl's face, caught in the garden that day, has been reproduced over and over again. Newspapers. TV. Internet. The sides of lorries barrelling along the country's motorways.

Right now, Ella's all anybody's talking about.

Despite police criticism, the *Mercury* has launched a reader appeal offering £100,000 for any information that will lead to the discovery of Ella's whereabouts. I've given our people licence to obtain information at any cost and it has been pouring through morning editorials. Dark information from dark places. A rush of it. Everything is moving so fast it isn't possible to break things down. Unpick sources. Hold them up to the light. Because right now we're all functioning a long way from the light, running on nothing but adrenaline.

'Sussex Police have had a sighting of a body in a lake.'

I check my phone – fifteen missed calls from Lisa.

My head hurts, the pain dense and heavy behind the eyes.

Getting untidily to my feet, I feel winded and dizzy with a blanket nausea. Then I'm sick in the bin, the force of it leaving me light-headed. A banana skin bobs, buoyant, in the terrible-smelling mess.

I get to Haversham as soon as I can, but it's already late afternoon when the door to number 6 Harvesters Close is opened in a rush. Dinkie slams herself against me, her arms in the stiff school blazer wrapping themselves around my suit jacket. She clings on so hard that I'm struggling for breath by the time she finally releases me.

And then I remember.

Today was her first day back at school. Her first almost normal day in a long time. Lisa spoke to me at length about it. The patent leather shoes shining on Dinkie's feet are something she insisted on for the occasion, knowing that this time round her mother wouldn't refuse to buy them. Perhaps some small part of Dinkie's thirteen-year-old soul thinks it's worth having a missing sister if it means new patent leather slip-ons.

These days, Dinkie is rarely refused anything.

Usually the easier of the two, she has become ungovernable, Lisa confided in a whisper, looking sick with guilt at daring to criticize her one remaining daughter. More and more like Ella with every passing day.

It's as if Dinkie has taken it upon herself to become both her mother's daughters.

I run my eyes over the familiar uniform. It hasn't changed.

'How was school?'

'Great. Like, really great.' Dinkie's glowing with excitement.

'I *sooo* want to board. I'm going to ask Mum – will you ask as well? A double-pronged attack.'

It makes sense. School has become the place she would rather be. A place with timetables. Adults in charge. Other children, who don't have missing sisters. I don't blame her. If I were Dinkie, I'd rather be anywhere than 6 Harvesters Close. I'd rather be in school by a long stretch.

'Where *is* your mum?'

'She's upstairs. I haven't had tea yet,' she adds, the magnitude of the day – despite its success – catching up with her at last.

Her voice wobbles suddenly towards tears.

She doesn't mention the fact that the police are investigating reports of a body in a lake – perhaps it's been kept from her.

'OK,' I soothe. 'Let's try and get something sorted.'

The kitchen is a mess from breakfast still. Dinkie slides onto a bar stool and watches as I clear up spilt milk and scattered cereal.

'I usually have toast when I get home from school,' she says, starting to hum a tune from a TV show.

She's more than capable of getting her own toast, but Dinkie's newfound helplessness is part of her coping mechanism – this is what the family's been told by a social worker. Being ten years old again is a place Dinkie would rather be. A safer place.

Following her directions, I manage to locate bread, a plate, spreads.

'How many slices?'

She holds up two fingers and smiles.

The fridge door is covered in bits of paper held in place by magnets: swim club timetables, an uncompleted permission slip for a long-past school trip, a postcard from the Algarve, a menu from Mr Li's Chinese Takeaway.

The only thing that feels out of place in this tumult of

family life is a list of questions written in felt tip by Dinkie and positioned next to the phone. The hoax and crank calls – the Walshes put their home number on the missing person posters – started only days after Ella's disappearance. People claiming that they'd seen Ella, or that they were holding her captive and wanted money. The police advised that Dinkie compile a list of personal questions – the sort of questions only a sister could know the answers to; from information traded in girlish whispers after lights out – in order to combat the calls.

'Will you talk to Mum – about the boarding?' Dinkie says as I attempt to spread butter and jam onto her toast, arms at an angle in order to keep my sleeves clear of the debris on the bench. 'She listens to you.'

There's a tightness to her voice that makes me think she has been told about the body after all.

I put the toast in front of her, aware that there are still no sounds coming from upstairs.

'Let me have a think about it. I'll just go check on her.'

Halfway up the stairs, I catch the scent of bubble bath. Following the trail, I peer into the rooms leading off the corridor, stopping when I come to Ella's. The door is open. Lisa told me that she opens and closes Ella's curtains each day. She does this religiously. Every morning at seven, the time she usually has trouble getting Ella to wake up. And every evening at ten, when she has as much trouble getting her to go to bed. But this afternoon the curtains are still closed. Despite this – and the fact that the police have removed a lot of Ella's things – I can make out a room crowded and colourful with girlish life. Photographs and posters. Stickers. Drawings. Certificates. The odd soft toy. Bags and scarves and beaded necklaces hanging from one of the bedposts. School textbooks arranged on the shelf above the desk, whose surface is covered in make-up and stationery.

It feels as if the room is holding its breath. Waiting.

Crossing the threshold, I pull open the curtains, a hard tug on each one, angry suddenly with Lisa for not having completed her ritual. Light falls into the room and as I turn around, I'm startled to find a pair of eyes staring back at me from the pillow on Ella's bed. Ginger, the Walshes' puppy.

I carry on along the corridor until I find the Walshes' bedroom. The curtains are still drawn in here as well, the bed unmade. It smells of their marriage. Floral top notes; dark base notes. Since Ella's disappearance there have, according to Lisa, been nothing but arguments. Day after day. Night after night. Lisa and Jack scratching away at each other's insides.

The Walshes have been on TV – two *Crimewatch* appeals for information with the couple sitting side by side. Lisa came out well; the camera liked her. Jack, silent and lost, not so well. I helped fix a *Newsnight* interview, but he was shifting and distracted throughout, unable to answer direct questions, staring about as if he had no idea where he was. Lisa answered for him, bright and focused, emphasizing her daughter's name, as she has been taught to.

Everybody watching saw Lisa's hand reaching out blindly for Jack's, grasping it in an attempt to animate her unresponsive husband, bring him to life in some way.

At one point, I thought Jack was going to stand up and simply walk off set. Perhaps Lisa did as well because she was careful to keep hold of him.

'Lisa?'

No answer.

'Lisa?'

I try the closed door leading to the en-suite, but it's locked. Aware of Dinkie downstairs, I bang as firmly as I can with the palm of my hand, the anger rising again combined with an old panic.

'Lisa?'

After a while there's an eruptive splash on the other side. Gasping. The wet slap of feet across a floor and then Lisa appears, turbaned and insubstantial in the cloud of steam filling the bathroom.

'Rebecca?' she says, confused, looking like she might be about to faint. 'I think I ran the bath too hot. I need everything to hurt at the moment.'

She half sits, half falls onto the end of the bed, wrapped in a white towel, her skin flushed pink and red. The furious poise of the past few weeks has gone; her well-toned shoulders, arms, everything bends inwards, while her wet hair hangs in thick strands.

'Sorry about this.' She gestures at the unmade bed, the stack of cups and glasses on the bedside table, her mobile phone balanced on top of them. 'The place isn't usually such a mess.'

In order to curb the last traces of anger, I open the curtains in here as well, glancing at the outside world, which seems an impossibly long way away.

Lisa, swinging her head towards the window, looks momentarily offended by the sunshine now falling into the bedroom.

'D'you want me to close them again?'

'No. It's fine.'

She watches herself in the mirror opposite, as if worried her reflection might betray her in some unforeseen way. The mirror is part of a small vanity unit, covered in a sparkling and disorderly array of jewellery and make-up. I imagine the girls sitting here trying on their mother's bracelets and necklaces, experimenting with her make-up. The mirror coated in their jostling reflections; a laughing dress rehearsal for the future.

Over the past few weeks, I've seen Lisa almost every day.

Press conferences, mostly. And I've thought – how does she do it? But the press conferences, I realize suddenly, have been the more bearable part of all these unbearable days.

Which start here in this bedroom, in this house. Every day. Day after day.

She shuts her eyes against the sun. 'It wasn't Ella – the body in the lake. The police phoned about an hour ago. The dental records didn't match.'

She sounds disengaged and after a while allows herself to fall backwards onto the bed. Letting out a hard laugh, she adds, 'Listen to me, chatting about dental records.'

'Oh, Lisa . . . that's such good news. More than good news. I don't know what to say.'

I stare out of the window, across the rows of gardens, but there's no view as such. I'd forgotten this about Haversham. There's nothing for the eyes to seek out. Defeated, I drop my gaze, squinting down at the disproportionately large kennel in the Walshes' garden, designed to look like a miniature Swiss chalet.

'Nobody does.' Lisa is lying curled tidily on her side, watching me. 'I guess that's why you're here.'

She pats the bed beside her.

I perch among the duvet's rumpled dents.

She says nothing for a while and when she does start speaking, it's to tell me how she and Jack met. She was seeing somebody else, and they were about to get engaged. Jack's company was printing the engagement invitations. It was a strange time, messy and upsetting, and then everything came right. The pregnancy with Ella and Dinkie – the shock when they realized it was twins – bound them.

She stares, preoccupied, at a laundry basket in the corner of the room. 'I wasn't ready, but then maybe you're never ready.'

Turning towards me again, her eyes seek out mine.

I start to stand up – wanting suddenly to put as much distance as possible between me and Lisa Walsh – but she catches hold of my hand, pulling me back down to the bed, a sudden, energetic movement that brings her into a sitting position.

'D'you want something to drink? I'll get us something.'

With an effort, she rolls off the bed and crosses the room to a chest of drawers – her feet, still wet from the bath, leave a trail in the carpet – pulling a bottle of vodka from the bottom drawer.

The bottle's half full. She grabs at a water glass and cup, peering into them before filling both.

'I've got to drive.'

Ignoring this, she hands me the glass, dropping back onto the bed.

'Can I tell you something?'

'Anything – you know that.'

'Part of me – a tiny, tiny part of me, but still a part – was hoping that the body would be Ella.' Her voice is shallow-sounding. Without depth.

We look at each other – she's frightened. Stripped back. Horribly naked.

'At least that way, she'd be found. And we'd know. It's the not knowing, Rebecca.' Her face is briefly bottomless. 'It's killing us. Jack and me, we're running on empty.'

'Where is Jack?'

'Work. He went in after we got the phone call saying the body wasn't Ella. Not that the offices are even open, but anywhere is better than here. He shut up shop. Sent everybody home. Apparently, the staff were getting constantly harassed by the press for information. Like – *any* information. What brand of toothpaste we use kind of information. He thinks the offices must be bugged. Phone lines, anyway. We think the phone here at home's bugged as well. I saw someone go through the bins last week.'

Lisa sounds tired. All used up.

'Jack used to think he was the luckiest man alive. Always home by six on the dot. On. The. Dot,' she says again, enunciating each word so that it sounds like mockery. 'Now he'd do anything rather than come home.' At last, Lisa lifts her head, turning anxiously towards the window, as if expecting to hear her husband's car pull up outside. 'And fuck knows where he goes when he isn't here.'

Instinctively, I turn in the same direction, only now becoming aware of the rain outside, the rush of it against the glass breaking up our reflections. From downstairs, the distant sound of the telephone.

'This morning was the first morning since Ella disappeared that I forgot to send her a text – I simply forgot. What does that mean?'

She finishes her cup of vodka, glancing at my still-full glass. 'You can tell me, you know. You don't have to keep it from me.'

'Tell you what?'

'That you're pregnant.'

There's a shy curiosity in her voice as she says this.

'I'm not pregnant. I mean, I haven't done a test or anything.'

I can hear how flustered I sound, the descent towards panic.

Ignoring this, she lays a hand on my stomach. 'You don't need to do a test. Women know. We just know.'

She's right. I do know. I know because I've become afraid of myself lately in a way I haven't been since puberty, when my mother bought me my first pack of sanitary pads and told me that this was how it would be now. And then she smiled. A secretive, triumphant smile. Life and all its troubles, that smile seemed to say, was coming my way whether I liked it or not.

I stand up in order to escape the unfamiliar pressure of Lisa's hand.

Offended, she says, 'Sorry to drag you all the way here for such disappointing news. I know you're waiting for a body, and you must have thought – this is it. You've probably got the pages mocked up already.' She snorts, her voice beginning to crescendo like she's standing on the edge of a cliff. Toes thrust out over the void. Contemplating a final jump. 'Don't worry, they will find a body, it's only a matter of time,' she shouts, hysterical now. 'Everybody knows they'll find a body. In the end.'

Dinkie's standing in the doorway.

I have no idea how long she's been there. But there isn't a trace of the elation she was full of downstairs, when I first arrived. Her eyes slide between her mother and me.

'A woman just phoned.' Tentatively, she crawls onto the bed in her new shoes and lies alongside her mother. 'She said she saw Ella running around the field with the stile the day she disappeared. She's told the police as well, but she wanted us to know – in case they don't tell us immediately.'

'Another crank,' Lisa says, uninterested.

'She described the butterfly T-shirt Ella was wearing and she got the right colour shorts.'

'She could have got that information from *Crimewatch*.'

Red blotches have appeared on Dinkie's cheeks. She's full of a young person's fury at not being listened to.

After a last long look at her mother, she switches her focus to me, impatient.

'The woman said that she walked on for a bit then turned around. By the time she walked back through the field, Ella was gone. But she saw something on the road beyond the stile – a blue van pulling away. She only noticed it because there was a picture of a castle painted on the side.'

# Haversham

There was a lake in the grounds of Chilston House, stretching from the school's boat sheds and diving platform to a remote wooded area where pheasants were bred to be shot. I knew this because I'd seen blue plastic feeders beneath the trees and asked one of the groundsmen my mother was friendly with what they were used for. He told me not to go into the woods. They were on private land that didn't belong to the school, and he didn't want me getting shot, he said, winking at my mother. So I avoided the woods after this, sticking to the southern shore where there were swans and a bird hide accessed via an overgrown path, built out over the water.

I liked the bird hide with its narrow wooden benches, observation hatches and posters of local birds. Birds with names I'd never heard of, that made the world feel big. From here, I could watch – unobserved – the senior school swim squad, girls reduced to nothing more than juddering rows of rubber caps as they ploughed through the algae-ridden water while a teacher, standing on the shore with megaphone in hand, shouted instructions at them. The swim squad trained throughout the summer in the roped-off section of the lake near the jetty.

One Saturday in July, there was a man sitting on the narrow bench where I usually sat, a canvas sunhat beside him.

I'd never seen anybody in the hide before, although it was clearly used by others. There were tell-tale signs, impossible to ignore. Initials had been carved on the wooden flaps covering

the observation hatches, and the kingfisher on the poster
had been given a large penis. Executed in blue biro. Even from
behind, however, I was certain that the man now sitting on the
bench in front of me was not the artist responsible for either
the carved initials or the kingfisher's penis.

The air inside the wooden hut was close, as if all of summer
had been shut up in there. My instinct was to retreat, and I
was about to let the door close again when he turned around.
I recognized him, vaguely, and took him to be a teacher I must
have seen around school.

He smiled and said, 'Have you come to watch the birds or
the girls?'

The question hung oddly in the small, wooden hut.

He held his smile.

I remained standing in the doorway, the sun on my back. He
patted the wooden bench beside him and then turned towards
the open observation hatch again. Through it, I could see girls
emerging from the water in their red swimsuits, pulling off
caps and shaking out hair. They stood on the shore retrieving
towels that were brittle from having been over-laundered.

I was jealous of the way they held his attention, standing in
small, complicit groups, giggling and calling out to each other.
If I got the music scholarship, I'd be among them, in a red
swimsuit of my own. I felt a worm of excitement at the thought
of him watching me from in here, and was pleased when he
said, 'Do you swim?' despite the abruptness of the question.

I was still a shy, mumbling child then. It took a lot to bring
me out of my shell and I found direct questions difficult.

I nodded mutely.

'Is that a yes?' he pressured me gently, his voice vague and
faraway-sounding as he turned back to the girls on the shore.

'Yes,' I managed at last.

I'd even thought about swimming here at the lake. One

particularly stifling day, I took off my shoes and socks and
stood at the water's edge among the swans but had been
alarmed at the mud. How quickly my feet sank into it.

'See you here next week,' he said in the same faraway voice
as he stood up to leave, his tone hovering comfortably between
question and command.

It felt like a promise, and I kept it close. All week I thought
about him as the days slipped past, restless with excitement,
the secret gaining weight. Gravity. Endowing me with a stature
I was sure I'd never had before.

My mother sensed it. A few times that week, she gave me
her sliding sideways look and said, 'What's up with you?'

Half worried. Half curious.

Not enough of either.

But in the end, I didn't go back to the bird hide that weekend. Or the next. I was worried, I think, that he wouldn't be
there, and wanted to protect myself from the magnitude of
the potential disappointment. I wanted the promise between
us to remain intact.

It wasn't until the autumn that I finally went back to the
bird hide.

It was a clear September day at the start of the new term.
Hot still, but not the bottomless heat of summer.

I was late because piano practice with Mr Crisp overran,
and I thought I'd missed the swimming session. But tearing
through the nettles lining the path, I could see girls in the
water.

Out of breath from having run all the way, I burst into the
wooden hide.

He was there, but something was different. I felt it
immediately – I think I *saw* it – even though he was sitting in the
same position and on the same bench as before, I felt surprised
somehow. And with this surprise came the overwhelming

sensation of having interrupted something. It was then that I saw her. A girl the same age as me jammed uncomfortably on the floor between the bench and the observation hatches, which were open as usual. I felt a twitch of jealousy.

What was she doing down there on the floor?

Why was his left hand on her head?

There was something about his other hand that bothered me. It was on the bench beside him, held over the girl's much smaller hand. Obscuring it, so that only a thin-looking wrist could be seen. A hairband was wrapped around it, light strands of hair caught in the elastic. The details of the moment were vivid, sun-picked by the daylight making its way through the observation hatches.

He turned around then and smiled. The same slow smile I remembered from last time.

The girl shifted, a quick succession of scuffles that made dust rise, her head bobbing briefly up. I wouldn't see that face again until the nightclub all those years later. Although by then, Lizzie Saltire no longer wore her hair in plaits.

I watched as his right hand took hold of one of the girl's fingers, bending it carefully – almost tenderly – back. This is what I thought I saw.

The girl flinched and sank from view once more.

'Everything's fine. You should go.'

I knew he was lying to me. It was what enabled me to leave the bird hide and step back into the September afternoon it felt as though I had left a long time ago. But as I started to move along the nettle-lined path towards the school, relief gave way to a new and thumping sense of urgency. I needed to get help. Now.

Time was running out.

Time was suddenly of the essence.

# A Baby and a Body

This time it's different.

The other time, when I was eighteen, I sat feeling torpedoed in a large waiting room full of girls and hard plastic chairs, our eyes taking shifty pokes at each other. When a girl was called, she disappeared down a blue corridor – everything was blue: blue linoleum, blue walls, blue curtains, blue gowns – and she didn't come back. The exit was elsewhere. I don't remember having to wait long for my turn. Everything happened with a muffled efficiency, and soon I was standing semi-naked under a blue gown, a draught blowing onto my bare legs beneath the cubicle's blue curtains. Beyond the cubicle, there were masked professionals and metal implements that clattered. People tried to be kind, but by this point the only thing I could focus on was the pain. Would the procedure, as everybody kept referring to it, hurt? I don't remember and my body has no memory of it either.

But this time, it's different. I feel cocooned. Money does that, it creates a hush around you. Phones ring at a distance. Voices become indistinct. Footsteps vanish. Money takes away the corners, making everything softer. Here, the surfaces are so soft and the colour scheme so far from blue that it hardly feels like a clinic at all. There are framed reproductions on the walls – a lot of Rothkos and Kandinskys. Nobody is in a hurry, and there are no traces of any medical smells in the room where I lie waiting for the consultant to come back.

The couch is comfortable. Everything in this padded world

is comfortable. Unable to remember when I last lay down like this during the afternoon, I feel myself start to drift off before being woken by the consultant's hand on my shoulder.

Patients often fall asleep, she reassures me, asking if I'm ready for the ultrasound scan. This is standard procedure and something we spoke about, but for some reason it catches me out.

Perhaps sensing this, she lays her hand on my arm again and gently, precisely, talks me through what's going to happen. The gel she will put on my stomach might feel cold. The screen will be angled so that I can't see it – although, if I do change my mind and decide that I want to see after all, this will be turned towards me. I can change my mind at any time. About anything. I'm in control. The voice becomes a touch less soothing. More emphatic. She wants me to know this, particularly. She's sitting very close on a small stool. I watch her mouth move over the words and wonder if she has children. When she finishes speaking, the hand is removed from my arm, leaving that part of my body colder than the rest.

Until she applies the gel.

'Twelve weeks. You're around twelve weeks.' She remains focused on the screen. 'Would you like to see?'

My phone starts ringing then. Instinctively, I sit up.

'Is that a yes?'

She starts turning the screen towards me, and before I'm aware of it my eyes are sliding over grainy flickers, already making sense of it. The outline of new life. 'No,' I try not to yell.

Already I'm standing, the gown sticking to the gel covering my stomach. I pad, barefoot, to the armchair in the corner of the room where I left my clothes and bag, fishing around for the ringing phone, irate.

Finally laying hands on it, I sit in the armchair staring down at my bare feet on the consultant's carpet. I listen to O'Dowd's voice telling me that a body has been found in woodland to the north of Haversham, close to the airport.

'Ella?' I whisper into the phone, holding it tight with both hands.

It's some time before O'Dowd speaks again. 'Yes.'

Later, when the police release their statement, they will say that Ella's body was discovered in its shallow woodland grave, unclothed. The body will be identified from dental records. It will be another two weeks before one of Ella's shoes is found beside a bus shelter in a nearby village.

But this detail has been withheld from Lisa for now, to protect her, and when she phones – I'm still standing in my hospital gown – the only thing she wants to talk about is the state Ella's clothes must be in, sounding ashamed, as if it reflects badly on her in some way. As a mother. She tells me that she's asked the police to send her Ella's clothes – the yellow butterfly T-shirt and the shorts, so that she can wash them – they must be filthy by now. But they're unable to do this. She can't understand why they won't send her Ella's clothes. After everything, she just can't understand it.

The consultant sits watching me, her left hand still holding the screen, which has gone blank.

The investigation has just become a murder inquiry.


At home that evening, I walk down the hallway towards the kitchen, following an unfamiliar trail of debris like crumbs through a forest – a child's socks, shoes that have been hastily discarded and tumbled on their sides, abandoned toys strewn haphazardly across the floor, the remains of a biscuit. There are screams and laughter and the smell of cooked food in the air.

For a moment, I'm close to hungry.

And worried that I've strayed into the wrong house. The wrong life.

The debris increases in the kitchen – a child's car seat sits on the table, and beside this, an open box of wet wipes. Handbag. Changing bag. Sprawl of car keys. Drinking cup. Plastic bowl. Spaghetti and puddles of tomato sauce, hardening under the early evening sunshine. Wine glasses – three of them. A cheese grater and a lump of Parmesan that couldn't possibly have been bought by either me or Rawdon.

Stunned, I turn my back on it all, open the fridge and pull out a carton of milk.

Everything feels brighter than usual, but then I haven't been home during daylight hours for months. I'm used to navigating the house in the dark. Often, I don't bother to turn on the lights until I'm upstairs. And then, only once the curtains have been drawn. Increasingly I've felt watched. Dark windows make me nervous. Especially in illuminated rooms when they fill with reflections. Echoes. Things that have no business being there.

A month ago, and without telling Rawdon, I had the house swept for bugs.

Unscrewing the lid of the milk carton, I take a sniff and then start to drink.

'Becky?'

I spin around, spilling milk over my feet. 'Shit, Rawdon. Where did you come from?'

'I live here.'

He's standing in the middle of the kitchen holding a football. His eyes graze the carton of milk. My coat. Shoes. He's barefoot and breathless, and he isn't pleased to see me – this is something else I notice. In fact, he looks caught out – as if whatever I've interrupted is in some way illicit.

We almost never run into each other like this. His work on the Prime Minister's communications team means that he's out of the house almost as much as I am.

As if on cue, he says, 'What are you doing home?'

'I live here too.'

'Oh. Yeah,' he agrees, nonplussed, crouching unsteadily while rummaging in the cabinet where the spirits and mixers are kept. The football rolls around the floor beside him.

Watching him, I realize that I have no idea when we were last in the kitchen together. But I'd like him to be surprised that I'm home early, for this to mean something to him.

'I'm making martinis – want one?'

He loses his balance then, laughing surreptitiously to himself as he tries to stand upright, a bottle of gin in one hand, vermouth in the other.

'What's with the football?' I ask.

I know I've made it sound like an accusation, puncturing our exchange with the sort of low-level hostility that can transform a meaningless conversation like this into a far more meaningful row. I can feel myself pushing us towards it now. A corner we'll have to fight to get out of, scratching and drawing blood.

'It's Jon's.' Rawdon passes an arm across his face, wiping away the sweat. 'Amelia's here.'

He turns his back on me and starts making the martinis, dribbling the football as he moves about the kitchen.

Of course. Today is the anniversary of Lizzie Saltire's funeral. Every year, he, Amelia and Dobbin – who we see a lot of these days because he works with Rawdon at Number 10 – mark it by meeting in Greenwich, Bermondsey or here.

Did he remind me, and I've forgotten? The truth dawns on me. He didn't even think to mention it.

'I wasn't expecting you home so early.' He eyes the pans, adding, 'We had spaghetti.'

We stare at each other as if he has just said something shocking. He would have preferred to keep the details of their commemorative lunch secret, I realize, for no other reason than the fact that Rawdon's become protective of his pleasures these days. As if sharing them with me might accelerate their disintegration in some way.

'You cooked?'

Propped against the central island, he gives the cocktail mixer a few vigorous shakes. 'No, Amelia cooked.'

Without knowing why, I laugh. A jittery laugh. The sort that might run away with itself. It has been a long day and I'm not at the end of it yet. I feel thin suddenly. And in an attempt to conceal this, I cross the kitchen to the bench opposite, leaning heavily against it. The milk carton is still in my hand.

Taking three glasses from the cupboard, Rawdon fills each of them in turn with martini before pushing one across the island towards me.

'You look like you could do with it – bad day?'

We no longer ask each other personal questions and he seems as startled as me to hear himself break the habit.

Now would be the time to tell him about Ella, but I don't do this. Why not? So that I can hold him to account later for not having somehow instinctively known? It's unreasonable, but I can't help myself.

Ignoring the martini, I finish the milk, aware of Rawdon's eyes on the carton.

'You could say that,' I murmur at last, before making my way towards the back of the house where the doors leading into the garden are open. There are scuffs and tears from the football game on the otherwise immaculate lawn – a lawn that Amelia's lying in the middle of, stretched out with unselfconscious abandon.

Gina's singing to herself and cartwheeling in a circle around her horizontal mother, as if casting a protective spell – hair flying, as happy upside down as upright. The soles of her feet are grass-stained, her thin arms effortlessly supporting her weight.

George's daughter has become a lithe six-year-old, obsessed with winning medals and trophies in gymnastics competitions. Amelia spends her weekends driving around the country from one fixture to another.

I watch, transfixed. Until she stops, mid-cartwheel, arms raised in the air, right leg thrust out.

Amelia, sitting up, raises a hand over her eyes even though the sun's left the garden. She gets clumsily to her feet, shaking out the skirt she's wearing. 'Hi, Rebecca.'

We kiss. As if we're pleased to see each other.

Amelia is better at this than I am.

She smells of sunshine and gardens and time suspended. She's less clear-cut these days, not so athletic. Her clothes, as always, are a mess. And yet there's still a part of me that feels inconsequential next to her.

Nobody else has this effect on me.

Gina, concluding her final circumference of the garden, crashes into her mother, wrapping her arms around her in an extravagant embrace.

'Where's Dobbin?'

'He had a dinner date.'

'Business or pleasure?'

I don't care either way and yet for some unaccountable reason feel like hurting her suddenly.

Amelia blushes. Then laughs. 'I haven't heard that expression in ages, do people still use it?'

And just like that, she has the upper hand, something that often happens during our sporadic exchanges. I've never worked out whether it's intentional on her part or accidental. But either way, it leaves me with the same feeling of having been somehow dismissed.

'We should go,' she says.

'Rawdon's made martinis.'

'Oh, that's sweet. Still, we should probably go,' she says again, keeping a tight hold of her daughter in the shaded garden.

Gina throws a smile straight through me to Rawdon. He has appeared with Jon in his arms, instead of the promised martinis. The child is half asleep, curled fists batting at his face as he attempts to wake himself up. He twists his head trying to get his bearings, instinctively seeking his mother and struggling out of Rawdon's arms towards her.

'I found him asleep on the sofa.'

'Oh my god, I completely forgot Jon.'

'Watch me!' Gina commands before setting herself in motion again.

Once he has relinquished Jon, Rawdon opens his arms and catches the cartwheeling Gina. A laughing bundle of man and girl, they disappear inside, followed by Amelia, who starts to gather their stuff together with her one free arm. Watching them all as they thread their way in silent syncopation between kitchen and hallway, I feel like the interloper in my own home. And then something becomes clear that should have been clear a long time ago. Amelia's familiarity with our house, her children's too – they've been here before. Many times.

'There,' she pronounces at last, laden with children and bags as the small gaggle of Osbornes gather by the front door. 'Sorry to leave you with all the mess.'

She staggers cheerfully towards the Volvo parked outside, which I missed earlier, Rawdon bringing up the rear with yet more bags. Chatting easily together. And then something else becomes clear that should have been clear a long time ago. Rawdon talks to Amelia. Shares things with her before he shares them with me. Amelia possibly knows things I don't.

I remain at the top of the steps.

Eventually car doors are slammed shut. Windows put down. The roof of the car given an encouraging pat by Rawdon, standing kerbside.

'You look well, Rebecca,' Amelia calls out unexpectedly then. 'Positively blooming. Not pregnant, are you?'

She waves, grinning, and the car pulls away.

Leaving Rawdon alone on the cherry-stained pavement, arm raised.

Rawdon makes a clattering attempt at tidying the kitchen. Pushing plates into the dishwasher. Scraping and emptying pans.

'Emmy forgot Jon's cup.' He picks up the lime-green beaker and stares at it for a moment. 'Can this go in the dishwasher?'

Without waiting for an answer, he drops the cup onto the haphazard stack inside the machine, puts in a tablet then switches it on. Washing his hands, he turns to face me while drying them with a tea towel.

'You're happy. Amelia makes you happy.'

'Her children make me happy.' He throws the tea towel onto the surface behind him. The slouch has gone. 'Children make me happy.'

'They make Amelia happy as well, so why not have a couple more together?'

'Because I don't want children with Amelia. I want children with you. Only you don't like children much, do you? Unless they're missing, of course.'

'Are we talking about Ella?'

'Ella's all we talk about, Becky.' He looks away, weary, suddenly not really in the room.

'I'm all she's got, Rawdon.'

He yawns. 'Shit, you really believe that, don't you? She has parents.'

Without thinking, I grab the almost empty milk carton I left on the surface earlier and throw it at him.

Rawdon lets out a single loud laugh. 'Let's go!' he yells, grinning and triumphant. There are streaks of milk across the surface of his T-shirt that he glances at but doesn't bother to wipe away.

Suddenly, we're alive to each other. Angry is how we connect. Angry, I notice things about Rawdon I wouldn't otherwise have noticed: his hair is going grey around the temples; his jawline has become slack. But noting these supposed defects, I feel an attraction towards him I haven't felt in ages. More than attraction. Something much deeper. Grounding. I want him to take hold of me, but don't know how to ask him to do this. His failure to read my mind feels like rejection, so I keep my distance.

There's a puddle of milk growing on the kitchen floor where the carton has come to rest.

'Since launching the campaign to bring Ella home, circulation's gone up to almost four million.'

He starts to clap, flinging his arms towards me as he speaks. His voice switches, suddenly, to perpetual loud. 'Yes, and there we have it! The real reason for all of this. Circulation figures.'

I leave the kitchen, walking through the puddle of milk before I can stop myself, trailing white footprints into the hallway. Rawdon follows.

'Where are you going? We only just got started.'

'To bed. I'm tired.'

'So am I, Becky. So very, very tired.'

At the foot of the stairs, I stop, turning to face him again. His eyes are bright in the gloom.

'Ella's body was found today.'

Keeping a hold of the banister, I slide onto the bottom step, wrapping the other arm around my stomach.

Without a word, Rawdon sits down beside me. I drop my head onto his shoulder.

When my phone starts ringing, he says, 'Leave it. Becky, just leave it.'

He takes hold of my hand and we remain pressed close. Like children, the two of us – children who have made a creeping, late-night descent in order to spy on the unsuspecting grown-ups downstairs.

'She was found by a group of ramblers.'

I imagine them – this group – passing through the woodland in twos and threes, their light chatter trailing them until they discover the girl lying buried in last autumn's leaves, staring up at the underbelly of aeroplanes passing overhead. One too many bodies in the damp, secretive undergrowth that day.

'Hey, you did everything you could,' he says, wiping at my cheeks with his thumb.

'It isn't that. This isn't about Ella,' I sniff. Knowing then what I've known all along – that I'm keeping the baby. 'I'm frightened.'

Instinctively, he glances down at my arm as I sit hunched over it.

'Becky?'

His face for a moment is unbearably naked, cut through with a reverence that hasn't been there for a long time. Not since our beginning when we would arrive home together in the back of taxis, loud and eager, unable to keep our hands to ourselves; silently mouthing filthy things at each other across the wide berth of seat.

I've missed him looking at me like this.

'I'm pregnant.'

# Manhunt

The hunt for Ella's killer is on and we're all feeling the pressure. It's building now around the violently white table. Oval, like a two-dimensional egg. Two of the meeting room's walls are floor-to-ceiling glass. One overlooks the atrium and the other has views into the newsroom. Too much light. It makes the room feel floodlit and a fight's already broken out between News and Features. Stationery and empty coffee cups have been thrown.

'OK!' I shout. 'We need to talk about the name and shame campaign: Ella's Law.'

The recently appointed head of news, Shane Macalister, sits, arms crossed, on the edge of the table, a foot balanced on his knee, studying the sole of his shoe. He's young. Fast. Ambitious. Talented. A background check carried out by Paul revealed that he's also a high-ranking member of the Magic Circle – in his spare time, he likes to pull rabbits from hats.

'I think we should hold back on the campaign.'

He watches me while keeping hold of his shoe.

I don't like to be challenged. It makes me flush. Immediately, I feel undermined; a forgery, exposed. I won't forget this.

'Why would we do that? Why would we do that when we now know that since Ella's abduction, Sussex Police have been systematically interviewing all known paedophiles and sex offenders on file in the area?' The file I'm talking about is the poorly coordinated, badly managed List 99, the secret register of those barred from working with children by the Department of Education and Skills that the *Mercury* is campaigning to permit parents access to. 'If Lisa and Jack had had access to this register, their daughter might still be alive,' I remind him, letting the word 'alive' hang in the bright white room, my voice uneven with rage. Soon, my hands will start to shake. To counteract this, I grip the back of Shane's empty chair.

But the room has fallen silent. People – even O'Dowd, who I brought back from the dead, and who's ready to die for me – are going to wait and see how this plays out.

Shane continues to watch me, his bent knee jolting rhythmically up and down.

'We've already revealed the names and addresses of all paedophiles living within a ten-mile radius of Ella's house. The decision was to go national with this. So, we carry on – we said we'd hit them hard,' I remind the room. 'Publish photographs. Personal details. Look, the campaign was always going to be contentious. I get that.'

'But we're not even getting the facts straight. There have been cases of mistaken identity.'

It's then that Malcolm speaks. 'Shane's got a point.'

I catch him looking across the room and wonder why it is that he wants to impress Macalister. Why it is that he has become unexpectedly dogged in his reporting since his return to work (he got a six-month suspended sentence for pleading guilty). Relentless, even – I often come in to find him asleep on one of the sofas in reception. A wash of grey – grey hair, grey skin, grey eyes – for the first time in a long career, Malcolm has earned himself the accolade of a nickname. Nosferatu. Although he's still chasing the promotion to chief reporter that we promised him. We didn't make good on that. Worse, when he returned, I moved him to the news desk. Now I wonder if Malcolm's going to become a problem.

He's standing at the back of the room next to a flip chart

I've never seen anybody use, a cryptic message written across it in green marker pen: *One random act of kindness.*

'What if Ella's death was completely avoidable?'

'Portsmouth is on fire. You've got lynch mobs roaming the streets hunting these men down.' Shane, again.

At last, O'Dowd rears. 'Well, fucking yeah. I fucking hope so. When I think of that little girl . . . That little—' There are beads of sweat on his forehead. 'People need someone to loathe,' he bawls. 'How fucking good does it feel to loathe these fucks?'

'*You* need to get your fucking facts straight, Shane,' I jump in, raising my voice. 'The so-called lynch mob is a group of mothers from an impoverished housing estate who took to the streets to protest. What most of the media – apart from us – has failed to report is what these mothers discovered: namely that the man they've been complaining to the authorities about for years is a paedophile with fourteen convictions for raping and abusing young boys between the ages of four and nine. But nobody listened. Nobody ever listens.'

Ignoring Shane and Malcolm, I turn to the room at large.

'Hands up if you're a parent.'

The hands start to shoot up. At least two thirds of the room.

'Tell me something – if I were to give you the names and addresses of all known paedophiles living within a ten-mile radius of your home, is that information you'd be interested in having?'

At this the room breaks loose with a roar.

'Because here's the bottom line. The absolute bottom line. As parents, surely you'd want to know if there was a convicted paedophile living next door?'

Everybody's suddenly getting to their feet, chairs tipping and falling to the floor. Tensions have been running too high for too long. O'Dowd makes straight for Shane Macalister. Rage and muscle memory send him sprinting through the bank of

section editors and reporters, tripping over fallen chairs. He
slams himself into Shane. More for support, initially, than
anything else. But he soon finds his balance, grasping at the
younger man as if about to break him into pieces. Shane
struggles. Clamped together, they move towards the window
overlooking the atrium. O'Dowd, surefooted and gasping.
Shane, trying to break away as he understands – too late – the
choreography of O'Dowd's intentions.

The window has been opened and O'Dowd is attempting to
feed Shane through it. Shane, made slow by his own disbelief,
tries to catch at the window's frame.

'Things have probably gone far enough,' I say loudly, as
Shane's head and arms appear – upside down – on the other
side of the glass, his hands grabbing at the window's sheer
surface, frantic now. He lets out a series of screams, swallowed
by the cheering crowd.

Trish puts her head around the door then, grinning at the
mayhem. 'I've got the PM's wife on the phone.'

Back in my office, I listen as the Prime Minister's wife tells
me that she isn't able to endorse our campaign, Ella's Law,
permitting parents access to List 99. After all. That her husband, the Prime Minister, isn't able to support the campaign
in Parliament. After all.

Nervous, her excuses come out in a rushed gabble. Teeth-
filled sentences. Traces of an old impediment that made a
good part of her childhood hell, only to be cured by ambition. First, speech therapy. Then, elocution lessons. Drunken
confessions I collected at a birthday party held at Chequers,
the Prime Minister's country residence. Along with the bleary,
early hours admission that, no matter what she spent on hair
and skincare products, she was convinced the smell of the
chip shop hung about her still. The chip shop she grew up in,

working alongside both her parents until the day she left for Oxford.

Not only that, but she hopes she might be able to persuade me to tone things down. Back off. There have been – she tries to find the right word – issues with the campaign currently igniting our nation.

Like one of our people confusing a paediatrician for a paedophile and publishing his name in the paper. His flat getting burnt down. Those kinds of issues.

'Mistakes have been made,' I admit, 'but you know me – I'm not going to stop. This isn't going away. This is Ella we're talking about.'

'Rebecca, the police haven't made any arrests yet. This could go off in any direction. The campaign could look seriously misguided.'

'You're pregnant with your fourth child!' I yell. I'm beyond cajoling her. These days, I don't have time. 'This is exactly the campaign you should be getting behind.'

I ring off before she has a chance to respond, turning to Trish.

'She's not backing the campaign. Neither is the PM.'

'So, it's too late to send this to Number 10?'

Trish and I stand contemplating the cot that was delivered this morning, its bare mattress empty-looking, the vital component missing. She has a roll of Sellotape in her hands and a stack of today's *Mercury* – the front page covered in photographs of known paedophiles, the headline 'Welcome to the Paedo-hood' – on the floor by her feet.

'It's never too late. Do it,' I say. 'Wrap the whole thing in newsprint and have it delivered.'

She uses the edge of my desk to lower herself to her knees and shuffles through the stack of newspapers, pulling out the front page of each, tearing off strips of Sellotape with her teeth and sticking them to the cot's frame while humming 'I've Got a Little List' from the Wandsworth Amateur Operatic production of *The Mikado* that she's currently starring in.

I kneel beside her to help, reaching the floor as the office door opens.

George is standing there. His eyes shift from the cot, to Trish, to me. 'You're really going ahead with this?'

'We're just finishing up – then getting it couriered over to Number 10,' Trish puts in loyally.

'You're in the wrong office,' I add, still on my knees.

Smiling, George slides around the door, letting it shut behind him.

'I heard that the PM isn't interested in supporting the Ella's Law campaign.'

'You heard fast.'

'You're not going to get any traction with him, Becky.'

'So, that's why the *Courier* isn't joining the campaign.'

I get untidily to my feet, feeling winded.

I'm aware of Trish struggling to make herself vertical again as well.

'Coffee?' she exhales at last.

I nod, wait for her to leave the room then turn back to George, who's sitting at my desk idly opening and shutting drawers.

'Ever since Ella was reported missing, Sussex Police have been interviewing convicted paedophiles with a history of abusing and abducting children. All the loopholes and inconsistencies in the 1997 Sex Offenders Act have left these men totally unmonitored by any authority. What I'm saying, George, is that Ella was a tragedy waiting to happen. Doesn't that bother you?'

I'm not angry yet – despite the fact that George is rifling through my desk. I hold on tightly to my sentences. Breathing in the right places. Pausing in the right places. Emphasizing the consonants, as my voice coach taught me. It's a delivery I've perfected over the years. Lectures. Award ceremonies. Press conferences. Boardrooms full of men. Impassioned but rational. A voice that will make my audience think I'm informed. Sane. Sanity is important. Because at the end of the day, there's no such thing as an angry woman. Only a madwoman. We're all just crazy cunts waiting to happen.

'You're not speaking to a room full of people, Becky. It's only us.'

This is a surprisingly astute observation for George. Astute enough to make me briefly paranoid. My previous comment was taken verbatim from a memorial lecture on campaigning journalism that I'm meant to be giving tomorrow night to students at the London School of Printing, which is listed under 'Education' in my *Who's Who* entry.

'What if Ella turns out to have died because of a failure in legislation? How many more children have to die before legislation changes? The public deserves to know about these failures. Our readers deserve to know. We did a MORI poll – the results overwhelmingly favoured parents having a right to know if there were paedophiles living close by. The law needs to change – the List needs to be made available in the public realm, so that parents like the Walshes can make informed decisions. I think that's worth fighting for.'

'However you spin this, Becky, the only thing you're fighting for is circulation figures.'

'Which are up, way up. Unlike the *Courier*'s.'

George spins away from me, gazing at the photographs filling the shelf behind my desk.

'This isn't a fight, it's a total fucking farce. Every day this week you've ignored all advice and gone ahead and published the names, photographs and addresses of vulnerable people.'

'Convicted paedophiles.'

'Who are breaking off contact with probation officers, moving from addresses monitored by police, altering their appearance in an attempt to disguise themselves, failing to attend treatment programmes, and adopting habits that signal a return to offending.'

'And we'll carry on publishing names, addresses and photographs until the law changes and the List is made available in the public realm. I gave fair warning, but nobody listened.'

'You're receiving death threats,' he says, his voice dropping. His face is suddenly serious.

How does he know?

'So, that's what this is about?'

'Yes, that's what this is about. And you should take them seriously. The campaign – it's a step too far, even for you. Even for Matilda.'

I drop messily onto the edge of the desk, arms folded, barricading myself against the idea of Matilda's disapproval, which comes as a shock. 'She hasn't said anything to me.'

'She says you don't listen to her any more.' George shakes his head. 'I don't know what makes her think you still listen to me.'

'Matilda asked you to speak to me?'

He ignores the question. 'And what about Rawdon? The PM must be leaning pretty heavily on him to get you to drop this.' He pauses, weighing up what he's about to say next. Deciding whether to risk it. 'Surely that's the only reason they gave Rawdon the job. So that he can run you from inside the Cabinet Office.'

He leans back in the chair, smiling, arms behind his head, legs outstretched.

'Rawdon doesn't run me. Nobody runs me.' I slide off the desk so that I'm standing over him. 'And besides, Rawdon's got other things on his mind right now.'

'Like what?'

'Like becoming a father.'

With an effort, George holds the pose, but his face is slipping away from him. 'So, that's why you haven't been returning my calls. When were you going to tell me?'

Within seconds he's navigated the desk and is trying to take hold of my arms as I twist away from him.

'Not here, George. For fuck's sake.'

'Is it even his?'

'Does it matter?'

It's then that O'Dowd appears. He takes in George, pauses. 'We need to talk, boss.'

George stares from me to O'Dowd.

I nod at him to leave, and after another few seconds' hesitation, he pushes past the bulk of O'Dowd, who remains fixed in the doorway and makes no effort to move.

Once he's gone, I listen as O'Dowd tells me that the police think they've found the blue van seen in the field the day Ella disappeared. Forensics are going over it at the moment. I can hear in his voice that there's more to come.

'The van belongs to a maintenance man working at that boarding school you used to go to – Chilston House. He runs a bouncy castle hire business at the weekends. Thought you'd want to know, boss.'

# Chilston House School for Girls

The school office feels much smaller than I remember. Nothing more than an overcrowded cubicle separated from the corridor by a stretch of panelling and shatterproof glass. And hot, like it was that day.

'I've come to see Miss Pinkerton,' I say. 'A surprise visit from an Old Girl.'

A clattering electric fan blows piles of loose paper about the desk. The woman sitting behind this has just slipped the glasses from her sweating face. She smiles brightly at me, eyes dropping to the bump in my dress before flicking back up to my face. A practised glance. Measured.

Good figure. Good tan. Good dress. Dark. Sleeveless. The dress, I think, couldn't possibly have been bought in anticipation of this cramped office in a boarding school for girls. This office feels like the far side of a bad divorce – a place where she has unexpectedly found herself, after decades of marriage, in need of a salary.

She stands up, runs her hands over the creases in her dress and then turns around to look out of the window at the car parked on the drive. Mehti is leaning against it, smoking, a hand tucked under an armpit.

The sight of the car and driver seems to affirm something, but she remains uncertain. She's uncertain because Miss Pinkerton is not currently in her office.

'Oh, I'm happy to wait. I would have phoned, but I was passing and . . .'

She wavers.

'A surprise visit,' I repeat.

She wavers some more and then brushes a hand through the air between us, dismissing her previous doubt, showing me, with purpose, into Miss Pinkerton's study.

'Can I get you something to drink?'

'Just water, please.'

She starts to retreat, the door closing. Then it opens again, her head reappearing. 'Who shall I say?'

'Amelia Sedley.'

After the institutional decor in the office outside – magnolia walls and green carpet tiles – Miss Pinkerton's study comes as a surprise. The dark floribunda twisting, trailing and blossoming across walls, curtains, sofas, cushions and lampshades. This I would have remembered. The room must have been redecorated since I was last here as a lean, agitated thirteen-year-old whose thin arms were laced with bramble scratches, little bubbles of blood forming a neat pattern where thorns had punctured skin.

The bay window behind the desk is three quarters full of green Weald.

I must have stood where I'm now standing that day. The view vanishing behind tears. Shoulders shaking. Eyes and nose running.

How long did Miss Pinkerton wait before pushing the box of tissues towards me?

I remember the box of tissues. Still there, on the desk, the top one pulled into graceful ripples, waiting. Passing my hand idly over this, I feel it. The anxious excitement that has been building ever since Mehti turned in at the school gates.

The photographs on the wall I also remember – the deceased Princess, an alumna of the school, tight-lipped and blushing in royal blue. It was a signed photograph on the occasion of her engagement to HRH the Prince. Next to the royal couple, on the same stretch of wall, is Margaret Thatcher during a visit to Chilston House, in the company of a young, shimmering Barbara Pinkerton.

The shimmer has gone.

I see this as soon as she enters the room. Despite the Dior jacket, Barbara Pinkerton is sliding towards dowdy.

She extends an energetic arm – she has seen the car on the drive, and Mehti.

'Amelia!'

We shake hands and Miss Pinkerton keeps a firm hold as she peers intently, searching for me in her memory and failing to find me. I can see it in her eyes.

'Amelia, Amelia!'

Perturbed, she gestures towards one of the armchairs grouped around an empty fireplace but doesn't move towards them herself, drifting instead behind the Georgian desk whose mahogany surface stretches the length of the bay window.

I remain standing.

'So, you would have been a Leaver in . . .'

'Eighty-eight.'

'Eighty-eight,' she repeats. 'Of course.'

A hot, bright sunlight falls into the room.

Through the open window, the sound of a whistle being blown, the crack of hockey sticks, a raised voice shouting instructions across a pitch. The excited scuffles of a new generation. Life carrying on. She lifts her head towards these sounds, as if to reassure herself, before slowly turning back to me.

'You'll forgive me, Amelia, it's most unusual – when it comes to my girls, I have a photographic memory – but I'm afraid I can't quite place you. Most unusual,' she repeats. Her smile narrows, becoming less substantial, all the initial enthusiasm now gone, doubt and suspicion creeping in. She splays her fingers along the edge of the desk.

I turn away from her. 'This room has changed since I was last here.'

The eyes she flings around her study are close to frantic now. 'Yes,' she struggles, losing her bearings fast. It's as if I've tampered with her magnetic north. 'New wallpaper and—'

'We had tea,' I cut in, 'and cake. The last time I was here. Remember the cake?' I'm unable to keep the disappointment out of my voice as Miss Pinkerton shakes her head. 'It doesn't matter. I didn't come here to talk about cake. I came here to talk about Ella.'

At this, the hand wearing an emerald ring – I remember the ring – goes out for the phone on her desk. She picks up the receiver, holding it against her. 'You're not Amelia Sedley.'

'No.'

'And you were never a pupil at Chilston House.'

'No.'

'What's your connection with Ella exactly?'

'I'm the editor of the *Mercury*.'

This pretty much undoes her. The eyes widen. The mouth, above sagging chins, opens. She replaces the receiver and lowers herself into the seat behind the desk, hovering for a moment before allowing herself to drop.

'I'm also a friend of the family. The Walshes. It's a shame you refused all our attempts to get an interview with you.'

'We issued a statement to the press when Ella first went missing and I have no further comment.'

'Only the missing persons inquiry is now a murder investigation.'

'Yes,' she falters, 'a terrible tragedy. Our thoughts and prayers are with Ella's family.' The words come out hollow-sounding. 'I've spoken to Mrs Walsh, naturally.'

She says this as if hoping to appease me.

'Naturally, and I'm sure that made a whole lot of difference.' I remain standing in an oblong of sunlight, my hands holding on to the back of a chair. 'To a woman whose daughter's naked body was found buried in woodland.'

'I'm going to have to ask you to leave.'

She reaches for the phone again and grapples with the buttons for a while, but her fingers won't do what she wants them to, and after a few seconds she gives up.

'It must have been pretty bad for you. When Ella went missing.'

'There was concern, of course. I'm responsible for the spiritual and mental wellbeing of our whole school community, so it was essential to contain the anxiety. But your newspaper has made that impossible. Every day the flames are fanned.'

'I'm talking about the backlash. Parents threatening to withdraw their children from the school.' I throw a hazy glance around the upholstered study, a thread of nausea pulling at my stomach. 'But you seem to have weathered the storm.'

'Numbers have never been an issue for us, given our reputation. The Princess . . .' Miss Pinkerton murmurs from on high. 'The calibre of our alumnae.'

She reaches a small patch of solid ground here and clings to it, briefly sure of herself. She thinks she might just swing it, turn the tables on me. I can see this thought taking hold. The hands, which have been reaching blindly for random objects on the desk in front of her, are clasped once more.

'You mean, one dead schoolgirl isn't going to make all that much of an impact?' I plough on through the studied impassivity. 'Well, I hate to be the bearer of bad news, but after tomorrow's headlines, numbers are going to become a serious issue.'

She stands up, shunting the chair back with such force that it teeters dangerously for a moment before coming to rest on all four legs once more.

'I think you should leave.'

'I think we should talk. Like you, my concern is for the mental and spiritual wellbeing of the whole school community. That's how you put it, isn't it? So, I'm interested to know what sort of checks you have in place – when it comes to recruiting staff – to safeguard that community. Presuming, of course, that you do have checks in place. A priority, I would have thought, in a school. Especially a school like this. Girls. Boarding. Does the name Lester Hayes mean anything to you?' I move the chair out of the rectangle of sunlight, but remain standing.

'Not immediately, no.'

'It's the name of the man the police apprehended yesterday in connection with Ella's disappearance and murder.'

'How do you know that? All they said was that a suspect was being held.'

'What can I say? Information has a habit of finding me. I wanted to do you the courtesy of letting you know in advance that Lester Hayes is in *your* employment. He works in the maintenance department here at Chilston House.'

I watch as she collapses back in her chair, as if flung there by the explosion of a long-buried bomb from a forgotten war.

'The thing is – he isn't the first, is he? There was a school chaplain as recently as 1998 – Father Robert – who we've tracked down in the Scilly Isles. I hear Scilly Isles and I think fields of early flowering narcissi, not paedophile bishops. Did you know he had become a bishop? Then there's the geography teacher, everyone called him Byron – nobody we've spoken to seems to be able to remember his real name – who used to take the girls for swimming. And Mr Todd, who would apparently encourage the younger girls to—'

'Who have you been speaking to?' She stares at me. Waiting.

'Ex-girls mostly. The ones whose lives look nothing like those promised in your glossy prospectus. Topless models, cocaine addicts . . . like Lizzie Saltire. Remember Lizzie?'

'Lizzie? Unfortunately, she—'

'Choked to death on her own vomit. Family's still in an uproar over it and devastated to hear about the abuse she suffered at school.'

Using the chair's armrests, she pulls herself upright. I expect her to flare up, but she remains eerily calm, as if preoccupied by something else entirely.

'I know you,' she says at last.

'You're still not listening, are you?' I pick up the chair and bang it against the floor. It's all I can do to stop myself throwing it at her. 'You're responsible for what happened to Lizzie. You had a duty of care towards her, and you failed in that. You failed all of them . . . and now Ella, who should have continued to flourish and grow. Ella, who would still be Ella if it wasn't for you. Rather than a body buried in woodland.'

I can hear myself screaming at her, and I see her get to her feet, but it's as if these things are happening at a distance. She says something that sounds like 'stop it' or 'shut up'. But nothing is going to stop me now.

'Don't say I didn't warn you, because I did. I tried to tell you what I'd seen in the bird hide that day . . . I stood right here in this exact spot.'

The door opens then and the woman I spoke to earlier – Miss Pinkerton's PA – asks if everything's OK. She knows it isn't. Her eyes loom large behind the spectacles she's wearing once more. She will have heard me shouting from the office outside.

Miss Pinkerton stares at her without speaking until the woman retreats, closing the door carefully behind her.

'I know you,' she says again, all the padding stripped from her voice. The bent arm drops, her fist falling away from her hip. Her face becomes animated as confusion gives way to fear. 'Sharp. Rebecca Sharp. Your mother used to work here. Now I have you.'

'No, Barbara' – she winces at the 'Barbara' – 'this time, I have you. We are going to be tireless in our coverage and it's going to destroy you. Ella is going to destroy you.'

# Haversham

I carried on running, away from the bird hide. Tearing through the green sunlight beneath the trees towards the sloping lawns and bulk of school buildings. Crashing out of the woods at last and into the open. Somehow propelling myself uphill through the heavy heat. Only vaguely aware of the activity around me as I streaked through it all. Bodies moving on the tennis courts, bodies playing ball games on the grass. Music coming from open windows and little puffs of laughter rising from groups of sunbathing girls. I had no idea where I was going, apart from away. This was the command my mind had given my body while frozen in the doorway to the bird hide. Get away.

My child's soul was having trouble accommodating the choreography of what I'd seen. It felt extravagantly wrong. The world was suddenly full of possibilities that hadn't been there before, and although my pounding feet were desperately trying to carry me away from this knowledge, my mind reached towards it. By the time I hit the thick bank of shade offered by the cloisters, I had no idea what I was running away from any more, only that I must on no account stop running. Something was trying to catch up with me that I instinctively knew I wasn't ready to bear the weight of.

Which is perhaps why I didn't immediately come to a halt when the woman walking towards me said loudly, 'No running in cloisters!'

Or why I carried on running even after she shot out a hand and grabbed me by the arm, forcing me to a stumbling standstill. Out of breath, my ears full of the sound of someone sobbing close by, I watched her mouth move without being able to hear what she was saying.

'Down in the bird hide . . .' I tried. Then, again, 'The bird hide . . . there was a girl . . . man . . .'

It wasn't until she let go of my arm with the impatient instruction to 'Stop it!' that I realized the sobbing was coming from me.

I stood in the stony shade, lungs bursting.

The woman flicked her head about, her face tight with something. Despite the heat, she had a cardigan draped over her shoulders. Taking hold of this with one hand, she held the other behind my back – without touching me – and guided us out of the cloisters, her heels loud; insistent-sounding.

We continued across the gravel drive towards the school's main entrance, which I had never used before, climbing the steps between planters full of hot-looking flowers. And it was then that I recognized her. Not just from her photograph in the prospectus, which had been taken on these very same steps. But she had been there at the Hunters' party as well. This was Miss Pinkerton, headmistress of Chilston House. She was ahead of me now and walking at such a pace that I had to run to keep up.

We reached some sort of office where a much older woman sat behind a desk and typewriter. She automatically got to her feet when she saw Miss Pinkerton, like a soldier standing to attention, making the cup of tea on her desk wobble and spill. She asked if we needed anything.

'Water,' I managed. I was so very thirsty.

But Miss Pinkerton simply waved dismissively at this before pushing me through a doorway into another much larger and lighter room.

Leaving me standing in the middle of the carpet, she positioned herself behind a desk filling the bay window, sitting down and clasping her hands across some neatly arranged papers. In the office outside, I could hear the banging click of the typewriter starting up again.

Miss Pinkerton smiled, as if she had made her mind up about something. Then she stood up, brushed down her dress and said, 'I'm forgetting myself. We haven't been introduced.'

She came to a stop in front of me, holding out her hand. 'Miss Pinkerton.'

I stared at the hand, then the face above it, which was not kind, before shyly stretching my own hand towards her. 'Becky.'

There was blood on my arms from where I'd torn through the brambles outside the bird hide. The sight of it panicked me and with the panic came the delayed hurt. Beyond the hurting, however, was the far greater fear that I would drip blood on the carpet. This, I instinctively felt, would be unforgiveable.

But Miss Pinkerton didn't seem to notice the blood patterning my arms.

Her cold spider fingers grasped my childish stubs.

Up close, she had all the feminine trappings: make-up, perfume, a dress, high-heeled shoes. And yet, without knowing why exactly, it felt to me like a fake sort of femininity.

Still holding on to my hand, she told me to stand up straight and put my shoulders back. I tried to do this but was concentrating so hard I forgot to breathe. There were dark spots. I felt dizzy and close to tears again, and had a terrible feeling that we weren't going to talk about the bird hide at all.

'Well, you're not one of our girls.'

Her voice sounded much lighter, suddenly. The smile reappeared, like make-up applied to her already made-up face. For a moment, I thought she might even break into laughter.

'Which begs the question – who are you?'

'Becky. Becky Sharp.'

'That means nothing to me. What are you *doing* here at Chilston House?'

'My mum works here. In the registrar's office.'

'Ah,' Miss Pinkerton sighed.

It was a sigh that screwed me even tighter to the spot. My sandaled feet sank further into the carpet's deep pile. And although I felt that I had betrayed my mother in some obscure way, by telling the truth, I was relieved that this information satisfied Miss Pinkerton enough to return her behind the desk once more, where, preoccupied, she moved an already immaculately positioned pen from spot to spot across the uncluttered surface.

'So, what's all this about a bird hide?'

Some voices draw you out of yourself, towards them; others make you burrow deep inside and close up. This was what happened now. I felt myself retreating.

Receding.

Until I was hardly there at all.

Miss Pinkerton waited.

'Please may I have some water?' I tried again, the words sticking in my dried-up mouth.

She waved this aside, impatient. The same gesture she'd used with the woman outside.

So, I told her about the man – that I'd seen him before in the bird hide, and that I guessed he was a teacher at the school. I paused here, expecting her to interrupt and ask the sort of questions that would enable her to establish his identity. But she didn't and I carried on. My voice was nothing more than a mumble now as I described the kneeling girl and the way her face had risen from the man's lap. But already, I could feel my memory betraying me. Parts of what I had seen were too distinct, other parts too indistinct to articulate. Each statement became a question as I both sought and hid from any sort of explanation.

I didn't need to worry. No explanation was forthcoming. In fact, Miss Pinkerton looked so distracted as I spoke that I wondered if she had even heard.

Worse still, in the silence that followed, I started to doubt that I had seen the girl at all. Perhaps I had simply made her up.

'Rebecca – what were you doing in the bird hide?'

'I . . . It's just somewhere I like to go.'

'So – your mother has given you licence to roam at will?'

I wasn't sure that I understood the question, but what I did understand was this: my mother was somehow being implicated in what had happened this hot afternoon.

'Do you know what a trespasser is?'

'Yes.'

I thought she might force me to give a definition, but she simply nodded. 'Good. A trespasser is someone who finds herself in a place where she doesn't belong. True or false?'

'True,' I whispered.

She was right. I didn't belong here.

'So, getting back to the bird hide. You haven't painted a particularly vivid picture, Rebecca. I'm still confused. What exactly did you see?'

'I don't know.'

'You don't know.' She nodded again, her voice softening for the first time. 'I think you saw something you didn't understand – if you saw anything at all. And in the absence of understanding, you simply saw what you *wanted* to see.'

I remained silent.

'Rebecca, I'm concerned.'

My shoulders had started to rise, an involuntary flinch every time she said my name.

'I think we should bring your mother in and have a talk.'

'No!'

Memories of my mother being called into school after the incident with Louise still haunted me. She would be frightened, and she would be upset if she was called into Miss Pinkerton's study. It would take weeks to get her back on track.

'I've been meaning to speak to her anyway – that unfortunate incident at the Hunters' party.' Miss Pinkerton picked up the phone and started to dial.

'No,' I yelled this time, starting to cry. 'Please.'

She stopped dialling. 'But Rebecca – how do we stop you from telling others what you think you saw in the bird hide today? After all, you've already completely confused me.'

'I won't. I promise I won't. Just – don't say anything to my mum.'

The words came out thick and wet through streaming tears. Gulping. Snot-filled.

She made her way towards me again and without thinking I lifted my arms up. A protective gesture.

'All right, I believe you,' she said, touching me for the first time and pushing my arms gently down. 'Tea. We need tea.'

She guided me towards one of the room's armchairs. Suddenly exhausted, I flopped into it. Perhaps I fell asleep then. I don't remember. But what I do remember is a tray appearing on the side table next to me. It was a beautifully laid tray. Silver teapot, silver milk jug, cups and saucers. A door closed. We were alone once more.

Miss Pinkerton reappeared in my line of vision and sat down in the other armchair, her legs together, slung to one side.

I watched her pour the tea. When this was done, she sat drinking hers, soundlessly.

'Do take a slice of cake,' she said in a faraway voice, staring into the fireplace, which was empty.

The cake, dusted in white sugar, was perfect. But I wasn't

hungry. All thumping heart and no appetite. Even more alarming was the shining serving utensil that I knew I was meant to use. Impossible. My hands would shake. Something would break. I might break.

'Oh dear, Rebecca,' she murmured, still in the same faraway voice. 'We have our music scholarship exams a week from today. If I remember correctly, you're down to sit for them? Piano, I think?'

She didn't need to say anything else.

What had I been thinking during all those hours of piano practice? My former hopes and aspirations weren't just laughable now, they were humiliating. I discarded them then and there.

Miss Pinkerton looked on, amused, as if she was able to see them as they fell on the carpet about my feet.

Until at last, I pushed myself out of the armchair and fled the room.

I hauled at the study door, which was heavier than I'd anticipated, and banged my shoulder, bruising it. I would have the bruise for weeks.

Long after I made the decision not to sit for the music scholarship.

Long after I vowed never to return.

# CEO
# 2010

# Beth

The day's colour has been drained by the heat, the only respite
a thin breeze coming through one of the room's many open
windows – along with the smell of diesel. The gravel drive
is banked with lorries and generators. And in the distance, a
stretch of sparkling water. The lake towards which Rawdon
and our nine-year-old daughter, Beth, along with Amelia, Gina
and Jon, are now headed. For a while, I allow them to distract me. Rawdon and Amelia are easy together, even at this
distance. Talking about the children, I imagine. It's all they
ever talk about. The young Osbornes, although both teenagers
now, are still boisterous and streak ahead, while Beth clings to
Rawdon with both hands. Her dark, tangled hair – Beth's hair
is always tangled – emerges from beneath a white sun hat.

I continue to watch their progress across the West Lawn – as
it was known when this was still Chilston House School –
where a marquee is being erected, along with fairground rides:
a request from Beth after a party she went to recently where
there were horses, a helter-skelter and carousel.

I came here once after the school closed. There was a sale and
I bought Barbara Pinkerton's desk. I combed through it when
it first arrived, my fingers catching on forgotten paperclips,
staples and rubber bands caught in the corners of drawers,
along with a dried corsage – worn at the Princess's wedding? –
which crumbled when I lifted it out. I was half hoping to find
a letter with my name on it, a scribbled missive written in a
moment of private defeat, acknowledging me as the victor of

our war. Because for some reason, despite the relentless way we kept Barbara Pinkerton pinned to the public eye throughout the Lester Hayes trial and the closure of Chilston House School, her downfall hasn't brought the catharsis I hoped it would. Even now – standing in the apartment that used to belong to her – I'm not able to lay her to rest.

The truth is, I'm not sure that I want to.

The loneliness, after Chilston House closed and Barbara Pinkerton disappeared, caught me out, threatened to unbalance me for a while. It was as if I'd lost some fundamental part of myself that I hadn't anticipated losing, and still haven't found the means of addressing.

The building remained empty for years after the sale, an eerie testament to communal living gone wrong, until it was turned into a country hotel and spa. Booked, by Matilda, in its entirety, to mark my fortieth birthday.

Despite the renovations that have taken place, the row of cottages that once housed the school's maintenance department is still standing. A waiter from breakfast showed me the cottage Lester Hayes used to live in. He said guests often ask staff if they can see it – the home of Ella Walsh's murderer. I did this before Dinkie, who I've remained close to, arrived. But now, the visit to Lester Hayes' cottage weighs on me.

Seating plans for tonight's celebrations are in a folder on the coffee table, having been meticulously prepared by Trish. Next to each guest's name is a summarized biography, along with personal interests and suitable topics of conversation. I've spent most of the week going over the plans and have almost every biography memorized. But it's hard now, to pick up where I left off a few minutes ago.

Unpinning the sheet showing the Prime Minister's table plan from the board, I drift back to the window. This plan was particularly difficult to draw up given the *Mercury*'s flagging support for him after we broke a property scandal involving his eldest son.

As I start fanning myself with the sheet, I notice writing on the back:

*Mummy were at the Lake. join Us. It will be Nice.*

The uneven, lopsided letters are multicoloured. Some upper case, some lower. And around the message, a border of flowers and stars has been drawn. The seating plans were piled on the coffee table earlier. Beth must have grabbed a sheet without thinking. At some point, she would have seen the seating plan on the other side and panicked. I imagine her pushing it clumsily back into the pile, desperate to leave the room before I returned.

*Mummy were at the Lake. join Us. It will be Nice.*

Briefly, I allow for the possibility that she decided to write it herself, but the idea of Beth wanting to leave me this message is too much of a stretch, I know. Rawdon would have suggested it and Beth, sighing and reluctant, would have traipsed into her room to retrieve her new scented felt tip pens.

She wrote this to please him.

She drew the flowers and the stars to please him.

Kneeling on the rug, tongue curled over her upper lip in concentration, she would have talked herself through the spellings and been anxious about getting them right. Beth is not an academic child and it's painful watching her push a bitten forefinger, word by impenetrable word, across the page. In my darker moments, I see something almost wilful in her underachievement. Nobody can be *that* stupid.

My impatience with her makes Beth trail after me, talking rapidly. It makes her hurl wild promises at my back in an attempt to catch hold of me in some way. Until her little face becomes flooded with tears that she babbles apologies through. Those same two words, over and over again. Sorry, Mummy.

Sorry, Mummy. Maddening and devastating. This continues until she grows short of breath and has to gulp in lungful after lungful of air, drawing up her shoulders and chest with the effort.

It doesn't have to be like this.

We both know it doesn't have to be like this. But over time we've crafted roles for ourselves in this familiar drama, roles we've learned by heart and fall back on with a relief that is almost clarifying. Me, caught up in horror at myself, yelling, 'Go to your room!' Beth, yelling back through snot and tears, 'I hate you!' before running for sanctuary in a distant corner of the house, where she will curl up in a cocoon of misery, waiting for Rawdon to find her.

After the storm has passed, a strange tranquillity often reigns between us. An intimacy, almost. And it's during these brief interludes that we play at being a family.

I move to the table and picking up one of my own pens, insert an apostrophe in 'were'. Then I underline the correction, before returning to the window, still holding the seating plan.

On the lawn below, Rawdon is breaking into a run after Jon Osborne, turning the haphazard dash towards the water into a whooping pursuit.

Someone else has joined the small party – a tall girl, arms thrown wide as she and Amelia clasp hold of each other. Beth is jumping excitedly up and down on the spot beside them, unusually demonstrative as she tries to find a way into their embrace.

It takes me a while to recognize my old charge in the girl towering over Amelia – Violet Crawley. In the past, we would occasionally run into each other at family events, but since her parents' divorce and Rosa's remarriage to a TV chef, she's become confrontational, prone to dramatic outbursts and even more dramatic departures. These days, she has little to do with any of us. Not even Matilda. Especially not Matilda, in fact. Although Beth still receives birthday and Christmas presents, and I know that Violet's in touch with Rawdon.

She now goes by her mother's name, Dawson.

For professional reasons, she claims, and in an attempt to put as much distance as possible between herself and the Crawley family. She turned down a job at the *Mercury* on ethical grounds, opting instead for our arch enemy – the *Post* – which has given her a platform from which to wage war against us.

The truth is, I find her unnerving, and was suspicious when she accepted the invitation to my birthday party. I'm becoming increasingly paranoid these days.

From her younger sister, Lulu, I've heard nothing.

Violet has hold of Beth's hand. This, I know, is an achievement. Beth shies away from most physical contact, unless it involves her father. She holds her breath when I kiss her. As Violet and Beth carry on towards the lake, hand in hand, I feel a sudden flush of irritation for my awkward daughter who wants for nothing.

No, it's more than irritation. It's resentment for her ignorance, which is essentially what innocence is. I resent my daughter for the things she doesn't know, the things she hasn't had to survive, something I first felt at her ninth birthday among the balloons at Smollensky's. It came over me suddenly, while everybody was singing 'Happy Birthday'. An urge to whisper in one of her small red ears – all the attention was making her blush – and tell her how on my own ninth birthday, I received no presents at all.

What on earth would she make of that?

Although there were never balloons or parties or games or cakes, I usually woke on my birthday to a couple of presents wrapped in gift paper saved from Christmas. These would be pushed among the debris on the kitchen table, like unseasonal contraband. But that year, there were no presents for me to poke at, excited, while my mother watched me with tired eyes. There were no presents and there was no mother. She had holed herself up in her bedroom because of something that had happened in her complicated adult world. Something to do with a man; it was always to do with a man.

So, I drifted, restless, through the day, until by 4 o'clock, I found the courage to stand in the bedroom doorway, picking at the paintwork, down through the coloured layers until I uncovered an improbable blue.

My mother, finally sensing my presence, heaved over in bed. Her hair was wild and her face creased from where she'd fallen asleep crushed against the pillow. Everything smelt of drink and tears.

I said, 'The baker's shuts soon.'

Iced buns had become a birthday tradition.

Groaning, she let a hand fall over her face. And for a moment, I thought she'd fallen asleep again. But then the hand was lifted. 'Your birthday! Shit!'

The duvet was thrown back and my mother hauled herself from the bed, briefly unsteady on her feet.

'I'll go now. Get us some buns.'

I ran, pounding down the corridor to the kitchen, and returned with her handbag.

She fished out her purse, unclasped it and, sniffing, shook the change into the palm of her hand, squinting down at it.

'Shit,' she said again. 'Never mind. I'll make it work.'

She grinned at me, made suddenly beautiful by her determination.

She was gone a long time but returned shining and triumphant, holding almost more paper bags than she could carry.

'They gave me loads,' she panted, as if she'd been running.

'It was the end of the day, and they were clearing everything out. I got this stash for next to nothing.'

I wanted to stay nine for ever. Because of some iced buns and my mother's excitement.

Down on the lawn, Violet comes to a sudden standstill, scanning the sky while keeping a tight hold of Beth as the sound of a helicopter fills the air, signalling Matilda Crawley's arrival.

Matilda fills the corridor outside like an exaggerated version of herself. There are other people with her, but they become obscured as she moves in for a kiss. Her hands clasp my shoulders hard, and she slides her face against each of my cheeks, smelling unsettlingly of baby powder.

The sheet of paper I'm holding, the one with the PM's table plan on it, crackles between us until finally, we pull apart.

'So, this is the school you shut down.'

She peers past me, eyes glancing around the suite of rooms and beyond to the shimmering line of Downs through the windows. Matilda gives an ambivalent grunt before turning her back on it and beckoning towards the people left stranded in the corridor outside. 'There's someone I want you to meet.'

A couple file into the room, tailed by Wenham.

There's a flurry of effusive greetings – sticky handshakes and jumpy eye contact.

I already know him – the opposition's new leader – but it's the first time I've met her. The wife. A glossy woman who stops just short of sleek. Very different from the current Prime Minister's wife, who has until recently always been so hungry for intimacy and friendship. Instinctively, I sense that there will be no drunken confidences with this woman. No Chequers sleepovers or wild, late-night laughter. Later, at the trial, I'll discover that soon after this meeting she started referring to me as 'that bloody woman'.

But I can see what it is about them that has been getting Matilda so excited – the freshness and authenticity. The extraordinary fact that they're in love with each other still. It's clear, even in a crowded room, that he'll always know where she is.

'Prime Minister,' I say, without hesitation.

He laughs readily – everybody laughs on cue for me now – his face flushing with colour. There's a boyish eagerness to him that will be the first thing to go when he comes to power and that he'll spend the rest of his life trying to retrieve. But he doesn't need to know this. He'll find it out soon enough.

'Steady on, we haven't even had a general election yet.'

'We can make that a foregone conclusion,' I put in.

'Be careful what you wish for.' Matilda's hand is spanning most of my back. 'Rebecca never makes empty promises. She doesn't move like ordinary people. You won't see her coming.'

The future Prime Minister is momentarily at a loss as he tries to work out whether he has just been threatened (he has). Because he has been a little too easy with his laughter. A little too self-assured. He has made himself too comfortable too fast. I know this. His eyes meet those of his worried wife, who has left a severely disabled newborn baby in hospital in order to be here this afternoon. Both are evidently surprised to find themselves out of their depth suddenly.

And it's then that my daughter runs into the room.

She stops, startled, as she registers the unexpected gathering of people.

'A savage in our midst!' Wenham calls out in his broad Lancashire accent.

It's true. Somewhere between the lake and the house, Beth has lost both her hat and her shoes. Her hair's in even more of a tangle than usual and her bare feet are filthy. She could almost be a different species. A pygmy forest-dweller, who has spent the morning climbing trees. Climbing trees is the sort of thing Rawdon encourages her to do. The sort of thing she likes to do anyway, to impress him.

Everybody laughs.

I laugh.

Beth looks lost at the laughter and says to nobody in particular, 'I want to go swimming. I've come for my costume.' This is delivered in a lisping monotone, eyes boring into the floor.

But an explanation isn't what Wenham wants. Wenham – and by default Matilda, who dislikes children – wants sport.

'It speaks!' he bellows.

'It speaks!' Matilda echoes, delighted.

Everybody apart from the future Prime Minister's wife – to her credit – laughs again, on cue.

Beth clamps her mouth shut. A defiance at odds with her hunched, sunburnt shoulders and curling toes. I've encountered it before, this surprising defiance, and try to catch her eye. But she doesn't look in my direction, hasn't once looked in my direction since first running into the room.

Wenham persists, intent on Beth now. 'Does it bite?'

She stands frozen to the spot, unmoving, as Wenham mimes a series of theatrical bites while tossing his head from side to side. He advances on her, Matilda clapping alongside him.

'Does it bite?' he says again, much louder this time.

Beth's eyes are wide and fixed on both of them as they continue to close in. With each snap of Wenham's teeth, she flinches. Her eyes grow darker by the second, her skin paler, like veined porcelain. She looks breakable.

The future Prime Minister and his wife glance at each other, unsure. And then they glance at me. Neither of them is laughing any more. Their older children, I know, won't be breakable, like Beth. They'll be well-groomed and buoyant. Robust. Resilient. A flurry of frustration at this thought is followed by an unspeakable tenderness and desire to protect. And I wonder, not for the first time, if this is my real issue with Beth. In her company, I'm constantly torn and exhausted. Trapped in the present moment.

Wenham, ruffled at Beth's lack of response, is now circling her, shoulders raised, arms hooked like claws.

Matilda contemplates them both, smiling.

'Does it roar?' he demands.

'Beth,' I urge, trying hard to temper the flutter of rage and smile encouragement at the stranded child. *My* stranded child. All she needs to do is turn this into a game. Bite back. Roar. Run, laughing, from him. Why can't she just work the room?

At last, she drags her miserable eyes from Matilda and the circling Wenham to me, flat and unexpectant.

My heart buckles. For a moment, it really does buckle, and I allow myself to feel everything a mother should feel. I could take hold of her hand, I think. I could take hold of her hand and we could roar together. But already, she's turning back to Wenham.

'Roar!' he commands, coming to a halt in front of her.

Part of me wants more than anything for Beth to roar, get it over and done with. But another part of me hopes against hope that she'll hold out.

Beth refuses to roar, silently shaking her head at him instead, her mouth still clamped shut.

And for a moment, Wenham hesitates. But he has started this, and he can't give up now or he'll end up looking ridiculous.

Throwing his head back, he lets out a long, animal sound.

Beth jumps – everybody jumps – clamping her hands over her ears, quivering all over like she might just shatter on the spot.

'Enough,' the future Prime Minister's wife says, making for Beth. 'That's enough.'

Despite looking shocked himself, her husband tries to lay a restraining hand on her shoulder. There's more than a child's misery at stake for them here in this room. But she shakes him off, glaring at Wenham and throwing an arm around Beth, who grabs handfuls of her immaculate shirt, pushing her face into it as she starts to sob.

The future Prime Minister claps his hands and starts rubbing them nervously together, his eyes sliding between all of us. Gently his wife turns Beth around in her arms and propels her towards me.

Beth stumbles obediently across the room, rubbing at her face with the palms of her hands.

'Sweetie!' I call out – where on earth did that come from? – holding my arms open. The seating plan flaps limply in my hands.

This brings her up short. Trembling with the aftershock of tears, she blinks vaguely in my direction – her eyes darting, fearful, to the seating plan – before pushing straight past me and breaking into a run. Her bare feet pound the corridor outside for what feels like a long time.

'Rebecca, I don't understand,' Matilda says at last, the words falling, languid, from her mouth, 'how did you come to have such a dull daughter?'

# Rawdon

Rawdon emerges from Beth's room in underpants, struggling with the buttons on his shirt. Coming to a halt in the middle of the suite's main room, he stares for a moment at the seating plans spread across the coffee table, squinting.

'D'you want me to get your glasses?'

'No. The last thing I want to know – in advance – is who I'm spending the night jammed between.'

Tucking his chin down, he makes a concerted effort with the buttons as I slide off the bed and cross the room to where he's standing, gently batting his fingers away and taking over. Even with my head bent, I can feel his eyes on me. The shift in his breathing. Both of us are quietly elated by this small act, the proximity to each other. Before the trip to Venice last weekend, it would never have occurred to me to help Rawdon do up his shirt. I would have simply watched him struggle and kept my distance. This is new territory. For both of us. Since Venice, an old shyness has crept back into our relationship. We're being careful with each other, and not taking anything for granted.

Strange as it may sound, I feel married to Rawdon for the first time in our marriage.

'You promised you'd behave,' I goad him gently. 'It's my birthday.'

'This isn't your birthday, it's a corporate event being held by my family in order to celebrate your promotion to CEO,' he goads me gently back. 'It was your birthday last weekend. In Venice.'

Venice took us by surprise. We spent the flight there just about as far apart as it was possible for two people to be while sharing a private jet (Matilda's). Me, working. Rawdon, sullen and already drunk. In the launch that took us to the hotel, I sat on the starboard side, Rawdon the port, making no effort to talk as we bounced across the grey lagoon. Rain mixed with sea spray as water streamed down the windows, all horizons lost to the oncoming storm. The launch's captain was anxious and muttering, so that it was a relief, almost, to arrive at the hotel.

Relief made Rawdon loud and high-handed. Nothing, he decided, was right. Staff were shouted at and sent scuttling as our arrival descended into red-faced chaos, and I stood in reception counting out the hours left in the sinking city.

By the evening, Rawdon was yo-yoing between catatonic and spiteful while I was thinking about leaving after lunch the following day. Something's come up, I would say. Something was always coming up. And then out of nowhere, the sound of the flood horn, blasting out its hollow warning. What a fucking godsend. We were all going to drown. We caught each other's eye, briefly excited as the dining room cleared.

In our room, we watched from the balcony as water swept silently into the city while the horn continued to sound.

We found ourselves by the bed. Rawdon sat on the end of it, pulling me towards him and burrowing his face in my stomach like he was trying to suffocate himself. Falling backwards, we made love for the first time in months, as the water level in the piazza below rose. And that's how it was all weekend. I forgot my departure plans and Rawdon buried his spite. We holed ourselves up instead, like honeymooners. Everything beyond the room a grey squall.

We made love as if time was running out, with a new and furious tenderness that it was hard to come back from.

Even more impossible to pick up the pieces of everyday life afterwards, which isn't something I've ever had trouble doing before.

Venice has left us undone. Since our return, we've remained wrapped up in each other in a way we haven't been for years, going through our separate days smelling of each other. It has made me unfocused, and this isn't something I'm used to either. The unspoken consensus between us is that our old life no longer fits, but we have no idea how to go about building a new one. This past week's seen us happily stranded between both worlds.

Beth has found our intimacy confusing, observing us with a mixture of fear and pleasure, her face a puckered frown. I often catch her humming to herself, and I like this new way of us all being together, which is why the incident with Wenham earlier was so upsetting.

'There.' I finish doing up the last button on his shirt and we kiss. 'You should get dressed. I've got the hairdresser coming at seven and he'll jump you looking like that.'

Moving across the room to the dressing table, I start to put on my make-up, aware of Rawdon's bare-legged figure in the mirror.

'Beth's unsure about her dress,' he says after a while.

I turn around, mascara in hand. 'She'll be fine.'

'I don't know.'

'It's just a dress.'

'Precisely.' He smiles suddenly, as if I've taken him by surprise. A wide, far-reaching smile that includes everything we've become to each other since Venice.

Beth appears then, hovering on the threshold of the room in a dress that isn't the one we chose together for this evening. She's anxious, her bottom lip bleeding from where she's been picking at the loose skin. Dropping her head to hide this from me, she pushes a foot forward through the carpet's deep pile, drawing a dark line. But behind the anxiety, there's courage, or she wouldn't be putting herself through this. And then I realize what this is really about. Revenge. For Wenham earlier.

Flicking her head up, we exchange a look I can only describe as complicit. She knows that I know. The room becomes suddenly still. The summer evening, a pinprick in time.

Rawdon is watching me.

Beth is watching me.

And the hairdresser will be here soon. So, it's almost against my will that I hear myself say, 'I want you to change.'

Beth draws her foot slowly back across the carpet. Immediately, I sense something a lot like excitement unfurling in her, and it occurs to me – not for the first time – that she might actually enjoy these confrontations. Need them, even. Perhaps we both do.

'Doesn't she look beautiful,' Rawdon insists, trying to keep his voice light. Trying not to let it fray around the edges.

He's right. She does look beautiful. Our daughter. But it's no good. We're all on the alert now. Who knows where we might go from here? Always, there's the possibility of uncharted waters when we're together like this. Bad weather.

'I want you to change into the dress we bought together, Beth.'

My voice sounds unusually plaintive because I need this to mean something to her. It was a good day. Even though to start with Beth had stomach ache in the back of the car. For the first hour, as we crawled through traffic towards Sloane Street, I felt as if I was kidnapping my own daughter rather than taking her shopping. I half expected to see her open the door and make an escape every time we stopped at a set of traffic lights.

But things got better.

Over lunch, which I was dreading, Beth eventually broke

her vow of silence and started to chatter, haltingly at first, but fast becoming a torrent of school and horses and a girl called Christie, who meant the world to her and who made her life hell. She chatted at speed about all the things that dominated her nine-year-old world, the habitual stiffness vanishing.

She came alive. She made me laugh. She took my breath away.

And somewhere in the middle of the afternoon, we chose the dress that she would wear to my birthday party tonight.

'We bought it together,' I say again. 'You chose it.'

There's anger in my voice now.

'Well, I don't like it any more.' She smiles a barely-there smile. The corners of her mouth flutter with it before concluding, 'In fact, I hate it.'

Turning away from her to face the mirror again, I try to finish putting on my mascara, but my right arm is shaking. It's ridiculous. Just about managing to screw the cap on, I drop the mascara into my make-up bag, picking up a blusher brush instead. Something large and easy to wield.

To her reflection, I say, 'Go and get changed.'

'I'm not wearing it.'

Still holding the blusher brush, I get to my feet, forgetting the one thing I can't afford to forget – Beth is *my* daughter. She isn't going to back down.

'Rebecca,' Rawdon pleads, looking suddenly exhausted, 'can we just let it go? Can we please just let it go?'

He makes a strange, prayer-like gesture, both hands pushed together. 'It's just a fucking dress,' he finishes, softly.

Beth, startled, clamps her hands over her ears.

'You're right, it's just a fucking dress. Like it's just my fucking birthday. Like it's just my fucking promotion to CEO.'

'Don't argue. Please don't argue,' she gibbers, spinning between us both.

Rawdon's face empties unexpectedly then. He slides untidily down the wall until he hits the carpet, crouching, his hands holding his head. Crying. It takes me a while to understand this. Rawdon is crying.

Beth disappears into her room, reappearing seconds later, wearing the dress she refused to put on.

'Look! Daddy, look!' she commands, running to where Rawdon crouches, jaw hanging loose, face red and streaming.

She turns frantically on the spot in front of him, but his head keeps flopping back onto his knees, as if it weighs too much. Giving up, she manages to somehow bundle herself into his lap until his legs give way, sliding out from under him. After a while, he rolls his head towards me.

'I wasn't expecting you – anything like you – in my life.'

'Oh, I'm nothing much,' I throw out, hearing myself and hating myself.

'You're everything, Becky. Everything I've ever needed is here in this room with me right now,' he mumbles, wetly. 'That's the difference between us, and I could live with that if occasionally – once in a blue moon – you were able to make me feel the same way.'

'I don't understand – is that a request? Are you asking me to make a choice?'

'No, I'm not asking you to make a choice. I wouldn't do that. Come on,' he urges, offended. 'You're a brilliant editor. Probably the best there ever was. It's who you are, and I would never ask you to give that up.'

'So – what is it exactly that you want from me?'

We watch each other from a long way away, over our daughter's head. The question hangs between us, unanswered.

Until, wiping hard at his face, Rawdon attempts to unpeel Beth from him, but she's clinging on too tightly and won't let go. In the end, he has to do it finger by finger, limb by limb, gently easing her onto the carpet so that he's able to stand. His shirt is creased from where she's tucked herself against him.

'Don't leave me,' she yelps, clasping him around the waist and burying her face in his shirt.

This, I realize, shocked, is the one thing she's afraid of – Rawdon leaving. Her fear briefly fills the room, making it seem possible in a way it never has before.

He stares down at her head, stroking it absently.

'Course I'm not leaving, silly.' Then, looking up at me: 'I don't want anything from you, Rebecca, I just want you.'

He holds my gaze for a few seconds then looks away. Through the window, beyond the line of pines, the fairground lights up, the illuminated rides starting to come to life.

Rawdon says, 'How about a turn on the Big Wheel before supper?'

The invitation is for Beth, but I know that it's extended to me as well. A last chance.

There's a knock at the door to the suite, which we all ignore.

Beth stays pressed into Rawdon, her head juddering as she burrows in as far as she can, her breathing loud.

'Hey,' he says, gently prising her upright. 'Beth, come on.'

Her face is red, her fringe wet with sweat and sticking to her forehead. She stares at me. Not quite a glare, but a hard stare. I have trouble holding her gaze, and always have done. She knows it as well. This is something she has on me. It started when she was a baby and I was afraid of what I might find in her features; what I might *not* find. Some days, I would convince myself that I could see George in her, or – as she grew older – he might come out in something she said, a gesture she made. But the truth is, there are no traces of him in Beth, who is Rawdon's daughter through and through.

Rawdon says, 'Go and get your shoes on.'

After a moment's hesitation, Beth finally disappears into her room.

It strikes me then – as my daughter vanishes – that I never look for myself in her.

'So.' Rawdon lifts his arms, helpless, into the air before letting them drop back down. 'Are you coming for a ride on the Big Wheel with us?'

'You go. I'll catch up.'

Another knock at the door as Beth reappears with a pair of shoes in her hand, worried about leaving us alone together. She sits on the sofa, sombrely pushing her feet into them.

'Come in!' Rawdon yells, louder than I think he meant to, lunging for the door, which is already starting to open, threatening to unbalance my hairdresser, Barry.

'Oh, I'm sorry . . . Should I . . . ?'

'No, she's ready for you. We were just leaving.'

Rawdon grabs the pair of dinner trousers laid out on the bed and pushes his legs into them, Barry watching in the mirror.

Beth waits for her father to finish dressing. Her eyes flit with a curiosity she's trying to fight over Barry's tattooed arms. A dense twist of roses runs from bicep to wrist. Drops of blood hang from the end of each thorn, creating the illusion that Barry's skin has somehow been pierced by the inked flora.

Finally, throwing his dinner jacket over his shoulder, Rawdon moves towards the door.

Beth gets to her feet, trailing after him. Until at the last moment, she peels away. A pair of small arms are thrust around me, and I feel her childish lips wet on my cheek.

'Happy birthday, Mummy,' she says in a flash.

Then she's gone.

# The Last Party

From our table, I scan the whole shimmering crowd inside the marquee. A jumble of dinner jackets and bare shoulders and painted faces. *My* crowd. We're our own small universe, and practically untouchable. Summit crawlers, each and every one of us. We know what the last ten metres feels like, those final steps we had to take to get here. Any sense of victory or triumph has been completely frozen out, leaving behind nothing but this hard-to-fathom numbness. It's like I no longer belong to myself. A gasping lung is how Messner described himself when he first climbed Everest without oxygen. The thought that terrified him most: that he would no longer recognize his own family when he returned to sea level.

George, sitting to my left, leans in and whispers something I don't catch at first. I'm having trouble bringing him into focus. It takes him three attempts before I manage to make out the words he's now hissing with impatience.

'Rawdon's not happy.'

'Rawdon's never happy.'

Apart from Venice. He was happy in Venice. But this is my secret.

George grins. An intimate, colluding grin. Although I didn't say it to please him. It was meant dismissively. To put him off the scent.

Disloyalty is something George has become much more insistent about during the last year. As if the sexual and emotional betrayal weren't enough. In fact, without either of us explicitly mentioning it, we've come to understand that it's almost a prerequisite of our continuing relationship, an endgame that will force us into making a choice, and that's proving to be far more corrosive than I'd anticipated. Since Venice, I've made no attempt to contact George, which is why tonight he's becoming dangerously insistent. Dangerously drunk, also. He's practically nuzzling my left arm.

'Rawdon's not happy around successful people,' he corrects me. 'And you're a successful person, Becky. Probably *the* singularly most successful person here tonight.'

There's genuine admiration in his voice. George left envy behind a long time ago.

'Your point being?' I whisper back.

'My point being that it's only going to get worse. His unhappiness. It's going to make you both miserable.'

Looking up then, I see Amelia's eyes stray towards us across the table. Dreary. Defeated. They fix on me for a few seconds as she allows herself to see me properly for the first time, her face wobbling – she knows, I think, now she knows – before going blank. I can't remember when I last saw her socially. George is always telling me how much she hates parties, and how she usually manages to avoid them. This party, however, was one of the unavoidable ones, which is why she's already halfway to drunk.

She's spent most of the evening talking to Dobbin, who has readily abandoned his latest girlfriend – a minor royal who likes to party – to Pitt. Dobbin's long string of girlfriends have all been famously unsuitable.

And anyway, Pitt and the minor royal already know each other. He's friends with her father, a duke who also likes to party – with girls much younger than his daughter. I've got quite a file on the duke in my darkroom. In fact, I have files on almost everybody here tonight.

The current Prime Minister and his wife, naturally. Next to them, Tom Crane, lead singer of Apocalipsis. Tom would rather not be here but was too afraid to turn down the invitation. He knows what we have on him. The au pairs, long-legged Slavs with horizon-busting eyes, that he takes to Brighton hotels for weekends of erotic asphyxiation. This, from a twenty-year-old Bratislavan in our pay, who was asked by her employer to strangle him with a pair of tights. Things which have been kept under lock and key in my darkroom, but that could come to the surface and make their way into the public domain at any moment.

Back at our table, Amelia is already slurring her words. Her dress, a precarious arrangement of stiff angles.

'Happy birthday, Rebecca, and congratulations!' She raises her glass suddenly in a toast, tilting towards me. Her eyelids are heavy and fluttering, something she would never permit them to be sober. 'I spent my fortieth alone with a microwaved fish pie, and—'

The table, startled, holds its breath.

Rawdon, I think. Know. They must have spent Amelia's fortieth together. On cue, Rawdon and Dobbin exchange glances over Amelia's swaying head – and Dobbin was there as well.

Then Rawdon looks at me. Our eyes meet, look away.

'My wife's a simple soul,' George exhales after a while into the table's suspended silence. 'Easy to please.'

The future Prime Minister laughs happily at this before his wife nudges him.

Encouraged, George adds, 'Strange, but that's far more draining than you'd think,' before leaning confidentially towards the centre of the table and dropping his voice to a silvery whisper. 'It's pretty much sucked the lifeblood out of me, actually.'

'That's p-p-probably enough,' Dobbin says softly.

George moves his head mournfully from side to side. 'And as for the in-laws—'

'George, stop it,' I say, taking hold of his wrist and pinning it to the table. I'm so used to laying claim to him physically that I do this without thinking.

Quickly, I move my hand away as he twists his head towards me, a distant smile on his face.

'Not my parents,' Amelia cuts in.

'That's e-e-enough,' Dobbin says again, still softly.

The two men hold each other's gaze across the table as around us an exodus starts from the sweltering marquee.

George breaks into a wavering smile, the first to look away. But he's in a brutal mood tonight.

'Lost more than his money, old Sedley,' he persists, loudly. 'Last time I saw him – which was, admittedly, some years ago now – he recited all of Longfellow's "Hiawatha" for me.' Then, wheezing, he starts to mimic an old man's shaking rendition of 'Hiawatha'. 'On the shores of Gitchee Gumee, of the shining Big-Sea-Water—'

'For God's sake, shut up.' Rawdon brings his hand down hard on the table. Bang. Things rattle. We all flinch.

'Yes, Longfellow doesn't really cut it any more.' George turns back to Amelia. 'Afterwards, he mistook you for your mother, d'you remember?'

Amelia, twisting her wine glass between bitten fingers, looks away, her jaw loose and quivering.

The shadows inside the marquee have grown tall and hotel staff are now moving discreetly from table to table, encouraging people outside, into the gardens.

Rawdon stands up, shunting his chair away with such force that it falls backwards. He holds his hand out to Amelia, pulling her up beside him. Dobbin is quick to bounce to his feet at the same time.

They stand together, all three of them, staring down at George and me.

'Lizzie was right about you. She was right about everything. You two deserve each other,' Amelia says.

They start to move away, soon disappearing into the crowd being corralled by uniformed staff, Dobbin loping after them.

I get up to follow. George tries catching my hand, but I snatch it away.

'What the fuck are you doing?'

'Trying to leave my wife.'

'Not on my account, you aren't.'

I move before he has time to react, joining the crowd spilling into the remains of the day, forced by those around me across the dew-ridden lawn towards the sound of music coming from the pavilion by the lake. The less sober are teetering and unsteady on the uneven ground. Close by there's a squeal of laughter. A girl topples over in a flash of silver and is helped back to her feet. When she's upright once more, I recognize Violet Crawley.

'Violet.'

'Rebecca.'

Putting a hand on my shoulder to balance herself, she pulls her shoes from her feet with a graceful carelessness, towering briefly over me.

Quick to step away, I say, 'Have you seen Rawdon?'

She peers down at me. 'Rawdon? Yeah – he was with Amelia. And Dobbin. They seemed in kind of a hurry. Wanted to know if I'd seen Beth – last time I saw her, she was down in the pavilion with the other kids. We danced together.'

'You danced with Beth? But – Beth never dances.'

Violet laughs as if she doesn't believe me. 'Seriously? Your daughter can *move*, Rebecca.' She stares at me for a moment, lightly swinging the shoes in her hand. 'She was dancing with Ella Walsh's sister too.'

Although there's no reason why it should unsettle me – the thought of Dinkie dancing with Beth – for some reason it does.

'I'm surprised she came, given the venue. Must be strange for you as well. Being back at the old alma mater. Doesn't it give you the creeps?'

Violet's her father's daughter, asking me questions I'm almost certain she has the answers to. Just as Pitt used to do. I'm convinced it's a trap – the 'alma mater' was pure mockery – and yet, despite this, I feel an absurd desire to walk deeper into it rather than away.

'It was all so long ago, but it's hard to forget.' Turning on the spot, I move an arm across the horizon, pushing back twenty to thirty years. 'That was the chapel. Hockey pitches over there. Tennis courts on the other side of the house.' Pointing to a dark window hung in the back of the illuminated hotel, I add with assurance, 'And I'm almost certain that was my room.'

Violet looks, following the direction of my outstretched arm.

Both of us wait, inexplicably, for something to happen. A light to go on. A girl's face to appear.

Violet smiles. It's a smile that makes me feel exposed suddenly. As if all my flaws and imperfections, the ones I've been so careful to hide over the years, have just become visible.

'Well, I'd better head to the pavilion,' I conclude, running my eyes over the drift of people still filing past from the marquee. The whole crowd, us included, is washed in twilight's silvery pallor. No sign of Rawdon or Amelia. 'Thank you for coming tonight,' I add, meaning it.

I liked her, as a child. Still like her.

'Are you kidding? I wouldn't have missed tonight for the world.'

She means it too, I realize, feeling threatened suddenly by her sincerity.

But before I have a chance to consider this, there's a touch on my elbow, and turning around, I find myself facing Wenham.

'Matilda's leaving – she wants to see you.'

'I just need to find Rawdon, and then—'

'Now,' Wenham cuts in, 'she's leaving now.'

I follow him to where Matilda's car is parked – the helicopter is taking the future Prime Minister and his wife back to Oxfordshire – and slide onto the back seat. My hands rest on the manufacturer's transparent protection, which hasn't yet been removed even though the car is several years old. The interior still smells of new upholstery. Matilda, I've noticed, has a fear of spoiling things. Of leaving traces.

One of her earliest pieces of advice to me was, 'Remain invisible.'

And apart from the publicity garnered during the Ella Walsh campaign, it's advice I've stuck to.

She continues to peer through the window at the floodlit facade of Chilston House. 'I heard that there's been some sort of row and that Rawdon's leaving?'

'He'll be back.'

Although suddenly, I'm not so sure. I'm not so sure at all, which is why I need to find him before he disappears with Beth.

But Matilda brushes this aside with a flutter of stubby fingers. Her face is unreadable in the dark car. 'Well, it's a shame things had to blow up tonight. More than a shame.' She tails off, turning to me. 'Rebecca, you know the board's decision to make you CEO was unanimous – but you should also know that I offered CEO to Rawdon first.'

This is such a ludicrous thought that before I can stop myself, I laugh. I know how strongly Matilda feels about family. But still.

'He didn't tell you?'

She looks sideways at me, genuinely curious.

Shaking my head, I turn towards the window in order to hide the shock.

'He turned it down. Of course.'

'Of course,' I echo, squinting across the darkening lawn, certain that I can see something moving at the fringes of the rhododendrons. A child, pushing her way deeper into the bushes. My finger presses the button for the window before I'm even aware of it.

'He told me to give it to you for your birthday.'

I stare at her for a moment, but I'm distracted now. By the child. I need to warn her. The urgency of this is overwhelming suddenly as I lean out of the window, calling into the night, 'Beth!'

I thread my way through the dancers at the pavilion, pulling on their moving arms, shunting myself between their bodies. I yell above the music to ask if they've seen Rawdon with Beth – or just Beth. Amelia, even. I look for Dinkie but see no sign of her, no sign of anyone who might be able to help me. Images of my daughter dancing with Ella Walsh's sister stick in all the wrong places. The strings of lights marking the temporary structure's boundaries swing in the rising wind. Beyond the lights, darkness. Night proper now.

Common sense tells me that Rawdon's probably back at the hotel with Beth, packing their bags. Or already in the car, heading towards London. Is Amelia with them as well? But somewhere between Matilda's car and the pavilion, I've become overwhelmed by a dark fear I can't shift – that Beth is now actually missing and in danger.

I run down the steps and into the woods separating the pavilion from the lake. Moving fast through the undergrowth, my heels sink into leaf mulch, sharp straggling branches catching at my dress and arms, leaves flapping against me with intent. I'm convinced that the summer woods have formed a barrier between my daughter and me.

I carry on running in the direction I'm certain the lake lies, although the trees seem to be moving and shifting in the wind that's becoming stronger by the minute. Eventually the woods give way to something more cultivated that feels like a garden, surrounding the dark outline of a building.

In my panic, it takes me longer than it should to realize that this is the old boathouse. Now it's a yoga studio. After grappling with a gate in a high hedge, I find myself stumbling over stones and almost losing my balance. The lakeshore. It feels cold, suddenly, down near the water, although it's almost impossible, given the darkening night, to see where land ends and water begins. I twist clumsily then towards the almost mechanical sound of beating wings. A swan, maybe. Startled by something? The next minute, footsteps. Slipping and uneven. I can just make out a white shirt suspended in the darkness, making its way towards me. A man.

'Hello?'

The shirt comes to a halt, tips to one side then sways upright again, regaining its balance.

'Becky?' Rawdon's voice. No longer angry, simply scared. 'Is Beth with you?'

'No, I thought she might be with you. I've been looking for her . . . Violet said they were dancing together in the pavilion.'

'I already checked the pavilion.'

'Me too.'

'Fuck . . . This is all just . . . Fuck.'

'Did you check the hotel?'

'Hotel. Fair. Pavilion. Marquee. Grounds.'

The white shirt remains where it is, the voice coming and going as Rawdon swings around peering into the dense dark surrounding us. The only lights, distant and moving, are from the pavilion and fairground behind the treeline.

'The bird hide,' I say suddenly, my voice small.

Without waiting for a reaction, I slip off my shoes, dropping them among the stones, and try to cut up the beach. But progress is slow.

'Rebecca!' Rawdon shouts behind me.

Holding my arms out straight, I try not to lose my balance as the soles of my feet seek out stone after stone. If I don't get to her . . .

I have to get to her. I'm her mother.

I'm not aware of Rawdon following me, then suddenly he's ahead, moving away in a different direction. From memory, the bird hide should be here somewhere, but I must have strayed off course. Something shifts and oozes between my toes. The water's much closer suddenly, and brackish-smelling. There's another smell too, so sweet and sickly that it has a density to it. An image of the lakeshore seen through one of the bird hide windows comes to mind. The muddy beach made wide by summer's drought crowded with Canada geese. I must be among them now – I can feel feathered bodies shunting against me, an unnatural interloper in their midst. I begin to panic, so that I slip and slide across the muddy shore. The birds becoming increasingly unsettled, the jabbering growing louder and louder until they rise suddenly through the dark as one. Their dense, fetid smell rises with them. For a moment, I'm in the middle of this avian maelstrom, brushed all over by feathers until I worry that I've perhaps sprouted feathers myself and am about to give flight.

And then they're gone.

'I've found her,' Rawdon's voice calls out close by, relief weighing it down. 'Becky? I've found her.'

Dimly, a child takes shape against the dark shifting backdrop of the lake.

The geese have brought me to a standstill, and with each second that passes I can feel my feet sinking further into the mud. My first thought is that Rawdon's talking about Ella. Somewhere between Matilda's car and the lakeshore, the line between Ella and Beth has become blurred, my eyes trying to pick out the shorts and yellow butterfly T-shirt that Ella was wearing the day she disappeared. But the semi-visible child on the beach between me and the water is wearing a dress. She's younger than Ella. And her hair's longer.

'Beth,' I try, unsure whether I've said her name out loud or not. 'Where did you go?'

I feel dishevelled, disorderly suddenly, and I don't want to frighten her away because Beth, I know, startles easily.

'I was exploring and then it got dark.'

'I'm going to take Beth back to the hotel. We'll probably head home.'

For Beth's sake, he's trying to keep his voice light.

'You can't be leaving? Rawdon, this is ridiculous.'

'So – leave with us. It's the last time I'm going to ask.'

'You said you wouldn't do this,' I explode, 'but here you are making me choose.'

'You chose a long time ago, Becky. I just don't have the energy to pretend otherwise any more. I thought something shifted in Venice.'

'Venice?' I laugh into the dark.

I immediately regret it, aware that I've forfeited something I can't afford to lose. Too late.

'I'll call you tomorrow, Rebecca.'

'Wait,' I almost scream this time. 'Beth, wait!'

But the two figures on the shore have become one united outline, and they're moving away from me back towards the lights and music on the other side of the lake.

I try to pull myself upright, out of the mud, but find it hard to move my legs – any part of me.

'Rawdon, you can't leave me at my own birthday party.' I pause, listening.

There's silence for a moment, only undercut by the lapping of the lake and the heavy beating of wings as the Canada geese land around me again. I can't make out Rawdon and Beth any more. It's as if they've vanished completely, and for a moment I worry that they were never there at all.

# Breaking

I leave sleep reluctantly, rising to the surface before slipping under again. The sensation is repetitive and soothing and unfamiliar. It has been so long since I allowed myself to wake up rather than being woken. My eyes flicker open, then shut against the close air in the room. My head is heavy and hurting.

Although the bed beside me is empty, I can hear movement beyond it.

I would like it to be Rawdon, but he left last night.

Wenham organized a media blackout across the entire weekend – anything to do with company security comes under his jurisdiction – so no phones. And satellites have been jammed. The blackout made it safer than usual for everyone to drink, and after Rawdon left, I became very drunk very fast. Something that makes it hard now for me to remember exactly what did happen last night.

George. I remember dancing with George in front of everyone, fixed under the pavilion's lighting. And it's George's familiar sweat on me, that I can smell as I turn my head.

I sit up carefully, becoming aware of voices outside. Chairs scraping on the terrace below. Distant aeroplanes. Birds.

The curtains are drawn but the sunlight outside is strong. There's a freshness to it, a playfulness that makes me realize it's far earlier than I first thought.

Pulling the sheet around me, I survey last night's debris, clothing that looks like it has been blown about in a gale before coming to rest on furniture and floor. My chest, shoulders and arms are criss-crossed with brittle-looking scratches that feel strangely familiar. So familiar that for a moment I wonder if they're old wounds risen to the surface. And my right foot, which has slid out from under the duvet, is filthy. A patchy memory of dancing without shoes last night rises.

The bathroom door opens, and George appears.

'Seen my shirt?' he asks without enthusiasm, conducting a half-hearted search of the bed before sinking onto the end of it, his face breaking into a smile. 'Well, we fucked up last night.'

Numb, I watch his hand move towards my face. Fingering one of my earlobes, distracted, he says, 'We weren't careful, and I'm glad. This has been a long time coming, Rebecca.'

There's a knocking at the door.

Rawdon, I think.

I imagine him stepping into the room in one of his smoky vicarage jumpers, the wool unravelling at the wrists. Old cords with indeterminable dark patches across the knees. Threadbare tennis shoes. His hair still in sleep-ridden clumps.

I imagine us making for each other. A bounding rush across the room. Both of us having slept off last night's row.

But George would bring Rawdon to a standstill. Startling him. A spectre. Then his eyes would shift to the bed, its messy contours, before jerking back to me. Blank for a moment but becoming gradually more focused. Staring at me. Through me. And then he would leave. Again.

Another tap.

George is already on his feet, instinctively retreating into the dark bathroom. 'Don't answer it!'

Ignoring this – what's done is done – and keeping the sheet wrapped around me, I tread carefully through the mess and open the door.

In the corridor outside, a young man stands beside a

trolley laden with breakfast trays and newspapers. I notice that he looks petrified and that he's passing me a copy of a broadsheet – the *Post*. There's a photograph of Ella Walsh on the front page. It's the photograph we used in all our publicity and appeals, cut off just below the nose where the newspaper has been folded in half.

'Happy birthday,' he gabbles while attempting a three-point turn.

It's then that Wenham appears from nowhere, approaching at speed.

The two of them are framed briefly in the open doorway, like a haphazard arrangement for a still life. But I barely register Wenham, all my attention taken by the newspaper I've just been handed.

'Wait,' I call out to the boy's fleeing back, light catching at the buckle on his waistcoat, 'who's this from?'

And then lots of things seem to happen simultaneously.

A flash from somewhere.

A photographer, I think, stunned, not quite believing it as another round of flashes goes off. Instinctively, I cover my face with the newspaper. The other hand grips the sheet, trying to keep it pulled around me. This image will be reproduced in tomorrow's papers. Over and over again. Taken by a photographer who shouldn't have been able to get access in a million years.

Unless access was given. But, who? Pitt? Possibly. Wenham? Possibly. On Matilda's instructions? Possibly. The more I think about it in the split second between the flash going off and Wenham grabbing at the newspaper and pushing me back into the room, the longer the list grows. Malcolm? Rawdon, even? George? Amelia? Violet, who said she wouldn't have missed my party for the world?

The door slams shut.

I remain fixed on Wenham, aware of an errant breast flopping out of the side of the sheet.

He stares flatly at this. His face, for the first time ever, is without even the hint of a smile, and although he's standing still there's a sense of urgency about him. He looks hurried somehow. His eyes slide towards George in the bathroom doorway, barefoot and bare-chested, before jerking back to the newspaper he's holding.

The headline – MURDERED ELLA'S PHONE HACKED – is clear enough from where I'm standing. And below it, a photograph of me with a smile that in the days, weeks and months to come, the media will start to refer to as cryptic.

'Who . . .'

Breathing comes hard. The pressure from the headache has now become a migraine, blinding.

I grab at the paper, ripping through it, scanning the headings and sub-headings. They've gone all out for the *Mercury*. Me. George, for his time there. Others as well. Claiming that hacking was rampant. Not just Ella but royals, politicians, celebrities. It's Ella, however, that they keep coming back to. I check the by-line – it isn't Violet, but she must have known. Surely. Only Violet isn't here.

Struggling to fold the newspaper back up, I hurl it across the room at Wenham. It misses, hitting the side of the bed instead, before sliding to the carpet where Ella lies face-up staring at us all.

'Media blackout?'

Stalking to the window, I pull at an edge of curtain before letting it drop quickly back into place.

'Matilda's called an emergency briefing. We're leaving now,' Wenham concludes, nonplussed by my fury.

I watch, confused for a moment, as he starts to move among the room's debris. Sifting. Collecting things into piles. Finding

George's shirt among the bedding and giving it an inadvertent sniff. Agile. Adept. Practised. And finally, it catches up with me. He's removing all traces of George from the room. This sort of clean-up operation is not unusual for Wenham.

'Matilda has no idea about this.' He flaps his hand between George and me, clutching the shirt to his chest as if anticipating a fight over it. 'She won't like it. So, we should keep it quiet.'

I follow Trish through the front door and into the hallway of her Fulham house. Her hair, now entirely grey, is scraped back in a girlish ponytail. Her make-up-free face is so unguarded that I feel as though I've taken her by surprise, even though I phoned on the way here and asked to see her.

Worried she might be about to change her mind, I grab at her, forcing us into a clumsy hug. Her six Yorkshire terriers – the reason she wasn't able to come to my party – thread themselves excitedly through our ankles. Physical contact isn't something I usually go in for, but it's a relief to hold on to someone.

'Thanks for seeing me – we've got ten minutes. Wenham's outside and Matilda's waiting in Wapping.'

I've been phoning home and Rawdon's mobile all morning, leaving messages. I've also been trying to get hold of Dinkie, but the hotel staff said she checked out in the early hours.

Trish leads the way through rooms that smell of toast, dog, furniture polish and floral air freshener, rooms overstuffed with furniture, paintings and china ornaments that feel inherited – as if everything in the house has been transplanted wholesale from her childhood.

I was expecting tidy neglect. A well-trimmed emptiness.

But the rooms we pass through feel homely, lived in.

'What a Shitanory,' she announces as we reach the kitchen, the dogs snapping around our ankles.

She sounds almost cheerful as she jerks her head towards the copy of the *Post*, folded on the table.

My eyes meet Ella's before straying to other things – a teapot under a tea cosy, a half-full toast rack, trails of crumbs. She must have been in the middle of breakfast when she got the call from me. There are crocheted cushions on the chairs and postcards stuck to the fridge door. Potted geraniums line the windowsills, and on the walls there are posters of past Wandsworth Amateur Operatic productions that Trish must have sung soprano in.

I watch as she fills a kettle and puts it on the hob to boil.

The feeling of safety is overwhelming. I would like to stay in this room and never leave it.

'So, what happens now?' I say after a while, to the vast spread of her back as she finishes making the tea and pours two cups to the brim, easing herself into a chair and pushing a cup across the table towards me.

'You know what happens. Investigation. Arrests. Hearing. Trial.' She runs a tongue over two tidy rows of teeth, enunciating each word carefully. 'In that order.'

I remain standing behind the chair on the opposite side of the table, tipping it gently backwards and forwards against my stomach. 'It isn't going to go away, is it?'

'Not this time. The scale of it.' With one deft swipe of her hand, the copy of the *Post* is opened. She turns the pages at random before training her eyes on me over the raised cup, looking worried for the first time. 'Ella's only the tip of the iceberg. We're talking about the phones and personal data of hundreds – if not thousands – of people. Public figures. The royal family. According to this, we've been listening in on the whole wide world.'

'Ella isn't the tip of the iceberg, Trish. Ella *is* the iceberg – she's going to sink us.' A scuffling – something being knocked over outside in the dank patch of London garden – although when I jerk my head to look, there's nothing out there apart from a sundial surrounded by ferns. 'Isn't she?' I demand, turning back to Trish.

'Well, she's certainly brought us to our knees. For now. Becky, sit down.'

I can't remember when it was exactly, but around a couple of years into my editorship, Trish accidentally called me Becky one day. And it stuck.

I pull out the chair I'm standing behind and fall into it, reaching for the tea in front of me and taking a few sips.

'D'you think I should resign?'

This is the reason I wanted to stop in Fulham on the way to Wapping. I realized, as soon as I got into the car with Wenham, that Trish's answer is the only one I care about.

'You're in shock – give it some time. Matilda hasn't asked you to do that.'

'She shouldn't have to . . . it's the right thing to do. Isn't it?' I push.

'Since when have you been interested in doing the right thing?'

I try a different tack. 'Why didn't I see this coming, Trish?'

'Whether you saw it or not, you wouldn't have been able to stop this. It's too big an opportunity to miss. For a lot of people.'

'Which people?'

'Becky – you're the best editor I've ever worked with. But you've made enough enemies on the way up, and now they've decided it's time to bring you down. You got too good too fast.'

When I first became editor of the *Mercury*, I thought Trish would refuse to work for me. Her loyalty lay – had always lain – so absolutely with Pitt. So, I was surprised when she accepted my offer. Until finally, I understood that there was one thing she loved more than Pitt, and that was the *Mercury*. This was our common ground.

'You need to protect yourself.' She pauses. 'And you need leverage.'

Her voice is unhurried. She makes it sound no more complicated than taking the dogs for a walk. But we both know that it's a lot more complicated than that. And although I nod in time to everything she says, my mind is running in too many different directions and her words remain out of focus. Insubstantial.

'Don't trust anybody. Not even me.'

'I thought you were the only person I *could* allow myself to trust?'

Trish finishes her cup of tea and pours another.

We sit in silence.

'I'm still trying to understand what it is I did wrong. All I wanted was to bring her home. I just wanted to bring Ella home. You see that, don't you, Trish? You believe that?'

# Arrest

Our Notting Hill home is dark and empty. No sign of Rawdon or Beth. Dropping the suitcase I hastily packed at the hotel this morning, I close all the curtains. Then I try phoning him. I phone again and again – the mobile, the Oxfordshire landline. It goes straight to answerphone every time. Rawdon hasn't returned any of my calls today.

But then, there are calls I haven't returned either. Lisa Walsh has tried me seven times and left two messages I can't bear to listen to. George also. Nothing from Dinkie.

Downstairs, I leave purposeful trails through the kitchen in order to make it feel occupied. Lived in. To make myself less of a ghost. I've never felt alone in the house before, but I do tonight.

I need the shocked stupor to wear off, but I can't shift it. The most numbing thing of all is the sense of betrayal. Who knew this was coming? Anyone but Rawdon. Please. My usual information channels, the ones I've come to take for granted over the past fifteen years – senior police officers, Paul and his team – have dried up suddenly. The day has disintegrated into panicked phone calls, clumsy meetings and careless emails. Nobody has been available to take my calls, despite the years spent building relationships. The gifts. Holidays. Watching each other's children grow. During the course of a single day, the web-like intimacy of it all has vanished without a trace. I haven't felt this abandoned since childhood.

The only person I *am* able to get hold of is the Prime Minister.

We've always got on well, but I didn't expect him to pick up after the recent coverage in the *Mercury*. This is the last panicked phone call of the day and I've pretty much given up hope.

But we're on the phone together for over an hour. The fact that he's taking my call at all means he thinks this will blow over. A supreme vote of confidence on a dark day. He's remarkably calm, but then this is the man who started a war, I remind myself. He tells me to launch an internal investigation into misconduct and wrongdoing at the *Mercury*. It's good advice. I tell him that I won't forget this. I won't ever forget this. He says he knows that. One of the many things he admires about me is that I say what I mean. There's an almost flirtatious pause after this before he tells me to take sleeping pills. You won't sleep otherwise, he says. Speaking from experience. But this advice I don't take, and sleep is thin. Brittle. Easily broken.

I lie in bed, the blood banging in my ears, convinced that every noise outside must be the harbinger of a dawn raid. In the rain against the windowpane, a trespassing fox, the slamming of car doors in the street below or a bin lorry making its early-morning rounds, I hear syncopated footfall and the hushed anticipation of trained men with the authority to break and enter.

I dream of arrest. Of uniformed people, impassive and resigned, leading me along the corridor downstairs. The front door opening onto bright sunlight and a bank of waiting photographers, crowding the pavement beneath the cherry trees, all yelling my name. And buried somewhere in the middle of the throng is the car we need to make our way towards. But suddenly the flight of steps leading from front door to pavement becomes an obstacle I'm unconvinced I'll be able to navigate. Terrified of tripping, slipping, falling, I pull back. The thick hands holding my arms tighten their grip, propel me forward into the waiting photographers. Instinctively, I try to raise an arm and hide my face. This is the shot I've been afraid of. The one Matilda has warned me to avoid at all costs. The one I'll never recover from.

We start our descent and as the waiting car finally becomes visible, I see that there's somebody already sitting in the back seat. A child. But just as they turn their face towards me, I wake up. Sweating and disorientated.

Lines of sunlight make their way around the sides of the closed curtains, fuzzily touching on the piles of discarded clothes, the suitcase that hasn't yet been unpacked, competing with the lights I left on last night. Stranded on the outskirts of sleep, I hear my phone ringing. Rawdon. This is my first thought. The hope that I'll pick up and hear his voice.

It isn't Rawdon.

It's Amelia, and she wants to see me.


I shuffle nervously around the semi-dark kitchen, curtains drawn, not daring to switch on any lights. Hands shaking, I haul at random cupboard doors in search of cups and coffee. I'm like a stranger in my own home and painfully aware of Amelia watching me.

Our initial shock at the sight of each other has only just worn off.

'Rebecca, here,' she says, pulling out a bar stool with a clatter. Patting it. 'Sit down.'

A bag from a boulangerie we get weekend pastries from has appeared.

'I thought we could do with something sweet.'

She pats the stool again.

I give up trying to navigate my own kitchen and sit down. I've barely eaten. Last night I scavenged a pack of instant noodles way past its sell-by date from a forgotten corner of the larder. Yet somehow the place is a mess.

'You don't have to do that,' I say, watching as she restores order with a quiet efficiency I would have seen as strategic in anybody else. But not Amelia. Amelia, I realize suddenly, is one of the few people I trust. One of the few people I've ever trusted. Despite having wronged her more than most.

'No,' she agrees, continuing to wipe a cloth across the kitchen surfaces before swinging open the fridge.

'I'm out of milk,' I say. 'Out of just about everything, in fact.'

Amelia's face remains hidden by the fridge door. 'I'm scared.'

'I'm scared too.'

It's a relief, the admission of fear.

Letting go of the fridge door at last, Amelia holds up a bottle of wine. There's a shy flash of complicity before her face twists shut again.

Glasses are poured.

Pastries eaten.

'How's Beth?'

She blushes as I say my daughter's name.

'And Rawdon? He's not returning my calls.'

Amelia stretches across the surface for the wine, pouring us both a second glass.

'They're staying with you, aren't they?'

Blushing still, she says, 'He's in bad shape.'

'And George?'

'I asked him to leave.'

I move my head from side to side in disbelief.

'I did!'

'So, where's he gone?'

'Dobbin. He's the only person who would take him in.'

She laughs. I laugh back. The laughter gaining momentum, spiralling towards hysterics. Soon we're both sobbing for breath and wiping at our wet cheeks. We carry on like this for a while, giving in to the illusion that we're nothing more than a couple of teenagers talking about boys. Until we remember.

'How are they taking it all – Gina? Jon?'

'It's Gina I worry about. You know how she feels about George.' The eyes flicker towards me, then flicker away. 'And now this hacking stuff. I've tried to screen them from as much of it as I can, but the things they're saying . . .' She won't look at me.

Slipping from the stool, I cross the kitchen towards the sunlight banked behind the closed curtains and tentatively pull them apart. I'm half expecting the view to have changed since yesterday.

As I let the curtains fall back into place, I hear myself say, 'Is that why you're here? An emissary from Rawdon?'

'No,' she says, the earlier poise gone. Then, again, 'No.'

'More wine?' I open a second bottle, hope fading, holding the bench as I slide back onto the bar stool. 'So, what do you want?'

'What I've always wanted. George.'

'I thought you kicked him out?'

'That's temporary, to give us both time to think things through, but he'll be back. He always comes back. Rebecca, I need you to tell me that he's going to be OK. That we're going to be OK. Me and him. You can do that.'

'None of us are going to be OK. Not this time. Not him. Not me. Not you.'

'But I love him. And I think . . . I think you love him too.' Her eyes fix on me, terrified. Tears start that she tries to shift back.

'Amelia, I don't love George.'

'You don't love George,' she repeats softly, with something close to wonder, before letting out an unbalanced laugh.

'It's why we work so well together.'

'I don't want to talk about it.' Her voice rises, irate, as she

claps her hands over her ears, flying fingers catching at the
wine glass, tipping it over. She squeezes her wet eyes shut.
Quick, childish gestures.

'Yes, you do. It's why you're here.'

'I'm here because I want you to tell me that George will
be safe. Rebecca, I need you to be kind,' she sobs, shoulders
juddering. Her face is a wet mess, sucking at the air. The last
twenty years of her life have been wiped away in a handful of
words – my words – that she'll never be able to unhear.

'I am being kind. Amelia, the only reason George married
you was because Dobbin told him to. George can never be who
you want him to be. It's not how he's built.'

Suddenly she's standing. Swollen. Shouting. 'You couldn't
stand the things I had, could you? I'll never forget the first
time I took you home to Clapham. Those eyes. The way they
rested on things. And then George . . .'

She stares at me for a moment before grabbing her bag and
throwing it over her shoulder. 'I don't know why I came here.
You'll never change.'

She makes a banging retreat from the kitchen, losing all
coordination in her desperation to leave.

'Amelia, wait. Wait.'

I pursue her up the hallway until she reaches the front door,
where we come to a halt, breathless. She wrestles with the lock
for a moment before going still suddenly, her head dropping.
Drawing it back up again with an effort, eyes empty, she says,
'Is George Beth's father?'

'No. Beth is Rawdon's daughter through and through. She's
his life – you know that.'

'Yes, Rawdon's a wonderful father.' She won't look at me.

I fall back against the wall, my hand holding loosely on to
her arm although she has stopped trying to run – is barely

moving at all, in fact. 'You have Dobbin, Amelia. You've always had Dobbin – you must know that.'

'Why are you telling me this?'

But before I have a chance to answer, the door swings open and, shaking my hand off her, Amelia stumbles out.

Later that week, they arrest George in the newsroom at the *Courier*. They turn up with warrants. I hear this from O'Dowd.

Later still, there's live footage on the news of him leaving a London police station. He's nothing more than a smudge of pale face behind a car window. They keep playing it. The same piece of footage, repeatedly. He's not allowed to contact me, isn't allowed to move from Dobbin's house without notifying the police, and has had to hand over his passport.

I stand watching with the remote in one hand, as if this will enable me to somehow change the sequence of events. In the other hand, a cup of black coffee.

And then the photograph of Ella. Eyes staring. Locking on to me. The corners of the smiling mouth lifting. I hate her. I hurl the cup at the screen and coffee runs across her face until I turn off the TV, unplugging it from the wall as well.

My mother used to unplug all the appliances and switch off the lights during electrical storms. Someone she knew as a child lived in a house that went up in flames when the TV aerial was struck by lightning. It left her terrified.

We would sit huddled on the sofa together in the dark, jumping and squealing at every rumble, every illuminating flash, counting out the seconds between.

# Another Arrest

Rawdon doesn't use his keys to let himself in; he rings on the doorbell, arriving with an overnight bag. I notice the bag immediately.

'How's Beth?'

This is the first thing I say when I open the front door.

In the outside world, beyond his shoulders, there are people playing tennis on the courts in the square. Evening is shifting towards night. He slides quickly into the house, the hallway hung with a golden haze that makes it easy for him to avoid looking at me.

'Not good. Doesn't want to go to school. We've had temper tantrums and her eczema's flaring up again.'

I picture the dark creases behind Beth's knees and at the elbows, the wounding red that will have crept across her skin. And suddenly I feel an intense yearning for her, a physical need for her taut young body with its decisive shoulders and thin arms. The possibility of her.

'She's wet the bed a couple of times, as well.' He shrugs, his face full of an old sadness. 'But – she's holding out.'

We move cautiously towards the kitchen. I was in the middle of preparing supper when he arrived. I actually gave tonight's meal a lot of thought. Too much, I realize suddenly, panicked by my own efforts. I shopped nervously in Fortnum's earlier, my hair pushed under a cap. The things I bought look dead and ugly laid out on the surface under the bright lights, smug in their turquoise wrappings.

'Hungry?'

'Oh.' He looks terrified. 'No, my appetite's fucked.'

Yesterday – Friday – I received summons to present myself at Lewisham police station on Sunday morning. It was this summons, finally, that prompted Rawdon to respond to over a week's worth of unanswered calls.

It is unusual to be given so much notice.

Unusual, also, to be summoned on a Sunday.

These courtesies have been extended me not because of my relationship with the Met's Commissioner, but because of the diaries. The police have scoured company archives for the rumoured 'darkroom' diaries that so many people have asked for under so many different auspices, without results.

'We should probably just . . .' Rawdon's eyes dart towards the bottle of wine and, grabbing it, he retreats from the kitchen to the sitting room whose curtains have remained closed all week, collapsing onto a sofa. I follow with glasses, unable to remember when we last sat on the sofa together.

He stretches towards a sidelight, switching it on before pouring the wine.

'Rebecca, there's a very real possibility they're going to arrest you tomorrow.'

True as it is, hearing him say it feels like a betrayal. 'We don't know that for sure, my lawyers haven't been able to confirm it. And I can't get hold of Paul – so, where are you getting your information from?'

Ignoring this, he says, 'There's going to be a trial.'

His voice is soft, almost soothing.

'Rawdon, did you know this was coming?'

'Does it matter?'

'Yes, it matters.'

'D'you want to know what matters to me – the only thing

that matters in all of this? Whether or not the allegations are true.'

He pours another glass of wine.

'Are you wearing a wire?'

'What? Jesus, no.' He laughs, baffled. 'Jesus,' he says again, putting down his wine and undoing his shirt. He becomes increasingly angry with each button until they're all undone, the shirt ripping as he pulls it off, balling it up and hurling it as hard as he can towards one of the room's many dark corners.

He holds up his arms – 'Happy?' – before grabbing at his glass and collapsing, semi-naked, back onto the sofa again. 'That's the problem with you, Rebecca. Your priorities are all wrong, always have been. Shit, if I'm being honest, there's a part of me that's actually glad they've caught up with you.'

Something stirs behind the curtains. I'm certain I sense movement. A faint billowing. I stand up, feeling the need suddenly to move about the room, put some distance between us. 'If there's a trial—'

'There's going to be a trial,' he says again.

'They'll be prosecuting us for telling the truth about people who told lies. That's absurd.'

'Yes, but it's how you came by that truth. You really can't see it, can you? They're saying that the *Mercury*'s been hacking into the phone messages of a murdered schoolgirl.'

I lower myself into a chair opposite him. 'But even if that's true, we didn't know that then.'

'Fuck.' He presses his hand over his mouth. 'Rebecca, you must see. Your newspaper crossed a line. Other people's pain. Grief. You had no right to that, and you certainly had no right to trade in it. It isn't a . . . a . . . commodity.'

'Our coverage of Ella Walsh had one goal, and one goal alone. We were trying to save a child's life.'

'Compelling.' Rawdon leans forward, spreading his knees

and clasping his hands between them. His stomach falls into a couple of tight folds. 'But you're in denial.'

'I'm not in denial, Rawdon. And this isn't about Ella. Not really. It's about power – they think we've got too much. We're changing things that nobody wants changed. Things that need changing because life's unfair – and why should anybody's story end there? That's the fight. It's always been my fight. You want to know what this is? It's a big, costly, public slap on the wrist for stepping out of line.'

Rawdon's phone starts ringing. Glancing at the screen, he takes the call, disappearing towards the kitchen.

I listen to his voice, the brushing intimacy of it. Beth. He's talking to Beth.

I follow him.

In the kitchen, he paces, semi-naked still.

'Can I speak to her?'

'Hang on a minute. Beth? I've got Mummy here. Oh. OK.'

He shakes his head, but I make a grab for the phone anyway. 'Beth? Beth?' I listen to her laboured breathing for a couple of seconds before the line goes dead. 'She cut me off.'

I stare at the phone in my hand, keeping hold of it.

'Rebecca, we need to talk about Beth.'

'She cut me off,' I say again.

He reaches for the phone, gently prising it off me and pushing it into a pocket. 'What we tell her, and what we do if it comes to a trial. Look, there's something I've been thinking.' He pauses. 'You should consider pleading guilty in order to negotiate a reduced sentence.'

'Why would I do that?'

'Beth. Some of the charges you could be looking at come with a long sentence.'

'How do you know what charges I could be looking at? Wenham? Tell me who your source is. Rawdon, tell me,' I repeat, pushing my face against his chest, clawing at him. He catches at my wrists. I try to reach his mouth, but he twists away. Undeterred, I start kissing any part of him I can reach.

'Stop. Rebecca, stop.'

'You want to. I know you want to.'

'We're not doing this.'

'Why not?'

Keeping hold of my wrists, he takes a step back. 'When did you stop loving me?'

I laugh, stare at him. Let myself go limp. 'Not now, Rawdon. I can't talk about this now.'

'You don't know how to love.'

'I love,' I hear myself shout suddenly, as if everything depends on it. 'I *do* love.'

'So, say it.'

He stands, waiting.

The next morning, Rawdon emerges fully dressed from the spare room, shaking his arms so that the shirt cuffs settle in just the right place beneath the jacket's sleeves. Caught in the corridor together, our eyes skate over each other. Both of us are in black. Wearing too much money, I think. In the kitchen, we drink our coffee standing propped against opposite benches. Stiff, silent and preoccupied.

Neither of us eats.

I can't imagine ever feeling hungry again.

Abandoning our cups with a clatter in the sink, we leave the house. Rawdon steers me down the steps and across the pavement towards the car with a hand on my elbow. I miss the feeling of his hand when he lets go, disappearing around the back of the car to the other side.

It's early. The light is bright and unpolluted still. By midday, the park's burnt grass will be strewn with sunbathers. I feel

myself stretching briefly towards them, these anonymous figures with their books and phones and music.

We pause before getting in the car, staring at each other
across the glinting roof. It's the last thing I remember with any
real clarity. The empty, early-morning street.

Everything after this is a tumult. Crossing the river, the
London skyline becomes low-slung. Halal chicken shops, nail
bars, Turkish grocers, power churches. Lewisham police station with reporters already banked against the security gates,
despite the Sunday summons. My name being yelled. An
orchestrated media bloodbath.

'Did you know this was coming?' I say, repeating last night's
question.

Rawdon puts his hand on my arm again. 'Walk. Just keep
on walking.'

The heat inside the police station is unbearable, the few
plug-in fans doing nothing apart from making the blinds rattle
and piles of paper flap. Everything I lay eyes on is chipped and
scuffed and battered, reminding me of the flat I grew up in. I
re-read the same cautionary drugs poster Blu-tacked to the wall
in reception, eyes trailing the out-of-order sign on the coffee
machine. The empty water dispenser.

Rawdon was right.

I am arrested.

Then escorted to an interview room that seems impossibly
small. So small that in my memory I'm sure I crawled into it
on hands and knees.

# Haversham

It was a couple of weeks before Christmas. I don't remember when exactly, but I do know that it was the afternoon, and that her bedside light was on.

Standing at the foot of the bed, breath held, I felt it immediately – an overwhelming sense of departure.

My mother – an untidy sprawl of limbs at strange angles, with her face turned towards the window. It was as if someone had attempted to tidy her away in a box that was too small and given up. She had lost her skirt but was still wearing the shirt she had come home in yesterday. Her hair was a sweaty tangle covering her face.

Keeping to the left-hand side of the room, I picked up the empty pot from the bedside table. For once, the lid had been screwed neatly back on. When had she done this? Last night while I slept next door? This morning while I was at school? After making her mind up, she must have felt momentarily calm, to have screwed the cap back on so carefully. But it couldn't have lasted long. There was nothing calm about the way she lay. The way she lay signalled a struggle of some kind. That in the end she had fought. And lost.

This, I realized suddenly, was what defeat looked like.

Staring at the pot, I read out her name, which had been handwritten across the label. First name. Surname. As a whole, the name looked unfamiliar. But saying it out loud, I felt a heavy tenderness I had no outlet for.

My first thoughts were practical. 999. Ambulance. Police.

Whoever it was you were meant to call when you thought somebody might be dead. Out of habit, I shut the bedroom door as quietly as I could. I tiptoed my way along the corridor to the kitchen where the telephone was, lifted the receiver and dialled the first 9. The second 9. And then I replaced it, soundlessly. What if I made the call and people in uniforms arrived and my mother turned out not to be dead after all? Imagine that. The ridicule. How she would laugh. It could even be a trick, I reasoned. She liked to play tricks on me.

But standing beside the bed, I'd been *certain* my mother was dead.

Mark, the one man in her life she had held out for, had finally decided to end the relationship yesterday. After five years.

When I arrived home from school last night, she was drunk and furious, hair wild, her face a dark smudge of mascara. In the kitchen, plates that had been left on the draining board after breakfast had been swept onto the floor. As had a bottle of milk. I could smell it as soon as I opened the front door. In the lounge, curtains had been pulled from their railings and a lamp lay on its side. The tasselled shade was crushed. She'd left bloodied footprints on the carpet after she'd trailed, oblivious, through the broken glass and china.

I'd cleaned since then, but the stains remained. Perhaps this was the real reason I rang off. Violence had taken root in our silent home. And what if they'd asked me why I'd left her alone, in the state she was in, with a full pot of sleeping tablets? Could I have prevented it? Was I in some way culpable? Complicit even? What if they asked me a whole host of twisting, turning questions that would lead them to those things I was trying to hide from myself? What if some small part of me had wished for this?

I rang at Angelina's door, pressing on the bell even though

there were no lights on in the flat. Continuing to press even after remembering that Angelina and Paul had gone north to Manchester for Christmas.

I'd left the house without shoes and my socked feet were soon soaking wet – my face as well. There were tears hanging from the edge of my chin. Useless. They weren't going to illuminate the dark windows in Angelina's flat. I gave my face a frustrated swipe that stopped just short of a slap. Returning home, I stripped off the socks, leaving them on the mat by the front door, and made my way, barefoot, back towards my mother's bedroom. I stopped halfway up the corridor, convinced I could hear running water coming from the bathroom. A sudden updraught of hope saw me pushing open the door with real expectation. The bath was almost full and at the sight of this – the water lapping at the rim – I felt duped.

The seal on the cold tap was broken. You had to twist hard to stop it from dripping and she'd forgotten to do this. Five minutes later and it would have flooded the entire flat. I turned off the tap and pulled the plug. The water I plunged my arm through was icy. She must have run the bath hours ago. Stamping and banging my way back into the bedroom, I started yelling. Yelling at her.

All the things I'd ever wanted to say. Recriminations. Accusations. Torrential. Nonsensical. Circling the bed with one sleeve rolled up, my right arm wet from the bath. It was the last rage of childhood. Afterwards, I collapsed on the end of the bed.

While I was shouting, caught up in my rage still, I wanted to hurt her. Physically hurt her. But now, curled up and spent on the end of the bed, I simply rested a hand on one of her unnaturally cold ankles. And as my breathing calmed, I became aware that the room felt heavier somehow. That's the only way I can describe it. As if everything in it had gained weight during my brief absence. Even the mascara-blackened tissues balled up on the bedside table looked like they would be impossible to lift.

I stared at my hand, loosely clasping one of her ankles.

If I hadn't been certain before, I was certain now.

I felt it then – the childish need for an adult.

Leaping up, I ran from the room and along the corridor as if I was being chased. Pushing my bare feet into a pair of Dunlop Green Flash trainers by the front door, it took me a while to find the car key, which wasn't hanging from its usual hook on the wall.

It also took me five attempts to get the car started, while gabbling to myself and shuddering with the cold. In the rear-view mirror, I could see the light still on in my mother's bedroom.

Mark was the adult who came to mind.

The cause of all this, and yet – he knew me. Her. Us. He would help me, I thought, as I left the house, the street and my childhood behind.

# The Trial of the Century

The court is full.

The media – most of them linked to this room via screens that have been set up in Court 19 to cope with the overspill – have dubbed it the trial of the century.

I made the mistake of wearing black at the hearing – a simply cut McQueen tunic dress. But as the charges against me were read out, the cut of the dress felt increasingly dramatic. Too late, I realized that the white Peter Pan collar made me look like something out of Salem.

I went viral.

All these months later, on my first day in the witness box, I've been careful to wear unassuming browns and whites. Colours that make me look like the depressed first wife of a celebrity golfer. Colours a woman wears in order to make herself invisible.

Gone are the black patent leather Louboutins because I now know that when asked to stand in court, my legs shake uncontrollably. These have been replaced by a pair of flat pumps. My trademark restless hair has been pulled back from a make-up-free face. I'm glad. After months pinned under glass in the dock at the back of Court 12 along with George and Malcolm, the witness box feels exposing.

William Thackeray, QC, is heading up my defence counsel and gives me an ambiguous glance. By some strange accident of fate, he was also the prosecutor responsible for successfully convicting Lester Hayes of Ella's murder.

The first time I met him, he had bandages on his knuckles. He'd spent the weekend surfing with his daughter in Devon and come off his board in turbulent waters. He is one of the few QCs to have been to a comprehensive school. His mother was also a cleaner. I can't remember whether he told me this himself, or whether I found out elsewhere. But it's something we have in common.

'Stowaways,' he called us at that first meeting.

Only a few days ago, he had his wig stolen from the robing room. 'Just a prank,' he said, his face briefly flat with a child-hood pain.

Today, he's wearing an emergency wig he had to buy from a theatrical supplier. The irony of this isn't lost on either of us as he swears me in. The stupor that has settled over the court during the past three months of prosecutions has finally lifted. The pursuit of the truth, it turns out, is a tedious business. And it's the memory of this tedium that William has decided to pit himself against. It's a strategy that's already paying off. At my appearance in the witness box, the mood in Court 12 has lightened. I've been careful to make eye contact with the eight women jurors and received an unexpected swell of sympathy.

Opposite the jury, high up in the windowless courtroom beneath the curved and peeling ceiling, I can see Amelia and Dobbin. No sign of Rawdon. I don't look for Jack and Lisa Walsh. Or Dinkie. But I know they're here, as are all of us, because of Ella. She has brought the Crawley empire, the government and a whole country to its knees. Just as Trish said she would.

Because children, more than anything, are what this trial is about.

Lost children. Childhoods.

Standing now through the hush full of staring eyes, I say my name. 'Rebecca Sharp.' My hand is trembling on the ledge in front of me, beside the silver and black microphones. My voice catches. Laddered.

And then, for the first time ever, I promise to tell the truth. The whole truth.

A long time ago, Rawdon asked me for this. He assured me that it was the truth he wanted and that it wouldn't change a thing. But the truth changes everything. There's such an awful intimacy to it. A banality, even. Perhaps this is why the one time I actually – publicly – tell the truth, and not just to this room of forty or so people, but to the hundreds and thousands beyond it, I'm accused by the media of delivering a carefully scripted performance.

The performance of a lifetime.

# Haversham

Somewhere on the road between our flat and Chilston House School, it struck me that I was now alone. The sluggish rain turned to snow. It was only the third or fourth time I'd driven the car by myself, and I couldn't find the switches I needed to get rid of the condensation building up on the windscreen. Instead, I kept rubbing at it with the sleeve of my coat. Visibility was terrible. The snow was already settling, and it was becoming hard to see the edges of the road. I was chattering to myself in a nervy litany. I sounded like a crazy person, and just as I made the decision to turn around and go back home, I saw the swans on top of the entrance gates to Chilston House School. The crest of snow on their heads had turned them into a different species.

The place felt abandoned, dark windows and dark trees shifting in the wind. It was something I should have anticipated, but in my shock at what had happened that day, I'd forgotten. Term had finished and although a lot of staff lived on site, there didn't seem to be anybody around.

My tyres slid across the snow as I drove past the music block towards the Crisps' cottage. It was one of the few inhabited buildings, light shining from almost all the windows. A lone fox crossed in front of the headlights and I banged on the brakes, skidding to a stop as it disappeared. I stepped out into the snow, feeling unbalanced and strangely breathless.

My trainers were soon soaked through, although I was only vaguely aware of the pain in my feet as I pushed open the gate and stumbled across the silent white garden, trying not to trip on the jumble of wellingtons in the porch before banging on the front door. A curtain was lifted, and a woman's pale face appeared. I moved into the illuminated patch of snow. We stared at each other through the glass.

The curtain was dropped.

Nothing happened for a while.

Then the front door opened a crack and Mark appeared, bewildered. Seeing him in context for the first time was a shock. The woman from the window stood behind him with a tumult of little Crisps around her ankles. Mark's family. The house was warm and shimmering with festive greens and reds and silvers. Christmas chez Crisp was all the colours Christmas should be. I imagined being invited in, being wrapped in blankets in front of a blazing fire, encouraged to slip off my wet shoes, plied with hot chocolate.

'Mr Crisp?' I ventured, breaking the stunned silence at last. The breath from my mouth formed a puff that hung in the air. And for the benefit of Mrs Crisp, 'It's Rebecca. Rebecca Sharp. I used to play piano.'

Nobody spoke. Having been preoccupied for the past few minutes by my wet shoes, the Crisps en masse shifted their gaze, staring beyond me into what was now a blizzard, as if worried I might bring more than just myself in from the cold.

Once inside I was quickly ushered into a study, away from the rest of the family. Mark gestured towards a sofa whose print of birds on branches became threadbare up close. He sat in the desk chair opposite, elbows on the armrests, hands together, fingertips pressing into his lips. It made him look attentive. Concerned, even. He had turned down the volume on the record player, but carols were still playing at a whisper. I have no idea what I said, only that I somehow managed to convey to him that my mother was dead. Saying it out loud, I felt shocked for the first time. And then before Mark had time to react, Mrs Crisp arrived with a cup of tea.

They left the study together. Soon, I could hear the strained squeak of their conversation through the wall. I stood up when it rose into an argument and drifted across the room to the piano where a book of beginner's pieces was open. Keeping one hand wrapped around the warm mug, I picked out some Schubert with the other while glancing around the study, anger biting at my fingers.

Where on earth did my mother think she was going to fit into all this?

Mark reappeared alone. He stared at me for what felt like a long time. The snow was getting worse. It was best I went home, called an ambulance. He was happy to drive me. He said this loudly, for Mrs Crisp's benefit, I guess.

'No,' I said, more urgently than I meant to. 'I can't go home. I have to stay here.'

He shook his head, distracted.

'She's dead, Mark! Don't you even care?'

I grabbed hold of his arm, thrusting myself up close to him as I carried on pleading. For a moment he was startled. Then, changing tack: 'Is she definitely dead? I mean, she can be quite the drama queen when she wants to.'

'Why don't you come and see for yourself!' I shouted.

'Shush,' he mouthed at me, making a calming motion with his hands through the air, then starting to sob uncontrollably. 'OK,' he said, trying to calm himself, to stifle the betraying sounds he was making. 'OK.'

We were both breathing heavily.

Then, in a voice that was almost normal, he said that it wasn't going to be possible for me to stay. Unfortunately. Christmas.

Family commitments. He crossed to the study door, opening it, and couldn't look at me as he spoke.

I stopped listening. My feet hurt. My fingers went back to picking out Schubert. But, he said, looking up at last, he would make all necessary arrangements to deal with the situation. By 'situation', I guessed he meant my dead mother. He jerked his head. Defiance? Grief? I wasn't to worry, he announced. His voice wavered.

I followed him into the hallway, where he started to gather the things he would need to drive me home. An anorak and a pair of gloves.

'You coward,' I yelled. 'You fucking coward!'

Before wrenching open the front door, crashing back over the wellies and heading out into the frozen night towards my mother's parked car.

As I pulled away, Mrs Crisp's worried face loomed at the study window. Through the condensation inside the car, the cottage had been reduced to a glow in the dark. I didn't want to leave that glow. Returning home was unthinkable. As the engine finally came to life, the panic closed in. There had to be somewhere, anywhere else I could go.

I drove slowly through what was fast becoming a whiteout. Visibility was so poor that it was impossible to tell where the edges of the road lay. It took me almost an hour to crawl back into town, using the Ciba-Geigy pharmaceuticals factory as a navigational beacon. George lived in a street of bungalows just behind this, something that had surprised me when I drove him home a couple of months ago while his car was in the garage. I'd always thought that he lived in one of the outlying villages, although when I came to think about it, I'm not sure why I thought this. He hadn't specifically said anything, simply dropped hints at the pub and given the vague impression that this was the case. Or perhaps it was the way he dressed and the way he spoke that led me to that conclusion.

Tonight, I didn't care. I just wanted him to be home.

His car was parked outside and there was blue light from a TV coming through the front window. I'd lost all track of time and – worried that the lights might flicker out at any moment – pulled clumsily on the door handle, thrusting my sodden trainers into deep snow. The world felt empty and full of a heavy silence as I crunched through the gate, hanging lopsided from its hinges.

I stood beneath a porch light that I doubted was ever switched on and rang the doorbell, triggering an ugly buzzing on the other side. When the sound died down, all I could hear was the TV. In the orange glow coming from the factory, reflected into the sky by the snow carpeting the streets, I had an impression of all too familiar neglect. I rang again. This time I heard shouts, followed by banging footsteps.

The door swung open, and George stood there staring out at me. His eyes slow. Features stung-looking. Bringing the smell of pot with him. The house – apart from the TV's light – was dark.

'Becky?'

His voice sounded stupid rather than surprised, like it was about to collapse into giggles. And although I realized that it was unreasonable of me to expect him to know what I'd been through that night, for some reason it offended me that he didn't.

'Can I come in?'

He nodded yes but said no, stumbling against the open door like he was having trouble keeping his balance. 'Now's not a good time.'

'George, come on,' I pleaded.

'What the fuck, Becky,' he said, pulling his eyes across the snow-covered world beyond my shoulders, and then me. 'You in trouble?'

'Yeah, I'm in big trouble.'

We watched each other for a while.

'Seriously,' I added, before saying again, 'can I come in?'

He pulled me across the threshold, shutting the door as quietly as he could and putting a finger to his lips, despite the volume of the TV. Gunfire. Police sirens. The screeching tyres of a car chase.

'George – who the fuck is that at this time of night?' a voice heavy with drink cranked out over the sound of the TV.

'No fucking idea,' he yelled back, keeping his eyes – bright in the hallway's gloom – on me.

'And where's my fucking food – you're taking your time.'

'Coming!'

Putting his finger to his lips again, George took hold of my hand and we crept towards the back of the house. He flicked on a harsh strip light that buzzed before unevenly coming to life to reveal a kitchen. There was a white plastic garden table and chairs filling most of the available floor space and stretches of brown packing tape stuck to the carpet – to conceal worn patches, I guessed. The air smelt bad. Stale lives and unemptied bins.

I watched George push a ready meal into the microwave and get a six-pack of beer out of the fridge. There was something different about his silhouette and it took me a while to realize that he was wearing a substantial number of layers. There was good reason for this – it was freezing cold in the house. Little difference, in fact, between outside and inside. Our breath hung in the air.

As the microwave pinged and he took out what smelt like macaroni cheese, he whispered, 'Stay here.'

He disappeared with the steaming carton, some cutlery and

the six-pack towards the sound of the TV, then reappeared, jerking his head in the direction of the dark hallway. I padded after him towards a room that turned out to be his bedroom, no longer able to feel my feet and holding my coat tightly around me.

It wasn't until he closed the door that he exhaled at last. Leaning against it, he shut his eyes then opened them again, as if double checking to make sure I was still there. For a moment, I worried that he might ask me to leave, but then he grinned.

Exhausted, I dropped down onto the unmade bed, careful not to sit on the cassettes caught up in the duvet's messy folds. He started to gather the things strewn across the bed, floor and desk chair, as if they were incriminating evidence, hauling them onto the floor and then kicking them energetically into a corner of the room. He put on a Smiths album and lit himself a cigarette before throwing the box and lighter at me. He didn't ask me any questions about the trouble I'd said I was in, and I didn't offer an explanation.

He simply watched as I threw glances around the room, taking it all in. The CND posters, the mural of a matador painted on the wall behind me, and bookshelves full of French writers: a lot of Sartre and Camus.

'You look freezing.'

'I am freezing.'

He bent over a gas heater and after a few clumsy attempts managed to light it with a match. It let out a toxic smell and not much heat.

I said, 'I can't feel my feet.'

Without warning, he slid onto his knees and grabbed my right foot, slipping the trainer off. 'Jesus, Becky – no socks?'

'I didn't have time.'

He stared at me for a while and then nodded, pulling my

feet onto his lap, against his groin where it was warm. Rubbing them, blowing on them.

'Get into the bed.'

I fell back with relief, able to pick out the smell of him caught up in the duvet, sheet and pillows. Going floppy, I let him pull my coat off me, making no effort to help as he struggled. Once the coat was off, he bundled me under the duvet.

'Shove up,' he said, trying to fit himself onto the narrow bed beside me.

I shunted myself as far back as I could until I hit the wall with the matador on it.

We lay squeezed together and finished our cigarettes, blowing smoke over each other, ash falling onto the duvet. When we were done, he leaned over the edge of the bed and stubbed his out on the carpet, before taking mine and doing the same. Then he pulled the duvet over us, and we disappeared from sight. The last thing I remembered was pressing my face into his jumper.

At some point we must have fallen asleep. Because later, we woke. I was much warmer by then, and George was awake as well. We pushed the duvet back, but the air temperature had fallen even further and the house was oppressively silent. I could feel the weight of the snow covering the world outside. Pulling the duvet over us again, we tried to trap the heat inside as we clawed clumsily at our clothes in the narrow bed, George trying not to fall out.

His hands all over me.

My hands all over him.

Flushed and impatient suddenly. Prickling all over and no longer worried about getting it right. No longer afraid. Stretching and shuddering. Aware of myself crying in the hot dark.

# The Verdict

I lie on a couch in the matron's office at the Old Bailey, waiting – along with the rest of the world – for the verdict. My hands are clutching at the cardigan I'm wearing, crushing the red Remembrance poppy on its lapel.

The phone never seems to stop ringing. When it does, Matron picks it up and says things like 'of course' and 'I see' and 'not to worry'. And 'I'll be with you soon.'

I feel privileged to be party to these small, inconsequential exchanges, their very smallness protection from big words like innocent and guilty.

She ends the call she's on now with a soft sigh, before putting down the receiver and getting to her feet in one smooth movement. She crosses the room between desk and couch with the same unhurried speed that she does everything.

'There now,' she murmurs, laying a hand on my shoulder.

Matron manages to take a good look at me without making it feel intrusive – after the hundred and thirty-five days spent in court, I can't bear to be looked at. But this is different. Her face hovers somewhere between smiling and serene. She gives my shoulder a squeeze and I try to put a hand over hers to keep it there. But she slides it firmly away.

There's to be no more holding on to each other – I've had my fair share of that.

'How are we?' she says brightly, starting to move about the room now with a new efficiency, before announcing, 'I'm making tea.'

I watch her do this. The quiet clatter of kettle and teapot – like a still afternoon at a favourite aunt's house. Only I never had an aunt, let alone a favourite one.

During the trial this room has become familiar. A retreat from panic attacks, loss of voice, and the time I thought I'd gone blind. A hysterical blindness that saw me unable to find my way to the witness box.

'What just happened?' I say after a while. 'I remember crying.'

The tears came in a shuddering burst at 10.30 a.m. when it was announced that they were deferring the verdict until the afternoon. I thought I was going to fall over. I felt myself start to topple, but before that happened, Kathleen – Matron – took hold of me. I fell into her blue uniform instead, pushing my face against her pocket watch.

I remember her arms around me. She had hold of me. She had hold of all of me when she leaned in and said, 'We're going to walk out of here, Rebecca. You're going to do this. Let them see you walk out of here.'

Now, she holds a cup of tea towards me but changes her mind and puts it on the desk instead. 'It's here if you want it,' she says.

I nod, distracted, worried that there's something she's not telling me. Worried that I embarrassed myself in some critical way. Lost control.

'Oh, there were tears,' she agrees, sounding happy about this as she sits down at her desk, taking a few contented sips of tea. 'A river of them. But I wouldn't worry about that.'

Tears, in her book, are a good thing, a good sign – and she is a great believer in signs. She is a great believer in many things.

'So, nothing else happened?'

She gives her head a calm, decisive shake, our eyes meeting

above the raised teacup. 'We left court. Came here. And here we are. Your tea,' she reminds me.

With an effort, I leave the couch and pick up the cup she has placed on the desk for me, taking a few sips before putting it back down.

Through the window I can see the copper dome of the Courts of Justice. Shuffling across the room, I peer cautiously at the world beyond the courthouse.

Windows and doors have become daunting.

Outside, I watch a storm break. They've been promising one for days, and the furious sky finally gives way over camera crews, reporters, police. The whole crowd of them.

Nobody moves from their spot.

Nobody seeks shelter.

Down at street level, I think I recognize one of the security guards. Matthew, who always jokes that my wedding ring can't be real gold because it sets off the metal detectors when I arrive at court.

The rain is hard and vast.

'Kathleen, have you got children?'

'Oh. Yes.' Her eyes are bright, briefly full of something.

The rain outside becomes even harder, the din of it making the tannoy announcement – 'All parties in Sharp and others to Court 12' – distant-sounding and somehow inconclusive.

'What happens now?'

My legs are shaking. It feels as if there aren't enough things to hold on to suddenly.

'We'll just take a few minutes and then we'll get you back to court.'

'Will I have to stand?'

'They won't deliver the verdict until you're standing, Rebecca.'

For the first time, she sounds severe.

I overheard two journalists in the canteen the other day, trying to work out how much the trial's cost. They estimated that ten million had probably been spent on barristers alone, but that the total cost must be closer to twenty-five million. I wonder what Matron's thoughts on this are. And I almost ask her – not what she thinks the verdict will be, but what she'd like it to be. Kathleen's opinion of me suddenly matters more than the verdict itself. Instead, I say, 'Becky. I told you to call me Becky.'

I enter the dock slowly and deliberately. Almost everything that isn't a flat surface has become hazardous. Kerbs, steps, staircases. Which is why bearing my own weight must be done purposefully and with real concentration. I barely look at my fellow defendants: among them George and Malcolm. Paul is a noticeable absence – they arrested his partner, Hugo, instead.

I can tell from Justice Heaton's face that this time it's real, unlike the morning's summons, which turned out to be a false alert. And despite the stampede after the announcement calling us back to court, the atmosphere as Heaton explains the earlier delay is eerily calm. The jury had only been able to reach partial verdicts, agreeing on some counts and disagreeing on others. Given the jury's indecision, he felt that there would have to be reporting restrictions, in order to control the impact of media coverage on the jury's ongoing deliberations. Over lunch, however, he'd decided to hear the verdicts and then discuss whether they could be reported. He's tired. We're all so very tired. The trial's lasted almost eight months. One of the longest criminal trials in history.

The jury enter then, and the atmosphere shifts again, becoming taut with expectation. Never have I studied twelve faces so carefully. Eight women. Four men. Odds worth playing to, William had observed when the trial began. We also speculated which of them were *Mercury* readers.

In the past months, I've taken to measuring my life in numbers. The number of steps from my front door to the car; from the car to the side entrance at the Old Bailey; from security to the dock; from the dock to the witness box.

I estimate the number of steps if the verdict is guilty: this route involves me being taken through the padded and studded green door that I'm sitting next to and down a dark staircase leading to the cells below.

And the number of steps if the verdict's not guilty: leaving the dock and exiting the courtroom through the fire doors at the back.

But as William warned at the beginning of the trial, no matter which door I leave this glass dock by, some part of me will remain for ever in Court 12.

For the first time since entering the dock, I twist quickly towards George, but he keeps his eyes on the jury. We barely exist beyond ourselves, reduced, each and every one of us, to our lowest common denominators, the knowledge of which we will have to live with for the rest of our lives.

The court clerk stands up. 'Have you reached a verdict on which you are all agreed? Please answer yes or no.'

The lead juror, in a striped jumper today, also stands. Many times during the trial, she's caught my eye. Smiled.

Malcolm – guilty of conspiracy to intercept communications in the course of their transmission without lawful authority. Beyond the glass, the courtroom erupts as the first verdict is read out. Justice Heaton has trouble calling order. I feel a deep need suddenly to get away from all the noise. Somewhere dark and quiet. I imagine burrowing under the duvet in the bedroom of my Notting Hill house. But an improbable number of steps need to be covered between here and there.

George – guilty of conspiracy to intercept communications in the course of their transmission without lawful authority.

Out of the corner of my eye, I see him slump. His head dropping down. His hands with their bitten nails, white-knuckled, before he unclasps them. Stretching them open and rubbing the palms along his legs. I can smell the fear coming off him.

Hugo – guilty of conspiracy to intercept communications in the course of their transmission without lawful authority.

Three guilty verdicts. For an awful moment, I worry that I've slipped from my chair – it's such an effort to stay seated. I have to glance down at myself to check, half expecting to see my legs splayed and broken-looking across the courtroom's green carpet.

And still, the courtroom holds its breath. Waiting.

'Rebecca Sharp.'

I shut my eyes. When I open them again, it's impossible to make out anyone apart from Dinkie Walsh. She's strangely still, the clothes she's wearing odd-looking. Unsuitable and yet familiar. Clothes more appropriate for a child than a grown woman. Shorts and a yellow T-shirt with a butterfly on it. The legs and arms thin and girlish suddenly. Her entire silhouette shrinks against the ceremonial backdrop. People in black costumes rise and leave with a well-rehearsed formality. Everybody looks very grown-up. Dinkie is childlike and impish in comparison. Loose-limbed and grinning. A terrible power emanates from her, as if she might just upturn this unsatisfactory charade of dark-robed adults and enact a far more terrible revenge of her own.

Until it's Ella herself I see, skipping through the crowded courtroom like it's the hundred-acre wood. Her yellow butterfly

T-shirt and shorts are covered in dark and aggressive stains, becoming filthier and filthier. Dead leaves fall all around her, huge and impossible piles of them that she dances wildly through. Arms raised. Grinning still.

Chanting over and over again, 'Not guilty, not guilty, not guilty.'

Everything on the other side of the glass is now obscured by falling leaves.

The child, vanishing. Free.

2012

# Birthday

A summer's day in Greenwich Park. I recognize them immediately, the couple in the distance, horizontal across a picnic rug beneath the trees, at the tail end of a party. Beth's, in fact. She's eleven years old today. The invitation came from Rawdon, the first direct contact I've had with him for almost two years, during which time the only correspondence has been through lawyers. But there's no sign of either Rawdon or Beth.

Only Amelia, on her stomach, trying to read.

And Dobbin, lying beside her.

Dobbin, who has waited a lifetime to do just this: lie in the sun, close enough to Amelia to distract her by nuzzling her ear. A choreography of intimacy he will never take for granted. She bats him away, smiling, giving up on the book and rolling onto her back. Already, she's capitulated.

George made it easy for them in the end, unravelling when he came out of prison and vanishing down the tunnel of reality TV. Presenting a celebrity survival show.

Coming to a standstill, I watch at a distance as Dobbin starts to lean over her. They're interrupted suddenly by a scream close by, forcing itself through the heavy humidity of the afternoon.

Followed by a child, falling from a tree.

Landing in a stunned clutter on the ground, arms and legs thrust out.

Beth, I realize with a jolt, starting to make my way across the grass. But already Amelia and Dobbin are pulling apart, scrambling to their feet and breaking into a run. Dobbin is still impossibly tall but far more graceful than I remember.

Two more children drop from the tree. They grow so fast when you take your eyes off them, but I just about recognize Gina. And Jon.

They crowd around Beth and help her into a sitting position.

The group shift together as a dog comes bounding over, jumping up at Beth, who hauls the animal against her. The dog's long ears fall over her thin arms.

Another couple approach, along the path running between the avenue of chestnuts, loosely swinging clasped hands, letting go of each other as they see the group gathered around Beth. Rawdon jogs across the sunburnt grass, Sophie following – long strides behind him – as he scoops up his daughter and the dog.

There are some straggling tears, but already it feels as if the moment has passed.

Nothing broken.

The group – a tight, happy bundle – drift back towards the picnic rug, dropping into the fading shade – the sun is fast retreating behind cloud. Dobbin sits with his back against a tree, Amelia inside his legs, his face in her hair. Beth lies across Sophie's lap. Rawdon pushes through the debris of food and drink. I remain beneath the avenue's pooled shadows. Undecided.

Until, with an instinctive jerk, Beth sits up and stares straight at me.

Even at this distance, I see the shudder of something cross her face. It isn't shock – she must have been told I was coming. It's fear. My daughter is afraid of me. Is that why she was in the tree? Was she hiding from me? On the lookout, perhaps, so that she could give fair warning of the enemy's approach. Did she try to persuade Rawdon against inviting me? Did she rage against his decision with one of her stampeding tantrums? It's a humid day with a low, grey sky that I feel trapped under suddenly, unable to take a single step forward as Beth and I continue our long-distance observation of each other.

She gives her head a quick shake. It's a dismissal. She wants me to leave before I'm seen. By Rawdon in particular, I guess. What will she say – that I must have changed my mind? Yes, this is the story she will tell, turning me into a ghost, and perhaps in time she'll come to believe it herself. So that my presence here today becomes an uncertainty in her mind. Maybe she saw me, maybe she didn't.

Perhaps this is what all parents are – nothing more than figments of their children's imaginations. My mind goes briefly to my own mother. And Lisa Walsh, who once told me that without Ella in the world, she felt like she didn't exist at all.

Already I feel dangerously insubstantial, but I also understand something else now. Beth is allowed to shake her head and dismiss me because I've forfeited any natural claim I have to be her mother. That decides me. I'm going to have to wait until she's ready to come looking for me. But what I can do today is start to leave a trail. One that she may or may not choose to follow.

I carry on walking without looking back.

Behind me I can hear a dog barking. Children's voices. Lazy and inconsequential now the danger's past.

Through the trees, beyond the observatory's dome, the tidy white symmetry of a house built for a queen. Beyond this, a wide, shining river and all of London.

All over again.

The city from up here is tall and defiant-looking.

I'll send Beth's present to her – the first crumb in the trail.

# VANITY FAIR

## Rebecca Sharp

*Uncorrected Proof*

*For Beth*

## AUTHOR'S NOTE
## A NOVEL WITHOUT A HEROINE

*Becky* is a story I've carried inside me for a long time, but I can pinpoint its origins to the relationship between two eighteen-year-old girls about to embark on the great adventure of life. One, a real girl with dreams of becoming a writer, at the end of the twentieth century. The other, a fictional character from the Victorian novel *Vanity Fair*, set at the beginning of the nineteenth.

From the moment she hurls her dictionary out of the carriage window as she leaves Miss Pinkerton's Academy for Young Ladies, I fell in love with William Thackeray's Becky Sharp. An eighteen-year-old orphan with no friends in the world and even fewer prospects. The odds are stacked against her, but Becky is determined to make her own way in the world.

And is the world that Thackeray's Becky comes of age in so very different from our own? The questions the novel raises about female identity being defined by marriage and maternity, and the categorizing of women as good or bad, remain unanswered. When I first started work on *Becky*, my contemporary retelling of Thackeray's classic, I found the parallels to be both urgent and compelling. At a glance, the Regency period appears to be one of elegance and excess, extravagance and eccentricity following on from the economic boom and certainties of the Enlightenment. Not dissimilar, in outlook, to the garish optimism of the 1990s. But lurking beneath the surface – in both cases – were the turbulent twins of uncertainty and unrest. A lot of the issues *Vanity Fair* explores and exposes are – if anything – even more relevant today: gender inequality, the legacy of colonialism, an obsession with celebrity culture, corrupt politics, a rotten Establishment, and a growing Wealth Gap.

In 1810 – around the time *Vanity Fair* opens – George III was declared insane. The raving and forgotten king became England's dark secret. In 1997 the sudden death of a beloved and troubled Princess sent out similar shockwaves that battered the royal family and left the country in crisis. Triggering a collective outpouring of grief on a scale that is still – even with hindsight – difficult to understand. The closing years of the twentieth century were ones in which the media set the country's emotional and political agenda. Newsprint was at its zenith, racing from scandal to scandal, and Princess Diana spearheaded a whole new brand of celebrity culture. Her death in a high-speed paparazzi chase felt like a reckoning and the shadow that spread from the Pont d'Alma tunnel heralded a slide from optimism into political and moral turmoil. This is the stage onto which my Becky steps. A stage that echoes the Regency one Thackeray's Becky stepped onto.

*Becky*'s structure, I owe to *Vanity Fair*. I've retained all of Thackeray's original names – Becky Sharp is an aptronym that still rings true – just as my story follows his original blockbuster rags to riches and back to rags plot. *Vanity Fair* charts almost twenty years of Becky's life and as I passed my own life milestones of marriage and motherhood, career hits and misses, different parts of Becky's story resonated with me. I knew that I wanted you – the reader – to have a similar relationship with the main character in my novel. This is why I've kept the same timeframe as well as plotting around characters and their relationships, and why I owe the debt I do to Thackeray. But it should be said that the characters in *Becky* are all my own – entirely fictitious, despite the events that inspired the novel, and autonomous. They have taken on a life of their own – this is what characters do. And I've reclaimed Becky's voice by stripping out Thackeray's male narrator and writing her in first person. Laying her bare so that she appears, unfiltered. Herself.

The heart of Thackeray's novel, however, remains. My Becky, like her namesake, is a penniless orphan who starts working life as a nanny to the Crawley family. The impact of both poverty and lost childhoods are impossible to escape in *Vanity Fair* and this is also true of *Becky*. The Crawleys are no longer peers of the realm. In *Becky* they become the Crawley Corporation – a powerful media conglomerate and owners of bestselling tabloid, the *Mercury*. It is into this Nineties tabloid world – very much a man's world – that Becky, a hungry young journalist, launches herself as the novel charts her meteoric rise to become the *Mercury*'s first female editor.

I hope that I've done justice to the struggles that Becky faces, and that we have yet to find fixes for. Just as I hope Becky speaks to you as she speaks to me. Keeping us company in troubled times.

# Acknowledgements

Firstly, I thank William Makepeace Thackeray for writing his Victorian blockbuster *Vanity Fair* and bringing Becky Sharp to life. I've spent six years in her company and never once grown tired of it. Eternal gratitude to my agent, the incomparable Clare Alexander. Grand duchess, hand-holder and long-time companion on this literary adventure. Also at Aitken Alexander Associates, my thanks go to Amy St Johnston for her astute early edits one dark February.

I am forever grateful to the extraordinary Sophie Jonathan. For her vision and ambition. Becky – as she is – would not exist without her. To Roshani Moorjani, for being there from the beginning. For her unshakeable belief in both me and *Becky*. Rosh, you have made my writerly world a brighter place. To Anna Jean Hughes for her precision editing, deep dark sense of humour and even deeper darker laugh. To all the team at Picador and beyond, notably Joanna Prior, Gaby Quattromini and Emma Bravo.

To Rebecca Carter, dear friend and one of my first readers, I am indebted beyond measure. The following people I thank for their time and insight into all things journalistic: Caroline Shearing and Katherine Faulkner. Thanks must also go to all my Faber Academy students, past, present and future, for continuing to challenge me. You have helped to shape this book in more ways than you can possibly imagine.

And lastly, again and again, Benj . . . for putting up with the ménage à trois that writing *Becky* has turned our marriage into over the past six years. Be careful what you wish for.